# THE RUBBER ROOM

# THE RUBBER ROOM

## Ivan Bosanko

**ARPress**
45 Dan Road Suite 5
Canton, MA 02021

Hotline:  1(888) 821-0229
Fax:        1(508) 545-7580

Ordering Information:
Quantity sales. Special discounts are available on quantity purchases by corporations,associations, and others. For details, contact the publisher at the address above.

Printed in the United States of America.

ISBN-13:       Softcover        979-8-89330-810-5
                    eBook            979-8-89330-812-9
                    Hardcover       979-8-89330-811-2

Library of Congress Control Number: 2024901933

# Table Of Contents

Most of the people I know can proudly point to an occurrence, event or happening as to when their career started. In my case, my writing career started as a suggestion.

At the ripe old age of 12, after the Christmas break, we brought our presents to school for a class "show and tell." When I showed the other kids my printers set, my teacher suggested I put my printer to good use and print something. But what? How about printing a community newspaper? And I'll even help you.

Every Saturday night the wheat farmers in my hometown brought their cream cans in and used the money to buy food, school clothes and small equipment items. Every other Saturday night, I sold my newspapers for 20 cents. And so my writing career began. In the eighth grade, I wrote an essay about the first wheat farmers in our county. I called it, "Solders of the Soil." A Minneapolis newspaper paid me first prize money.

In 1980, I had my first book printed. It was titled "The Sea of Grain." It was a love story about a Quaker country school teacher ( my mom) unusual courtship and the needed change in order to marry my dad. Movie director/producer Stanley Kramers wrote me saying, "Ivan, your story has movie written all over." Contract talks between my publisher and Hollywood broke down which meant my book never made it to the silver screen.

I married in September 1952.  Six weeks later, I was drafted into the U.S. Army Signal Corps.  I resumed college classes in 1955 under the GI Bill with a double major in electrical engineering and technical writing.  Through my lifetime I have accumulated over 10 years' worth of college credits.  Those college credits really paid of for me later on.

In 1978, The Boeing Aerospace Division sent me to Cape Kennedy to straighten out a contract mess on the Apollo/Saturn space program.  I solved the problem with NASA's new director Werner Von Braun.  I became friend with one of his staff and learned some shocking things about the new director.  He had been a Nazi during Adolf Hitler's regime.  The big man's ego matched his size.  When this info leaked out, the other contractors disliked him immensely.

Today's calendar tells me I have been an author, writer and engineering specialist for over half a century.  Not too shabby for a small town boy!!

# DEDICATION

To those who doubted-- my thanks because you challenged me.


To all the rest who believed in me--Thank God, because you were my inspiration.

# PREFACE

The 1950's marked the beginning of the most dramatic social and economic changes our country has ever experienced. Everything we ate, wore, talked about, and even prayed about became "fair game" by those who proclaimed "the new dawn of enlightenment." Nothing escaped their scrutiny! Better than a century of well-founded traditional and cultural values were attacked, questioned, or challenged by first, second, and third generation sons and daughters who followed these social and economic experimenters through thick and thin, believing that they offered the best of every facet of life. Change was good for the nation they adamantly proclaimed and you must accept this as man's best efforts to date. The old country standards of thrift, hard-work ethics and savings literally went down the drain as in swept a new tide of credit aptly dubbed "plastic money." Credit was everywhere! Why wait became their hue and cry? Soon the effects of such radical change left our country drowning in a "sea of red ink," so much so that both our state and federal bankruptcy laws were either rewritten or changed so that the stigma of failure carried far less impact than before.

American industry underwent unparalleled change too, as one by one, our nation's established giants of trade and business were toppled by waves of foreign investors, foreign capital, and foreign competition. These icons were besieged at every turn of the day. Soon a new breed of businessman appeared on the scene, "The Corporate Raider." They sold-off long-standing stocks, inventory, and even goodwill. Company pension funds including health and vacation accounts disappeared overnight through theft, embezzlement, and/or "creative bookkeeping." Once these raiders had leveraged everything of value they could lay their hands on, they disappeared into the "woodwork" as easily as they first appeared! Gone were the hopes and dreams of thousands of loyal company employees who had faithfully served their employers. Finally, to save face and appease public outrage, a few were eventually hauled into court and given light sentences that hardly fit the nature of their crimes. Thus the slow moving and inept "white-collar justice system" were also exposed along with those few who became "the public scapegoats." The so-called golden years had been reduced to mockery status for these victims!

The railroads were especially hit hard. Mergers, takeovers, and downsizing became everyday events. Those who were left to collect a paycheck were treated to or they heard about a whole new experience: The Rubber Room Treatment! This century old practice was brought out of the railroad industry's closet once more. Many were bounced around from job-to-job and location-to-location by a very select, all-powerful few who played God with every aspect of their lives! Those who stood up or fought this treatment learned that their employment had been turned into a living hell here on earth! Soon article after article hit the headlines and all the other news media. So much so, that railroad management, quickly, coined or added a new catch-all phrase, "alternative worksite or location" to lessen the public outcry over such tactics or treatment. And so from such shoddy treatment, came my story, *The Rubber Room.*

"OVER HERE MOTHER! HURRY!" For all her thirty-seven years young, Mary McCray had never seen her daughter, KateLynn , so excited as she kept pointing to the exquisitely dressed mannequin. "Oh Mother, this is the formal I want. Four long years of waiting forever... ...hoping.. .and even praying."

Mary took her own sweet time looking over her daughter's wonderful find."Well, Lass, I'll give you this, it sure matches that dark brown hair with the reddish wisps you got...from my Brannigan side of course."

"Let's go in to get it before somebody else snatches it up. The mint-green shade will be perfect on me." KateLynn exclaimed excitedly.

Mary walked on down the sidewalk in front of Sacramento's leading department store, giving each of the six mannequins more than her usual close inspection. When she reached the last one, she motioned for KateLynn to come join her.

"What is it Mother? What's wrong now?"

"The price tags, Lass! They've turned 'em so a'body can't see what they're chargin.' And you can bet there are high prices hiding behind those tags, if we dare go in. And all this for what? A dress you'll wear but once! Right daughter?"

"It's called a formal. And you and Daddy did promise, remember?"

"I don't care what it's called. Let's go shop at Penny's or Monkey Wards for a nice, new Sunday-go –to-church dress that you will wear for a good long time. The McCray money will get a fightin' chance over there."

"But you promised! You and Daddy!" KateLynn wailed.

Mary started to walk away. KateLynn had to practically run to catch up. "I'm not going to settle for just a new dress. Do you hear me, Mother? NEVER!'

Mary waited for the pedestrian light to change at the crosswalk. "In that case shoppin's over. And when we get home I'm gonna tell your father about the shenanigan they tried to pull on me. He'll back me all the way."

Five days passed without so much as a kind word between mother and daughter. Aaron McCray had had enough. He packed his pipe, lit it, and walked into the kitchen where the two McCray women were busy doing the supper dishes in stone-cold silence. "The house of McCray used to be a home filled with kind words and good thoughts. It will be again. When we McCrays give our promise, we keep it no matter what. Tomorrow both of you will go to that little dress shop that KateLynn's friend, Molly, told us about and YOU WILL COME HOME WITH THE KIND OF DRESS THAT KATELYNN WANTS! "

The thaw began between mother and daughter at a deli across the street from the dress shop. Over ham-on-rye sandwiches and hot navy bean soup, the two started to open up to each other.

Mary beamed with immense pride in what KateLynn had accomplished. "Lass, your father 'n me are so proud that you'll be graduatin' next week. Your father has put aside enough money so when you meet the cold, hard world, you'll be more than ready we're thinkin'. 'Tis to Business College he has in mind for you, eh? A good payin' job will surely follow this schoolin' and then you'll be set to meet the right kind of young man."

KateLynn was pleased by her mother's comments. "I hope Daddy has in mind a good business college in Sacramento."

"He has Lass, he has! There's money put aside for your schooling. So you see, dear daughter, we've provided for all you'll be needin' in the near future."

KateLynn put down her soup spoon. "Sacramento will fit into mine and Jerry's plans just great, Mother! Just great! I know he hasn't come right out with it, but right after graduation I'm sure you'll be seeing much more of him at our house."

Mary threw up her hands. "Jerry, Jerry, Jerry! That's all your father 'n me have heard for two long years, KateLynn! He's just a boy, the same age you are! Listen to me, he's a nice lad, I'll give you that, but it's time you took a hard look at life, the one that's comin' to knock on your door. Aye Lass, it's a man you best be thinkin' 'bout, one that has a good job, comes from the right kind of family, and has good prospects for the future, and of course, goes to our church."

"Jerry's not really eighteen, he's much older than his age and he's all man!"

Mary had a mother's worried look about her. She didn't care one whit where KateLynn's defense of Jerry was headed. "Oh and how would ye be knowin' such a thing? Please tell me you and Jerry are only good friends and there's nothing more between you. You're father 'n me have such high hopes for you."

"Relax Mother, I'm not ready for another lecture, not today anyway. I think it only fair to warn you, Jerry and I are very serious about each other."

Mary shook her finger at KateLynn. "Daughter, day dreamin'll get you nowhere! It's rollin' up your sleeves and gettin' sore knees that pays the bills and puts money in the cookie jar. Aye, now Lass, don't deny it, your Jerry's never been inside a proper church, much less our own Catholic one! No Lass, 'tis time to give him up. A little pain and heartache now are much better against all that hurt later on."

KateLynn's Irish flared. "You were sixteen when you married my daddy, and you had me just after your seventeenth birthday. I'm eighteen and I've been working at the five and dime for two full years saving my money. Maybe I've bent a few, but I've tried hard to obey all your rules. I'll bring pride and purity to my marriage bed when the time comes."

Shhh, Lass! That kind of talk's not proper in a public place. It belongs at home between you, me, and your father."

"All right let's get my dress." KateLynn replied heavily.

The two McCray women left the deli on good terms, each aware of just where the other stood on certain matters. Yet through their near-blow-up, a closer bonding of sorts was formed between the two. One that both hoped fervently would last far beyond next week's graduation. This time KateLynn matched stride for stride with her mother as both put their five-foot-three frames to good purpose.

When they reached the dress shop, KateLynn rushed up to the small front window of the shop. "Look Mother," she gushed, "it's perfect for me! Just my size and the right color too. Light blue."

Mary McCray took her own sweet time looking over the only dress in the window."You're right, the color goes good, matches your hair very well."

KateLynn hugged her mother. "Oh thank you! Thank you, Mother! Another ten pounds difference and it would fit you too! Let's go inside!"

The shop owner handed the light –blue creation to KateLynn and pointed to the dressing room. Five minutes later, she returned for her mother's inspection and okay.

"Turn around, Lass, let's have a good look."

"Why she fits into it like a glove" said the shop owner." Won't even have to take in or let out one bit."

Mary nodded in agreement. She opened her purse, got her checkbook out and then asked for a pen. She finished filling in the amount, then a second thought hit. "Surely, there's a piece that comes with it to cover the top, right?"

"No mother, that's the way all formals are."

"But there's nothing but a lot of imagination and darned few threads holding it up. And it shows way, way too much of your breasts, love, without something to cover them up."

"That's the way all formals are made," the owner replied.

"I don't care how they're made when my daughter's reputation is at stake. Why, why it shows everything but her nipples! NO, NO! COME, COME, KATELYNN! I'VE SEEN MORE THAN ENOUGH! PROMISE BE DAMNED! WAIT'LL I TELL YOU FATHER WHAT THEY EXPECT YOU TO WEAR!'

KateLynn left the shop in tears.

The next evening, while KateLynn worked at the five and dime, Aaron drove Mary back to the dress shop. Another twenty minutes of hard sell, and Mary DID write the check over her very passionate objections. On the way back to their home, Aaron had his say. "Mary McCray, the reason we came to this country was to start our new life in America. And after our daughter was born, we both promised each other that we'd try to be as American as our neighbors."

***

KateLynn's bedroom was a beehive of activity with Mary McCray more than making her presence known. She clucked and fussed over her daughter all the while dispensing her motherly wisdom in bits and doses. "Your freckles, Lass, what's to be done about them?"

Her daughter's smile, reflected in her vanity mirror, told Mary that she had everything under control. "Look over in my evening purse Mother, I got some new make-up at work this week. It's supposed to block them out."

Carefully, the application was applied midst growing amazement on Mary's part. "Oh Daughter it's workin' ! It's working! What a lovely young lady you are my sweet! My Lord, Lass, your father's lost his tomboy for sure tonight!"

KateLynn turned around on her vanity bench, an absolute vision of loveliness. "I'm so pleased you like what you see, Mother. I only hope Jerry will think so too!"

"Well he'd better my dear, after a solid hour of brushing and primping since you put on that evenin' dress…Ooops! I mean your formal."

KateLynn smiled. "That's pretty good, Mother." With eyes that dared to gather a bit of mist, KateLynn felt a special tug at her heartstrings. "Mother, I want you to know something. I think you're the most wonderful mother any daughter could possibly ever have or want. I know I've apologized since our little flare-up, but let me apologize once more for what I said last week in Sacramento. And to think of what you did… going back to that little dress shop and not only buying my formal but a matching evening purse and patent leather black shoes too… well, you're simply the best!"

"Tell you what, Lass. I'll trade two of them apologies for one tiny little hug, darling!"

KateLynn rose in her formal, eager to oblige.

A tear graced KateLynn's cheek while they hugged. "Careful my love, don't want to spoil up a good hour's worth of work.'

They came out of the bedroom, both women's cheeks aglow, down the hall they walked, KateLynn right on Mary's heels. Even the swish from KateLynn's formal added its own special luster to such an important occasion. Her perfume was joined with that of another scent, an aroma of pipe smoke.

A hush filled the room loaded with anticipation. Aaron McCray rested his newspaper on his lap, and then he laid his pipe on an ash tray next to his tobacco humidor. A most pleased expression crossed his rugged though handsome face. A slow smile found home in both corners of his mouth. His eyes telegraphed his love for the two most important women in his life. There was no need for words, yet they came.

"Well, Mary McCray, what have we here?"

"Aye, Father, there was to be an Irish pixie hiding behind me, but no more. Now you best know that an Irish princess has taken her place, and she's beggin' to make your acquaintance."

Out from behind Mary McCray stepped KateLynn, truly the reincarnation of her mother minus the eighteen years. "You do the house of McCray proud this night. Come closer! If I'm to lose my tomboy, don't you think a hug would be at least a fair trade?"

KateLynn slipped into her father's lap as easily as he moved the newspaper. Two soft, creamy, lotioned hands encircled his muscular shoulders before her cheek came to rest gently against his. The immense pride etched clearly in his manner took hold while he returned an affectionate peck to her cheek.

"Careful, careful Father!" cautioned Mary. "The freckles are covered, now easy goes with her dress!"

He looked at the tiny card dangling from her thin, small wrist. "What have we here?"

"It's my dance card, Daddy! See, I've already filled it out for the evening!"

Mr. McCray glanced at it carefully. "But there are only three names on it! Surely you'll give more of the young buckos a chance than three?"

"I've saved two dances for Ricco, two for Greg and the rest are all spoken for by Jerry. It's the last dance for our foursome, the Amigos!"

"Amigos! What foolishness is that?"

"Aye Father, you remember me tellin' ye years ago? KateLynn, Ricco, Greg and Jerry put this kind of play on, been callin' themselves the Amigos every since!"

Aaron McCray was not amused in the least. "KateLynn, enjoy tonight, but remember, we're expectin' big things from you and tonight's the end of it! Next week you graduate and then we'll help you make your way into the real world out there!"

"I know Daddy, I know, and I'm ready for it! Been dreaming about this night since the fourth grade and planning on it since my junior year. I have big plans too! After graduation, I hope to have some good news."

Aaron shot a glance over to his wife. She shook her head, as if to say: *Aaron McCray, you best keep a lid on your thoughts, let our KateLynn have tonight, she's earned it, what with all her late bloomin' and such into a right proper young lady. You dare spoil it and you'll have me to deal with!*

KateLynn left her father's lap so he could repack his pipe. She watched his callous hands, thickened and hardened by years of hard labor, refill, and light his pipe with ease. She marveled at his obvious physical strength. Yet none of this backbreaking labor had robbed him of his zest for life.

She positioned herself as close to the front parlor window as possible, waiting for Jerry's arrival.

Mary sat down beside her on the couch with her knitting basket. Once, twice, her mother had to restrain KateLynn from rushing to the window when a passing car slowed down. "Your young lad will show when he's a mind to and that's that! Turn to me, let's have a second look! Aye, the straps are too thin, and I still think you dress is cut way too low in front. American style or not, it still shows too much! That's not proper to my way of thinkin'!"

"Motherrr! We've been through all this before and you DID buy my formal, remember? Now if Molly were here, then you'd really have something to talk about."

"Oh, 'tis bust comparin' time, is it? Shame on you, KateLynn McCray! I dare say Molly McCarren's got a wee bit more up front, if ye catch my meanin'. Nevertheless, I'm thinkin' you'll more than hold you own, as of late, for being a small-figured young lady."

Aaron knew it was high time to change subjects. "KateLynn, where's your lad?"

"I don't know Daddy, Jerry's sure running late. Maybe Bettingers had extra grocery deliveries tonight, and that's probably making him extra late."

Aaron blew a smoke ring high above his newspaper. "Maybe so, but being on time counts pretty heavy with me, especially when he's keeping our lovely daughter waiting!"

KateLynn went to the telephone. "Maybe I'd better call Bettingers to check on him, see when he'll be through."

"Sit down, KateLynn! Sit down!" KateLynn knew her mother meant it! "No daughter of mine is going to call any lad, and that's all there is to it!"

They waited, and they waited, and they waited some more. Aaron rose, bent on double-checking their grandfather clock next to the door. He stood in front of their only expensive piece of furniture, then turned all five-feet ten inches. "Daughter, maybe I best be taking you, your lad is running far too late. After your ball is over, you call me when it's time to come for you."

"Please, Daddy, not yet! Jerry'll be along, something must've happened."

Then all heard it, the screeching of tires, brakes grinding to a halt, and the resounding slam of the door. KateLynn shot off the couch to make a beeline for the parlor door,

"Get back KateLynn! Get back! You've been warned!"

She took one look at her mother's knitting needle and knew she dared not risk her mother's Irish temper.

"I'll handle this," said Aaron, "it's about time I had a talk with your young lad, KateLynn. Try to impress upon him that around here being on time is very much a way of life."

He opened the door just as Jerry got ready to frantically pound on it. "Oh, er, good day, Mr. McCray, I'm sorry I'm late." He looked past Aaron in KateLynn's direction. "Got held up, Katey, sorry about it!"

Aaron grabbed him by the arm. Mr. McCray's arm strength jerked the good looking blonde around to where he could finish what was on his mind. "We haven't finished talking, Lad, and I'll thank you to call my daughter KateLynn, that's her proper name. If her mother and I wanted to name her Katey, we would've. Now then, I'd like to hear more about why you're so late, and why you had our daughter on pins and needles wondering what's become of you."

"Won't happen again, Mr. McCray," Jerry blurted out, still trying to catch his breath. "Too many orders at the grocery, Sir. Had to deliver them before Mr. Bettinger let me use his pick-up for the rest of the evening."

Aaron eased his vise-grip on Jerry's arm. He took that as a signal he was free to pass by and enter the parlor. "Good evening Mrs. McCray, I'm sorry about this, everything was a mess tonight. Please accept my apology."

Mary smiled at the tuxedo-clothed lad. She liked the fact that he took the time to show her a proper amount of respect. "Your apology is accepted, Jerry. Now then, your date is patiently waiting. KateLynn."

Both parents watched Jerry's eyes and his expression as KateLynn rose. "Wow, Kate---er, KateLynn, you are really something tonight. Man oh man!"

Her heart beat in triple time, her cheeks blushed a bit of the rose, oh how captivating she looked, so grown up, so confident, so sure, and so ready. "I'm glad you approve, Jerry." Then she looked past him. "You didn't forget my corsage, did you?"

Out behind his back flashed a cellophane covered box. Mary wasn't about to let this lad get even a finger anywhere near those two thin straps. "I'd better pin it, we wouldn't want to start your evening off on the wrong foot, now would we?"

KateLynn's mother deftly pinned the corsage where the strap met the front of the evening gown. "There now!"

KateLynn nodded her head and rolled her eyes slightly in her father's direction as a reminder to her mother. Mary turned toward her husband. "There's a matter your daughter would like to address on such an occasion as this."

"Yes KateLynn, speak up."

KateLynn tried her best to show that she was not nervous in front of her father; however, she worked her hands over and over again. Finally the words came. "Jerry's such a good driver, Daddy… has a perfect record driving Bettingers pick-up for two years. We were wondering… could we borrow the car tonight?"

Jerry lent his support. "I promise I'll drive extra careful Sir, you can definitely count on that, Mr. McCray. Just for this one special night, Sir!"

Aaron McCray felt three pairs of eyes trained on his trying their best to ferret out his reactions. He turned quickly to Jerry. "If you're to be a man about something, don't expect the women folk to do the heavy part of the question for you." His cold stare froze Jerry in his shoes; his eyes narrowed and he raised a forefinger. "Come Lad, follow me to the garage, there's something you need to see."

While mother and daughter couldn't possibly guess what Aaron had in mind, Jerry dutifully followed Mr. McCray outside. Once there, Aaron turned on the garage light and stood beside the car waiting for Jerry to catch up. Then as though to really drive home the point, he kicked the tire closest to him. "This is a new car Lad, our first. It's a 1950 Chevrolet. KateLynn's mother scrubbed floors, washed clothes and took in ironin' for our first car, a used 1937 Ford. Know how we managed to pay for this one?"

"Certainly Sir, you worked for it!"

"Well said, Lad. Now let's not keep KateLynn waiting a minute longer!"

Again, Aaron led the way. This time Jerry caught up before they reached the front steps. "Mr. McCray, please wait up, Sir."

Aaron hesitated. "What is it? Speak up Lad!"

"I… I know you think I'm just a boy, Sir, but Mr. McCray, I'm a man. I'm ready to work hard, save my money, get ahead. I'm very serious about your daughter, Sir, and I aim to tell her that soon. I have plans, good plans for our future. All I need is a little time, Sir, to prove myself to you and Mrs. McCray. I think the world of Katey… I mean KateLynn."

Aaron McCray clamped two hands down hard on Jerry's shoulders. "Lad, there's only one thing you can do for Mrs. McCray and myself tonight, and that is bring our KateLynn safely back to us the minute the ball is over. That's it! Nothing more and nothing less will be accepted. As for serious intentions, Lad, the man our KateLynn marries someday had better come prepared to show us he has a car, money saved in the bank, a good job with fine prospects, and he'd better be a damned good Catholic! No one else need show up! Are we clear about this, Mr. Landis?"

Aaron led the way inside. The two women's faces lit up expecting good news. "Mother, get an extra blanket for the front seat of that pick-up parked outside. No need adding a dry cleaning bill to the money we put out for KateLynn's dress."

KateLynn followed her mother into the bedroom, she was near tears. "Why does he have to be so mean, Mother? Just one time, you'd think he'd do it for me, if not for Jerry. Just this one time, that's all I asked!"

Mary handed KateLynn a blanket from the closet. "Now, now Lass, your father loves you very much. True, at times, it's a strange way of showin' it, he has! He's goin' to be testin' your Jerry, so you must be prepared for it, KateLynn. Today's the first round. If your Jerry's the man you claim he is, he'll answer for the final bell with your Father. One more thing Lass, I know your Jerry's intentions are honorable, or else you'd have nothin' to do with him, but he will want you, and you must resist all temptation 'til you wear your wedding dress. Aye, tonight you look almost ready for it! I'll keep the two of 'em separated long enough so they can size each other up and get to know each other as men instead of barnyard roosters! It's your job to keep your innocence and protect your purity."

Jerry bid KateLynn's parents goodnight. Aaron stepped forward and put some change in his daughter's hand. "If there's drinkin,' call me and I'll come get you! That's one thing I will not stand for. I read the papers too, and I know what goes on at these graduation dances."

"Daddy," Katey assured her father, "Jerry and I don't party or drink. We don't have time for such stupidity!"

"And when will the dance be over?" asked Mary.

"Around midnight, Mrs. McCray," Jerry quickly answered.

"Daddy, Mother, this is our big night, can we stay out later, maybe get something to eat after?"

Aaron looked at his wife to check; she didn't say no. "All right, two hours, and then you be home safe and sound. We'll be waiting up!"

Mary and her husband watched the two walk out the front door, Jerry about the same height as Aaron McCray, a full seven inches taller than their daughter. "Aye, Father, 'tis a nice lookin' pair they make. Him with the blonde hair and such deep, dark blue eyes. I read his face, Father, there's honesty and hard work there all right. Good lookin' lad too! How might you see him?"

Aaron mused a mite at his wife's observation, he wasn't as easily swayed. "The proof'll be in the puddin' Mary, and the fixin's ain't even bought and paid for yet!"

# CHAPTER TWO

The two sweethearts headed down the road toward their high school graduation ball. Once out of the driveway, KateLynn scooted over to Jerry. "Didn't get a chance to say it, but gosh, you're a big, good-lookin' handsome hunk tonight. You look kinda different in your tux. What did Daddy say out in the garage?"

He drove on before answering. "All I know Katey, is that I never want to get your father mad at me. Boy, did he ever lay the good word on my shoulders tonight! I mean he spelled it out! BING! BANG! BOOM!"

She thought a few seconds before volunteering her thoughts. "Okay, now that we know what it's going to take, question is, what are we going to do about it?"

He shifted the pick-up down and braked to a stop off the road's shoulder. "I know what I'm going to do about it right now, Katey McCray. You need kissing and I'm just the man to make sure that happens."

He found her eager lips and pulled her close, then settled in for a long, juicy, deep kiss. "Jerry! Stop that! No more right now!"

He let up and resumed a more gentle approach, one that Katey found much more to her liking. Finally, their lips parted long enough for him to breathe, "God, you're a knockout, Katey!

"I think you've had enough humble pie for one night. We're late and the rest of the Amigos probably think we fell in. Move it, Landis!"

They parked the pick-up a block away from the high school gymnasium. Suddenly, it was there, the culmination of twelve long years, of being together, of textbooks, homework, and teachers, some whom they admired, others they barely tolerated, yet through it all they were the product of their homes, their families, their cultures, and most of all, their classrooms. Katey rechecked her lipstick with the pick-up door open, taking advantage of a nearby streetlight as it reflected into the tiny mirror in her compact case. "My lipstick's fine, Darling, let's find the Amigos!"

Gaily decorated bells, twisted rope ribbons, and the Rushton High School colors hung down from the ceiling and stretched across the gymnasium. On stage, a small dance-band combination tooted, drummed, twanged, and strummed its music as fifty couples did their best to keep up with the jumpy beat. A huge banner hung down on suspended ropes over the band with the caption: '1950 – THIS IS OUR TIME.'

"Over here! Over here!" shouted and waved the robust six-footer with the sun-bleached hair. Jerry helped seat Katey. "Hey you two," said Greg Hibbard, "we've been holding up the whole evening on your account. Let's get to it!"

"Sorry, Greg," replied Jerry, "got held up at work."

Greg nodded to his date beside him. "Hey, Jerry Landis and Katey McCray, this is Rhonda Dearing from East Sacramento High."

The introductions taken care of, Greg tapped on his empty punch glass with a pen. "Okay, Amigos, this will be our last official meeting. We have some old business and some new business to take care of, so let's get to it! The music's hot, our dancing shoes are cold and time's a'wasting! But before we hit the dance floor, each Amigo has something to say."

One hilarious incident after another was recalled during their twelve years together, first as classmates, then as the Amigos. Molly went first. She handed Katey a pair of girl's pink panties, a token of her tomboy status when she first let Jerry have a peek or two. Katey followed next. The minute she took a small pair of scissors from her evening purse, Greg turned beet-red Then she talked about the out-house tipping time and how their fearless leader, Greg, managed to fall in when the toilet had been moved ahead on a dark, rainy Halloween night. After the laughter subsided, she went on to chide poor Greg about making new cut-offs once he crawled out of the hole. Jerry took his turn by handing Ricco a tube of deodorant. Ricco had flunked their teacher's "sniff-test," thereby cancelling the social graces and beginner's dance classes. Greg went last. He handed Molly a small package. Curiosity got the best of her. Out popped a girl's training bra as she was the first to use one in their class.

Greg raised his glass. "Amigos!"

Everyone responded with punch glasses held high.

Jerry whispered out of the side of his mouth to Katey. "What's with Ricco's beard?"

"Shssh, I'll tell you later."

"Raise your glasses!"

"Amigos!" came the response in unison.

Greg took charge once more. "Now, for some old business. The last official piece of unfinished business for The Loyal Order of Amigos." He handed Jerry an empty Coke bottle with a note wrapped around it with a thick rubber band. "Jerry, this isn't meant to be funny or embarrass you in any way, shape, or form. Please accept this in the true spirit it was meant and given, as a long overdue explanation to you. It's our apology, so please remember it that way."

He slipped the band off the bottle and opened the note:

"It took us 'til the fifth grade to figure out our tomboy Katey was right, it's not what you're wearing that counts, it's who's wearing them that really makes the difference. Anyway, those mysterious J.C. Penney clothes packages that showed up on your doorstep came courtesy of Sam Moore's Pool Hall. While Katey stood watch, Ricco and I filched enough bottles out of his storage room and re-sold them to Sam to buy your clothes, so you wouldn't have to wear WPA clothing any longer. Some would call it stealing, but I've got a hunch if he had caught us, he'd probably have told us to go ahead after we confessed why we did it. Anyway, please accept our sincere apology from the bottom of all our hearts. Signed, all your friends, your Amigos."

There wasn't a dry eye at Greg's table, including Jerry's. He raised his glass and turned toward Jerry.

"From the bottom of our hearts, Jerry, here's to you! Amigos!"

The dance band cut into the somberness. Ricco and Molly got up to dance. "Hold it! Please indulge me a minute longer," Greg said. "Let's do a little crystal ball gazing. Starting with Ricco, what do you think you'll be doing a year from tonight?"

Ricco replied, "I plan on working for my father at the local union hall, I'll be a trainee right here in Rushton."

Molly could hardly wait to blurt out her answer so she could be on the dance floor. Eyes riveted on Ricco, she gave her stock answer, "I have other plans, but in any event, I'll probably be in the secretarial typing pool right here at the headquarters of The California Central Railroad for awhile."

"And you, Jerry?"

Jerry answered Greg's question with ease. "Starting a week from Monday, I'll be a tax-rate and freight-rate clerk for The California Central. After I get established, I plan on going for my accounting degree through the evening division at Sacramento State College."

"Katey?"

Katey had the same riveted look at Jerry that Molly gave Ricco. She was hoping her plans would be changing too. Her stock reply, "I'll be finishing classes at the business college in Sacramento within the next year. After that, I'm not sure at this point."

Greg gave his answer. "I should be through my freshman year at Sacramento State College; I plan on majoring in Railroad Transportation Management. Oh, one other thing! Molly, how about you keeping tabs on everybody a year from now when we throw our first anniversary party? Okay Amigos, let's dance!"

And dance they did; the evening hours floated right on by, and before they knew it, the big clock above the basketball scoreboard told the happy participants their time had dwindled down to a precious last few dances. Katy and Jerry watched the couples gradually sift out of the building. Greg and his date said goodbye, and then they watched Ricco gallop right on out too, dragging a gushing, blushing Molly after him.

"Hey Katey, what's goin' on?"

"Ricco and Molly are going to stay overnight at a fancy motel in Sacramento. I'm supposed to cover for her in case her mother calls my home tomorrow morning. He's let his beard grow, wants to look older."

"No matter how you cut it, Katey, that's a shack-up job, pure and simple," said Jerry as he guided Katey away from the nearest couples so they could talk while dancing.

"You got it all wrong. Molly's so crazy about Ricco that she can't stop making love with him. All she wants to do is get married, settle down and have his babies."

"Katey, Molly may call it making love, but it's all give on her part. She needs to wise-up! Still don't see how he's managed to snow her time after time with all that bull he's been throwing at her. You're her best friend, tell her there's one sure way to find out who's right. She needs to cut him off and tell him no more 'til he comes across with a wedding ring, then let's see how long Ricco sticks around. I dare you to tell Molly that. He'll drop her so fast, she'll still be in free-fall while he's checking out the next skirt. C'mon Katey, I dare you!"

"It's their life, Jerry, not ours!

"Okay! Okay! But I'm just telling you they're way past 'playing house.' Somebody's going to get hurt and it sure as heck isn't gonna be Ricco! I just call it the way I see it, Amigo."

They danced on, each reluctant to speak their mind, for fear their perfect evening might end up in an argument or a shouting match. Jerry held her a little closer, Katey read him perfectly, his way of saying I'm sorry. She looked up in his face and he saw her tonight for what she was, an ex-tomboy, complete with freckles, who somehow transformed herself into a beautiful, desirable young lady. A young lady he knew that had definite plans of her own, waiting patiently for him to supply some of the answers.

"Do you love me, Jerry? Say it, please!"

He bent down, brushed his lips past one cheek, and kissed her ear lightly. "You know I do Katey, it's always been you."

She turned just enough to phantom kiss his lips. "Say it, Darling. I need to hear it."

He whispered as he brushed her lips. "I love you… give me a chance Katey… that's all I ask."

They danced on, Katey wanting to get close, Jerry wanting the same, but stern glances from one chaperon nearby convinced him he was close enough.

Suddenly he burst out with his thought."NO MORE KATEY! I'VE HAD IT! I'M SICK OF THE WHOLE MESS! I'VE MADE OF MY LIFE!"

"Jerry, quiet down," Katey cautioned. "What's the matter with you? Everybody within thirty feet heard you!"

The music stopped. Jerry led Katey back to their deserted table. "Let's blow this place, Katey. I'm ready to explode if I don't get this off my chest."

"Okay, okay, if you feel it's really that important!"

Outside, he escorted her down the block to the parked pick-up. He opened the door, picked her up and planted her on the front seat.

"Katey," he said, "your father really got to me tonight. I know what I must do, and tonight's the night I change my life forever. FOREVER, KATEY! DO YOU HEAR? FOREVER!

Katey thought she could guess, but she wanted to hear him say it. "Okay, Jerry, tell me!"

"No more crutches, for my mother! Not one dime or dollar for her anymore! Starting tonight, I'm taking charge at home. She comes across with her paycheck or I turn her over to the social workers for neglect and they'll put my two little sisters in foster homes. I don't care what she calls me, hell, I've heard worse before! From now on I row my own boat. I'm saving every dollar I can get my hands on! I've got plans too, Katey! I'm tired of being poor! Well, what have you got to say?"

Katey came alive. "I saw it in your eyes tonight after you and Dad had that little talk. I saw it in the way you acted tonight, and out on the dance floor I knew I was right about you. You have changed, Jerry. I've waited and hoped and prayed for two years that this day would come, and it has. We're both ready for the next step, Jerry."

He felt in his pocket. "Katey, I'm a little short on money tonight. It's still early, if you'd like to go for a sandwich I'll need a short loan 'til next payday at Bettingers. Promise to pay you back then."

"I'm really not very hungry. I'd rather talk. I've got a great deal on my mind too. Is there some place where we could talk alone?"

"Yes, it's real quiet out there, discovered it on one of my deliveries last week."

They headed out on the north side of Rushton, while Katey snuggled up on Jerry's shoulder. Down Bleeker Road they went 'til he found the spot he wanted, a small bluff at the end of the road, overlooking the city lights of Rushton below.

He rolled down the window on the driver's side. The cool, fresh air stimulated his thoughts. He had so much on his mind he wondered where to start.

Katey removed her corsage and put it safely away in the glove compartment. "I know we came out to talk, but I'd better play it safe… just in case."

He read her double meaning and decided tonight would be the night, the right time to pledge his love for her in a most honorable and respectful way. To Katey's surprise he opened the door to get out, and then went around to her side of the pick-up. He opened her door to see his Katey better. In the soft moonlight, she turned to him, eyes dancing, a radiance of its own making, bathing his face and her features in a glow that captured the epitome of the moment. She was something all right. He knew that if love had a name it had to have belonged to one KateLynn McCray that night.

"Katey, please scoot over to the edge of your seat… please."

Her eyes riveted on him, but she had to say it anyway. "Why do you want me to move over?"

"'Cause I've got something to say… something to ask you tonight… something that needs saying… you're so set on things being proper…"

She knew what was going to happen. Heart beating sixty miles a minute, adrenaline coursing through every vein, she moved over quickly. "Okay, here I am Jerry… go ahead, I'm ready!"

"Please Katey… your formal is blocking my way… was gonna use the running board to kneel down on…"

"Okay Love, I'll move my legs so you can kneel down between the folds. Wait! I'd better lift my formal a tad so you won't wrinkle it. My folks would have a tizzy if it came back looking all crushed and beat up! Remember dear, that's as far as you go… right, Jerry?" He nodded accordingly as they were both on the same romantic page

Now she knew for sure what was on his mind, the answer to more than two years of wonderful dreams and serious prayers. How could she refuse? He looked so grown up, so right for her, so ready to take the big step. Carefully, ever so carefully she opened up, making sure there was enough room for him to fit… to kneel on the running board between the folds of her formal and yet leave her plenty of modesty and no permanent wrinkles or creases that could never be explained.. "Okay Jerry, I'm ready," she breathed, "kneel down easy like… easy… please."

He found the room he needed and looked up into her sparkling eyes, flushed cheeks and soft forgiving lips. His heart too, was on fire.

"Katey, I know you've been patient with me, and I don't have much to offer you tonight except all my love, all my thoughts, and all my desire. Ever since I first looked up the word love in the dictionary I've thought of you. That word describes you perfectly. You've always been there for me, always been my friend, and now I'm hoping you'll say yes to being my wife. Will you marry me?"

She saw in his eyes not an eighteen year-old youth trying to be gallant, but a man ready to commit, eager for responsibility, wanting to share their love and their lives forever. How could she refuse?

Her adrenaline put on overload, her feelings, and yes, her passion overflowed. "Yes, yes," she whispered, her voice choked with so much emotion she barely got the words out.

He slipped his senior class ring on her wedding finger. "I promise Katey, my love, that if you'll put your faith and trust and love in me, I'll never disappoint you."

He rose up between the folds as she fell into his arms, her tears of joy never more beautiful, and her love for her man never more real than at that moment. "Gerald Landis, I love you, I love you. I want to be your wife, the best wife I can possibly be. Come sit by me, we need to make plans, such wonderful plans!"

No two lovebirds ever enjoyed each other's company more than Jerry and Katey did. "Katey, you go ahead, tell me what's on your mind."

"Kiss me first, like you really mean it, and then I'll talk!"

This time, their lips touched and connected, oh how they connected. He was deep, past her lips, taking every drop of pleasure she so joyously offered up to whet his appetite again and again. Finally she came up for air. "Wow! Now that was French kissing! Oh Jerry you do things to me when you do that!"

He put his arm around his Katey. "Okay, shoot! What's on your mind?"

"I know we both want the same thing, to get married as soon as possible. I've also got a pretty good idea about what my folks expect out of you before they'll go along, so here goes. I'm going to start summer quarter in business college, so I can get through as soon as possible Then next spring we can get married, I've got it all worked out. I'll get the jump on the good jobs, and then I'm going to help put you through college to get your degree. We'll be married, but we'll have to be on a real tight budget. We can make it if we really save every dollar between now and the next twelve months. What do you think, darling?"

"I'm going to hold down two jobs, Katey. Mr. Bettinger will let me deliver evenings and weekends besides my regular day job at the railroad, I've got to make up for lost time. I'll be able to buy a good used car by Thanksgiving and get you a real diamond engagement ring for Christmas. From that point on every buck I make goes into our saving account for our wedding. Katey, there won't be extra money for a honeymoon. I hope you can understand that."

Their two hearts beat as one, and so did their minds. "Jerry, I have a dowry coming, and so we can figure on some help there, and then I've got some things already saved in my hope chest." She laughed. "Molly and my mother keep calling it my hopeless chest but not anymore! I'll add to it as I can afford. By next spring they'll be surprised what I'll have in it for us!"

Both stopped talking at the same time, their faces, and their minds aglow with the excitement of planning their lives together, and the enormity of those plans and the changes that will and must take place. He kissed her again for reassurance. "We can swing it Katey, can't we? I mean by next spring?"

She gave him her best smile, the reassurance he needed. "Yes, my love. When two people want to be together as much as we do, we'll find a way!"

"Jerry?"

He knew that tone of voice and he knew Katey wanted something out of him. Only question on his mind was how deep she was going to dig concerning his past. "Before we started going steady, I know you dated Shirley Dawson and that checkout gal at Bettingers. And when you borrowed Greg's car to take them out I knew why. What I must know is what it meant to you. Please be honest with me when you answer."

Straight across to her shoulders keeping his gaze fixed on hers trying to gauge the depth of hurt and pain his answer would surely inflict upon the most wonderful, beautiful and trusting face he'd ever known. "Katey, it wasn't so great…at least I didn't think so. I wish I could've taken back what happened and saved myself for you, because that's how much I love you. YOUR'E THE ONE I'VE ALWAYS LOVED! NO ONE ELSE! Now if you can't or won't believe that then I truly am sorry for you."

He knew he'd hurt her, yet she had a wonderful look about her. Her soft words rang out true and clear. "Thank you for what you said, especially that part about wishing you could've saved yourself for me. You'll never know how much that meant. I was hoping and praying that your answer be something like that. Come back inside, my Love, there's more I'd like tell you."

Jerry got back in the pick-up. "Okay, let's hear the rest."

"Kiss me first, and then I'll tell you what I truly believe about us."

They sealed it, all their kisses; with all the love two people who ever loved could feel for each other.

"I know why you weren't satisfied with those two."

"You do? Why?

"When two people who truly love each other make love, it's the most precious and wonderful thing that could ever happen between them because it's part of God's plan for a man and a woman."

"You really believe that don't you, Katey."

"With all my heart and soul! And tonight, I'm going to prove it to you."

It took a full thirty seconds for the implication of what was said and offered to sink in. Jerry was speechless. Could his Katey really be willing to prove it with action instead of words? Caution was still Jerry's master. "Look Katey, you've held me off more times than I can count… sure this is what you want? I've waited this long, twelve more months isn't all that long now that I know we're gonna be married."

A demure, confident smile played across Katey's face in the moon's semi-bathed light. Passion building by the second, she sensed Jerry was about one kiss away from fulfilling everything she had ever wished or wanted. "I need your love now. I need to know for sure that I'm ready for your love…" Her words trailed off.

He held her close then kissed her hard, his way of showing his Katey that he was on fire. Next he blew his breath over the exposed cleavage on her formal. Suddenly he stopped to look for something.

"One other thing, Jerry, before we make love. It must be God's way, or not at all. I know what you were looking for and I won't ever allow you to wear one. If you want me, then it must be my way. Well?"

He looked down at his petite-figured Katey, his for the taking. Then something went off in his mind: *No matter what you do, above all else, you must be kind, you must take your time and you must be ever so caring and considerate.*

They finished redressing in silence outside the pick-up. Katey hummed away, her heart and thoughts soaring like a white dove winging its way across the heavens. Arm in arm, they returned to the pick-up. Once inside they studied each other, trying to sort out their feelings from their emotions trying to relive what had just happened.

"Any regrets Katey?" He whispered.

She blew him a kiss. "Oh my love, oh my love," she cried in exaltation, "now I know I was right… oh so right . You made everything so wonderful…and so beautiful with all your patience…"

"Sure it was safe? You do know about such things, don't you, Katey?"

"Well my super bean counter, just because I'm not going to be an accountant doesn't mean that I can't count my safe days. Been keeping close track ever since we started going steady …just in case."

Katey's reassuring answer was all Jerry needed. He smiled at her then proceeded to insert the key back into the ignition."

"Don't start just yet my love, there's still one very important question I need to ask you tonight."

His finished inserting the key but didn't crank the engine." I thought we covered all the questions, at least we both have the answers to your big one."

"Do you believe in God?"

He'd never been asked that before. More surprises from his Katey. "I don't know…up 'til now I never could see how He could really affect our lives' "

"God will always be a part of my life Jerry. I will have it no other way. Someday He will be a part of yours too. Do you believe in the Ten Commandments?"

"Boy Katey, you're really pitchin' 'em straight into the strike zone. I've never thought about that either… no, wait a minute, I take that back. Yes, yes, I believe the Ten Commandments are the way to go, the way we should live our lives. I believe in family values, too, that kind of life. I've never had a real family, but that's what I want. Katey, you don't really know how lucky you are to have the kind of parents that worry about you, who love you and who want you to be happy and succeed in life. If I'd had parents like that, maybe I wouldn't have strayed so much, did things I'm not very proud of, lead a much better, moral life."

She liked his remarks. "From now on, my love, our life is going to be pure between us, I know you're sincere, you've changed, or else you'd never have proposed to me. Tell me you love me again and again. Oh darling, I could never tire of you saying that to me. Such precious words when they're spoken from the bottom of our hearts. Such ugly, terrible words if they're spoken to get something or posses somebody."

Jerry looked down at his petite Katey. "Let me say this about the woman I'm going to marry, the same one I made love to only a few minutes ago. What a change! Four short years ago you were all tomboy, but I'll give you this, you sure didn't back down when I double-dared you down by the levee in Ormandy Park. Of course there wasn't much to see…a couple'a knobbies and a bit of peach fuzz."

He smiled then broke out into prolonged laughter. Katey's sharp jab to his ribs cut short anymore laughter. "Darned you Jerry Landis! Just couldn't leave it alone could you? I ran home and cried each night for a week straight. My mother finally broke down and bought me my first training bra even though I didn't have anything to train 'cause all my friends were already wearing them."

"I'll never forget what you said when it came my turn! Just two words! Holy cow!"

They both roared! "Oh my gosh! Oh my gosh! What time is it?"

nstinctively Jerry looked down at his left wrist. "Jerry! Where's your watch? The one I gave you last Christmas?"

"Left it at home. Oh God, Katey, your folks'll kill me!"

"NOT JUST YOU! ME TOO!"

Down Bleeker Road they drove neither certain of the late hour, only of their love for each other. A mile from home, Katey nudged Jerry. "There! There! Pull in! Texaco stations always have clean restrooms, I'd better double check."

He drove past the gas pumps and parked a short distance from the restrooms. "Here, don't forget your corsage Katey! Make everything look as normal as possible!"

She blew him a kiss and disappeared inside the ladies room. He got out, stretched his arms and legs and asked the attendant what time it was. "Two-thirty," he replied. "Say, how come a feller like you, one all duded up who drives a beat-up old pick-up, ain't got no watch? How come, huh?"

"It's a long story," said Jerry. "But tonight it's gonna change."

The attendant cracked a near-toothless grin. "Yeah I've heard that line more than just a few times too."

Katey got back in. "Everything's fine, not to worry. Even managed to find the same pinhole on my strap for the corsage. Did you find out what time it is?"

"Yeah, two-thirty!"

"That's not too bad. They'll understand, I hope!"

He saw her again in the light from the station, radiant, confident, make-up back in place as though nothing had ever happened between them.

"Are you sorry it happened, Katey?"

She looked so kissable, when she turned to him and quietly answered. "No, just remember, it can never happen again, it must not 'til we're married. Now I have the answers, and I'll be ready on our wedding night, ready with all my love for you my Dear, only you."

He turned the key, the engine cranked hard; it gave Katey time to say something. "We're only a few minutes late, a few more won't matter now. Don't start just yet, there's something else that needs to be said between us."

Again, another surprise for Jerry. "I can't imagine what, and I used to think I knew you so well, your every thought, the way you'd act or respond. After tonight, I'm not so sure."

"You still do," she smiled, "only tonight was different because it had to be, to be so special between us. Remember I said no more secrets between us, because we now believe it's an important foundation of our marriage. Now it's my turn. Remember those two movies they made us go to when we were sophomores?"

"Yeah, I remember, VD and teenage pregnancy. Boy that's where 'ol Jerr got the good word and smartened up in a hurry! Carried protection from that day on! So what's your point Katey?"

"I was worried sick about you and those two you were dating, because I knew you were the kind of guy who would live up to his responsibility if either one got pregnant, so I had to do something drastic to win you back."

"So what did you do, Love?

"Right after that VD movie, I cozied up to Shirley's best friend, Mimi Rogers, and she did the rest for me."

"So what happened?"

"I told Mimi that the county health nurse was looking for you 'cause you were on their list of the ten worst cases of VD in the county!"

"KATEY McCRAY! YOU DID THAT! NO, I DON'T BELIEVE YOU'D EVER DO SUCH A THING!"

"I had to Jerry, those two were ruining all my plans and prayers! I didn't dare wait any longer! I did it for us, don't you see?"

Katey watched for his reaction. She didn't have long to wait. First Jerry began shaking his head, still mired down by what his ex-tomboy had done to win him back. The more he thought about it, the more he was humbled by just how far his Katey was prepared to go for him.

" You're not angry at me are you, Jerry?"

He touched her arm. "Actually, I'm pretty proud of you, Hon. Now I know why Shirley gave me the dodge!" He started to laugh, then a bit harder as Katey joined in too. It was obvious that she'd been forgiven and then some!

They turned into the driveway next to the garage in front of Katey's home. He looked at her as never before. "If you don't kiss me Katey, I'm going to explode. I'm the luckiest guy alive to have you for my wife-to-be."

Katey threw her arms around her Jerry. "Smear up my lipstick real good, gotta make that part look right after being out so late! They'll expect that!"

She broke from his passionate kisses just long enough to murmur, "KateLynn Landis sounds even better. Good night, sweet love. The extra pillow I sleep with and hug the stuffin' out of, I call it my 'Jerry pillow.' Boy, is it ever gonna get a real workout after I say my prayers and thank God for answering them."

"All your prayers?"

"Especially one certain one, He was right. Ours is a perfect union, everything fits together even when I refused to believe it at first."

The twinkle in her eyes, the stardust in her hair, the eagerness and vitality of her character completely mesmerized Jerry Landis. "I wish I believed in your God, Katey, you have such faith, such a way about you, and after tonight, I wonder if there isn't somebody or someone out there who can put all the pieces of our life's puzzle together."

Katey beamed as radiant as he'd ever seen her. "There is my love, His name is God. We're going to have such a good life, such a happy life, just wait and see! Our plan will unfold with God's help."

He started the engine. "Level with me Katey, about tonight I mean. Tell me what this night meant to you.""

Her answer flowed as easily as sweet, spun honey spread on warm toast. "My first time? Unbelievable! The experience? Beyond understanding! There are no words to describe the feelings I have for you, the gentleness and patience you showed me when I needed and wanted your love. You are my man Jerry Landis, tonight you made me your woman!"

Katey got out of the cab and leaned in through the open window. "Your night's not over, not over by a long shot! Is it?"

"I've just begun to turn my life around. I'm going to have it out with my mother right now. No MOS! That's been going on far too long. Far too long!"

"All right dear, let's have it, your 'Jerry-ism', your acronym for today."

"It's simple Katey, I'm not taking any more of the same old crap my mother's been dishing out. MOS! More of the same. No more! Not after tonight!"

She blew him a kiss as he backed slowly out of the driveway. He called out to her. "I love you, Katey! You're my Katey! Never forget that!"

Suddenly he stopped and waited for Katey to approach the pick-up again. "What is it Katey?"

She paused, then her words slipped out anyway. "Not having second thoughts?"

"Second thoughts? Never! My ring on your finger means more to me than you can possibly know. It's the start of my new life. It's everything. You said no more secrets, and now I understand and agree. Katey, about tonight, I mean earlier, I came home from my deliveries and found mother drunk as a skunk. She'd blown her paycheck, and there wasn't a dime in the apartment! My two little sisters, Stacey and Cheryl hadn't eaten all day! I hocked the wristwatch you gave me to buy some food and pay for your corsage. Then I stayed to fix supper and make sure they got something to eat; that's why I was so darned late. I promise to get your watch back next payday! It'll never happen again."

Tears welled up in Katey's eyes as she fought hard to keep them there. "Jerry, if you need money for more groceries, I can let you have some. I'm so proud of you."

"Thanks Katey, but we'll manage 'till payday, I can get credit at Bettingers. After that, every dollar, every spare buck I make goes to us and our future."

Katey lifted her formal slightly so as not to trip on the front steps while watching him drive away. The tail lights flickered and he was gone. She stood alone in the moonlight, an enchanting night, a night filled with passion, and promises for a bright future, one that would have to be won by hard work, dedication, commitment, and love. She never felt more ready as she kissed the ring on her wedding finger and went inside.

# CHAPTER THREE

The clock at the bank corner chimed three as Jerry chugged past on his way to their two-bedroom apartment in the low-income housing complex, jokingly referred to by its tenants as 'The Highlands,' when in fact, it was anything but. He pulled up in front of the apartment, skillfully dodging between two trash cans that had been tipped over by stray packs of dogs who roamed the neighborhood in search of food scraps. Several cats scooted away, after trying to forage the dog-spilled leftovers for themselves.

He inserted his key and found the door unlocked. Not at all unusual for his mother rarely, if ever, used her key, preferring instead to often lean against it in her drunken stupor rather than give the neighbors a free show watching her fall down and dump the contents of her purse on the sidewalk looking for the lost key. Inside, he tripped over two empty whiskey bottles before his eyes adjusted to the darkness. His mind raced gathering his thoughts: *Aha! Mother must be 'entertaining', picked up some loser at a local bar and together they staggered home to sleep it off among other things.*

He groped in the darkness 'til his hand touched the kitchen sink, still filled with the same dishes from supper time his mother promised to do. Oh well, so much for promises from her, he told himself. He reached up to screw in the 15-watt light bulb over the sink that doubled for a sink and night light. It flickered all of three seconds and went out. *Par for the course*, he mused.

Down the hall he walked, stopping at the first door to his right to check on his two sisters in their bunk-beds. Stacey's blanket was on the floor. Like any concerned father, he picked it up and re-spread it over her, tucking it in along the sides, to make sure it stayed. Satisfied they were okay, he closed the door behind him, knowing full well he was about to encounter one hecku'va mess and confrontation the minute he stepped inside the next bedroom.

He flicked on the 30-watt ceiling light and found them in bed, one a stranger, and the other, his mother. On the stranger's side of the bed, he discovered another whiskey bottle; this one still had two or three good swigs left in it. Angrily, he ripped the covers off both of them, then kicked the feet of the stranger, shouting, "Hey Uncle Reuben, or Tom, or Dick, or Harry, or whatever the 'H' your name is, time to rise and shine! Mom's motel is closed from now on. No more tail around here! Get the message pal? Out of business!"

Jerry didn't wait for the cobwebs to clear in the stranger's head. He wadded up the man's clothes and delivered a major league baseball pitch aimed directly at the man.

"Hey, what the 'H' is goin' on?" the stranger blurted out.

"Get your butt out'a here, before I kick it right out the door!"

Jerry's mother stirred out of her drunkenness. "Get the 'H' out'a here you no good 'Sonofa B!'" she screamed. "Got no right bustin' in here. This here's Dan… he treats me good!"

"Yeah, I'll bet he sure does, a little piece here, a little tail there, some you'll never miss, right Mom?"

That got both of the sleepers' attention. Jerry jerked the man to his feet, stuffed his clothes into his massive belly, and headed him right on out the door, with his mother hollering obscenities after both of them.

At the front door, Jerry ripped the man's trousers from his hands, found his billfold, and took four 20's from it. "We're a little short of grocery money this month. You'll understand tomorrow when things will look a lot better."

"Hey! That's stealing! Gimme my money back! I'll call the cops on you! Gimme it back!"

Jerry shoved him out the front door and snapped on the outside light. He scanned the man's billfold. "Yes sir, Mr. Daniel Heiser, and it says here you live at 14037 SE Lynden Street. Well, well, what have we here? Must be pictures of the Mrs. and the little ones? Suppose they'd like to know where you slept tonight? By gosh, what'aya know? Must be your telephone number, 342-6149. How about me callin' and tellin' 'em to send a cab over here? That okay with you, Mr. Daniel Heiser?"

The stranger spouted his profanities at Jerry before he hurled the billfold in the stranger's direction. He avoided a sure fist-fight by slamming the door and sliding the bolt in place. Now it was time to take on his mother.

During the swift fracas with Mr. Heiser, Jerry's mother remained in her bedroom. She had heard more than enough. Staggering against the walls, bouncing from side to side as best her wobbly legs would carry her, she let her son have a full load of profanities from her pickled mind. It was worse than the proverbial washtub worth of gutter slime and sleeze. "Who put you in charge, you 'S-O-B'?"

Jerry calmly and very deliberately escorted her toward the kitchen table. "You keep calling me some of those names you just used, and first thing you know the neighbors will think you're beginning to like me just a little bit! I'd pick 'Sonofa B', sounds a lot better."

They made their way to the kitchen table, Jerry found the light switch. "Smart butt, Mr. Smart mouth," she shouted into his ear, her breath and her foul mouth nearly doing him in.

"Shssh. You'll wake the girls."

"Who gives a diddly dang. I'm up, by God they might as well be too."

He parked her in the closest chair, and then took an old broom that'd seen better days, and took one sweet, level major-league swing with it, clearing off the debris-laden table. Old newspapers, paper plates, two empty whiskey bottles, pieces of bread, and an empty box of cereal all went flying through the air. "There now, got a clean table, good place to hold our little pow-wow, don't you think, Mother?"

If she heard him, she could care less; she directed what little concentration she had on pulling the near-empty whiskey bottle out of her bathrobe pocket and sucking its contents dry.

Whack! Jerry knocked the bottle from her lips. "Sober up, Mother! I'll fix coffee, and then we're going to talk."

Through a bobbing, throbbing head and bleary eyes, she tried to follow her son's activity. She gave up a half minute later, and fished into her other bathrobe pocket, finally coming up with one bent cigarette butt, and an open book of soggy matches. Jerry stood back and watched the comic futility, a soused drunk trying to light a half-smoked cigarette with a whiskey soaked book of matches. He finally took pity on the poor woman and lit her up with a farmer match. She tried to say something, but the lit cigarette stuck to her lower lip, burning her. "You 'Sonofa B' she screamed in his face, "You made me burn my lip!"

Twenty minutes and three hot coffee refills later, Jerry faced his mother across the table. "Here's how it's going to be, so listen up. From now on, I'm in charge around here, you're going to hand over every paycheck to me. I'll pay the bills and make the decisions. Got it? You either go it alone or else you lose Stacey and Cheryl."

She sat stupefied for a long minute. "Ain'tcha gonna help out like you used to?"

"Not anymore, every dollar I make goes into my savings account. Katey and I plan on being married a year from now."

It took a full minute to let Jerry's message sink in. Then all kinds of heck broke loose. She picked up her half-filled cup and flung it as hard as she could in his general direction. He saw it coming and ducked in plenty of time.

"You worthless 'Sonofa B' ! Finally get big enough to do me some good… help around here a little bit and what the hell happens? You're gonna walk out on me! You not only look like your old man, you're pulling the same crap on me! First he deserts me and now you! Ain't that something!"

Jerry got up, went to her bedroom and came back with a hand mirror off her dressing table. Seething with anger, he vented his rage. He grabbed her once glorious head of light brown hair, shoved the mirror in her face and exploded. "Take a good look Mom! A darned good look!" Twice he jerked her head 'til some of the dullness left the hollow grey sockets that passed for her eyes. "If you aren't the sorriest excuse for a woman God ever laid eyes on! No wonder my father deserted us! Who would want to come home to something that looked like you?"

The minute Jerry let go, her eyelids closed as she slumped over, hitting her head on the table. Again he jerked her back into reality, his world, not hers. He shook his head in disgust at the bag of bones that took up space inside her nightgown and bathrobe. His Mother.

He tossed the mirror aside then concentrated on getting her attention once more. Two quick slaps to her cheek hurt him almost as much as it did her as he discovered her cheek bones jutted out now more than ever. He put one hand behind her head to steady it, and then doubled up the other fist in front of her sickly looking face and let his fist do the talking, waving it back and forth a scant inch in front of her nose. "As for helping out, dear Mother, every dime I've made since my first paper route when I was twelve 'til now, I've spent helping out. Six year's worth, Mother! Got that? I'm sick of being poor! Of doing without while my friends are doing just fine! No more, Mother! No more! You go it alone, or I'll run you in for child desertion and neglect! You'd better hear me good 'cause you're going it alone from now on."

Jerry's mother got in her two-bits. "Said it to your old man, an' I'll say it to you! You ain't worth the spit on the public park bench, Gerald Landis! Never will amount to a damned thing. Go ahead, walk out on me! Go ahead! Who cares? Marry up with your little Irish whore, see if I care! Surprised she ain't knocked up by now! How come she ain't Jerry? Yea, how come? Ain't man enough are ya?"

He slapped her alcohol-drained, shallow face. Back and forth, her head bounced from shoulder to shoulder like a ping-pong ball. Then he grabbed her hair and stuck his head right in her face. "You're not fit enough to kiss my Katey's month-old footprints! She's the best thing that's ever happened to me! I'm the luckiest guy in the world to have her because she believes in me, and I love her."

Jerry released his grip on his mother; she folded up into her chair. "Go to 'H' Gerald Landis! Why don't you pack up and walk out now? Go to your little Irish bitch! Live with 'em! See if I care!"

"Don't tempt me, Mother. If it weren't for Stacey and Cheryl, I'd be long gone. I'd pull the quickest Hank Snow you've ever seen by moving on. You got one last chance, shape up or I ship my sisters out. Which is it, Mother? C'mon, make up your mind."

For the first time, Jerry's mother was in the driver's seat. A cruel smile slithered across the corners of her thin, ugly mouth. "Well Mr.

Smart butt, you outsmarted yourself this time. You'll have to wait 'til next payday to find out, won't'cha?"

Jerry wasn't about to let her end their conversation on a winning note. "You bring one more of your bar buddies in here for some sack time and I'll run you in on a morals charge. Then we won't have to wait 'til next payday, now will we, Mother dear!"

# CHAPTER FOUR

Sleep was next to impossible for Katey, she rolled and tossed and turned in bed. Even kissing and hugging her extra pillow didn't help much this time, it just wasn't real enough anymore, not when she'd hugged and kissed and held the real McCoy, Jerry Landis.

At 6 A.M. sharp, she got up, did an impromptu Irish jig, letting her nightgown flare and billow out, and then sidled over to her hope chest. There she opened it to set the upper tray out so she'd have a clear view of the contents in both the tray and the chest bottom. She hummed and sang to herself. Never in all her young years had she been so happy, felt so good about herself, or loved her Jerry more than she did at that moment. Remembering how grateful she was for her good fortune and the blessings bestowed upon her, Katey knelt in front of her chest and offered a silent prayer of thanks to the Almighty.

Mary rose to put on the coffee pot and glanced inside Katey's bedroom as she'd always done each morning. "Lass, what are you doing up so early? You come in at the wee hours and look at you, you're fresh as new-baked bread!"

Katey ran to her mother. "Oh I can't hold it in, I'm so very, very happy! See my ring? Jerry proposed last night! Oh Mother, my dreams, all my plans, they're coming true!"

Mary was far less excited or enthusiastic. "KateLynn McCray, get your head out of the clouds. Wait'll your father sees what you've gone and done. He has such big plans for you."

Katey was very unconcerned. "What, you mean go to Business College in Sacramento? No problem. That fits right in with Jerry's and my plans. Only difference is that I'm starting summer quarter next month instead of in the fall. I'll be through by spring break next year, and then I'll hit the job market early to land a good position to help put Jerry through college. And of course we'll be married by then. It's all worked out, Mother! Isn't it exciting? I can hardly wait to start Business College!"

There was no shutting Katey down, and her mother sensed the futility of offering any further argument. "Jerry's awful young to be proposin' KateLynn. Suppose you've taken that into consideration, have you?"

Katey beamed a toothpaste commercial smile. "No he's not, Mother, he's a lot older than you and daddy think, and he's all man, ready for marriage and responsibility."

"Aye Lassie, maybe so, but 'tis your Jerry ready to be a good Catholic?"

Mary's question brought Katey back down to earth. "He will be if I ask him, he's never belonged to any church, so that shouldn't be a problem."

"Come Lass, while I put on the coffee."

Katey, still on cloud nine, followed her mother out to the kitchen. Mary put the coffee on and popped another question. "Tell me the truth, now has Jerry ever been to church?"

Katey started setting the table. "No, I don't think so… but why should that matter? He knows he must be Catholic in order for us to marry."

"Ah, KateLynn, and there's the rub. Maybe he'll take one look inside our church and bid you good-day, then what? Eh KateLynn? You should've brought him to our church before you accepted his ring. The damage may already be done."

"I… I hadn't really given that much thought… always assumed he'd go along…"

Mary laid out the bacon strips in the broiling pan. "Take the ring off 'til you're sure, Lass. I'll not mention this to your father for now, no need to upset him."

"NO, NEVER! JERRY'S RING STAYS ON, MOTHER! I accepted it and I won't take it off… not after…"

"Not after what, KateLynn?"

For a split second the mother confronted her daughter, trying to get an accurate read. "Is there something you should be tellin' me?"

"Of course not," KateLynn sharply replied. "What I meant was, not after we both committed ourselves to marriage and our plans."

Mary let KateLynn's remark pass for now. "Come make the toast and put out that new jar of jam from the fridge. I'll go wake your father."

After breakfast KateLynn helped do the dishes and then went back to her room. Mary followed, KateLynn's remark disturbed her. She closed the door. "We're alone now KateLynn, and I'm still wonderin'."

Katey was up tight. "Why is it every time I try to make things work out, get some happiness for a change, you come along and poke and prod and needle 'til you almost take most all my happiness away? Why, Mother, do you do that?"

Mary tried to comfort her daughter. "Tis your stage of life that's botherin' me Lass. A mistake here, a bad decision there, and your life's changed forever. Can you not see that? Your father'n me want only the best for you, surely you can see that too."

The following week passed without further questions from Mary and no open conflict between the McCray women. Graduation wasn't until the following Saturday, so KateLynn spent the week working at the five-and-dime earning extra money. Both mother and daughter made an extra effort to get along and enjoy their time together. For as Mary so aptly pointed out, "We go 'round but once Lass, let's make sure we stay in the same circle."

Graduation Saturday was a marvelous day. Warm, late May breezes helped make the outdoor graduation exercise all the more enjoyable at the high school football stadium. Fifty graduates gathered with their parents, friends and relatives on that day, and were challenged by the keynote speaker not to look back, but to face tomorrow with dedication, determination, and desire.

Aaron had a tear in his eye as he and Mary heard the name KateLynn McCray called out. How proud they were to see her walk across the stage in cap and gown to accept her diploma. He looked down on his wife. "Aye Mary, the first of our family to make it through high school. Now would'ja not say the ocean voyage was well worth it?"

Mary squeezed her husband's muscular arm. "See how she carried herself, aye, she's a proud one, our KateLynn is."

"And she'll go far, too, I'm thinkin', Mrs. McCray."

"See how KateLynn looks, first to us, then to Jerry when they called out his name? Our KateLynn's taken by the young lad. She claims he's a man, ready for marriage and responsibility. Could she be right?"

He stroked his chin, and closed his eyes in deep thought before answering. "I think it's time we put him to the test. KateLynn's worried about us not inviting him when we eat out this afternoon. I think we should insist he join us, give me a chance to see what makes this lad tick."

All too soon, it was time for handshakes, hugs, and good-byes between the classmates, followed by last minute snapshots. The Amigos were no exception. Greg rallied his bunch around for picture taking, and then the sad good-byes. Jerry and Katey held hands and actually seemed to enjoy the so-longs and fare-wells as both saw only one another and what tomorrow would bring – their future.

The dinner went off far better than either Katey or Jerry expected. Aaron McCray had Jerry sit next to him and monopolized his every minute, pumping him with questions, getting good straight answers in return, and then moving forward with a new batch of questions.

Mr. McCray drove home after dinner with Katey and Jerry in the back seat. Katey was in near-shock when her father parked out in the driveway, got out and then waited for Jerry to emerge from the back seat. He handed him the keys and looked directly at Katey. "KateLynn, do you suppose Jerry could drive home and you bring the car back? There's some family business that needs tending to."

He shook hands with Jerry. "Enjoyed talking to you, Son, hope to see you soon!"

Jerry could hardly believe his ears. Katey had to give him a nudge. "C'mon Jerry, you know better than to keep my father waiting."

Down the street they went with Jerry driving ever so cautiously behind the wheel. Katey scooted over next to him. "Oh Lord, Jerry, it's happening. My folks are coming around. They like you. Hope you didn't mind dad's third degree?"

"Can you believe it, he called me Son! I'm driving his new car! No, I was ready for him when he started in on me. I could tell he liked my answers. Sorry he kept me so busy hardly had time to eat or look at you."

He turned off Maynard Avenue and headed toward the housing complex. "Hey Katey, what's with this family business bit anyway?"

Katey gave him a hug. "It's the best possible news for us. They're really gonna grill me about you. Depending on my answers, you'll be accepted into or rejected by our family. It's old country, but I don't mind, it had to come sooner or later, and I'm looking forward to it!"

"Shouldn't I be there? You may not know everything about me."

"No secrets, remember? Now you can see how it all fits.. You already had your grilling at dinner, and you passed. Now it's my turn."

Jerry pulled up in front of his apartment. He kissed her, and she responded immediately by moving her body into his. Her perfume, her cherry lips, the freshness of her hair, the closeness of her body stirred him. "Katey, I've got to ask this."

"I already know the question and the answer. Yes, I think about it all the time. I wasn't going to tell you, but every time I'm near you, you know what I want. Even if it hurts so much, it's the same thing we both want. The next twelve months are gonna seem like years, but we must hold back Jerry."

He touched the outside of her breasts ever so slightly, she almost came apart. "Please, please, I can't let you do that anymore... not after what happened... I have to keep control, if I let you have any more pleasure I won't be able to stop. That's what you've done to me. All because of what happened, all because I love you so much I can't keep away from you."

"I'm in the same boat too. I'm so crazy about you. So much in love with you. Good thing I have two jobs coming up, that's the only way I'll be able to keep away from you."

He slid the driver's seat forward before he got out of the car, and then opened the back door of the sedan to fetch a small cushion. "There Katey, it's all set up for you, so you can see to drive back safely."

Katey slid over onto the cushion behind the steering wheel. "How's it going with your mother since you had it out with her?"

He leaned back in through the open window. "Better than I expected. Last night was her weekly payday from the laundry, and believe it or not but she came home and handed it over to me. Then she tried to fix supper," he laughed. "She's a terrible cook when she's half sober or better, but I'll give her credit, she at least tried. Burned everything, but my sisters and I did our best to hack our way through it."

Katey started the car. "Gotta go Sweetheart, they're waiting on me. Oh, one last question, they're going to ask me sure as heck about you starting to attend church with me, what do I tell them?"

"I don't know anything about your God, Katey, even less about your Catholic Church, but you can count on me to do my part if it'll help swing the vote in our favor. Tell them I'm willing to do whatever it takes."

They kissed and Katey started to back up, Jerry hailed her. "Katey, I'm still worried about you-know-what. Sure it was safe?"

She blew him a kiss. "I can still add up the safe days. Bye Jerry, I love you!"

Aaron and Mary McCray were waiting for Katey at the kitchen table. Katey sensed the importance and the seriousness of their session when she saw her father's leprechaun -adorned tobacco humidor sitting on the corner of the kitchen table instead of resting in its usual spot in the front parlor. Aaron refilled his pipe, lit it, and then smiled reassuringly toward his daughter. "Before we get down to business KateLynn, your mother and I want to tell you how very proud we are of you graduating today. With Jerry with us, we didn't think it proper to do this in front of him." He handed her an envelope. "It's our graduation present to you. There's a check for all your tuition and books for the one year course to Sacramento Business College. We also included enough money to cover bus tickets and lunches. Your mother tells me you want to start summer time, and not wait 'til the fall. Is that right, Lass?"

She hugged and kissed her father. "Thank you, thank you, both of you! I want to start the summer quarter which means I'll be through by spring so I can help with Jerry's college expenses,"

"Your mother also has a little something for you."

Katey ran to Mary to put her arms around her.

"This is a check for five hundred dollars. We believe your hopeless chest could sure stand the help, my love."

She hugged and kissed her mother. "Oh you two are so good to me. Thank you, thank you, from the bottom of my heart!"

Mr. McCray got up from his chair, circled the room and stood by Katey and Mary. "One other small item, KateLynn. At your graduation today, we noticed how your friends kept calling you Katey and how you handled that name so easily. I think over here they call it your nickname. We kinda like it, and if you've no objection, we'd like to call you that too. Of course your proper name must always be KateLynn and we expect you to use that name on official things as before. Well Lass, what say you?"

She turned to her father, her adoring father. "Oh yes, yes! Oh Daddy, Mother, I love you two so very much, you two are the best parents in the whole wide world!"

Mary cleared her throat. "Now then, down to business. In-as-much as you've set your mind and your cap for Jerry Landis, it's time we found out more about him. Katey, are you sure the Lad's but eighteen? Your father'n me feel certain he must be older. Perhaps they held him back a year or two."

Katey was never more ready or proud of her response. "Jerry's eighteen, but only by the calendar. He's had to raise himself alone as best he could. His father deserted the family when he was six, so he's had to go it alone."

"What about his mother? Why wasn't she to his graduation, Katey? Surely she would've been proud of him, like we are of you. It's the proper thing to do."

Katey answered her mother's question. "Jerry and his mother have no use for each other."

"What? You mean there's no respect in their home? How can that be?"

Katey got up. "Mom, Dad, get a good grip on your chairs. Jerry's mother is an alcoholic, and as foul-mouthed a woman as you'd ever not want to meet. She keeps running him down, I guess because he reminds her of his father. She's drunk most of the time and brings home different men to sleep with her. How he puts up with that is beyond me. He has two little sisters who I'm sure have different fathers, but Jerry treats them like they're his very own family. He protects them from his mother, and I believe that's why he still sticks around home."

Mary's mouth opened, her eyes popped. "My goodness Lass, oh my heavens! No wonder the Lad never talks about home! Lord, he has none!"

Aaron's eyebrows furrowed. "That explains the home situation, but you've told us on several occasions that Jerry's worked since he was twelve years old. How is it that he has no money or savings?"

Again, Katey told it as it was. "Since Jerry started his paper route when he was twelve 'til last weekend, he's turned over every dime to his mother. She's blown it on booze and other men she picks up at several bars in the neighborhood. Little, if any, of that money ever gets spent on food or clothes for his sisters or to pay the bills. Jerry and his mother had it out with each other, and now Jerry's in charge since last weekend, and things are better for now at least."

Mary could only shake her head. "How did such a nice young man ever come from such a place like that, Katey?"

"Mom, Dad, all Jerry and I ask is that you just give him a chance! He's saving his money now, and by Thanksgiving he'll have his first car. It'll be used, but I know Jerry, it won't be a clunker. By Christmas, he will give me a proper engagement ring and wedding band, and by next spring, a year from now, we'll both be ready for marriage. We've done some homework and we can make it on our own by then. We'll have to live on a very tight budget, but we love each other very much; we're committed to marriage and we'll have enough money saved so he can start college then."

Aaron had more questions. "Today at dinner Jerry told me he plans on getting a degree in accounting with your help. Katey, we don't know much about this accounting business. Can you tell us something about it?"

Katey was oh so pleased to relate what she knew. "Jerry's taken every bookkeeping class they offered in high school as background for his future job in accounting. Accountants keep a company's financial or money records, but I know he wants to specialize in analyzing what to do and where to put that money to work where it will do the best job, or the most good. He has good ideas, so he'll do well once he gets his degree."

Mary had other questions. "Katey, once Jerry gets this degree, can he make a good living at it?"

Katey knew exactly what was on her mother's mind. "Yes, Mother, I'll be able to quit my job and stay home to have our babies."

"You do plan on having children, don't you?"

"Yes, Daddy, you'll have grandchildren, you'll just have to wait and be patient. Jerry and I both want a family. We do believe in family and the values it brings to our marriage."

Aaron was satisfied with Katey's answers so far. "Mother, we could stand a pot of coffee. There's much more that needs to be said."

Mary made coffee and the question and answer session continued. Mary spoke up. "Lass, does it not strike you as odd that Jerry will be dealing and handling money when up to now he's had so little of it?"

Katey couldn't help but smile. "All the better, Mother, because no one will take care of money and manage it better than Jerry, I'd trust him with my last dollar!"

Aaron had other thoughts too. "Marriage is serious business, and of course Katey, you must be absolutely sure he is the one for you. There can be no divorce, no mistakes, no second-guessing. Are you that sure about him?"

Katey got up to set three coffee cups around the table. "Yes, I agree marriage is serious business and we are both committed to making our marriage work. There are no secrets between us since last week, and we both believe that is the best way to start off a good, solid marriage."

Mary's ears perked up. "No secrets, eh Lass! And can you tell us about Jerry's morals? With him raising himself so to speak, and him being so experienced so to speak in life, have there been others, other women in his life?"

Katey didn't care for the question. "Come out and say it Mother! Yes, he's had other women, I told you there are no secrets between us!"

Aaron tried quickly to defuse the situation. "Katey, surely you must realize we meant no harm in your mother's question. Jerry's been on his own for all these years, and you've just told us he's had others. How will that affect your marriage?"

"Yes, it bothers me considerably he's been with others, but that's in his past and neither of us can change that. I've forgiven him and for two years since we've been going steady he has never cheated on me, and that's a pretty good basis for trust and understanding. There is a purity between us now, and nothing is ever going to change that."

"Careful Katey, when you say that, I know you mean that now, but time can change things that were true only a short time before."

Katey would not be swayed by her father's remarks. "I still stand behind what I said, Daddy. It's there, it happened, and it will always be there. I will honor that purity with everything that's in me. So will Jerry."

Mary read Katey's double meaning and quickly turned to another question. "You told me lately that he's never been in a church, ours or any other. Can you say with a certainty Lass, he'll come to our church?"

"That's the last thing he told me this afternoon when I brought the car back. He said he'd be willing to do whatever it takes to make our marriage work, including going to our church."

"Aye, Lassie, but you told me yourself Jerry doesn't believe in God."

"That's true, but again, I ask you to give him a chance. He does believe in our Ten Commandments, and we will live by them in our marriage, and that too, is a pretty good basis for a good, solid, happy marriage. He also has told me that he respects my freedom of religion and will do nothing to oppose me or my beliefs."

Aaron went to the stove to refill his coffee cup. One last question, "Katey, and I'll put it to you straight. Suppose after going to church and it comes time for your wedding and Jerry balks at committing to his marriage vows in our church, what then?"

Katey never batted an eyelash or flinched a muscle. "I WILL NEVER LEAVE MY CHURCH NOR ABANDON MY GOD FOR ANY MAN! NOTE EVEN JERRY LANDIS!"

Mary and Aaron McCray were extremely happy over Katey's adamant reaffirmation. "Well, Mother, how say you?"

"I say our Lassie has earned the right to invite her man to late Mass and early afternoon dinner each and every Sunday."

***

For three weeks, Katey and Jerry buried their thoughts and feelings in good old-fashioned work habits. Sundays were the one exception, and the two spent every waking moment they possibly could together, enjoying their precious hours as though they were rationed out grudgingly, for in a sense they were.

On the fourth Saturday afternoon, Katey came home early as business was slow at the store. "Where's Daddy?"

"They called him an hour ago, a train's been derailed east of here, and there are new ties and rails for his crew that needs puttin' back."

Mary visited with her daughter while she changed clothes in her bedroom. "Think I'll go see Molly this afternoon, her mother's saving Betty Crocker coupons for me; hope there's enough so I can send for my spoons to finish out my silverware set."

"And Molly, what does she say about you wearing Jerry's ring?"

"She and Ricco have been fighting quite a bit lately. She wants to get married right away, and seeing my engagement ring hasn't helped matters any. Jerry says this is the time for Molly to test Ricco's intentions, but she won't risk it."

"Risk what, Lass?"

Katey looked at her mother. "I guess it's safe to tell you, now that I know you can keep a secret. They're making love all the time, like married people do."

Mary was shocked. "Katey, they must stop at once! 'Tis the work of the devil, this temptation of the flesh! Oh Katey, this is bad, very bad! Tell Molly when you see her that she must confess her sins at once. Then, no more!"

Katey let her mother quiet down. "Molly's been careful, her period happens like clockwork, and she only lets Ricco make love to her on the safe days. She sees nothing wrong with that as long as they plan on getting married."

Again Mary was shocked. She turned to Katey, eyes blazing, and lashed out. "What's this world comin' to? Your friends have turned their backs on the teachings at home and their church. This cannot go on, people will be hurt, lives will be ruined. Can they not see that? Only when they are married is such a thing proper between a man and his wife. ONLY THEN, KATEY!"

Katey slipped into a loose skirt. "I'm sorry I told you, now you're all upset."

Mary sat down on the edge of the bed. "Come, sit down with me. There's plenty of time to see Molly today, we have much to talk about."

Katey always hated it when her mother used that tone of voice with her. "Mother, please, no new lectures today. We've been getting along just great, don't spoil it now."

Mary was firm again with her voice. "KateLynn, we have to talk. Come, sit down."

Her daughter knew there was no getting around her mother's strong Irish will. She finished buttoning her blouse and reluctantly sat down. Katey took the initiative. "Jerry stopped by today during my lunch break. Oh Mother, you should've seen how proud he looked and felt when he showed me his savings passbook. Two hundred eighty-eight dollars already! I miss him so much, and love him beyond words. Do you know love can actually hurt? Yes, that's what I said, actually hurt. That's how much I love Jerry."

Mary put her hand on Katey's. "KateLynn, I know."

"You didn't hear a single word I said. Know what Mother?"

Mary rose, a troubled look etched deep in her face. "I'm going to fix your father's favorite, his roasted chicken. I'll be busy in the kitchen. Come to me when you're ready, and we'll talk about it. Maybe there's a chance your father needn't find out."

Katey blushed crimson. She broke out in a sweat across her forehead. Suddenly she felt a gnawing, sickening lump in the pit of her stomach. How could her mother know? Was she bluffing? No, Katey knew better, when personal or private family matters were at stake, Mary McCray never minced feelings or words. She definitely knew something, but what?

Ten, fifteen, twenty, long excruciating, agonizing minutes passed while Katey stayed glued to her bed.

Mary worked quietly, confidently in the kitchen. She knew getting a confession out of Katey was akin to pulling teeth, but she waited patiently for her daughter's belated appearance. First would come the flood of tears, her lower lip would curl just a tad, then the begging for forgiveness followed by one giant-sized bear hug from such a small person. It had always followed that pattern since the fourth grade, when Katey's teacher sent home a note requesting that Katey wear bib overalls for the remainder of the school year. Seems her tomboy had been caught lifting her dress at the top of the stairs at school during recess so one certain boy, pretending to drink at the water fountain below could look up and see a pretty pair of lace panties exposed for all his own personal viewing. It wasn't 'til years later, she found out that boy was named Gerald Landis.

# CHAPTER FIVE

Tears cascading down both cheeks, Katey rushed into her mother's arms. "Please, please, don't tell Daddy. I love Jerry so. Please, please, don't tell! He'll make Jerry go away! Please, please, don't tell"

"Let me put the chicken dinner in the oven, then we'll talk."

Into Mary's bedroom, Katey followed her mother. She closed the door and between sobs, she blurted out, "Mother, it only happened once."

Mary held her daughter close and they rocked gently together, much as Mary had done when Katey was a baby. "I know, I know. You put your dainty in the laundry and I noticed a bit of a blood stain, and lots of Jerry's manhood dried on the inside. You should've hand-washed them if you didn't want me to find out when you came home after your graduation ball."

Katey cried her heart out, begging forgiveness, and promising it would never happen again. Mary listened intently, never doubting for an instant that Katey would keep her promise. "What do you think I should do about this KateLynn?"

Mary got up to get KateLynn a hanky from her dresser drawer. Soon the sniffles were more or less under control.

"I know you think it's a sin of the flesh and that I must be weak, but I'm not. All my life, I've had to wait to become a woman, to try to catch up with the others. Molly told me just how wonderful it felt to her, and I couldn't wait, not after Jerry gave me his ring, and his promise and commitment. I only did it because I wanted my wedding night with Jerry to be extra special and now I know I must get help for it to be really the way I want it between us after we're married. Jerry didn't force me, I asked him to… it was more my idea."

"Katey, 'tis a sad lot we women have to take on. We endure the pain of our first time with our man, then, later, comes the pain of birthin' our babies and all the monthly pain thereafter. "Tis a nasty, dirty business, but if we don't submit, we may wake up to find our husband's shoes under another's bed. Aye, and that's worse yet!"

"Dirty business? Is that what you really think making love with each other is? Oh, it hurt, boy did it hurt. But I've never felt anything like it, and the pleasure we gave each other, Mother, it was unbelievable!"

Mary stood before her daughter dumbfounded. "Katey, are we talkin' 'bout the same thing?"

Katey was surprised and shocked. "You and Dad…never thought much about it before, but I never see you and Dad touch much or kiss either, for that matter. How come?"

Mary did not appreciate being questioned. "That's private business KateLynn, it belongs behind closed doors, and that's where it stays between your father n'me."

"When Jerry and I marry, I want to be touched and caressed and kissed and held tight, and when nobody's around, I hope he does even more to me. I can't wait to give him all the pleasure he wants, and in turn there's plenty of things he can do to me that I might like, too!"

Mary was flabbergasted. . "Oh, the Saints preserve us. My daughter has become a worshipper of the flesh! Sins of the flesh, Katey!"

"Stop it, Mother! That's a lot of hooey Grandma Brannigan passed on down to you, it's enough to scare the liver out'a most decent women. No wonder you don't like it, and no wonder you and Dad don't show any affection toward each other. Give yourself a chance. Find out, explore, touch, caress, search! I'll bet you and Dad have been missing out on one heckuva lot of pleasure, and not to mention all the good love-making too!"

"So, my Katey, my KateLynn's become the bedroom expert! And after one night of sin, no less! How's that for gall?"

"Okay, it's confession time, so Mother, here goes! During the first year we started going steady I made sure that Jerry never got anywhere. I was testing him and he seemed to understand it that way. This last year I've been gradually, oh so gradually letting him explore a little bit at a time. I made sure he could only have my breasts and you know what dear Mother? I get as much pleasure as he does. I don't have the right words to describe how wonderful it feels!"

Mary squirmed and fidgeted during Katey's most personal confession. Up came a warning finger in Katey's face. "I don't care how much you or Jerry enjoyed it! This must stop at once! You're not a married woman! Remember that Lass! I knew you were never a Saint but this …this cannot go on! I don't care how much of this pleasure you say you get from doing this. You must see Father Murphy at once! Do you hear me?' I'm shocked that you've been doing such things!" Mary went to the bedroom door.

"Hold it Mother! Before you go check on the chicken, do me one favor! Please!

"Daughter, I don't think my ears can handle much more! They're about to catch fire now from what you've told me."

"Okay, okay. Think back in your life since you've been married and see if there wasn't one time. One incident maybe, that you wanted dad to do something more or maybe explore a little farther, but your modesty or your Brannigan old wives tales wouldn't let you! Betcha' you'll come up with something! Mother, betcha!"

Katey helped set the table. Neither of the McCray women said one word to each other during this time, and that worried Katey. After all that had been exchanged between mother and daughter, nothing had been resolved regarding Mary finding out about Katey's one night of love-making with Jerry. Katey feared that all her poor mother could do was meet her husband at the door when he came home and dump the whole problem in his lap for the meting out of swift justice as he saw fit. In that case, Jerry's Sunday visits would be history.

"What are you going to do about telling father?"

Mary raised her apron to her forehead to wipe her brow. "Aye Lass, 'tis a puzzle dealin' with the likes of you. Do you have time for the tellin' of a tale, perhaps?"

Katey grabbed two cups. Then mother and daughter sat down together. "Okay, you have all my attention."

Mary tasted the coffee. "Go get the Irish whiskey, Katey, the tellin' of this is gonna take a stout heart!"

Katey's mother laced her cup with a good shot and dropped a small dose in Katey's cup. "Your father'n me married at the worst possible time, Lass. The potato famine had done its dirty work, even though it happened years before. Times were tough in our village and most of us were barely getting by. Thank God for the money my older sister Rose and her husband, Kevin, sent from Chicago. But times in Chicago were hardly better, the soup lines stretched down for blocks, sometimes as far as the eye could see! Your father's seed had taken hold in me by the time we arrived in Chicago to live in them beehives, places unfit for neither man nor beast! Never hated a place so much as them beehives!"

"They're called tenements, Mother."

"Whatever! Anyway, the short of it is I had to find work, and I did, helpin' the cook at a cheap restaurant nearby. Your father finally found work 'way down on the south side in the cattle yards by the slaughter houses. By the time he rode the bus to work, he was gone a good 18 hours a day. How he stood them hours I'll never know. My feet swelled something awful, especially around me ankles. After supper one evening, your father goes down the hall to the community toilet and shower on our floor to fetch some water to soak me feet in. He comes back with a pail and pours the water in a basin. The poor man was half-dead, but he wanted to do for me. Anyhow he drops to one knee to rub my feet. Next thing I know, he's touchin' 'n kissin' my stomach where you are. He's got a funny look on his face, like he's askin' me permission to do more, but no words have I for him. I was shocked by such behavior, I tell you!"

"Mother, don't you see? Dad wanted to know if it was all right."

"He moves on down and wants to kiss! Katey, I was near panic! I pushed his head aside and told him in no uncertain words that if he had kissin' in mind, he was headed in the wrong direction! He got angry, and rose up. He accidentally touched my breast to steady himself. That one touch, my breasts were already heavy with milk waitin' on your arrival. Well, Lass, they near exploded from your father's touch, they were on fire! That's where he should'a been!"

"Did he ever do anything like that again?"

"Never! I had shamed the poor man! Katey, I was still sixteen and pregnant, I knew nothing 'bout such goings on! My mother, God rest her soul, had told me only to submit to him when he needed to do his business, nothing else!"

Katey could only shake her head. "You and Dad! What a waste of real pleasure between you two all these years! No wonder he's afraid to show you much affection or attention."

"So, is it too late?"

"No, Mother, but you'd better start real slow with Dad, like maybe holding each other tight at night and then tell him you love him very much."

"Katey, all we ever do when he needs me is turn out the light, he does his business, and then we turn our backs and go to sleep!"

"That's it! Oh Mother! When Jerry and I get married, I'm going to let him touch me, kiss me, and love me anyway he wants to. We'll explore, we'll make lots of mistakes, but we'll move on to find out what to do, what really gives each of us pleasure. We'll do that 'til we come up with something else that gives us even more pleasure., What a wonderful sentence, marriage will give us, a lifetime of holding each other close, of getting more and more pleasure and satisfaction out of each and every day! It's all part of God's design! I can't imagine anything closer to paradise here on earth than having the freedom that marriage allows!"

Mary now realized how much of life and love she'd been missing. "Lass, I can't approve of what you did, but I do see what you're tryin' to tell me. Some business, eh Lass? My daughter knows more about this love making business than I do!" Her expression and tone said it all. "Katey, I am your mother, and what I'm about to say is still the right thing! No more givin' pleasure, not 'til you're married! Are we agreed?"

"Yes Mother, we are agreed. Since we made love, I have to say no because I must be in control, and if I let him start in, I won't be able to say no. I want his love that much, pain or no pain."

"After the proper engagement ring shows up, Katey, then it's off to a woman specialist with you. I want to go with you, and maybe I can learn a thing or two."

The two McCray women were never closer than on that day. It was a unique bonding, the old world ways meshing with the new thinking of more personal liberty and less social constraints. Yet within limits, to be sure, for Katey was a blend of both.

Mary checked the oven while Katey double-checked on the pudding in the refrigerator.

The mother smiled and turned to her daughter. "I'll give ye this, love, never have I met two young people more ready for marriage than you and Jerry. I can't abide by the way it came about, but there's no arguing with the result. I can see now how you've carefully dreamed and planned to get to where you are today; come now, there can be no denyin' it, eh Lass?"

"I've set the standards I want to live by and I've carefully groomed and tested Jerry to meet them, for I'll have him no other way. Remember, man can only take what woman wants to give. I want our marriage to be more than a union. I want it to be fresh, stimulating, and romantic. I think that Catholic women make the best marriage prospects because divorce is not an option with them. Jerry will never fail when he tackles a meaningful challenge in his career or in our marriage for that matter, I won't let him."

"About them little red hearts you put on your calendar in your bedroom? What do you mean by them?"

Katey blushed. "They're my safe days. If Jerry and I were married today, those would be my safe days so we could make love."

"But KateLynn, you've never been regular on your cycle. How can you be so sure?"

"Mother, trust me. That's what I told worry-wart Jerry. I know what I'm doing."

They finished setting the table by adding the bread and butter, condiments, and napkins, awaiting Mr. McCray's arrival. "If your father doesn't come soon, we'll have to turn the oven down. Must've been quite a derailment."

"One question Mother, dad always talks about after you arrived out here from Chicago, but not how you got here. What happened?"

"After we paid every penny back to your Aunt Rose, and after you were born, we saved every red cent for six months. Your father said the West was the place to start our new life, so we bought tickets for as far as our money would take us. With only twenty dollars to our name, we got off the railroad car in Sacramento. We found a cheap hotel, and at first light your father kissed me goodbye and set out lookin' for work. That night it was late when he returned, he'd found work as a gandy dancer on the California Central Railroad. They were layin' new track all the way to San Francisco. Two months later, he challenges his foreman on the crew, saying he's a better man for the job. The road superintendent hears this, and the crew is divided up. He picks Chinamen to work on his crew, and after one week his crew has done almost twice the work. Your father's been a foreman on the maintenance crew ever since. Even today, I still believe your father could outwork any man he's ever had on his crew."

"Oh Mother, what a story, no wonder you're so proud of him."

An hour later, a tired and thoroughly disgusted Aaron McCray washed up and brought his weary bones to rest under the supper table. "Not such a good day, eh love?"

Aaron reached out to touch his wife's hand as she passed by to set two bowls on the table. Mary nearly dropped both bowls as she was surprised by his effort to communicate. Even Katey noticed. "The derailment was bad enough, and my two new-hires were worse!"

"What do you mean 'worse,' Daddy?"

Aaron looked worn out; he'd begun to show the years of back-breaking toil. "It's those your age Katey, there's little or no hope for 'em, I say. They're lost, have no respect, don't want to work, laugh about responsibility and their women, and they'll do anything to make a buck if they don't have to work for it!"

Katey poured their tea. "According to you Daddy, we'd be called the 'lost generation'."

"Mr. McCray, let's not be forgettin' those new hires you took on are probably the leavins'. Those like Jerry and Katey will bring us pride."

Mr. McCray was not swayed. "Before we set out, my boss comes to me and says do something with 'em, we gotta 'cause our union contract says so. Now I'm as good a union man as the next, pay my dues and most of my decent wages came about because of our union. But this! This makes no sense!"

His daughter sat down. "It's called 'feather-bedding' Daddy; the unions are so strong that they can demand the railroad keep the labor count to a certain level."

"Anyway, I takes these two out on my section car with our regular crew. I tell you it wasn't worth it, couldn't get a lick'a work out of 'em. Up to the first one I goes, and I said lend a hand, help my crew to reset the rails. He says it's too hard on his back, so go ahead and make out a layoff slip when we get back, but I'd better not fire him 'cause if I do he can't draw unemployment compensation. Now ain't that the beatinest?"

Mary sliced the chicken. "You said you had to take on two, what about the other?"

Aaron picked up a piece of bread to go along with his first slice of chicken He poured gravy over the meat and bread. "Oh that one was really something. Used that word what starts with F, he did! Used it so much, had to tell him to button his lip or I'd close it for him. My crew knows I won't allow such language, why let him get away with it?"

"Then what happened?" questioned Katey.

"I got one what won't work, and the other's a braggart about his women who can't talk or eat without that word poppin' out. Anyway, come lunch break those two gets together and has a high old time by themselves, lookin' at my crew n'me, laughin' and sayin' things about women that'd curl a mustache on a man. I tell ye, it was somethin'!"

"Do we dare ask in a roundabout way what was said about womenfolk?"

Aaron cut into his meat and downed a boiled potato with gravy. He cleared his throat. "I'll clean it up as best I can. This young buck brags and brags about how many times he's... well, you know what I mean... he's slept with his girlfriend. Now, she's 'knocked up,' he calls it. Right then I collared him and told him where I come from when a man does that, he'd better expect to at least take on the responsibility of raisin' the child even if he won't marry the lady."

"How did that go over, Daddy?"

Aaron reared back on his chair and snorted. "'Lady' the young man says, 'she ain't no lady, she's my shack-job!' Now comes the topper. He then informs me in no uncertain words, that he ain't about to support either the baby this woman is carryin' or the woman. 'Let welfare take care of 'em, I sure as "H" won't!' And this is the one what really did it! Now, after he tells me that, he goes right on braggin, sayin' his girlfriend's no good anymore, so he's been sleepin' with the mother, a divorced woman, and he hopes she ain't knocked up, ' cause she's the best he's ever had!"

For the next five minutes, the three McCrays ate their supper in silence; Aaron had said quite enough, thank you.

Mary broke the silence. "Mrs. McGinty, Joe's wife, is ailin'. The church called today, perhaps after Mass tomorrow we could stop by'n pay our respects at the hospital. Jerry and Katey could drop us off and then come get us when we're visited up."

"Speakin' of Joe McGinty, I met him comin' by the boiler rooms on the way in today. Said he had to change from the night shift, couldn't take it no more."

"Couldn't take what, Daddy?"

"It's worse in the boilermaker's area, Lass, than on my crew. There's six of 'em, come in and roll up paper and bed down for the whole shift. Don't even bring a lunch, Joe says. When the whistle blows, they punch out like the rest and collect their paycheck on Friday nights like they'd put in the hours for it.. Two of 'em showed Joe some new kinda credit card. They buy on this card and never pay for nothing. Won't save a dime, live from payday to payday 'til the finance company comes to get what they wouldn't pay for."

"They don't save? What's this would comin' to, Aaron?" Mary questioned.

"I tell ye, Mary, it's movin' too fast and in the wrong direction to boot!"

Katey got up to get the dessert out of the fridge. "I'm so glad you and mother made me put some of my five-and-dime money aside. Without savings, Jerry and I would have no future, that's for sure."

"Aye Lass, and your business school money came from your mother's sore knees and the sweat off me back, make no mistake about that."

"Did Joe say anything about his brother-in-law in Kansas City? The one what's a big shot in the railroad back there?"

"Yes, but I don't understand. Joe's says he's not the same anymore. The railroad got after him somehow, bent his mind, and said somethin' about makin' him work in some kinda rubber room. Says all railroads got 'em. When they can't get them to bend, they end up in this kind'a room where they break 'em for good.I never heard of such a thing before, and I've been workin' for the California Central for over 17 years. You ever heard about such a thing, or place. Katey?"

"No, but most of the railroads have a history of pullin' some pretty shady deals."

"Of course, none of ye know a thing about such shenanigans! 'Tis plain to see what happened to Joe's brother-in-law."

"We don't even know if there is such a thing as a rubber room, Mother! So how can you possibly say you know what happened?"

"Katey, 'tis plain to see as the freckles on your nose, Lass! The railroad swept the whole sorry business under the carpet with their lily white hands!"

Another week passed and Katey was pleasantly surprised at work when Mary stopped in. "Aye Lass, 'tis plain to see which department you favor, 'tis the baby department. A light comes to your eye, and there's a rosy glow about'cha no question on that."

"What are you doin' here Mother? Boy, it's my day for surprises, Molly dropped by during morning coffee break!"

"I'm in the mood for buyin' lunch Lass! Come, there's so much to tell about your father'n me, I hardly know where to start!"

They went to a deli nearby and ordered their BLT special. "Okay Mother, what's the big news? C'mon, out with it!"

Mary raised her purse in front of her mouth to shield her voice. "Last night, your father'n me had our first pleasure. Oh Katey, 'twas somethin', it was! Made me feel like a new person! Now it's far too private, it 'tis, so don't be tryin' to wheedle it outa' me, but I'll tell ye this, there'd better be more comin' or your father'll be wishin' he'd never started it!"

Katey squeezed her mother's arm. "I'm so happy for the two of you! Did Daddy say he enjoyed it or something like that?"

"You know your father, not too heavy on sayin' things like that, but after the pleasurin' was done, I asked him what he thought. First off, he said it was okay. Katey, the man was on fire but he wouldn't say as much. Before he got up to turn out the light, he allowed it was better than okay. I also stated a new rule, no turnin' our backs to each other until we kiss goodnight and say we love each other. Oh Katey, I'm a new person, I am! After we turned our backs, your father's voice come right at me outa' the dark and he says: 'Mary McCray that was some pleasure we had. Do you suppose we could try that again soon? Maybe tomorrow night?'"

"That's great! Maybe you could try something else next time."

"Katey, we'd better go at this a bit slow, this is all so new between us. But I tell ye this, we're gonna have at it as much as I can possibly stand! Never knew there could be so much pleasure between your father'n me. My goodness, I'm rattlin' on somethin' fierce, what's new with Molly?"

"She sees my ring and I know it's killing her. She and Ricco had another big fight, always over the same thing. She swears she'll never give in until Ricco marries her, but it always ends up the same old way. He gets what he wants, and she goes home and cries all night. Jerry says she must be livin' in 'La La Land' 'cause sure as heck her brains are in cold storage."

"He's right Katey, Molly will never marry Ricco, I feel sure. You and Jerry, you two did it the right way, there must be commitment between two people or it will never work."

Katey picked up their order and returned to the table. "Only eleven more months, Mother, only eleven more. You know, even after we're married, it's going to be a long wait before I dare to think about having our first baby, before I dare let Jerry get me pregnant. I do want a baby so bad! I've always wanted a baby!"

"Careful love, God has big ears. He may just grant you that wish."

They finished their sandwiches and Katey got ready to leave. "Any good news Katey?"

"I'm runnin' late, but then I did that a couple of months ago, so this time it'll be like that." Mary saw the worry lines on her daughter's face for the first time. "Oh Mother, I'm sure I'm okay, I just have to be."

Mary waited 'til they were outside the deli. "I say a special prayer each night for you and I hope He's listenin' 'cause I'd rather face the devil himself, three times over, than take on the chore of tellin' your father his pride and joy got herself in a family way!"

# Chapter Six

Another week managed to slip by, a mere ten days before Katey was due to start the summer quarter session at Sacramento Business College. Mary could wait no longer. No sooner had she shoved her husband out the door with his lunch bucket, than she camped on Katey's heels in the bathroom. "There'll be no going to work today, time to have a doctor look at'cha!"

"Motherrrr! I will not! I'm not pregnant! I can't be! I'm just real late!"

"We're goin' so gather up your things!"

Two hours later, Katey stormed back into her home and made a beeline straight for her bedroom. She went crazy. She tore the calendar off the wall and screamed at the top of her lungs. "LIES, LIES, LIES! That's all a calendar tells is LIES, LIES AND MORE LIES!" She ripped every page out and tore each into a hundred tiny pieces. "Never trust a calendar, they all LIE, LIE, LIE!"

Mary stood in the open doorway and watched the unbelievable spectacle. "Katey, get a hold of yourself, you're going to pieces."

Wild-eyed, Katey turned on her mother. "Molly does it all the time, and she never gets pregnant. She does it again and again and again and she's not pregnant! I do it just once! Not twice, or three times mind you, but once! JUST ONCE!!! Where's the justice in that? Huh? Where's the justice!!!"

She paced around the room. "Betcha I can't count the number of times Molly and Ricco have done it and she's not pregnant! No, she never gets pregnant!!!" Then she dove back into her pillow crying hard, her poor body shaking and jerking from such deep sobs. Her muffled cries came through the pillow. "It's not fair! It's just not fair!!!"

Mary waited for Katey's tiny fists to quit pummeling her pillow. Then gently, ever so gently she eased in beside her. Katey rolled over and went to her mother, her crying sounded more like deep gasps, dry choking. "Now, now my Lass, the end of the world's still a bit off. You'll survive, you have to now Katey! You must think of the baby that's growing inside you! You must stop'n think!"

"It's not fair Mother!" Then the crying started all over again. Mary rocked her KateLynn, it brought back good memories, precious memories of years ago, faded perhaps but not forgotten. "Katey, are ye able to listen, to understand?"

"I… I think so, Mother. I need a hanky."

Mary slipped out of their embrace. She handed her daughter several and sat down beside her again. "Lass, my schoolin' never amounted to much in the old country, but if ye never remember anything 'bout today besides being pregnant, please remember this, life isn't fair, it never was. Haven't the foggiest notion who said it was, but he was wrong! Dead wrong! Life is what you do with the hours, weeks, months, and years God gives you! Now you can either let this beat you or you can rise about it and accept it and go on. You still have a choice Katey, don't let yourself and your unborn baby down."

Aaron was surprised that evening when Mary started to serve supper alone. "I've already eaten, and Katey's in her room waiting for you to finish supper. We have some family business to discuss."

Mary stacked a few of the dishes, and then brought Katey out. Aaron could hardly believe his eyes, Katey looked terrible. She was a mess! "Now Lass, your mother tells me there's some family business that needs my attention." He motioned toward his daughter. "Come my sweet Irish pixie, come sit on my lap and tell me what the problem is. If it's a lover's spat, I'll speak to Jerry next time I see him."

"It's worse than that Father!"

Aaron looked at his wife, then to Katey. "Say, if he's hurt you in any way, he'll answer to me out in the garage next time he shows. I'll straighten him out you can be sure, or there'll be no Jerry Landis comin' 'round!"

"It's worse than that Daddy!" cried Katey.

Aaron still didn't know what to make of it. He took the sweet little face with the red, puffy eyes and swollen tear-stained cheeks in both hands. "Now Katey, I'm sure there's nothing that can't wait 'til I've finish my supper."

Neither Katey nor her mother could bring themselves to say another word, so Aaron proceeded to pick up his knife and fork to cut up his sliced roast beef. "Lass, if you're goin' to stay in me lap, please be so kind as to pass the gravy… your Mother's fine cookin' deserves just a wee touch of her good gravy to top off such a fine meal!"

Mary could wait no longer. As Aaron carefully poured the gravy, her words came in slow, deliberate, tunes. "Father, you best put down that gravy server… our KateLynn's in a family way…"

Aaron continued tilting the server. Suddenly, he stopped and looked squarely at his wife. "My hearin' must need some attention… for a minute I almost thought you said our Katey was with child… wouldj'a mind sayin' your words again?"

Katey threw her arms around her father's neck. Luckily the server found a level spot next to Aaron's plate. "Mother tried to tell you Daddy…" She burst into tears. "DADDY…DADDY! I'M PREGNANT!!!"

It took all of two seconds before the full impact hit Aaron between the ears. Katey bounced off his lap and hit the floor as he exploded out of his chair, sending it flying like a low projectile toward the kitchen sink. He hammered his fists twice on the table; it buckled under his mighty strength. Mary gasped at the sheer brutality he administered to her prize kitchen table. He went straight for the door. "Where is he? Where is he, Katey? I wanna get my hands on him now! Where is he?"

Katey made a lunge for her father, trying to stop him. She managed to hang on for dear life as she grabbed one pant leg. He lifted her along the floor like she wasn't even there!

"Killing him will be too easy. I wanna squeeze his neck 'til his eyeballs pop!"

Mary blocked his exit "SIT DOWN AARON McCRAY! SIT DOWN!""

He turned to his wife. "Sit down you say? Not when he's done this to our Katey! He'll never make it to his next birthday, not when I get through with him! Where is he Katey?"

Mary refused to budge. "You go after Jerry, and I'll call the cops on ye, Aaron McCray! I WILL! I MEAN IT!"

He could hardly believe his ears. "You mean you'd let him get away with this? I'm gonna put him in prison where he belongs, forcing my KateLynn They'll have to pipe in daylight 'cause that's as close he'll ever get to see the outside when I'm done with him!"

"Daddy, Daddy, please! Jerry didn't force me, it was more my idea!"

That it could be anything except forcible rape took him down a full three pegs. For a full minute he seemed unwilling or unable, or both, to cope with the naked truth. He wheeled upon Katey, demanding an answer. "When, Katey? When did this happen?"

She got up off the floor and flew into his arms, hoping to keep him occupied with her instead of bent on going after Jerry. "It happened after our senior graduation dance… I wasn't' going to let him, then he proposed and it happened!"

His Katey felt no heavier than a two-dollar sack of groceries as he stooped over long enough to pick up the chair with one hand, and with her still clinging around his neck he deposited her back at the kitchen table, or what was left of it.

He seemed stunned, not shocked by her announcement. "Each Sunday, he went to Mass with us, he sat at our table, we fed him, we treated him like family, and I treated him like a son… How? How Katey? How could he do this to you? To us? He's betrayed us! No, I never want to see him set foot in this home again! Maybe he doesn't belong in jail but he sure doesn't belong here either!"

Mary came at him straight on, shaking a warning finger in his face. "He's the same fine lad he was five minutes ago or five weeks ago, only difference is he and Katey made a mistake. Now, Mr. Aaron McCray, what are we going to do about it?"

"Do?" Suddenly he remembered what he had in mind all along. In no uncertain terms he shouted at Katey. "To your room, Daughter! Down on your knees! You'd better pray to God for forgiveness for your sin 'cause there's damn little of it you'll be getting from this table! You've disgraced the proud name of McCray! You've brought shame to yourself, to your mother and father! How could you KateLynn McCray! How could you do such a thing? Do? Why, you've done quite enough Daughter! Quite enough!"

Katey ran to her room, crying out with pain. Slam! The door shook! It was felt all the way along the walls and floor right up the hallway back to the kitchen itself.

Twenty, hard-fought minutes passed as the discussion teetered between Aaron and Mary, being on the verge of an all-out Irish free-for-all with some heavy concentrated what-ifs. When all was thoroughly hashed and rehashed, Mary told Katey to come out of her room, her father was ready to speak his mind.

Aaron waited 'til Katey stood before him again, humbled in the presence of her father and his final word on the matter. "Certain things have come to light between your mother and me, so Lass here's how I shall deal with you.

"First off, you'll be leavin' for Chicago day after tomorrow to stay with your Aunt Rose. Your mother's to go with you to see that you'll be settled and taken care of properly."

"I won't give up my baby, Daddy! NEVER!! I don't care what you and Mother decided, I won't give up my baby! NEVER!!!"

"KateLynn, there'll be no disrespect in this home, I won't allow it! Now then, what are you to do after your baby's born? Answer me that?"

"I'll do anything I have to, to keep my baby. I'll go on welfare or walk the streets to sell my body if I must, to feed my baby, but I WON'T GIVE UP MY BABY!"

Aaron pounded his fist hard on the table. "Welfare, you say? No, KateLynn, there'll be no more talk about welfare in this home, not as long as I draw a breath of life! I can promise you that, Daughter!"

Mary took her turn. "Walk the streets did'ja say? No, KateLynn, no McCray woman will ever do that as long as I've got two good knees and a sturdy back to work so I can support my grandchild! I never want to hear those kind of words comin' from such sweet, God fearin' innocent lips! Not while I'm alive!"

Katey was near tears again. "What then? What am I to do?"

Mr. McCray spoke his mind. "You still have your business school money. I suggest you use it to go to a business school in Chicago after you birth your baby."

"Why can't I go to school 'til my baby is born? Other women do!"

Katey's mother held her at arm's length. "Listen to my words Daughter! While you were dressing at the doctor's office, I had a conversation with the doctor. He said you will have a very hard time carryin' your baby to full term. You stand a good chance of losin' you baby unless you're off your feet and stay in bed. So school's out 'til you either birth our grandchild or face the worst possible news. Are we clear on that?"

Katey nodded she understood. Mary continued. "Now then, there'll be medical expenses and room and board at Aunt Rose's. We McCrays always pay our way. So, best your father'n me has figured you'll be gone most of two years…"

"TWO WHOLE YEARS AWAY FROM JERRY!" She screamed. "Why not make it twenty?"

It was Aaron's turn again. "KateLynn, listen to me! No matter what I think of Jerry for puttin' you in this situation, I now believe he's an honorable young man. However, there's the rub, he's in no position to marry you or support you at this time. Your mother and I have a proposition to put to you. Hear us out and I believe you'll agree it's best all around. If you tell Jerry about the baby, you'll be forcing him to marry you. Now then, is that what you really want?" He watched her face for any reaction. "Don't you really want him to come to you of his own free will when he's ready to give you a good life and a good marriage? Your mother's told me how you've planned your life around him and how you've brought him along to this point, surely you don't want to throw that away? Think on this carefully before you answer, Daughter!"

While Katey was deep in thought, Mary interjected her own observation. "No matter how you look at it Katey, Jerry will be in a much better position to marry you two years from now. Surely, you can see that! What your father'n me are really asking is, can your love for each other stand to be tested for two years?"

"Our love is solid and true, I have no fear about that. What I don't see is how am I going to tell him I must say good-bye for two whole years without telling him the truth?"

Mary McCray's words came out slowly, but deliberately to emphasize her point. "Daughter, you must tell him anything but the truth or else you'll be forcing his hand."

Katey saw the dilemma she was in. What to do? "I still don't see where all this money is coming from to pay for my medical expenses and room and board."

Aaron spoke his mind. "Katey, the money you're so worried about is coming from our hard-put savings. If it's not enough, your mother will go back to work to help out 'till you're through schoolin' and can start to pay us back. How say you Lass? Is this not a fair proposition?"

How could she refuse? Indeed, even from the pain and suffering she inflicted on herself and her parents, Katey knew deep down this was the only logical way to go. "Okay, you have my promise to go along with it. I don't like it one bit, but both of you are right, forcing Jerry into a marriage at this point is not the way to go. When we do marry later on, there must be no room for regrets, with or without my baby!"

The next day saw a flurry of activity in and around the McCray household. Hard-put savings were withdrawn from the bank. Aaron used his railroad pass to purchase discount-priced railroad fares for Katey's one way and Mary's roundtrip to Chicago. Under Mary's capable hands, the last-minute clothes washing and ironing were done, and Katey was told to pack only her loosest fitting skirts, blouses, and dresses. Then came time for one phone call, the one Katey dreaded making all day – the one to Jerry, asking him to stop by after work.

It was late when Jerry showed up, dog tired after working at the railroad all day, and doing the late evening grocery deliveries for Bettingers Super Market. Katey met him at the door and quickly stepped outside with him. "Hey Katey, what's up? You sounded kinda distant. Anything wrong? How come we're standing outside, instead of invitin' me in?"

She broke down sobbing her poor heart out. He gathered her up in his arms and tried to kiss away the tears and make her hurt feel a bit better. "Oh Jerry, Jerry," she cried out, "I've made a terrible mess of everything! Can you possibly forgive me?"

"Whoa! Wait a minute, slow down! Goin' a bit fast for old Jerr. Now put it in reverse and start over."

"The folks found out about us making love. I didn't think about doing my own panties. Mother found the telltale signs in the laundry next day."

"So why didn't they come unglued back then? And your father's been treating me really super. Doesn't make sense Katey!"

"Yes it does when I tell you that Mom didn't tell Dad 'til yesterday, after I came back from the doctor."

"The doctor! Oh my God Katey! Not that? YOU'RE PREGNANT! RIGHT!"

"No, but I've got some female problems that have to be taken care of soon and the folks are pretty upset over the whole mess. They're shipping me off to Chicago to go to a business college there and take care of my problems. I'll be gone about two years; they're going to test us and I told them we're up to it!"

He kissed her soundly. "You bet we are Katey! Oh God, why oh why did I have to have you that night? Now look what I've done to you Katey? Your big blond stud really screwed up first class, Katey!"

"Stop it Jerry! You know how I hate that word! As far as the rest goes, about making love, I'm not sorry. We both wanted it and that's why we went ahead."

"Yeah, but look what happened! Can you ever forgive me, Katey? Lord, how I love you, and two years is a long, long time between kisses."

"You better make sure my kisses aren't the only thing you're going to miss, Jerry Landis."

They embraced; his lips searched every corner of her mouth, tasting the nectar of love that passed between them. She moved her body into his, trying to give him a farewell reminder of what it'd been like, their bodies taking the warmth from each other. Time for pleasure was over … time for one last kiss. They made it count.

Inside, after Jerry's emotional good-bye, Katey faced her mother with salty tears lodged in the corners of both eyes.

"And how did it go Lass? The good-bye?"

"THE BIGGEST LIE I'VE EVER TOLD! IT'S BARELY TWO MINUTES OLD, AND I'M SICK OF IT ALREADY!

Early next morning, Aaron stood on the railroad station platform, three suitcases and one small train case nearby.

"Board," called the porter.

He quickly handed them to the porter and returned to Mary and Katey. To his surprise, Mary launched into him to gave him a resounding smack. "There now, Aaron McCray, that'll have to do ye 'til I get back. And when I do, mind'ja there's gonna be some more changes when we close our bedroom door. So don't get to feelin' too smug about things as they are, for its more out of our bedroom I'm wantin' and you're just the man what can make it happen!"

Father and daughter faced each other for their tearful good-bye. Each seemed hesitant to make the first move, each wanting to spare the other more hurt and pain. "Daddy, could you please find it in your heart to forgive me someday for what I've done?"

He never bothered to answer, instead he picked her straight up, hugged her, then put her back down with the same ease he'd lifted her. "KateLynn, there's too much hurt goin' on between us now, but as for the forgivin' part, it happened the minute you came to me and told right out what happened. The forgettin' part's gonna take a mite longer to work out between us, but it'll come with time. I was wonderin,' there's a small favor I need to ask of you."

"Name it, Daddy, it's yours!"

"It's about your mother, she's not much on letter writin'. Could you see your way clear to sittin' down at the other end to write me a letter? Never had one from you before!"

"First thing when we get there, I'll do it, Daddy… right after I write to Jerry!"

Aaron helped the two McCray women get aboard. Katey made sure she found her seat next to a window. She saw her father standing alone on the platform and waved to him. She was privy to something she'd never seen before.

"Aye Lass, take a good look at your father. Oh, he's hard as nails and maybe twice as strict, but he misses you already. See, look at him! Now he'll turn his back a wee bit so you'll not see any tears, but he has 'em for me and for you. That's the Aaron McCray part of the man I admire the most!" Mary replied calmly.

The train eased away from the station platform. Katey searched up and down the platform in vain. "Lass, you said your good-byes last night, leave it at that!"

"Jerry said he'd try to make it if he could. Oh where is he? Where is he?

"LOOK DOWN KATEY! BELOW YOU! DOWN HERE!"

The platform sloped down and there Jerry was, running alongside, under her window trying to keep up. She pressed her hand against the glass, and he reached up to match hers. The train was picking up speed, but Jerry gave it everything he had trying to keep pace. Katey mouthed her words in perfect sync: "Never forget I love you!"

He dropped from view, having reached the end of the inclined part of the platform. He stood with one foot on the rail, feeling its vibration run up his pant leg until it lodged deep inside his stomach and then within his heart. He held a steady gaze down the tracks watching the end of the caboose melt into the two rails until the three meshed into an ever smaller, disappearing speck. Then nothing. He turned away to bring his shirt sleeve up to his face while he wept unashamedly, not caring whether any spectators on the railroad platform saw him or not.

Jerry half-stumbled back to the open door of the pick-up. He dropped on the well-worn cushion, with his bleary eyes focused on the ignition keys jumping in crazy fashion when his weight hit the truck seat full force. He looked around, a desperate lonely feeling overwhelmed him. For the first time he could remember, he felt alone – truly alone; stripped of the one person he truly loved, the one person he could always count on, and the one person who'd stood by him no matter what.

He fiddled with the rearview mirror without really knowing why and to his surprise a visitor, a most unwelcome visitor entered his troubled mind long enough to take shape before his eyes. His intruder's words taunted him like never before. *"See! I told you!"* mocked the voice. *"JUST LIKE YOUR OLD MAN! YOU AIN'T WORTH THE SPIT ON A PUBLIC PARK BENCH!"*

# CHAPTER SEVEN

The two McCray women heard clickety click, clickety clack, clickety click, the resounding beat of the wheels on the rails beneath their railroad car. Ten, twenty minutes passed as Katey's sobs were gradually reduced to a series a sniffles, nose blowing and puffy cheeks with complimentary red eyes. Mary returned with a cold wash cloth from the restroom, thanks to an ever alert porter. "Here, put this across your eyes and cheeks, Lass. You'll be fine in no time."

Katey put on a brave smile and accepted the washcloth. "Thanks Mother, I never knew saying good-bye could hurt so much." She tried to stem a new spread of mist in her eyes. "It's… It's just that I love him so very much…"

Mary sat down and put her arm around Katey. "One thing about it, Darling, you're never really going anywhere without him are you?" She looked down at Katey's stomach. "There's a part of Jerry growing in you as we speak, Katey. I just wish you had waited 'til you had a proper ring on your finger…"

Neither spoke for a few minutes. Katey broke the silence. "I'm not ashamed of what I did, Mother, I just never believed it could happen to me… not this way… not now… not after all the planning, and all the dreaming…"

The train sped eastward, a mixture of black and white smoke curling and cascading down over the passenger cars as they entered the foothills to the High Sierras, the mountain range separating California from Nevada. Late that afternoon, they answered the first call for dinner in the dining car. Mary watched Katey pick at her food. "Listen to me, Katey, you must eat more so you'll have a healthy baby. There'll be no forgettin' you're eating for two from now on. Each time you feel full, take at least three more spoonfuls… it'll pay off in the long run, you'll see."

"First thing I'm going to do when we get to Chicago is write Daddy and Jerry. The next thing I'm going to do is buy a plain gold wedding band, there'll be no stares or snickers behind my back. I want to feel proud I'm carrying such a precious little life inside me! I can hardly wait to hold my baby in my arms…"

Mary squeezed her daughter's hand. "And you'll make a fine mother, KateLynn McCray, a fine mother! I'm glad to see some of the sparkle return to your eyes and a bit of color come out from its hiding place in your cheeks."

Katey forced another bite of food into her mouth.

She was pleased about her mother's concern. "You and Daddy really want me to have this baby don't you? I'm glad you feel that way."

Mary finished her cup of tea. "Your father doesn't know it, but when I get back there's going to be more changes besides in our bedroom. I'm going back to work, there'll be new baby things to buy… your father will be repainting your bedroom, and of course I'll be needin' ticket money to get back to Chicago to see our brand spankin' new grandchild born… and a camera so I can bring pictures back to show your father…"

Katey laughed. It was her first since boarding the train. "Mother, I see that Brannigan look about you and I know whenever I see that,

Daddy's a dead duck. He doesn't stand a chance. I'm so glad you'll be here with me then… I only wish Jerry could too…"

Mary poured Katey another cup of tea. "Last night, your father said something to me… about you and Jerry being tested… really tested to show your commitment to marriage and each other… am I makin' sense?"

Katey had a wistful look about her. She put down her cup just as the train whistled. "I think I know what he's getting at, most couples fall in love, get married, have good jobs, and then have their babies. With Jerry and me, it's all backwards… it's like we've been singled out for something different. I don't know how all this fits in, yet I feel God is a part of it… and He always will be with me."

"Remember Katey, God is with us always, never forget that! Maybe He has something else in mind for you two… time will tell."

Katey felt reassured by Mary's comforting words. "When you get back, make sure you tell Daddy that I'll pay you two back for helping me and Jerry out of this… I'll never rest 'til you two have your money back again."

Mary folded her napkin and got ready to leave. "Katey, there never was a smidgeon of doubt in our minds or hearts about that. As for payin' us back, look what we're going to be getting! Our very own grandchild to hold, spoil and pamper. You know your father made me promise to tell you when you come back you have to stay with us. About that, he'll have it no other way, KateLynn!"

They left the dining car to return to their seat. Katey watched the fence posts, trees and buildings flash by as the first shadows of evening claimed their rightful place on the back side of ravines, hills and man-made cuts in the landscape where the tracks followed. She saw her own reflection in the window and half-whispered out loud, more to herself than to her mother. She vowed, "When my baby is born, I'm going to make darned sure the birth certificate says Jerry Landis is the father and KateLynn McCray Landis is listed as the mother."

Mary McCray smiled. "Now who's set in their ways, eh Katey?"

"You bet, because I'll have it no other way!"

They ate their breakfast on the last call, late in the morning of the third day. Chicago with Aunt Rose waiting would be but four more hours away. The McCray women shared a table with a young married lady traveling with her six-week-old baby. Katey marveled at how well the young mother handled herself and her baby. There was hardly a whimper or barely a fuss from the infant. The mother finished her breakfast, and then turned her attention to feeding time for her child. She turned her back on the McCrays, faced toward the window to gain a little privacy before unbuttoning her blouse. She then reached back into a small bag resting on the vacant chair next to her and tried to pull a small baby blanket from the bag, but it caught on the bag's zipper. Katey rose from her side of the table to free the blanket.

"Thank you," the young mother said, reaching over her shoulder for the blanket. "Thought I was better organized, should've got my blanket out first."

Katey stood there watching the mother cover her breast and the baby with the blanket. Twice during feeding time, the mother moved the blanket just enough to make sure her baby was sucking properly. All anybody heard was a couple of lip smacking sounds followed by a gurgle or two, and then all was quiet. "May I ask you a personal question?"

"Sure," replied the mother, "if it's not too personal."

"Are you wearing some kind of a special bra?"

"Yes, it's a nursing bra. Boy, what a lifesaver! If you like I'll show you when he's through feeding."

Katey sat down and exchanged glances with Mary while the young mother nursed her baby. Soon no more smacking sounds were heard and the mother turned her head to Katey. "He's asleep. I'll lift the blanket so you can see for yourself."

From that moment on, the two hit it off like they'd been best friends for years. After the young mother left, Katey mused out loud. "Remind me to buy a couple of those bras, Mother, I only hope I'll have enough milk for mine. Did you… for me?"

Mary McCray answered, but her voice seemed distant, from another time, another era. "Yes, my Katey, I had plenty… and then some. Funny, but 'til now, 'til I saw that young mother nursing, I haven't so much as given a moment's thought… My breasts not only nursed you, but they paid for our first Christmas in America."

Katey had that inquisitive look about her. "Tell me, Mother, I'll bet it's a doozy!"

Mary surveyed their breakfast plates. "Katey, there'll be no tellin' a tale 'til you do a better job. Why, I see two gulps of orange juice left in your glass… and… there's half a piece of toast just beggin' for a wee bit of jam to help it slide into your tummy. Do that and we'll see to the tale?"

Katey half protested. "Mother, I'm full…" She saw the stern look flicker across her mother's face. "Okay, okay, I'll finish, now tell me about your first Christmas."

Mary continued her somber tone. "Katey, I'll tell you one thing we're not going to do and that's waste money on good food. I'm waitin'!"

The tale waited until Katey's orange juice glass was empty and the last bite of toast had disappeared into Katey's mouth. Mary began her story. "'Twas our first Christmas season in Chicago and oh how I hated the place we lived in… stacked on top of one another in them beehives, we was… what did you call 'em?"

"Tenement houses, Mother."

"Oh yes, that's the name. We didn't trust the banks so I made your father turn over every dime he made to me so we wouldn't have to stay a minute longer in such a place. I'll tell you, Mr. Scrooge coulda taken lessons from me I was so tight with my purse. You were a wee tyke, hardly two months old, and I was back scrubbin' floors at the hotel while your Aunt Rose tended you in the daytime. Well, your father comes to me asking for some money to buy one Christmas present for me… and mind you I turned him down flatter than a pancake, I did! He said not to get him anything 'cause he knew getting another spare nickel or two outa' me would take an act of God, probably on the order of the partin' of the Red Sea. The short of it was, he left in a big huff and we'd had our first big fight. I cried for being such a miser n' treatin' him that way."

"Well, why did you? And where did your breast milk fit in?"

"I'm comin' to that Lass, I'm comin' to that! About a week before Christmas, I happened by a small buildin' of some sorts… comin' from work and there it was, big as you please, just there for the takin'! A sign said: 'Wanted: Breast milk for orphan babies.' I high-tailed it into that buildin' like the devil himself was gainin' on me and sold my milk. A'course from then on, I made sure you were fed first before I stepped inside that buildin'."

"Then what?"

"Comes the day before Christmas and your father barely has a civil tongue in his head for me, Katey, you shoulda' seen the look on his face when I opened my purse and out popped five dollars! Old Saint Nick himself couldn'a done a better job! So I says to your father that around the corner in a certain store, there's a fine, soft woolen coat, and that the price was four dollars. I shook my finger at him and said make sure he bought my coat first, and on the way back, I'd have no objection to him liftin' his spirits at a local pub with the extra dollar. Then I gave him a smack and told him when he returned I had a present for him, a fine shirt he'd had his eye on since we arrived from Ireland. Then outa' the clear blue, your father comes up to me and says bein's it's the holiday season n'all, would there possibly be somethin' more waitin' for him when he comes back? I winks back at him and happened to mention in passin' that there's only one way to find out… hurry back because the Brannigan women were known for changin' their minds if left alone too long."

"Speaking of Christmas, I'll never forget the look on Jerry's face when I gave him the only wristwatch he's ever had, last Christmas. I told him he was really special and boy did he prove me right. The big reason he was late picking me up for our prom was because his sisters hadn 't eaten all day. So my Jerry hocked his watch to buy food for them and stayed to make sure they got to eat. There's so much goodness in him, Mother."

"And now my love, we've left two awfully lonesome men back home. And they will be 'til each of us returns."

***

For Jerry Landis, time didn't stand still after Katey boarded her train to Chicago, it traveled in reverse. Gone out of his life was his freckle-faced little Amigo, the tomboy who wanted so much and tried so hard to be his sweetheart, and then his love, that she made the transformation happen right before his very eyes. Yes, the transformation was there, along with an awful lot of growing up 'til she practically begged him to make her a woman – his woman, letting him draw and take his pleasure from her until he finally paid the price.

There was no doubt in his mind that he'd hurt her terribly on their special night in spite of when she kept whispering and urging him to make love with her.

Jerry fell victim to the loneliness. That terrible gnawing pain that spreads like a disease that has no cure until that special person returns again to cast a spell, to remove, as if by magic, the very reason for having it in the first place.

With Katey gone, Jerry too, changed his plans, and he started evening classes in accounting at Sacramento State College.

The weeks dragged on as if tethered to something that couldn't be moved or rolled aside. He grew melancholy waiting for Katey's first letter, the one she promised to write, the one he never received, the one thing that would've made each passing day a bit better, a bit brighter for one terribly lonely, young man.

Finally, he'd had enough. It was time to take the bull by the horns and find out what had gone wrong, terribly wrong. During the next lunch hour at work, he looked Molly up, hoping she could shed some light on why he hadn't gotten a single letter from Katey.

They shared their lunch hour together, each brown-bagging it. Molly looked radiant, her long dark hair complimented by two dark-brown eyes that danced every time she spoke or tossed her head.

"So Amigo, what's happening in your life? Any news from Katey?"

Molly put down her sandwich. "That's a funny question, Jerry. I'm sure Katey has filled you in on Ricco and me. We've split up… as if you didn't know."

Jerry put down his apple. "Split up? You're kidding! Listen Molly, I haven't had one letter from Katey, and I want to know what's going on! We're supposed to be engaged… as if you didn't know!"

Jerry's words caught Molly off-guard. She cleared her throat, and then wiped her mouth with a napkin. "I don't understand Jerry, her letters to me are filled with nothing but how much she loves you and how she can hardly wait 'til she's back here again to reset you wedding date. Is this some kind of sick joke?"

He finished his carton of milk. "I wish it was. I'm gettin' a little fed up with the whole mess. . Next time you write to Katey, tell her I'd better see a letter damned soon or… or…"

"Or what, Jerry?'

"Or she can go to blazes as far as I'm concerned! Tell her she's got two more weeks and if I don't see some words from her, like at least five, lousy, stinkin' lines… that's all I ask…nothing big like a whole page filled with sentences or paragraphs, just five lousy lines! Now do you think she can handle that?"

Molly could sense the rage and frustration building in her friend. "Listen Jerry, and you listen real close, you hear? Katey has always loved you. I've never seen two people who belong together more than you two do. There's something crazy here… it doesn't make sense. Sit back and think about it."

"I have and all I'm getting is a lot of sweet nothing!"

Neither spoke as they tried to finish up their lunches. Molly asked Jerry if he wanted her cookie. He politely said no, and then offered her a candy bar. Molly changed subjects. "How's the rate clerk job going?"

Jerry lightened up as he dead-panned. "A piece of cake, Molly, a real piece of cake." He laughed. "Heck, if the railroad could train a monkey to flip to the right page they wouldn't need me. I've been in evening accounting since the fall quarter started, no point in waiting now… you might mention that in your next letter to Katey… maybe she's still interested, I don't know anymore…"

Molly was pleased for Jerry. "I will, we write to each other about once a week. Say, why don't you write to her instead of being such a moper? It'll do you good, Jerry Landis."

"Me? No way, Molly, no way in heck 'til she breaks down and gives me a least five lines… she promised to write first and I'm gonna hold her to it."

"God, you're one stubborn mule, Amigo, one big stubborn jackass! Katey always said that's the one thing about you she was gonna change if she had to put a bull ring through your nose and get your attention with a two-by-four between your ears. It's that damned streak of stubbornness in you. And judgin' by today's performance, you haven't changed one bit, Landis!"

"What are you doin' for social activity now that Ricco's out of your life for good?"

She folded up her lunch sack. "He's not out of my life for good… I'm dating a couple other guys… nothing serious, just letting him know that I'm not the pushover I used to be. He'll come around when he sees what he coulda had if he'da played square with me."

"Can I be totally honest about something, Amigo?"

Molly saw the seriousness in Jerry's face. "Okay, go ahead."

"Greg and I have known about you and Ricco for two years now … and Katey didn't breathe the first word, so don't go jumpin' her about it. Ricco only wants what he can get from you and when you cut him off he's lookin' for new skirts to chase… he's not ready to settle down, he's not ready for commitment, a home, kids and monthly bills like you and Katey are. I've changed… I'm ready for those things… Ricco's not. Can you see where I'm going? What I'm trying to tell you?"

Jerry's words cut deep, way too deep. Molly tried her best to hide the panic, her hurt feelings. "You're wrong Jerry, dead wrong! Ricco had it too easy with me, that's all, and… and now I've made my stand and now he knows what I expect him to do. He gets nothing from me until I see that wedding ring and some proper attitude and respect… the same thing you and Katey have going between you. That's all I ask… he'll come around, you just wait'n see!"

"Don't wait too long, Molly, 'cause I don't think it's ever going to happen with Ricco."

"Speaking of being totally honest, how about giving me a turn?"

"Okay Amigo, shoot! What's on your mind?"

"From Katey's letters it's not so much what she says… it's what she doesn't say. Katey and I were close, I mean really, really tight… and yet I get the definite feeling she's not telling it all… and I know her like a book. She'd never let you get to her without a wedding band… and that's what bugs me. Jerry, somehow you did, didn't you? She's pregnant, and that's why she's in Chicago. Makes sense from where I stand."

Jerry turned to make a basketball shot with his wadded up lunch sack into the garbage can. "I almost wish she was, Molly, at least I'd know where I stand. No, she's back in Chicago for two reasons."

"What then? You said two reasons…"

Jerry leaned forward and looked Molly square in the face. "First off, her folks talked her into waiting 'til she finishes classes at business college away from here and away from me… that's supposed to be the big test to see if we still care for each other… if we're still committed to marriage. You and I both know Katey, there'll be no second thoughts once she says I do, The other reason is simple enough; Katey's always had female problems… heck, why am I telling you? You've known that since day one with her, right? She's back there seeing some female specialist… that kinda thing has always been very personal, very private with her. Now does it all make sense?"

Molly looked at her watch. "Yeah Jerry, gotta admit it does. Lunch break is almost over, so we'd better head back to our work stations. How 'bout walking with me back to the typing pool and when we get there, let's hold hands and you give me a peck on the cheek. I told those old hens you're my new blond hunk… let's keep 'em guessing, give some of those dried up old heifers something to moo about. Okay Amigo?"

"Sure, why not! Tell Katey about it in your next letter, she'll get a charge."

They stood at the entrance to the typing pool, holding hands, each playing their make-believe role to the hilt. Jerry didn't have to stoop when he planted a meek kiss on her cheek midst the whistles and catcalls. Molly smiled and winked back at him.

"Molly?"

"Yes Amigo."

"Add another line in your next letter to Katey. Tell her if I don't get those five lines from her within two weeks, I want my class ring back and then she can really go to 'H' as far as I'm concerned… I mean it."

"Don't do this to her, Jerry. You're making a big, big mistake!"

"JUST WRITE IT!"

Two weeks later, Jerry arrived at his work station a few minutes late. There, at his desk, was his class ring with a note from Molly. It read: 'See, I told you so, you made one big mistake. P.S. Katey said to tell you she still loves you, no matter what. Love, Moll.'

Another month inched by, the sixth since Katey left, and Jerry was down in the dumps. On Tuesday and Thursday, he was in evening class after his day job, and on Monday, Wednesday and Friday nights he did the evening grocery deliveries for Bettingers Supermarket. This busy schedule kept him from spending too much time thinking about Katey and what might have been, except this Friday night. His last delivery took him within two blocks of Katey's house. A sudden impulse took a hold, "Aw, what the heck" he muttered out loud, "How about a nice unfriendly visit to Katey's folks? Worst thing that'll probably happen is that old man McCray will meet me at the door and threaten to shoot me if I don't vacate the premises immediately… but what the heck, I got nothin' better to do tonight."

He pulled into the McCray driveway and whistled softly as he knocked on the door. To his surprise, Mary McCray opened the door. "Hello, Mrs. McCray! Are we still on speaking terms?"

Mary seemed almost glad to see him, and then a scowl crossed her face. "I'd invite you in, but Mr. McCray's in a foul mood…job's been goin' hard and I'm not too certain you'd be welcome just now."

"That's okay, I understand, Ma'am. Any news from Katey? I never got any, but figured she'd at least remember to drop you two a line..."

Mary closed the door behind her. They stood on the front steps. "That's what Katey said in her last letter too... said she never understood it... Molly said the same thing..."

"You're sure she tried to write me?"

Mary's eyes opened wide, her jaw set. "Write you Jerry? How dare you ask such a question! The very day we arrived at Katey's Aunt Rose, I personally saw her sit down and write you. It was the very first thing she did! Oh Jerry, I only wish you could've been there to have seen the feelings pourin' from her heart into them words. I tell you, it was somethin' special and beautiful to behold; such love, such devotion and such commitment..."

"But did you actually see her mail my letters?"

His question stumped Mary for a few seconds. "Ah, I see what you're drivin' at, my Lad. The answer is no, but we get our letter as regular as paydays around here. And Jerry, I must tell you, you broke our Katey's heart; you took the life right out'a her soul when you asked for your ring back. She'll have a hard time gettin' over the likes of you, I'm afraid. Still writes askin' about you..."

"Well, you two were right. We failed your test on commitment."

Mary shook a finger in Jerry's face. "Katey didn't fail, you did Mr. Landis! Now my husband is very angry with you. He liked you, you know, and Mr. McCray is a mighty shrewd judge of character. That's where our Katey gets it, from her father, and she was so certain about you..."

"I know why Katey is really back in Chicago."

Instinctively, Mary clamped a hand over her mouth. "You do? How could you? Who told?"

"Look, Mrs. McCray, it's really no big secret. That one night, when you found out about us, I must've hurt Katey a lot worse than she let on. I'm responsible for her condition, right?"

Mary felt relieved. "There'll be no denying that, Mr. Landis. She wouldn't be where she is without you puttin' her there. What are you gettin' at?"

He took out his billfold and handed Mary forty dollars. "I'm responsible, so I'm going to help pay her medical bills… it's only right. Each payday you folks can count on another forty 'til it's all paid back."

"Thank you for the money, Jerry, you're a better man than we give you credit for. Katey's havin' a real hard time now, she's been sick a lot. We were going to call her this evening to try to cheer her up. How about you coming in to talk with her Jerry? It'd mean an awful lot for her to hear your voice… and I'll keep Mr. McCray in the parlor, away from you, while you're on the telephone. What'a ya say Lad?"

"I have nothing to say to Katey 'til I get my first letter from her. Since she can't manage to put a postage stamp on all those letters she's supposed to have written me, I just can't manage to find the time to talk to her. Gotta suggestion, the next time you write, how about sending some postage stamps along? Maybe she'll take the hint."

"Jerry Landis, I see it all now! Your pride is hurting you so bad that it's eatin' you up inside. You've nothin' left for our Katey or anybody else. I'll tell her that when her father and I speak to her shortly. Anyway, I do thank you for the money and I'll bid you good evening!"

He turned to walk away, but Mary had one last thought. "Jerry?"

"Yes."

"Katey said something in her last letter about your mother not even liking her a wee bit, especially after you told her you were engaged. Is it possible she's been keepin' Katey's letters from you?"

"I've thought about that too. You're right, my mother has no use for Katey at all, but I don't believe she'd do a thing like that… and even if she did, my two little sisters would've told me right away… we're buddies, they depend on me. No, I never got her letters… not even one. Somebody's lying, and it sure as heck isn't me."

"Hmm, and the hard part is I believe you're both right."

With Katey two thousand miles away and no longer occupying center stage in Jerry's mind, he gradually drifted back to some of his old habits and friends, namely Sam Moore's Pool Hall and Ricco Petrocelli. Both offered a tonic for what ailed him, boredom and loneliness. Jerry bought his first car-a good, used 1946 Chevy. To celebrate, he and Ricco partied behind the levee at Ormandy Park. Their chosen spot was ideal because it was a great place to unwind and get a lot of things off their chests without police interference. Ricco boasted about the number of times he made "whoopee" with Molly. Then he told his Amigo that he couldn't believe Jerry wasted over two years on poor, little Katey without "scoring" at least once. Considering the deep hurt and frustration, Jerry's answer was magnificent when he said he'd never touched her. They topped off the evening with Ricco wildly cheering Jerry on, as he heaved his class ring as far as it could go into the Sacramento River. Then he topped that off with a lusty "Go to "H"!

About three in the morning, Ricco woke up. He shook Jerry. "Hey, Amigo, it's gettin' late, you feel up to drivin'?"

Jerry stirred, tried to sit up, then he rubbed his bloodshot eyes. "Yeah, I'm okay. Guess I can navigate my Chevy good enough to get you'n me home."

From a distance, they looked to be about the same height and weight, both two inches under six feet with solid frames to easily carry one hundred sixty-five pounds. Together, they leaned on one another for support while they weaved and walked to Jerry's car.

The next two weekends, Ricco and Jerry partied 'til they ran out of money, booze and finally women. Ricco was the life at each party while Jerry tagged along to claim whatever female was left, willing and able. Try as he might to enjoy his conquests, Jerry always found himself trying to compare each one-night stand to a petite-built Irish Lass with a cute oval face and a few left-over freckles. The comparison didn't end there either, for none exhibited what he admired most and longed for, respect and attitude with more than a few brains above their brassieres. To Jerry, flopping in bed with a new partner each time didn't cut it, it just simply made matters worse. For all the freedom he claimed he had, he was totally miserable with himself and the results.

Two more months rolled by when Ricco paid Jerry a surprise visit at work. "Hey Amigo," said Jerry, "aren't you in enemy territory? We're supposed to be on opposite sides of the bargaining table. Speaking of negotiations, how's your dad doing?"

Ricco pulled up a chair by Jerry's desk. "Pretty good! Dad had me doing much of the leg-work lately before negotiations were reopened. I'm here to tell you that railroad management team of yours is a bunch of double-dealing shysters… that's all they are. We know they're makin' all kinds of profit, but the figures they show the union makes it look like we just opened Mother Hubbard's cupboard. Hey Jerr, the key operative words are 'Let us see!' Get it? Those railroad figures are phony as can be."

Jerry leaned back in his chair. "Has the union considered that maybe, just maybe, our railroad might be starting to hurt a bit? The airline freighters and highway truckers are bound to be cutting into our revenues. Add in the fact that railroad taxes are used to subsidize our competitors by building new highways for the truckers and new airport facilities for the airlines, and you can kinda get a picture of where California Central stands. It's not a pretty picture, especially when we get no tax dollars to maintain and operate our own road system."

"Hey, Amigo, I didn't come here for an overview of Cal Central's economic picture."

"Well then, why did you come?" Jerry asked quietly.

"Jerry, I hate to admit this, but take a look at my eyes. Notice anything about them? Like those bags under my eyes are nothing compared to the Samsonite luggage I carried under 'em last week. I feel all run down… lost four pounds. I gotta dump my Dad's secretary. She's too much for me to take on day after day. She's killin' me slow but sure!"

Jerry snickered, and then let out a big roar. "Yeah, you do look all dragged out. Never in my wildest thoughts did I ever think the Italian Stallion would cry uncle. So, what's next on your agenda?"

"Let's start workin' the Friday night dances at the Eagles. Should be lots of young stuff there for the pickin'. Are you with me?"

"I've had enough one-night stands to last me for awhile. What I'm lookin' for is a gal that doesn't roll over easy, likes to talk and have a good time, but won't club a guy over the head with 'I can't Jerry, not 'til we're married.' Get my drift?"

"Yeah, you're lookin' for another Katey without the church and God Almighty breathin' down your neck. Those kinds of gals are hard to find. Usually they're loose as a goose, or it'll take a stick of dynamite to get things to open up, even on a guy's wedding night. And that's after they lead you up to the altar where they make you put a ring on their finger while they put a bull ring through your nose."

Jerry poured a cup of coffee out of his thermos. He took a sip, and then put the thermos cup down. "Guess what I'm really looking for is somebody nice, somebody to keep steady company with, but with no strings attached for either of us. I want a decent looker too, no dogs! Most of all, I gotta be in control of the situation. The second I'm not, that's when I Hank Snow again by movin' on!"

Next Friday night, Jerry and Ricco frequented the dance scene at the local Eagles Hall. Within an hour, Ricco had his pillow gal, his target for the night, staked out. A saucy, sharp-looking little number from Sacramento who was visiting her cousin, a former classmate of Ricco and Jerry's. Three dances later, Ricco cut out with his date, leaving Jerry to soak up the evening's atmosphere along with several other wallflowers.

"Do you dance?" came a soft voice.

Jerry looked up from his chair into a pleasant round face with a touch or two of too much lipstick and rouge. She was about his size, had a very friendly smile and a good shape to go along with the more than passing good looks. She appeared older than most of the crowd, he guessed probably twenty-four or five. Her dark hair was beautifully groomed. "Yeah, guess I do."

She held out her hand to him. "You don't look like you're having much fun, and I promise to keep off your toes if you'll try to stay off mine. How about it?"

He shrugged to himself, mumbled something under his breath she failed to overhear, and tried his best to accommodate his new partner on the dance floor. After the music stopped, he was undecided what to do next. She read his mind. "My name's Carol Kingman."

"I'm Jerry Landis," he blurted out. "Hope I didn't step on you too many times."

Carol laughed. "No, matter of fact, you dance pretty well… maybe a bit rusty… what say we try it again? The band looks ready…"

They moved around to the beat, both much more relaxed and at ease with each other. When the band took a break, Carol again took the initiative. "Jerry, I feel a bit out of place here… you and I look somewhat older than this crowd. Any objections to having a cup of coffee, maybe a sandwich, and … and just chat?"

He couldn't believe his ears. She was exactly what he'd been telling Ricco he was looking for earlier that evening. "Fine with me, lead the way."

"I was hoping you'd have a place in mind, I'm still kinda new around here."

"Okay, let's go to Wally's, my car is just outside in the parking lot."

Over sandwiches and hot coffee, the twosome got along famously for being total strangers less than an hour ago. Jerry soon learned she was a commercial real estate agent and had just moved to Rushton from the San Diego area. Carol took another bite of her sandwich. "Say, I've been doing all the talking. What about you, Jerry?"

He fidgeted a moment, not sure just how much information he cared to part with. "I work days as a freight clerk for the railroad here, and on Monday and Wednesday evenings and all day Saturday, I work for Bettingers Super Market doing the grocery deliveries. On Tuesday and Thursday nights, I drive to Sacramento to take a couple of accounting classes each night. I'll finish my first year with this coming summer session, I hope."

"Wow, that's a lot of commitment!" Carol sensed that was a very poor choice of words. "I'm sorry, did I say something wrong? I meant to compliment you when I said commitment... I can readily see you don't appreciate that word..."

"Not like I used to," came Jerry's reply.

"Care to talk about it?"

"Not really."

Carol let the subject drop as she finished her sandwich. "I could go for some dessert, how about a piece of pie ala mode? The tab's on me, so order whatever you want."

Jerry nodded and slowly smiled. He too ordered pie ala mode. As soon as the waitress went to get the pie, she again broached him on the subject. "I don't mean to be nosey, but I get the definite impression you've been hurt very deeply by someone who used to be very close to you. Am I warm?"

He didn't answer at first, only looked away from his friendly companion. Finally he opened up a little. "Yeah, guess it shows, huh? That's what you get when you trust someone… when you wear your heart on a sleeve, and get it knocked off right back in your face."

"Is she a local girl?"

"She was. We grew up together all through grade and then high school. We had some big plans. She was brought up very strict Catholic with old world ideas and values."

"Are you very religious? A Catholic too?"

"Me? Heck no! Only started going to church to please her and her folks. They wanted us to wait awhile before we took the plunge, so they sent her back to Chicago to test our commitment. Well, we failed miserably, couldn't even get her to write five lines to me, so I threw in the towel."

Carol held her coffee cup up with both hands, letting her elbows rest on the table. "High school romances rarely work out unless you really know each other and are committed. She's probably found somebody else back there and just couldn't break the news to you. I'm surprised you said high school. You act much older. Are you?"

Jerry evaded the direct answer. "I took your question as a compliment. If I'm too young for your company, I'll gladly pick up the check and say so long. Where do you want me to drop you off?"

He started to reach for the check, but Carol snatched it away from him. "Hey, Jerry, I'm an agent, I meet a lot of nice people, and I'm generally a pretty good judge of maturity in people. You strike me as all of the above. I enjoy your company, hope you feel the same way about me."

He sat back. "I do. You're the first person I've met in a long, long time I feel comfortable with."

"Fine! Now let's enjoy our dessert and not miss out on each other's company and lots of good conversation."

They finished the pie and ice cream. Carol could see Jerry was getting a little apprehensive about where their conversation and particularly the evening were headed. She reached her hands across the table and gently squeezed his. "I'm going to be honest with you and tell you some more about me. I'm an Army brat, well traveled, and lived in four other countries while I was growing up. I quit college during my sophomore year, almost broke my dad and mother's heart because I decided to do my own thing. Dad's a retired Army colonel, and they don't have much to do with me anymore. I'm kind of a loner. I do as I please, and I live alone as I please. I just sold my first commercial property here in Rushton and like the area, so I plan on being here for awhile. I had a relationship with a guy a couple of years ago, it didn't pan out, and so we went our separate ways. Why am I telling you all this? Because I've been through just what you're going through."

Jerry fiddled with his spoon.

"You've got something on your mind, go ahead. I'll try to be a good listener."

"I got burned pretty bad and I'm not about to commit to any kind of a relationship. I'm also sick of one night flings. So anytime I feel I'm not in control of my own situation, I'm going to walk away."

Carol pushed her coffee cup aside. "Fine by me, just tell me when you've reached that point, that's all I'll ever ask of you. Fair enough?"

He liked her smile, he liked her attitude, and he liked the direction their conversation was headed, but most of all he appreciated her frankness. "I hope we become friends, maybe good friends later, in time."

He drove her back to the parking lot behind the Eagles Hall to where her car was parked. Jerry asked, "What are you driving?"

Carol pointed, "The last car on this row, the 1950 two-tone Chrysler."

He got out to open the door and walked her to the Chrysler. "Nice car. Guess those real estate commissions treat you right."

She smiled, and then added, "Yes, it's a good living. Drop by anytime, I work for Bazell and Broderick, you can't miss the purple paint job on the corner of First and Sycamore Street. The color's horrible, but it does get your attention and that's what commercial real estate is all about."

They shook hands. Then Carol surprised Jerry by planting a kiss where it would do the most good, on his lips. "Well, good night Jerry, see you around. Thanks again for the good company and conversation. Let's do it again, whenever you want to."

He closed the door after she got in. "We will, you can count on it. Goodnight, Carol!"

The Chrysler barely hummed after she started the engine. The window rolled down and Carol stuck her head out. "She must've been quite small, right Jerry?"

"Why, yes, how did you know?" Jerry questioned.

"The way you acted when I kissed you… you stooped way down at first… old habits are hard to break. Good night!"

Jerry watched the tail lights disappear around the corner. He smiled to himself and whistled all the way back to his own car. For the first time in months he felt good about his night and himself.

# CHAPTER NINE

Katey's time was at hand, her pain almost unbearable, until she saw the precious, beautiful little baby girl she welcomed into the world. Kristianne Marie McCray-Landis arrived at 8:45 P.M. on a Friday; the same Friday night her father met Carol Kingman, some two thousand miles west.

Mary McCray was at Katey's side during her delivery, and a prouder grandmother would be hard to come by. Katey finally drifted off to sleep only after the delivery doctor assured her twice that her baby, though very small, was normal and healthy in every way.

Next morning, Katey and Mary were the first to stand outside the nursery window anxiously awaiting the drawing of the curtain so they might spot Krissy. "There! There!" exclaimed Katey. "See, over by the corner, there's Krissy! Oh Mother, have you ever seen a more beautiful baby? What a precious, sweet little girl… it's a miracle! Oh I love her so much and I promised God last night that I'm going to be the best mother in the entire world."

"I'm so thankful you didn't lose your baby… twice Rose called me… had your father'n me on pins and needles wonderin' if you'd lost our grandchild."

Later that morning, Katey breast-fed Krissy while Mary looked on in a most maternal manner. "The nurse told me I have enough milk to probably breast-feed Krissy for at least six months until she's ready to drink from a cup. Isn't that great? Probably won't even have to buy bottles or baby formula."

Mary agreed. "Yes, that'll be a savin' there to be sure… and your own natural milk, Katey, there's nothin' better." Then she raised a finger in caution. "Aye, but you must eat the proper food or else your Krissy will not nurse enough."

The duty nurse stepped into the room. "Mrs. Landis, let me take your baby back to the nursery soon as she's finished. Let your baby nurse 'til she's had enough, she'll let you know."

All three women watched intently as Krissy finally stopped making a sucking sound. "Boy, when she wants to be fed she really goes at it! It's hard to believe those sweet little lips have so much suction! Did you bring the camera, Mother?"

Mary took the Polaroid out of her purse. She turned to the nurse. "Would you mind taking a couple of pictures? Her grandfather's chompin' at the bit! Says to me, 'don't come home 'til you get some pictures to show me'."

The nurse waited for Katey to hold Krissy up. Mary moved in beside them. "Okay smile, everybody! Now Grandmother, you hold the baby this time!"

Mary held the bundle of soft wiggles and squirms. "Oh Katey, darlin' you didn't have a baby, you had a baby doll, a real live, huggable baby doll.! Once you hold her, she'll melt your heart and steal your soul, that's what she does!"

"Hold it! Good!"

The nurse handed the camera back to Mary. "Time to take Krissy back. Has your husband been in to see his new daughter yet? Don't seem to remember seeing him around."

Katey shot a quick glance over at her mother. "My husband Jerry is out west, he won't be here until after I leave the hospital. His job keeps him tied down!"

"Does your daughter look anything like him?"

Mary handed Krissy back to Katey. "Yes, her eyes are just like his, deepest blue I've ever seen!"

Katey studied her sleepy bundle of joy" Her hair is blonde like his… never saw so much blonde hair on a tiny baby before, but her face is like mine. I still can't get over the small hands and feet, but she's a perfect baby in every way."

The nurse headed down the hall toward the nursery carrying Krissy. Katey let out a big sigh of relief from her bed. "Whew! I had to think of something! Sure glad I'm wearing this wedding band. Wonder how many other unwed mothers are doing the same thing? I'm so sick of lying."

Mary sat on the edge of Katey's bed. "I didn't want to bring this up Lass, but I called Molly a couple of times just before I came to see you. I'm afraid Jerry is out of your life for good… he's running around with Ricco… it's a pretty loose crowd he's picked to go company with. Oh Katey, he came to see me… never have I seen so much hurt and pride all mixed up in what used to be such a good, decent lad."

"Do you see him anymore?"

"No, just the once. He leaves two twenties in an envelope each payday. Slips it under the front door, but never a note with a word or two on it. I'll say this for him, he's a man about taking his responsibility, he is."

Katey turned away, biting her lip. Her eyes watered. "I miss him so much… even if he told me to go to blazes. I know he's hurting bad, but I DID WRITE! Still don't understand what happened between us. Why does life have to hurt so much? Be so cruel at times? Especially when you love somebody who says he doesn't care for you anymore?"

Mary squeezed her daughter's hand. "Maybe it's for the best, the way things worked out between you two. You know what the hardest thing will be when you leave this hospital?"

"When I have to leave Krissy with Aunt Rose after I start classes at the business college next week?"

"That's peanuts compared to when you finish school and leave Krissy behind so you can come home. That's when the pain will really hurt. Still think you're up to it?"

Katey put on her bravest smile before dabbing her eyes with a Kleenex. "I've had a lot of time to think this over and I'm going ahead with my part of the promise I made to you and Daddy. I've already checked into the business college. They offer an accelerated nine-month course instead of the regular twelve. I'm not wrong about him, Mother, he's worth doing this for. After I return home, I'm going to get him back, no matter what it takes."

"Even if you have to tell him he's the father to our Krissy?"

"No. I'll never force him to marry me, that won't work, you and Dad are right about that. When I marry, it will be for keeps, one man, one love, one lifetime together. I have the right man picked out; he just doesn't want to admit it."

Mary knew Katey meant every word. There was no use trying to persuade her to get on with her life. She'd seen that look before, that Brannigan look. "Katey, you're from good stock. You've a pride about you that'd make any man you choose as your husband proud as a peacock. I'm just afraid it'll take an awful lot of convincin' to get Jerry back in your life. Katey, he feels you let him down… his pride is hurtin' somethin' fierce, and when a man's pride is gone there's not much left to get back. He'll not be the man you remember. Can you see what I've seen in Jerry?"

"Yes, Mother, but there has to be some reason… some explanation for what's happened. I know what makes him tick. I'm still not convinced I was wrong about him."

Mary switched subjects. "Your father, oh is he ever the proud one, Katey! Before I left, he comes to me and these are his exact words, 'Tell Katey not to worry 'bout bein' a good mother to our grandchild… 'cause her mother was the best and our daughter takes from her.'"

Katey took the compliment as it was intended, a testimonial to the McCrays in general and to her in particular.

***

Molly showed up at Jerry's work station, the first time in many months. He saw an excitement in her eyes. "Guess what, Amigo?"

"Ricco's talked you into going out with him!"

"No, no, not that! Katey's back! Called me last night to say she's going to work for the railroad up at the Corporate Headquarters Building. Said she finished up her business training in record time. Know how many months she's been gone Amigo? Don't kid me Jerry, I know you're been counting them too, all eighteen!"

Molly's announcement stirred him, even though he tried his best to downplay it. "So what, Molly, why should that interest me?"

"Landis, you're such a jackass! Your old flame's back and all you can say is 'so what'? She's going to have lunch with me at the cafeteria. Care to tag along?"

"Not really. I'd just get in the way with all the gossip you two probably will rehash over the past year and a half. Count me out."

Molly could only shake her head in disbelief. "Well, anyway, I'll tell her you said hi. You and Katey are still friends, aren't you?"

"Maybe, don't really know… and don't really much care."

Jerry stayed at his desk, eating his lunch alone. He read the sports page, and then glanced up at the clock above his work station. Ten more minutes and he could forget about any encounter with Katey for at least another day.

"Hello, Jerry!" came a familiar voice.

He put down the paper and there she was. Lord, she was something all right! He almost choked on his emotions as his eyes did the traveling. Gone was her shoulder-length hair, replaced by a neat, short crop effect, one which made her look older, more mature. She wore a light tan woman's business jacket with matching skirt and high heels. Her blouse, a light blue creation, complimented everything about her, from the thin application of lipstick to the hint of rouge over her flesh-tone make-up which covered all but a few of the tom-boy freckles he'd remembered so well. Silver-clad clip-on earrings completed his vision.

"Hello, Katey," he managed to blurt. "Molly tells me you're headquartered up at the snob building, rubbing elbows with the brain trust of our railroad. You look very professional… new hairdo, new clothes, and such."

"I'm glad you approve, Jerry. I'm substituting for the Headquarters Division Manager's private secretary while she's on vacation. Then I'll be filling in for the other secretaries during most of this summer. If I do okay, they will keep me on. It's my first job… I'm kind of excited about it… a chance to make pretty decent pay."

He folded up the newspaper and laid it on the desk next to him. "You'll do fine, Katey, you always did have a knack for secretarial work."

"So, how are you doing? Molly tells me you'll finish your second year in accounting after this summer quarter. I'm so proud of you, Jerry, I always knew you could do it."

"Thanks, Katey."

She glanced at her wristwatch. "I'd better get back, don't want to make a bad impression on my first day on the job." Katey started to say something else, but wound up saying, "I know you told me where to go, and I know you think you have plenty of reason to think that way about me, but can't we still be friends? Please, Amigo?"

Jerry studied her face, her eyes, her expression, and thought about her words. Then the pain took over. Oh, how it hurt! "All right, Katey, but nothing more."

A great sense of relief cleared Katey's lips, as she exhaled. "I'm glad, Jerry. Say, if you want to call me, wait 'til I'm home after work. They're pretty touchy about using the phones for personal reasons. You still remember my number?"

"No problem."

"Good, I'd better go now. Talk to you later!"

"Katey?"

"Yes?"

"When I said no problem, I meant no problem because I don't plan on making any personal phone calls for you at home, or anywhere else for that matter."

# CHAPTER TEN

Katey returned to work, quite disappointed that her first meeting with Jerry hadn't been more positive. She had hoped that he might have welcomed her back, maybe not with open arms, but at least a warm smile, so she could get a read on his feelings. It was his true feelings that bothered her most. She saw the hurt in his eyes, the distrust written all over his face, and knew now for certain he'd put a protective shell around both his feelings and his heart. For her to penetrate, for her to ever stand a chance to break down the barrier that now was keeping them apart, would call for drastic action. Yet, the irony of it all slapped her in the face: hard. For she'd done nothing wrong to deserve this treatment, except love him and have his baby.

Summer days dwindled down to the first signs of autumn, and Katey was no nearer to reconciling their differences. She had to make the first move.

Jerry finished the summer session of evening classes and had registered as a junior getting ready for the fall quarter's evening session, which began in late September. He'd seen Katey only on four occasions since her return, and those brief visits came as a result of her stopping by for a lunch break with Molly. They'd exchanged cool pleasantries, nothing more, and left it at that, much to Jerry's indifference and Katey's dismay. It was after her fourth try of getting nowhere, that Katey made her move.

The last Monday in September dawned just like any other, the morning air was clear, cool, and crisp, sure signs that Mother Nature was in control of the calendar. Jerry reached his work station, only to find a pretty colored note conspicuously lodged under his set of rate manuals so there'd be no chance of it getting lost or misplaced. He unfolded the note. It read, *'Blue with white lace.'*

Each morning another colored note and each time another color combination. On Friday, it read, *'Black lace with see-through frills for thrills.'* Although the notes were typewritten, there was no doubt who was behind their sudden appearances. He allowed a smile to surface, then wadded it up and promptly deposited it in the round file, his waste basket.

That evening, he waited outside the Corporate Headquarters Building for Katey to get off work. He was surprised to see her waiting at the bus stop. She smiled, knowing why he was there. "Hi, Jerry," she called out to him, "What brings you up here?"

"As if you didn't know. Hey, that was fourth-grade stuff, it won't work anymore, Katey."

"Oh, I don't know about that, got you up here, didn't it?"

She saw him actually smile. "All right, what's on your mind?"

"I have to catch a ride downtown. I'm due at the Jackson Law offices in twenty minutes. Sure hope I didn't miss my bus."

"You working two jobs? Since when? I thought you told me the railroad pays decent wages up here."

"They do. It's just that I need part-time work to help pay off my folks as soon as I can. They dipped pretty deep into their savings to pay some medical bills and my room and board while I was back in Chicago."

"That much, huh? I didn't realize it took so much. Look, I've been paying a little, trying to help out. Didn't your mother mention it?"

"Yes, she did Jerry, and I want to thank you for helping. It's my problem… I didn't want you to feel obligated… well, you know what I mean."

"Hey Katey, I caused it, I should be the one to pay for it… not you. I'm sorry I put you in such a pickle… let me do some refiguring and maybe I can spare a few more bucks to help out after my fall quarter starts."

"Aren't you forgetting something? It took two of us, Jerry, not just you alone."

"Let me give you a ride downtown, Katey. No need for you to stand here waiting… it's the least I can do."

"Well okay. Where's your car?"

He pointed with pride to his car parked in the visitors section at the front of the company parking lot. "C'mon, follow me!"

"Gee, it's a nice car, Jerry. What year is it?"

He unlocked the door on the passenger side. "It's a 1946 Chevy and it's all paid for!"

He held the door open while Katey sat down on the seat and removed her high-heels. She let him take in a little extra leg than usual while changing to a pair of sneakers she had in her brief case. "Boy that feels good! High-heels are all right, but they'll never replace sneakers as far as I'm concerned. At the law offices, they don't mind what I wear just as long as I do their work."

Jerry got behind the wheel. "What kind of work do you do?"

"Mostly typing up depositions and legal briefs and doing some steno too, if they need something out right away. I like working for them, they've even offered me a permanent job, so I must be doing something right for a change!"

Downtown, he dropped Katey off in front of the law office building. She started to get out of the car, and then had second thoughts. "Are you busy tonight? Have a class?"

"No, not tonight, why?"

"I have two hours of work, and then I'll be through. If you don't mind sticking around, I'll treat for dinner… it's been a long time, Jerry. Maybe we could talk some, how about it?"

"Okay, but on one condition, if I don't like the subject, we drop it! Agreed? From now on, I call the shots… all the shots."

"Fine by me. See you at six-thirty. Thanks for the ride. Jerry?"

"Yes?"

"I like your car, it's exactly what I pictured your first car would look like. It's a reflection of you… clean, responsive, and most of all, it knows where it's going."

Their dinner started out a bit edgy, each trying to mask their feelings. Katey finally broached the first touchy subject, Carol Kingman. She finished a sip of tea. "Understand you've been seeing an older woman, a real estate agent… I think her name is Miss Carol Kingman…"

"Cut the crap, Katey! You know darned well who she is and what her name is."

The next question lodged in Katey's throat for a full minute. "Is it serious?"

Jerry put down his steak knife and finished chewing the piece of meat. "Serious? No way! I'm not ready for anymore commitments and don't figure on any at least until I finish getting my degree… and that's some time down the road. We're just friends, and that's all."

She hesitated, and then asked, "Good friends?"

He never blinked as their eyes met. "Yeah, I suppose you could say that. How about you, Katey? Anybody special in your life now? Maybe back in Chicago?"

Jerry's insinuation raised the Irish in Katey. Oh, how she longed to slap his face for daring to suggest such a thing. She drummed her fingers beside her plate and somehow controlled her temper with these words. "When I left for Chicago, I had somebody special in mind… nothing's changed my way of thinking… even though after I've returned, I find this special person that I still care about feels that I've somehow betrayed him, that he's gotten a raw deal, even though I've kept, yes, more than kept my part of our commitment."

He pounded his fist on the table. "That's enough, Katey! Knock it off! Time to change subjects or else I walk out tonight for good!"

She didn't back down. "So, that's how you're going to handle it, right Jerry? Whenever you don't like something, or you feel crowded just a bit too much, well, then Jerry Landis says, 'to heck with it, I'll walk out!' Life doesn't work that way, and you know it!"

"I think it's time I took you home. We're liable to say something we'll both regret. I'll still try to be your friend, but nothing more."

Katey put a twenty dollar bill on the table and they left without so much as one more word to each other. Choking with rage, Katey fought the flood of tears and anguish residing in her mind and in her body. She stared straight ahead; blinking hard, and tightened her lips for fear she'd be the one to utter the words "go to 'H'" this time.

Jerry drove to Katey's home in record time. He obviously wanted her out of his car and his life for good. The car stopped, but she just sat there making no move to get out. Without so much as a word between them, he reached across her body to open the door on her side.

On impulse, Katey grabbed him and wrapped her arms around him, blocking his path to the car's door latch. She found his face, and then his lips and she went to work like never before, pouring every ounce of love and feelings that she could muster into him. She tasted on every corner of his lips until she felt his response, he too wanted her.

They kissed hard, they kissed again, and again, neither's lips staying apart long enough to utter a sound. Katey moved in with her body, making sure he got the full benefit. Seconds later she felt his hand work inside her suit jacket. She nearly swooned from the feeling, it'd been over two years since she'd experienced such pleasure. It never felt better than it did at that moment.

Finally the words came, hot, and hurried, between more passionate French kisses, the kind designed to stimulate. "Jerry, Jerry," she whispered, her tone pleading for his response to be in concert with hers. "How can you deny our love for each other… how, Jerry?" She kissed on, saying, "I love you with everything I have… I love you… do you hear me? Say it, say it," she begged, "you know you do… please… Jerry… please…"

He could hold out no longer. She knew what was coming, yet she must hear his words, they meant everything to her… all the world to her. "Katey, Katey, I… I…I won't fight it… I do love you… God I hurt so… but I do love you… and I want you… why do I hurt so much? I want to forget what you did to me… but I can't."

"I'll give you the time you need darling, just say you love me enough to start over… to give ourselves the chance we both want… please Jerry, say it."

He pushed her away as suddenly as she had caught him off-guard. "What is it Jerry? Why are you doing this to me? To us?"

"I have to know something and please be honest with me. Those… those letters your mother said you wrote me… it was some kind of a test wasn't it, Katey? Level with me, you never did write them did you? Did you Katey?"

She lashed out, slapping his face once, twice; the second hard slap drew blood from his cheek when her fingernails raked his face. "HOW DARE YOU!" she screamed, "HOW DARE YOU THINK THAT OF ME!" Then she saw the blood. He grabbed both hands to keep her from hitting again. "I'm sorry Jerry, I'm sorry! I didn't mean to slap you… I lost my temper, I lost control…"

Calmly, very calmly, he gradually released his hold on her. "Sure you did Katey, you meant every damn slap and a hundred more if I'd let you get away with it…"

She threw herself into his arms once more, begging, pleading. "Jerry, I'll take an oath, swear on a stack of Bibles before you, or God, if that'll help, because I DID WRITE AND I DID SEND THOSE LETTERS… please…" she sobbed again, "Please Jerry, I did… please believe me… please…"

He looked down at his distraught Katey. Very carefully he raised her head up so their eyes met, so there'd be no mistaking his words. "It'll always be there, Katey… the mistrust, the doubt… the damage that has been done that can never be undone. Katey, listen to me, before we end up hating each other and not even being friends for the rest of our lives. Get on with your life… I have. Go find somebody else who will start over with you, someone who trusts you… I can't…"

"Do you love her, your Carol?"

"No, Katey, but that's not the point I'm trying to get you to see."

"That is the point, Jerry, the whole point. How can you walk away from all the years, the feelings, and the love that's been growing between us? How?"

"Simple, I'm not ready to commit and you are. You want to marry, settle down, and raise a family. I'm not ready… not now, after what's happened… and in truth Katey, I'm not sure I ever will be… again."

"So that's how we end it, huh? We both walk away from what we had and say sorry it's not for us. That doesn't cut it, Jerry Landis, and you know it!"

"It does with me! Goodnight Katey! Maybe see you around sometime!"

She got out of his car and slammed the door as hard as she could, trying her darndest to at least get some small satisfaction out of the effort she'd put forth. Jerry backed out and was gone, gone out of her life for good she deeply feared.

Katey grabbed her briefcase and stormed past Mary into her bedroom. Mary followed, right on her heels. "We couldn't even finish a meal without gettin' into it over those damned missing letters! So help me, next time I write, I'm going to personally deliver every darned one. I'll be the postman! Then there'll be no more screw-ups!"

Mary sat down calmly waiting for Katey's Irish to settle down. Isn't it time to bring Krissy home and get on with the raisin' of your daughter? Your father's been asking how much longer he must wait to hold Krissy in his arms. His waitin' is about used up."

Katey set her jaw and gritted her teeth. "That's a hechava lot more than that stubborn-headed Jerry Landis is ready to do. Awrrrh! I've never seen anybody so pig-headed, so set in his ways! He thinks he's just walked out of my life for good! Well, Landis, I've got a news flash for you, Buster! I'm going to have you pantin' to get next to me, pleadin' on bended knees to take me back and waltz down that matrimonial aisle. And you know what Mother? It'll all be for his own good… 'course now he'd never believe that."

Mary headed for the door.

"Did you have something more on your mind?"

"Not any more. I'll tell your father he'll have to wait a wee bit longer for his granddaughter to make her grand appearance. Katey, there's a mighty big streak of Brannigan willpower in you, 'tis plain to see. And when you add in the McCray stubbornness too, that young man of yours might just as well wave the white flag now. Think of the time it'll save!"

They both laughed.

Jerry was bombarded with pretty colored notes each and every morning when he reported to his work station. At first they found his round file.

Then curiosity got the best of him, like Katey figured it would, so he read them before they got his basketball toss. Her notes provided just the tonic that Jerry needed. They showed him that he was not "the forgotten man" in her life; regardless of the deep distrust that festered within. Her offers of you-name-it and I'll be there were 'last gasp efforts' as far as he was concerned. He now believed that his future lay in a different direction. True, every time they met, his heartstrings played an 'old refrain' one that was still deeply embedded in their past. Yet, little by little, upon those meetings, he fell a bit less under her spell.

# CHAPTER ELEVEN

It was Wednesday afternoon when Jerry rushed home from work to change clothes and grab a sandwich before he started the evening deliveries for Bettinger's Supermarket. Actually, he liked the routine, it kept him busy and since Katey's return, it kept him from thinking too much about her, thoughts that always seemed to translate into his chronic pain of distrust, no matter how little or how much he dwelled on her.

He cleared the dirty dishes off the counter, wiped it clean and made his sandwich. While eating he watched his two little sisters at play. Stacey, the oldest, had dressed herself up in her mother's old apron and was about to enter the make-believe store made out of two huge cardboard boxes stacked on top of each other. Cheryl, the youngest was the store keeper.

"Good day Mrs. Smith," Cheryl began, "and what can I do for you on this fine day?"

Stacey, a.k.a. Mrs. Smith, put on her best grown-up imitation and walked around the store several times before placing her order. "I'm really not very happy with the corn I bought here yesterday, so I'm returning it… I want my money back."

Cheryl pretended to take the corn back. "Now do you want me to pay you, or do you want credit on something else Mrs. Smith. We have some fine donuts… they're fresh, right out of our bakery…"

Mrs. Smith folded her arms in a most grown-up way. "I don't know… yes, the donuts smell good, so I'll take the credit on them. Oh, by the way, will you check to see I have any mail today. Been expectin' a check from my husband, he's in South America getting rich mining gold."

Cheryl went to the back of the store, where the two girls had used an old wooden chair with its spindles in the back as their post office. Between the spindles, they had put some old envelopes. She withdrew one and handed it to Mrs. Smith. "Yes, there's a letter for you, it's from South America. Open it. Let's see if your husband sent the check."

Mrs. Smith took the envelope but wouldn't open it. "It's mine! I'll take my letter home and see if the check's inside. He's my husband, not yours!"

At that point, the pretend drama broke down. Cheryl ran over to her big brother. "Jerry, Stacey's not playing fair! Make her open the letter. I want to see the check too!"

Jerry motioned to Stacey. "C'mon Stacey, it's only pretend. Go ahead and open it!"

"No, I won't," came the reply. "It's mine and I can do whatever I want with it."

"Then bring it here and I'll open it. That's fair isn't it?"

Stacey reluctantly brought the half-burned, dirty, crumpled up letter to Jerry. Cheryl clapped her hands in glee. "See, Jerry made you bring it to him! Ha! Ha! Ha! Ha! He's bigger'n you! He made you do it!"

"Did not!" Stacey yelled

"Did too!" Cheryl yelled even louder back.

"Hey, hey, you two, knock it off!" Jerry replied firmly.

Jerry reached for a table knife to open the old envelope. His jaw dropped, his eyes opened wide as he stared at the handwriting and address on the envelope. He checked the postmark, Chicago. It was from Katey. He questioned Stacey. "C'mon, where'd you get this?"

Little Cheryl quickly volunteered. "We got an old shoe box full of 'em, Jerry. Mommy burned most of them but Stacey fished some out of the fire so we could use 'em to play post office with."

Jerry again questioned Stacey. "Why did Mother burn them? Why, Stacey? How come you didn't tell me about these letters a long time ago?"

Stacey started to cry. "She said they came from a bad lady, a bad lady who wanted you to go away with her… she… she said if we told you… she'd put us in homes far, far away from each other… and they'd beat us every day… and nobody would feed us like you do, Jerry… and we'd never get to see you again."

He clenched his fists and slammed them down together with all his strength on the table. His half-eaten sandwich bounced a foot up into the air.

Little Cheryl mistook Jerry's anger and ran crying at the top of her lungs to her bedroom. "Don't hit her, please, Jerry!" begged the older sister. "She's too young, she didn't know!"

He lowered his voice. "Don't worry, Stacey, I'll never lay a glove on either of you. When I see your mother, I won't make any such promises. What time does she get home? I'm never here anymore, so you'll have to tell me!"

"About six-thirty, if she doesn't stop off somewhere first."

"Go get that shoebox, will you?"

Stacey went outside to the dog kennel next door. Inside, wedged up between a rafter, she removed a weather-beaten old shoe box half-filled with partially burned-up letters. Jerry sorted through the box, only two envelopes still contained complete letters. He read them with profound interest, and then put them back into the box.

"I'm going over to the neighbor's to use their phone, and I won't be going to work tonight. When I get back, I'll fix supper, and them I'm going to wait for mother."

Six-thirty came and no mother. About eight o'clock, Jerry's mother wandered in, half-drunk, reeking of whiskey. "What the "H" are you doin' here? Supposed to be workin' ain'tcha?"

"Girls, you better go get ready for bed," Jerry warned, "Mother and I have some talking to do. Better keep the door closed too."

Jerry launched into his mother with over two years' worth of rage. He really unloaded on her. "Where do you get off pulling crap like this?" He shoved the box under her nose. "If you were a man, I'd knock you on your behind for what you did to me and to Katey!"

Jerry's mother slouched down in a chair opposite him at the kitchen table. She fumbled through her purse for a cigarette, found a loose, half-bent one, and then went looking for a match. Jerry reached back on the counter and tossed her a box of farmer style matches. She promptly used the table instead of the striker strip on the box. Two puffs later, she let go with a volley of profanity that'd put a drunken sailor on shore leave to shame. "You know, Jerry, I try'n do you a friggin' favor and what do I get for it? Not a thank you, oh no! I get my butt-chewed out, that's what I get for tryin' to do the right thing… for being a good mother to all'a ya! I'm tickled to death I broke you'n that little Irish bitch of yours up… yes, plum tickled to death! And I'd do it again if I got another chance. Those Irish, they breed like rabbits, always got a pack of runny nosed kids trailin' 'round waitin' for some stiff-necked Catholic Father to forgive 'em and tell 'em to go out and do it again. Raise another batch of brats, then come see me, I'll take your last dime and tell ya to do it again."

"Mother, you're full of horse manure! Katey is the best thing that ever could've happened to me, and she's an only child, so where do you get off with all that runny-nosed brat crap, anyway?'

"Then her mother must'a let the church down 'cause they generally shuck 'em out like peas… don't believe in birth control ya know."

"Tomorrow morning I'm turning you in, no more covering for you. The way I see it, Stacey and Cheryl will be one hundred percent better off with whomever they put 'em with. You're no mother! Never was, never will be! You love your booze too damn much!"

Jerry's mother glared at her son. "You worthless 'Sonofa B'! Just like your ol' man, still ain't worth the spit on a park bench! Go ahead, turn me in! And get the 'H' outa my house! Never wanna see hide nor hair'a ya again!"

"With pleasure Mother! With pleasure! I'm staying tonight 'til I take the girls down to Social Services first thing tomorrow morning."

She got up to wobble and weave her way through the room's filth and clutter toward her bedroom. Ten steps from her bedroom door, she cussed at the cat, tried to kick it, and missed badly, landing on her behind for all her wasted effort. She saw Jerry snicker at her drunken antics. She told him off. "Go ahead, laugh, you worthless 'Sonofa B'. That's the last laugh you'll ever get watchin' me!"

He could hardly wait to let the words out. "I sure hope so, Mother, I sure hope so."

Mr. McCray picked Katey up at the Jackson Law Office Building. Katey could hardly believe her eyes when she spotted Jerry waiting on their front steps. She wanted to rush up to greet him, but decided against such an outward display of enthusiasm, especially with her father by her side. He parked the car and together they approached their visitor. Mr. McCray mumbled a decent hello, and continued on into the house. Katey stayed outside with Jerry.

"What brings you here, Jerry? Aren't you supposed to be in class? It's Thursday night!"

He motioned for her to sit down on the steps with him. "I'll only miss the early class… still have plenty of time to make the second class."

Katey set her briefcase down between them. "Must be pretty important to make you cut class. What is it?"

He handed her one of the crumpled letters. "I… I don't know what to say to you… except I'm sorry. I want to apologize for not believing you… I've been such a BHJ!"

Katey examined the signed letter. She recognized her own handwriting. She turned the crumpled and wrinkled envelope over and over in her hands.

"My mother burned most of them, but my little sisters managed to save a couple. I read that one and another last night, waiting to have it out with her. Welfare has my sisters now, and I filed a complaint against her for child neglect. She kicked me out, been stayin' at the YMCA since then."

"What does BHJ stand for?"

"Butt-Headed Jackass!"

"Well Landis, that's a pretty fair description of you all right. I could add a few more choice words, but that won't help either of us. Tell you what, I'll accept your apology on one condition, and one only."

"What's that?"

"You come to dinner tomorrow night. My treat. I want to see if you and I can get through a meal without somebody getting their face slapped or called a liar or getting their feelings hurt before I even get to open the fridge door looking for the dessert."

"Any strings attached?"

"None. I'll even have my folks disappear for the evening. Well, you BHJ, what do you say? Interested?"

"You're on!"

Friday night came, and it would be hard to find two more cautious people than Katey and Jerry. Jerry was beside himself, trying to help Katey finish setting the table, placing the silverware just so, down to the two smokeless candles Katey had bought for this special occasion.

Katey finally made Jerry sit down to keep him from getting in her way while she finished dishing up the food.

"Katey?"

"Yes."

"I love watching you in the kitchen. Did I ever tell you that?"

"No, but thanks for the compliment," Katey replied happily.

"Katey?"

"Yes."

"You look extra nice… no, make that extra special tonight. God, you look good enough to eat! Did I ever say that before?"

She finished setting the gravy and mashed potatoes on the table. "We'd better concentrate on the food first, don't you think, Jerry?"

They ate and talked, and then talked and ate some more, always being careful to skirt anything remotely connected to their feelings.

Both could plainly see how much they still enjoyed each other's company. "Great meal Katey, you're a pretty darned good cook. Did I ever mention that before?"

She smiled. "Yes, on at least two other occasions as I remember."

Before they realized it, they had finished dinner. "Dessert now or later, Jerry?"

"Later. I want to help do the dishes."

Side by side at the kitchen sink they started in on the dishes, Katey washing, Jerry wiping. Often their hands touched as Katey would hand Jerry a dish to wipe. Each would smile at the other and continue on, each keenly aware that the electricity between them not only was there, but was one flick of the emotional switch away from happening. Jerry stacked the last plate in the cupboard. "I never knew doing dishes together could be such fun… almost romantic."

Katey dried her hands and looked up at him. "That's because you and I have always enjoyed each other's company, like being around each other, doing things together."

"What's next Katey? What do you want to do?"

She hesitated, and then took the first bold step. "Let's go to my bedroom. I want to show you my hope chest. I don't believe you've ever seen it."

Jerry was uneasy with Katey's suggestion "Gee Katey, your bedroom… I dunno. Sure it's where we should be? Your folk's would never approve, I know that."

Katey tried to pass it off as nonchalantly as possible. "They won't be back for several hours yet. What are you afraid of Jerry? Nothing will happen unless we want it to. Right?"

"Right!"

He followed her into Katey's bedroom. "Wow! This is the first time I've ever been in here." Jerry looked around. "Neat as a pin too, 'course I should'a guessed that… and that perfume smell… what is it?"

Katey opened her hope chest. "It's a light lilac scent… bought it when I worked at the five-and-dime." She turned to Jerry. "Seems like a lifetime or two ago… so much happened between us, most of it pretty darned wonderful as I remember. You still feel that way?"

She'd casually but openly put Jerry on the spot. Heart racing, emotions on fire, she'd taken the first calculated risk. If only he'd respond with anything positive, she'd gladly settle for that.

Checking the contents of Katey's hope chest was the last thing on Jerry's mind… He lifted her up and knelt beside her bed as he gently deposited her down on her pillow. They never separated. He kissed her over and over, pleading, begging, and saying, "I love you, I'm sorry about everything, Katey, I want you back in my life… please Katey, please give me another chance… please…"

She responded by raising her legs high, her skirt fell off her thighs, giving him a glimpse of her beautiful black panties with the see-through lace around them. He kissed them as she held on for dear life. Then lady-like to the core, she sat up and pulled her skirt down. Her breathing came fast, matching his. She kissed him on the lips, then his cheeks, and then worked around to his ear lobes. She whispered. "I want you to touch me, I want to give you all the pleasure I can… but I can't let you make love until I have your commitment… your promise… until we're married… but you said you've changed your mind… you don't want commitment…"

Adrenalin pumping like never before, Jerry looked at his Katey, her skirt down, her knees locked tight, and her blouse half-open, everything depending on his word. His face and body flush with desire. He kissed her hard, trying to force the words out to match his passion. "Katey, I love you with all my heart and soul, isn't that enough?"

She pulled away from his feverish lips. "No, Jerry it's not enough. Let me up."

He watched her straighten her skirt, the dainty half-slip she wore, disappeared from his sight. She rebuttoned her blouse, and walked out of the bedroom. Katey poured two cups of coffee and carried them into the parlor, sat down and waited. Judging by certain signs, she knew it'd be a while before he would join her under much calmer circumstances and a clearer mind.

When he appeared, his face was still beet-red, a sure sign that wanting Katey's body was still very much on his mind. She handed him a cup as he sat next to her. "You're sending confusing signals to me. Tell me, what do you really want out of life? Where do I fit in? Or do I?"

He touched his lips to the cup but didn't sip. "Since I've moved into the Y, I've never been so lonely, or felt so alone. I miss my two sisters more than I could possibly have thought. I miss being part of my family, even the one I hated and detested. I want to belong, be a part of something I believe in. I want to come home at night and find somebody waiting for me. I want to share the day's events with somebody I love instead of talkin' to four empty walls. I want to hear laughter, help do the dishes, talk about tomorrow and plan the future. I want all this, but I'm afraid to commit. I'm afraid if I do, it won't be there someday when I need it most. I'm afraid Katey, can you understand that? I only believe in the now, what I can touch and take."

Katey moved closer, letting him drink from her cup. It was a beautiful gesture, and he responded to it, to their closeness again. "We're very much alike, Jerry, we always have been. We both want the same things, but I want one more thing, marriage with commitment. One night, one very special night over two years ago, I let you touch and take and you were not one bit afraid of responsibility or commitment. Matter of fact you welcomed it. We had such great plans and dreams. Now, we're both older, we should be more aware of what we want than ever before. We can be, if you'll believe in me and trust yourself to do the right thing. I've never been more proud of you than I am tonight. You've proven me right about you all along. I've known I was right about you since the fourth grade and since that special night when we made love. How can you deny your feelings for me and turn your back on everything you told me you want? How, Jerry, how can you?"

He took the cup out of Katey's hands and broke down crying. She held him in her arms and comforted him, then whispered tenderly to him, "Jerry, don't be afraid, I'm never going to leave you. I'll be here for you always. I'll promise that before you, and before God. Then nothing can ever come between us again because we won't let it."

She dug a handkerchief out of his back pocket and dried his tears.

"Okay Katey, I'm ready to believe in you, this time for good. Where do we start?"

"By being totally honest with each other. Where's your graduation ring, Jerry? The one I used to wear? I don't see you wearing it any more. Did you give it to someone else?"

He lowered his head and turned away. "Please Katey, you ask such hard questions. Anything but that… please."

"Jerry!"

Her tone told him only one thing, there'd be no peace until he owned up. "Aw Katey, I got to drinkin' pretty hard with Ricco, and I got to feelin' awful sorry for myself… well… well, we'd broke up and… and I got mad… I hurt so bad… well, if you must know, I threw it in the Sacramento River one night! There! Are you satisfied?"

She snickered, and then tried to remain serious. "Landis, you never cease to amaze me! At least you didn't give it to somebody else… 'cause if you had, I'd expect you to get it back."

"Yeah, Katey, that's like you… every loose end has to be tidied up and accounted for."

"Now Jerry, this is gonna hurt a bit more, and once you tell me, I promise that'll be the end of it. I know you chased around with Ricco and I know what that means. C'mon Jerry, how many? You know what I mean!"

"Please, Katey, not that again! I'm so damned ashamed of what I did… they were only one-night stands. Heck, I don't remember how many, or even their first names. Isn't that good enough? I quit it after only a few… it's not my style, Katey. You know that too!"

"How many Jerry?"

"Five or six. Honestly, I don't remember. Didn't care enough to even catch their names!"

"Yes, but you could've caught something else. You know what I mean."

"Katey. I swear I used… you're the only one I didn't use one on…"

"Do you ever think about our one special night, Jerry?"

"I've never forgotten about it… not for one day… it's still the most special night I've ever had…. Even though I hurt you terribly…"

"I think about it too! It's changed our lives forever, Dear… someday soon I'll tell you just how much it's changed our lives…"

"Katey, I know what happened and it's my fault. I know you had an operation back in Chicago… I know what that means. Katey… I know…"

Katey broke down, it was her turn. "Please Jerry, hold me. I have something to tell you… I … I can't… I can't give you any more babies…"

He comforted his Katey first by reassuring her. "I love you Katey… I know how much starting our own family has always meant to you." He tried to kiss away her tears. "I wanted kids too… always did. When we're set up a little better, we can adopt… a girl and a boy… and we'll still have that family we've always talked about. You said it wrong Katey, but I understand… please, I do."

"What did I say wrong?"

He let her snuggle up against his shoulder trying to control her sniffles. "You should've said, 'I can't give you babies anymore instead of any more babies'."

She looked up into his face. "I said that?"

"You did, but I know it's just a slip. You're forgiven, I understand."

Katey's near-slip about Krissy shut down their conversation dramatically for a few minutes. They concentrated on their coffee cups before Katey pushed on, determined to remove any lingering pieces of information in her mind to account for their twenty-six month separation. "Jerry, I have to know… about Carol… did you?"

He struggled with his conscience. This answer did not roll off his tongue like the others. "Katey, she's a fine person… is this really necessary?"

"Yes, if we're going to be honest with each other. I promise I'll never mention it again… I want to put it in the past, where it belongs. But I need to know, for my own peace of mind… please, Jerry…"

"Three times and I do remember each one because I pretended it was you… it got to the point I couldn't anymore because I felt guilty… like I was cheating on you somehow."

"Did you make love like we did?"

"No, like I said, you were the only one I've ever been… well, you know…"

She hugged him. "Oh Darling, I'm so glad I'm the only one that way… there's this purity between us and from now on it's going to stay that way."

"There now, I think we've answered all the important questions. Anything else still on your mind, Katey?"

"I was hoping that you'd be willing to let God come into your life from now on. Will He?"

He frowned, trying his best to answer. "I'm not ready to accept Him, but I know how important your church and His teachings are to you and your family. I want to be part of your family. I want to belong, so I'll agree to your church wedding so we can all be one family. You understand that's as far as my commitment to your church or God can go for now."

She hugged him again and again. "Oh, Jerry, you've made me so happy… thank you for being so understanding. You won't regret it, I promise. All we need is time, it's a great healer, you'll see!"

"Now, Katey, I've committed! Anymore questions?"

"I want to set our wedding date as soon as possible. Okay with you?"

"Aren't we forgetting one mighty big stumbling block? Your parents? If I remember correctly, they're waiting to be convinced I've passed all their tests? I can hardly wait to show them my savings account, clear title to my car, my last grade transcript from college and a check stub from my last payday."

Katey was pleased as punch. "Don't forget I'm going to mention the church wedding. You've agreed to marry in our church and that's the biggest, most important hurdle of all!"

Katey got up. "Let's have some dessert. I'm ready for it now! Oh, oh, I forgot the most important thing! You haven't proposed to me!"

She saw his looks, his bedroom eyes. "Jerry… we can't…not 'til we're married!

"Okay then, I'd like a little of both desserts tonight. Didn't you say, a short time ago, about wanting me to touch you… and you'd give me all your pleasure… except making love? How about me proposing to you, in there? Back in your bedroom?"

Katey didn't object. "Okay, if you carry me to my bed and propose to me first. Remember, you can only go so far…"

She peppered him with kisses as he carried her again to her bed. Down on his knees he proposed to her. "I love you Katey, and I want you for my wife, and from this day forward, we shall be as one, think as one and act as one."

He enjoyed her charms and as never before, such was his drive and his desire for his Katey. They lay together, cradled into each other's arms. Katey surprised him. "Jerry, I can give you pleasure if you'll only let me, and don't be embarrassed or ashamed. What we do and how we give each other pleasure will always be just between us. We'll make each time, each touching special and precious."

He didn't object, but was a bit bewildered. "Katey, how do you know about this?" After all, we've only made love once, and that was over two years ago."

She quietly wriggled out of his arms, out of their embrace and sat up. "I know you Jerry, and that's all I need to know about men." She stood up and removed her skirt. "I'll be back in a jiffy. Let's see if we can do this right without any more Fourth-of-July accidents all over me."

Together they made it happen. After, they lay together as one. She kissed him as tenderly as before. "Now, isn't this much better than fantasizing, wishing it was me? That's what you've done in the past and I do understand."

He didn't answer, but she knew and held him all the tighter. "Now, there are no secrets between us my love, except one, and that's a special one, and I promise you'll think it was well worth waiting for. After we're married, I will tell you."

Jerry didn't really listen. He was so caught up in the rapture of the moment. He nuzzled her, and softly said, "Katey, how could I get so lucky? You really do know me… everything about me… and I mean everything. No wonder when we're together, everything falls into place, like it's part of one big plan."

She smiled. "It didn't just happen. I spent a lot of years getting ready for this, a lot of years. But when I wear my wedding gown, and I see the wedding band you've slipped on my finger, then I'll thank God and our marriage will truly be blessed. Then, and only then will my heart sing, for our life together will be complete."

Aaron and Mary McCray found Katey curled upon the davenport fast asleep when they re-entered at the late hour. She wasn't about to let such wonderful news wait 'til morning. Katey jumped up and rushed to her father. Her eyes opened big as saucers, she could hardly wait to tell him. "Jerry's coming with us for mass and staying for dinner on Sunday, and you'd better act surprised and pleased because we're getting married very soon! Everything's been worked out between us… everything!"

Mr. McCray hugged his Katey. "I'm so glad, so very glad. Now at last we'll get to see our granddaughter. Soon, Katey, soon! Right, my Lass?"

"Right after Jerry left, I telephoned Aunt Rose. I forgot about the two hour difference, but Aunt Rose didn't mind. She woke Krissy up and she said 'Mommy, Mommy' to me over the phone! Oh, I'm so happy, so very, very happy! Oh life is so sweet! I'm sayin' a special prayer tonight before I go to bed!"

Mr. McCray continued, caught up in the good news. "Tell me Lass, wasn't it all worth waiting for? Now you'll have your young man and you'll be a family… a real family."

"Yes, yes, Father. At last! At long last, my life will be complete!"

Mary McCray wasn't about to be outdone. "And for sure we'll be spoilin' our granddaughter somethin' fierce, we will. And all the while knowin' Katey and Jerry will have to undo all we do to her. Oh this home will truly be a happy home once again."

Katey got ready for bed. Mary slipped in to say goodnight. "You should see your father, Katey. He got Krissy's picture out twice tonight and he says to me, 'Katey and Jerry are goin' to be watchin' their money close, so if my granddaughter needs something you see to it that she has it!' Well now, I turns to my husband, and I tells him right off, Krissy will be wantin' for nothing if I have any say in the matter, and I'll be remindin' you, Aaron McCray, that she's my grandchild too!"

Mary hugged her daughter. "Katey, you've done us proud, you have. Jerry's the right lad for you, he's proven himself, he has. Did everything go well tonight?"

There was no need for words, but Katey supplied them anyway. "Oh Mother, it's so good, so good between us… better than… yes, better than before… if that's possible. Oh I love that man so much, my heart is bursting with so much pride and love for him."

"One thing bothers me a wee bit. I noticed the wash machine had a hand towel and your dainty in it, Katey!"

She squeezed her mother's hand. "No, Mother it's not what you think! Not this time. I'm waiting 'til my wedding night just as I promised. I did give Jerry some other pleasures, well, a lot of pleasure for both of us… and it got very personal. That's all I'm going to say."

Mary smiled, all knowing. "Ever since you helped your father'n me to decide we'd rather hear more squeaks and less snores… … I've been doing the same thing… getting very personal."

# CHAPTER TWELVE

Jerry attended Sunday morning Mass at St. Stephan's Catholic Church with Katey and her family. They squeezed and held each other's hand on the sly until Mary gave the two love birds a disapproving glance at first, then relented and put forth her warm, not-quite-approving smile.

Noon found them eyeing each other across the dinner table at the McCray's, going through the formality of eating. Finally, Katey could wait no longer. "Father, Mother," she proudly and confidently announced, "Jerry has something he'd like to say."

Jerry rose, and said, "Excuse me, I'll be right back." He disappeared out the front door and returned with a business-sized envelope. He dumped the contents in front of Mr. McCray. "Sir, if you'll bother to look, I think you'll find everything in order… there's the title to my 1946 Chevy, there's my passbook savings account, and my last grade transcript from college and my latest check stubs from my railroad clerk's job and my part-time job at the supermarket. Next Friday night, Katey and I would be pleased if you and Katey's mother would kindly accompany us to Overjorde's Jewelry Store while Katey picks out her engagement ring and wedding band. She has already accepted my marriage proposal, but we want your blessing and permission."

Aaron McCray thumbed through the items, but never bothered to pick up one or examine it. He smiled and looked over at his wife.

"Mother, I believe we have a small problem on our hands. These two think they're ready for marriage, our KateLynn has already accepted Jerry's proposal. How do you answer to that?"

Mary went to hug Jerry. "Bless you my son, you did the proper thing by coming to us and asking for our permission." She turned around to her husband. "Tis time me thinks for some of our Irish coffee to seal the bargain."

What a round of stiff Irish drinks it was. Katey finally interrupted the festivities. "Father, do you have a word or two to say about my dowry?"

Her father put down his cup, raised both eyebrows, and answered, "This has given your mother and me more than a wee bit of thought, Katey. We will provide a proper wedding and reception for you and Jerry. Katey, you and your mother will work out the details. And when you decide to set up housekeepin,' your mother and me will provide the necessary things to start you out in your new life. Now then, there's one other bit of business that needs discussin' at this very moment."

Katey rushed to her father and threw her arms around his neck. "Oh thank you, thank you, for being so good to us! Now what's left to discuss?"

Mary had her say. "There's the matter of the money our Katey has promised to repay us."

erry jumped in. "I can assure you and your husband, we intend to repay every penny of it."

Mary smiled politely. "I'm sure it'll be repaid in short order. However, hear me out. If you, Jerry, were to go full time, starting next quarter, Katey tells us you could finish your schoolin' and get a proper good paying job with the railroad in just over a year and a half."

"Yes, that's correct. But if I go full-time days, it'll take most of Katey's salary to pay the bills and put me through school… there'd be very little left over to keep repaying Katey's debt."

Mr. McCray joined in the discussion. "Son, if we were to wait on that 'til after you graduated, wouldn't that help you and Katey get started quicker in life?"

Jerry turned to Katey, she nodded yes. "Yes, it would."

"Good, then it's agreed, we'll wait 'til then. Right, Mrs. McCray?"

Mary was pleased with the discussion and its frankness. "It's settled then. Time for dessert!"

"One more thing, Mr. and Mrs. McCray," Jerry stated.

Katey couldn't imagine what was on Jerry's mind. "Jerry, I think everything has been covered."

"I want to wait ninety days to get married. That way we'll have three more months to pay on Katey's debt and it'll also give us extra time to build up our emergency fund when I go full time."

Jerry's delay upset Katey. She'd counted on bringing Krissy home and introducing her to Jerry in no more than thirty days, tops. She exchanged quick glances with her parents. They saw the uneasiness in her composure, the deep frown on her face. Mr. McCray spoke up. "Son, if you and Katey have an emergency, we're more than willing to help out. Please put your mind at ease in that regard."

Katey saw how adamant Jerry was; saw his Landis way, the determination and pride take hold. She knew better than to raise an objection, she could only accept his well-intentioned idea and leave it at that. Krissy would have to wait. "Okay, Jerry, but I'm going shopping next Saturday for my wedding gown and this coming week I'll pack us a lunch so we can work out our budget and wedding plans during our lunch hour. I see no reason not to get started now." Her statement satisfied all concerned.

Wednesday evening, Katey came home from the Jackson Law Offices aglow with excitement. She and Jerry had worked out everything to their satisfaction. She poured over the details while setting the table for supper. Mary said nothing, letting Katey do the talking. "Mother, Jerry and I decided to cut way back on the wedding party. Big weddings aren't his thing… mine either for that matter. I'm just going to have Molly as my maid of honor, no bridesmaids. Jerry already asked Greg to be his best man and Ricco will be one of our ushers."

"I thought you told me Molly and Ricco weren't even speakin' to each other… and now you're gonna have them in the same wedding party?"

Katey set the tea cups. "Guess they patched it up again… that's what Molly claims, anyway."

"Yes, but for how long? Your wedding day's almost a full three months away. Think they'll be together 'til then?"

Katey could only shrug her shoulders and set the condiments on the kitchen table. "Soon as we're married I'm going to add Jerry and Krissy to my group medical coverage so we won't have to worry about that. We've gone over every dollar we have, you know what a stickler for details Jerry is. Being poor for so many years, has really put a keen edge on his thinking about money and finances. Believe you me, my Jerry doesn't miss a trick!"

"You should be glad Katey, he's going to be a very good provider. That's important to any good marriage, your father's the same way. You could'a done a lot worse than Jerry."

Katey opened the refrigerator to set the salad bowl out. "Here's how we figured everything. After Jerry buys my engagement ring Friday night, we're going to use his savings as our emergency fund. I'll pick out a ring to match my gold wedding band; we'll save some money right there. Besides, I like my gold band, even if it came from a Chicago pawn shop. I won't part with it for anything. It brought me Krissy and it's going to bring me Jerry, my very own husband to cherish, love, honor and obey."

Mary checked the pot roast in the oven. "You wouldn't happen to be a wee bit superstitious now, would'ja Lass?"

Katey joked. "No, not in the least bit. Anyway, I'm using some of my savings to buy our airline tickets to Chicago." She stopped a minute. "Boy, I can hardly wait 'til he sees Krissy and I tell him she's our daughter! He'll probably need smelling salts!"

"How'd you manage to steer him into flyin' to Chicago? Thought sure he'd want to go down the California coast or maybe up north to the Redwoods for your honeymoon."

Katey pulled out a chair to sit down. "That took a bita' doin' Mother. I told Jerry I had a sentimental reason for flying back there, that I wanted to show him the business college I attended and while we were there. I wanted him to meet Aunt Rose and Uncle Kevin."

"Well you pulled it off and when you return you'll be three instead of two!"

"I'll be so happy to hold Krissy again. Gosh, it's been over six months already. I miss her so much, so very, very much, and I love her so…" Katey began to cry.

"Now, now, it'll all be over in a few more months," said Mary, trying to lessen the pain Katey felt.

"I'll be so glad Mother, lies just aren't my bag. Jerry and I have no secrets between us, except one big one, and when that's over, no more! I've had it! They rob you of everything, every chance to live. Oh, that reminds me! How about letting Jerry and me spend the first part of our honeymoon here? Think of the money we can save before we fly to Chicago. We'll need some privacy, and motels just don't give us that. If we could be alone, we'd both prefer that. We'd sleep in, cook our own meals, make love, do the dishes, and then probably make love again. I'll decorate our bedroom up really pretty with those streamers from the five n' dime, and we'd have fresh flowers delivered to put in my bedroom. Well?"

"Katey, there's a practical side to you that's for sure. Your father has a cousin in San Jose that needs visitin'. We'll use his railroad pass and be outa your hair for the weekend. When we come back, you'll be gone to get Krissy."

Katey hugged her mother. "Thanks, Mom, you're the greatest!"

"When you come back, where do you plan on living?"

"Jerry's already checked into housing for married students at the college and we're on the list. Figure we'll live there so he can walk to his classes on campus, while I drive the car from Sacramento to Rushton to my job. I won't work part-time at the Jackson Law Offices then, not with Krissy with us. Jerry's a pretty good cook, so by the time I drive back to our apartment on campus, he'll have picked up Krissy from the neighborhood babysitter's and have supper already started. We'll have to watch our budget, but we'll make out fine... of course, we won't be eating steak very often, but we'll get by. I also checked my clothes, I've plenty to wear to work... should last 'til he's through school. Oh, yes, speaking of clothes, I stopped by St. Vincent De Paul's clothing department the other day. With Krissy growing so fast we'll buy good used ones for her everyday outfits. That'll save us a ton of money, and I have enough savings still left over to buy her some really nice dresses and outfits for Sundays and special occasions when we'll want her to look extra nice, like when we visit her grandpa and grandma. Did I mention that Jerry will still work Saturdays at Bettingers here in Rushton? He's already cleared that with the manager… that'll bring in a few extra dollars to our budget. Guess I covered it all pretty well, don't you think?"

Mary stood up, hands on her hips and let it rip. "Well, KateLynn Landis, so that's how it is, is it?"

Katey was perplexed. "I thought I covered everything. What'd I miss?"

"You missed Krissy's grandpa and grandma for starters, you did! While we're settin' here, gnarling up our hands, worryin' ourselves to death about our granddaughter's welfare, you're off workin' and Jerry's in school and both of you not carin' two hoots n' a holler about our feelings in this matter. But that's gratitude for you, never thinkin' nor carin' 'about what's important to us!"

Katey went over to her mother's chair. "I'm sorry. I didn't think it fair to ask you to babysit Krissy. Besides we couldn't afford to pay you what you're worth."

Mary barked back. "Ha, if it's money I'm after, I'll find myself another job. I'm talkin' 'bout feedin', and holdin' our grandchild. How dare you deny us that honor? I'd give anything to surprise Mrs. Feeney on the corner, and tell her in no uncertain words, this is my granddaughter I'm in charge of, and I'll be thankin' you to keep your hugs and kisses to the bare minimum, 'cause her grandpa's and mine take full priority."

Katey was pleased beyond words. "Okay, okay, Mother! Guess I could drop her off in the morning on the way in and then pick her up each evening after work. I'll expect to pay you something…"

"Fine, then it's settled. Soon as you leave for Chicago I'll have your father get your old baby crib down. We'll be expectin' the three of you here 'til you get settled at them beehives at Jerry's school. Understood?"

There was no arguing with the Brannigan look in Mary McCray's determined face. Katey knew better. "All right Mother, have it your own way."

"Of that my dear, you can be sure!"

There was no hiding the disappointment on Katey's face and in her heart when Jerry startled the McCray clan with his pronouncement that he preferred to wait three long months to marry while he feathered his savings account with a few more bucks and paid back a few more dollars on Katey's debt. For Katey this continued separation between mother and daughter seemed intolerable, almost unbearable, yet she told herself it must be endured if all the pieces in her life's puzzle were to be placed at last in their proper spaces. An emotional blow-up was the last thing she wanted to let happen now, too much was at risk.

# Chapter Thirteen

Friday night came and with Jerry at her side, she picked out her engagement ring, a beautiful diamond on a simple gold setting. Then she opened her purse, and to Jerry's surprise, produced a solid gold wedding band that matched her engagement ring perfectly. "When I sent your class ring back, I still felt we were bonded by our love, so I bought this at a pawn shop and I wore it every day at business college to prove my love for you. And now look at the money we're saving Dear." The word "saving" erased any doubt in Jerry's mind.

Despite Katey's consternation, shopping the next day for her very own wedding dress lifted her to a new high, she was at least two-thousand feet above cloud nine. With her dear friend Molly and her mother at her side, Katey thoroughly enjoyed every waking moment for this once-in-a-lifetime event, it was that special to her. All the years of waiting, of hoping, of planning, of dreaming, and most certainly of praying, had now culminated into that pinnacle of love lodged deep within her soul. The rose returned to her cheeks, she spoke with baited breath, there was an excitement, an electricity about her and everything she did.

Molly too, noticed this as the three women lunched together after Katey had selected her wedding gown. She gushed, "Katey, you now have everything you've always wanted. I'm so happy for you. You always knew Jerry would come through for you, you never gave up on him and now it's paid off."

Katey blushed. "Thanks Amigo. Someday your turn will come and good things will happen to you too."

Molly surprised them. "It already has! Next weekend, I'm going to the Bon and I'm registering in the bridal salon like you, Katey. Ricco's picking me up on Friday night after payday, and we're going to do it up right, just like you!"

Mary shot a worried glance over to Katey. "I take it then your man... your Ricco has finally settled down and proposed?"

"Molly, when did this happen? You never said a word about it before."

Molly's expression changed, she reddened a bit, and then strongly replied with certainty. "Katey, it's been settled between us, just like you and Jerry. I've had to lay the law down to him, there'll be no more chasing around. He's going to change, I can promise you that... he has too... I'm giving him no choice. Look how you've gotten Jerry to come around... He's ready for responsibility and commitment..."

"Molly, please listen to me," begged Katey, "Jerry was ready two years ago... he's always been more mature, more grown-up than Ricco."

Katey's best friend did not appreciate Katey's candor. "Oh, so you're saying Ricco's not ready for marriage, huh? And Jerry's all grown up now? Well, he did plenty of chasing around when you were gone Katey... you should've seen him... and Ricco too... I wrote you about it, remember?"

Katey tried her best to close the open wound in Molly's heart. "Yes, and I thank you for keeping tabs on Jerry. Jerry's and my breakup was a terrible mess over my letters... I told you about what Jerry's mother did. It's not the same thing between you and Ricco, now is it?"

Molly pouted at first, and then brightened up. "I'm sorry Katey, I've been under a lot of strain lately, deciding what to do about Ricco.

He's wild, but I won't let him go. I love him so much. I've always loved him, just like you have with Jerry."

Katey and her mother dropped Molly off and headed home. "Katey, I don't like what's happened to Molly. She's in big trouble, I'm afraid."

Katey pulled into their driveway. "I hope I read her wrong, Mother, I do really."

"What do you mean?"

"She's going to trap Ricco into marriage. If she's not pregnant now, she soon will be. I'd be willing to bet Ricco hasn't a clue about what Molly's got in store for him"

Mary opened the car door inside the garage. "See Katey! What did I tell you about this business of making love before marriage? It's trouble, Katey! It really is! You're very lucky Katey! You and Jerry will do fine… you both have faced up to your responsibility. Molly wants what you have, marriage, a faithful husband and a family."

Katey was sad. "But it's not going to happen and we both know it, Mother! She's going to either give up her baby or raise it alone without the father. I thank God each night because that's not going to happen with me!"

The countdown to Katey's wedding had reached day sixty, only thirty more to go. The telephone rang, interrupting the McCray's supper. Mary returned to the kitchen table with a long face. "Katey, it's Molly's mother on the line. She's in tears, Molly tried to commit suicide! Come talk to her! She needs you now!"

Katey telephoned Jerry at work. Ten minutes later he picked her up for the short drive to the local hospital. There they met Molly's mother and father outside her room. Katey rushed up to the distraught woman. "I'm so sorry, Mrs. McCarren, is there anything I or Jerry can do?

The poor woman was beside herself with grief. "Go inside and talk to her! Please Katey! She won't talk to either of us… maybe you… you're her closest friend."

Katey closed the door behind her and entered the most unreal situation she had ever come face-to-face with. Molly, heavily sedated, lay on the hospital bed, her wrists bandaged and strapped to the side rails. Two other straps, across her upper body and legs, secured her to the bed frame. Katey approached, trying to see if Molly was awake enough to be aware of her presence. She stooped low, over her face, "Molly, can you hear me? It's Katey, I'm here for you."

At first there was no answer. Then Molly's eyes fluttered a bit as she tried to speak. "Tell… tell Ricco I didn't mean it… I'm sorry…"

"Yes, yes, go on! What happened?"

"I'm pregnant… two months… told Ricco we have to get married…" Molly broke down, tears welled in her eyes. Katey tried to dry them as her dearest, closest friend lay helpless. "He… he called me a whore… said I slept around…" She cried out in pain. "He slapped me around… hurt me bad… kicked me in the stomach… said my baby… called it a bastard… said it wasn't his. He walked out on me… dumped me off at home… couldn't tell my folks… locked myself in the bath room. Oh Katey… what am I going to do? You're my best friend…"

A rage, deep within, erupted inside Katey. She was consumed by it and the tears that flowed easily down both cheeks. "Don't worry Molly, after you're feeling better, I'll come visit you, and we'll work this out. There must be a way… I'll talk to Father Murphy for you… we'll get some help."

Molly tried to force a smile. "You will? For me? Oh thank you Katey!"

The on-duty nurse stepped inside. She tapped Katey on the shoulder. "You'll have to leave Miss, I have to give her another shot… she'll be out for hours."

Out in the parking lot, Katey broke down, weeping as though it had been her instead of Molly who was laying down, strapped to a bed. Jerry tried his best to console her, to give her some measure of comfort. "I'm so thankful Katey, it's not you in there. I hate to say it, but we both knew what Molly was going to do when Ricco started going out with her again… never figured it would end up like this."

Katey turned to Jerry, "I need to borrow your hanky, used mine up on Molly." Then she broke out sobbing, "Oh, why do people hurt each other so? Why? Ricco and Molly should be together like we are. I've been so happy lately… and now this… it's upsetting everything…"

He kissed one of her wet cheeks. "Please Katey, we must go on with our lives, our plans. Let me tell you this, my love, Ricco is not the right person for Molly, he never was. He got what he wanted out of her and we both know why he came back. He told me a hundred times, when you were gone, she was the best he ever had."

Katey's Irish was up, "Go ahead say it, Jerry Landis! Say it, and I'll slap your face! All he wanted out of her was what he got from her, wasn't it?"

"You said it Katey, I didn't! Those were his exact words, said he had her so many times, he lost count."

"I still can't believe she let him all those times, why didn't she catch on? He was never gonna marry her. It was a line of bull and she bought it all the way. Damn you men! All of you!" Katey screamed.

Jerry backed away from Katey in the front seat of his car. He held up both hands in mock surrender in front of Katey. "Hey, let's not get so temperamental over this! Remember it takes two to make it happen…

gotta believe it's a fifty-fifty proposition… one pitching, the other catching."

Katey tore into him again. "It's not a baseball game, Jerry, and you damn well know it! She's gonna have his baby and he could care less even though it's his and he damn well knows that too!"

"Excuse me, but I think she tried to trap him and it backfired. How do you see it?"

She calmed down a little. "Well, you're right there… but that doesn't give him the right to slap her, and… and kick her in the stomach… and, and call her a whore… and then he calls the baby a BASTARD! Their baby! Can you believe it?"

"That's what babies are called that are born out of wedlock, Katey. Sorry, but you'll have to take that up with the Webster Dictionary people, not me."

"That's a terrible name and I never want to hear you ever say it, Landis! Just remember that! That other word, screwing, I can't stand it either! It's only one step above that F word… and don't you dare ever say that word around me, you hear?"

"I don't like it either. It has no place in any conversation as far as I'm concerned. Ricco always used the 'F' or 'S' word behind her back when he talked about Molly. Which told me he no respect for her whatsoever."

"I agree with you on that, Dear. Molly always said they made love, but she was only kidding herself. He was screwing her, not making love like…"

"We did once? Katey, what we did that one time… what we felt has no business in any conversation with either that 'S'-word or the 'F'-word."

She smiled again, feeling better. "I'm so glad you feel that way, sweetheart, 'cause I believe what we did was beautiful… it's the most perfect expression of love between a man and woman that God ever created… it had to be because I'll have it no other way."

Jerry backed out of his parking stall and headed out of the traffic aisle toward the main entrance of the hospital visitor parking lot. Suddenly, Katey called out, "Stop Jerry! Stop the car!"

He hit the brakes hard, nearly pitching both of them into the car dashboard. "I don't see anything or anybody coming. Why'd you holler stop?"

Katey pointed over to the next row opposite her side. "There's Ricco just pulling in! I'm gonna give him a good piece of my mind, tell him what I really think of what he did to Molly!"

"Let's stay out of it, Katey! We don't know what really happened. We only know…"

Katey bolted out of Jerry's car before he finished his thought. Sensing Katey was about to get into it with Ricco, there was only one thing he could do, rush over to pull them apart and try to keep them friends. By the time he reached Ricco's car, they were already arguing.

Ricco turned to Jerry. "Get her out of my face, Amigo, I don't need this!"

Katey doubled up her pint-sized fist and shoved it under Ricco's nose. "If I were a man, I'd clean your clock, right here and now, Ricco Petrocelli. How could you? How could you slap Molly around like that? Hit her and kick her in the stomach? She's not a whore! What the hell's the matter with you? Huh?"

Jerry pulled Katey back, away from Ricco. "I'm sorry, Ricco, Katey's having a pretty bad time of it after seeing Molly'n all…"

Katey turned on Jerry. "Take his side, why don't you? All you men stick together when it comes down to the knitty-gritty."

Jerry opened both arms in mock surrender. "Hey, Katey, maybe Ricco's got something to say. How about hearing his side for a change? That's all I'm saying"

Ricco opened up. "Hear me out, Katey, it's not the way you think…"

"Oh no? Tell me about slappin' her around, kickin' her and callin' her a whore. My God, you crazy fool! She's carrying your baby!"

Ricco waved a warning finger in front of Katey's nose. "She tried to trap me into marriage, Katey! I'm sorry I hit her and kicked her! I lost my head for a second, I made a mistake doin' that. But I sure as 'H' don't regret callin' her a whore, 'cause she's been sleepin' around – told me so herself."

"What did she tell you? C'mon Ricco, spill it!"

"Well, she said she's been datin' four or five other guys, trying to make me jealous I guess…"

"And that's sleeping around?" Katey shook her head. "Ricco, you wouldn't know true love if it hauled off and smacked you between the ears. Molly's only had one man and you damn well know who that is. What I can't figure out is why she's put up with your bull all those times, all this long."

Ricco's smug expression was the best barometer Katey ever saw of himself. "Well now Katey, I must say that I do have a certain amount of good looks that the ladies find hard to resist, and then there's that good old Petrocelli charm they just can't do without. Get my drift?"

"I get it all right! It's all restin' behind the crotch in your shorts! That's where you do most of your thinkin,' don't you? You egotistical stud! Someday you're going to meet up with your Waterloo, and then we'll see what you think about hosin' down every skirt that gives you the time of day."

Ricco smiled and looked over at Jerry. He cracked a smile. "Your Jerry ain't no piker in the crotch department, either."

Jerry laid a hand on Ricco's shoulder. "That'll be enough, Amigo… more than enough!"

Ricco let his remark about Jerry die. He turned serious. "All right Katey, here's the honest-to-goodness straight truth! Molly called me a couple of months ago… says she wants us to get together again… and she promises me there's no strings attached like marriage, family and all that jazz. One thing leads to another and next thing I know we're meeting three or four times a week up in a sleazy motel out on Dexter Avenue. I told her straight out, the first time, that there's no way I'm going to marry her." He kept shaking his head, "Dumb stupid woman! That's what she is! STUPID! She wouldn't let me wear my protection… got this thing from her church, some religious crap that it has to be natural. Ever hear such garbage, Jerry? Anyway, after all those years she and I made whoopee, I figured she must know what she's doin.' My poor little Molly wouldn't be dumb enough to get herself in a family way, now would she?"

Katey'd had enough. "YOU'RE THE STUPID JERK! Not Molly! She's so much in love with you that she'd do anything; even get herself pregnant so she could have you. The least you can do is offer to support your own baby even if you refuse to marry her."

He shook his head. "Now, now, Katey, there's where you and I don't see eye- to- eye. I still figure there's a pretty good chance Molly's tryin' to saddle me up with one of those other guy's fun n' games. No way! Old Ricco here's wise to that little scheme. I'm going in there and tell her I'm sorry about 'bout treating her the way I did but she'd better plan on lookin' for some other poor sucker to play daddy. I'm gonna miss her though. That was prime stuff!"

"Ricco?"

"Yeah, Katey?"

"Don't plan on coming to my wedding. I don't want you in any part of it, not even as our usher."

Ricco squinted his eyes, cocked his finger, pointed it at Katey, then Jerry, and made a loud bang sound with his jaw. "Got your message, Amigos, fine by me!"

The drive back to Katey's home was in absolute silence. Jerry parked in the driveway. "I believe him Katey, especially the part about Molly calling him, and meeting him and then making sure she trapped him. Molly did a very foolish thing."

Katey didn't answer. Instead, she looked out the window on her side, trying to make heads or tails out of the terrible human tragedy she and Jerry had just gone through down at the hospital. "They say love is blind… but Molly… I just don't know. It's all so crazy, so mixed up. Everybody's going to get hurt. No one's going to win."

He slid over in the seat and put his arm around her. She felt his warmth and cuddled up beside him. "We're going to win, Katey, and it's because of you. You were right to stick by your beliefs, your ways. I never, ever want our relationship to end up like Molly and Ricco's. I'm going to work my tail off to make sure our marriage works. After what happened today, after what I saw… the way Ricco talked about Molly… it was all so ugly… no respect, no honor …not a respectful thought anytime."

She turned to face her Jerry, to read his eyes, to see his expression and know that the sincerity in his voice was her passport to the love and security that nourished in her heart, mind, and soul. "It's really good between us, Jerry, and it will always be that way. I promise you I won't ever let if drift away, not for one second. We have our whole future, our lives, and our happiness depending on each other- we won't fail. Maybe it was meant for us to see what happens when there's no caretaker, when love is being passed around too easily, too foolishly. It must be used right, and that can only be God's way."

They kissed each other goodnight, each drawing on their strength, and the bond of love between them ever tighter, ever closer. Katey stood outside the car, started to wave to him, changed her mind and rushed up to Jerry's window. "What's up Katey?"

"I know your answer, just need to hear you say it.

"I'll sleep much better after I hear your words. Love, what would you do if you'd gotten me pregnant on our special night? What if I'd made a mistake and told you it was all right when it wasn't?"

He smiled. "I'm surprised you even bothered to ask, Katey, especially when you already know my answer. I'd kiss you first, then you'd probably let me kiss your tummy where our precious baby was, and I'd say, 'Okay, KateLynn McCray, I'm responsible for your carrying our baby, now let's do the right thing by getting married'."

She reached in to pinch him a trifle on the cheek. "You took the words right out of my mouth, darling."

***

Wednesday night arrived and Jerry paid the McCray household a surprise visit. Katey met him at the door. She gave him a most welcome kiss. "What brings you by sweetheart?"

"Decided to take some time off to talk to you when you're through with your meal."

Mr. McCray got up from the kitchen table. He motioned for Jerry to come in. "Good to see you, Son. Have you had your supper?"

"No Sir, but don't let me interrupt, I'll wait in the parlor."

Mary McCray joined Katey in the parlor. "We'll hear nothing of the kind. Come sit down with us. Katey, set your young man a plate next to yours. There's plenty of roast beef left and I'll reheat the gravy, it'll take but a minute or two."

Jerry joined the McCray's at the kitchen table. Katey let him heap his plate with mashed potatoes, roast beef and the gravy. "Have you heard anything about our apartment in student housing on campus?"

Mrs. McCray interrupted, "KateLynn McCray, let the poor Lad finish his meal, please! You'll have to forgive her, Jerry. Every night all we get is questions and more questions. Did you do this or that today? She's making a wreck out of us and there's still two more days to go 'till the wedding."

Jerry took a drink of milk. Mr. McCray spoke up. "Son, we can't say enough about how pleased Mrs. McCray and I are about the way you two have gone ahead with your plans and your life together." Then he winked first at Mary, then Katey. "But there is one small favor you could do for us."

"Oh, what's that?"

"Hurry up and marry her! I know there's only two days 'til your wedding, Saturday night, but let me tell you what we've had to go through for the last 30 days. First thing she does after work is go to her closet to see if her wedding gown is still there! Where else would it be?"

"Father," Katey protested mildly.

"And then Jerry, she opens up her hopeless chest and lays out every single gift she's got from the two bridal showers…"

Mary chimed in, "Then comes the sleep problem… She's lucky if she catches forty winks each night, she gets so excited thinking about the wedding and the honeymoon and your trip back to Chicago. Get the picture?"

"At least you won't call my hopeless chest, hopeless much longer. Only two more days after tonight…"

Everybody laughed at Katey's remark, even Katey.

Mary and Katey served the men dessert, a very moist bread pudding. Mary watched Jerry spoon his down practically non-stop. "Lad, you'll be pleased to know that our Katey's a very good cook, there'll be nothing lacking in that department when you two get situated in your apartment at college.""

Jerry put down his spoon and looked around. "I've eaten more than enough Sunday dinners here to know that Katey's been behind a good share of them. She should feel proud of her cooking skills."

Katey's face fairly beamed at the compliment. She tried to show Jerry how much she cared for him, and yet keep a smidgeon of modesty in front of her folks, so she pecked him on the cheek.

Katey's father took in the proceedings steeped in deep thought. Finally he put down his dessert spoon. "Son, this isn't all a social call is it? There's something or some reason for your visit tonight."

Aaron McCray's astute observation sounded the alarm in Katey. Quickly she focused on her fiancé, trying to ferret out any possible glitch in their wedding plans. "Jerry, is something wrong?"

Then she started to panic. "Tell me, tell me, Jerry, it's just the wedding jitters isn't it?" She raised her voice to show her concern. "ISN'T IT, JERRY?"

He searched three anxious faces seated around the kitchen table hoping for an ounce of sympathy or at least one grain of understanding. He got none. He reached in his back pocket and handed Katey an envelope. "Here," he said, "you'd better read this."

Katey's parents watched the expression on their daughter's face as her eyes traveled back and forth with each word, every line. Suddenly, she slammed the paper and envelope down and exploded. "NO WAY, GERALD LANDIS! YOU CAN'T DO THIS TO ME!"

# CHAPTER FOURTEEN

"I've been drafted! There's a war going on overseas in Korea. I have to report for induction next Monday morning."

Mary was completely in the dark about the conversation. "Jerry! Son! I don't understand, what is this draft business? Sure this is legal?"

Aaron answered as best he could. "Mother, Jerry has to serve our country. He has to stop what he's doing and get trained to fight."

"I mean can our government, really make him do that?" Mary questioned firmly.

Katey wasn't interested in the specifics of war or her mother's question. She let her Irish temper simmer down a wee bit. "All right, if that's the way it is, there's still no reason we can't be married this weekend, just as we planned. Right Jerry? I'll just cancel our plane tickets for now… I'm not about to let you join the Army and leave me behind, here at home, without a wedding band on my finger and my last name changed to Landis. Do you hear me, Jerry? Don't you dare walk out on me now… not after all we've been through… what's happened between us. And don't you be forgettin' our commitment to each other and our love… I won't let it happen… and you'd better not either!"

Mr. McCray understood the dilemma Jerry was in, even though he was more than sure his Katey would never accept or agree to any postponement of their marriage, no matter what the reason. He gave it his best try. "Jerry's not walking out on you Katey, all he's asking for is a little understandin' of the situation our country has put you two in, that's all."

Katey was in no mood for compromise. There was just too much at stake... too much to risk on waiting... too many days apart from Krissy... and too long since she'd been a woman ready for marriage with no fulfillment. No, she'd never accept any delay, no matter what the reason. She hurled her ultimatum at her perplexed lover. "Our wedding invitations were mailed three weeks ago, Jerry Landis!" Then she broke out in tears, the hurt and frustration came straight from the heart. "If you don't marry me Saturday night, it's over between us! I MEAN IT!"

Before Jerry could even open his mouth, Katey made a beeline for her bedroom. SLAM! The sound from the bedroom door left no doubt in anybody's mind, Katey meant business.

Mary ran to Katey's door, it was locked. "Katey! Katey! Let me in!" pleaded her mother. No answer. Mary ran back out to the kitchen. "Please Jerry, stay a little while longer! Go out in the parlor and talk to Mr. McCray. We'll work this out... give Katey some time to think about it... she'll come to an understandin'..."

Aaron McCray put his arm around Jerry's shoulder. "Son, let's just stay out of the boxing ring... round two's coming' up and only Katey's mother can answer the bell. Katey will listen to her... those two have always been close... maybe closer since our Katey's come home to us from Chicago."

Mr. McCray packed some loose tobacco in his pipe, lit it, and then settled back. "Son, there's time when it's best to let Katey's Irish have its way... this is one of those times. I learned that a long time ago soon after Katey's mother and I left a small village in County Cork in Ireland.

Times were hard, very hard, the bread lines were everywhere in America. My wife hated the big city life in Chicago, so she took charge of what little money we had. We didn't trust the banks so she was our watchdog and our bank. Katey's a bit like her mother, she'll find a way, after the hurt lessens a bit, she'll stand by you through thick or thin. Aye Lad, you couldn't find a better or truer mate for life than our Katey."

"I know Sir, but I just wish she'da given me a chance to explain that I haven't changed my mind one whit about getting married. With me going off to war, I don't want to leave a young widow behind, you know, just in case. It'd be the cruelest thing I could do to Katey…"

Mary finally gained entrance behind Katey's bedroom door, her inner sanctum, her place of refuge. She was shocked to see Katey open her hopeless chest and remove a manila envelope and a small photo album. "What do you think you're doing, KateLynn McCray?" Mary demanded

"I don't care anymore, Mother, I'm going to show Krissy's birth certificate and her baby pictures to Jerry and then let him decide what to do… I can't take anymore of this… all this waiting, planning, hoping, and dreaming… and for what?"

Mary stood toe-to-toe with Katey and then eyeball-to-eyeball. "You'll be making him do the very thing you vowed you never would do, force him to marry you. Is that what you really want, Lass? You've got a good head on your shoulders! Use it!"

"I want to see my baby sleeping safely in a crib in the same room with me at night… and when she's fast asleep, I want Jerry in my arms, giving me all the love I can handle as he makes me feel loved and wanted and fulfilled as his wife. Is that too much to ask out of life?"

Mary snapped back, "Sure you do, Lass, and those are proper wants and needs after you're married, after Jerry places that wedding band on your finger. You've come so close, Katey, don't give up on yourself or Jerry because he brings you news neither of you have control over. Think of him in this situation too… think how he must feel when he knows whatever he says or does he's going to hurt you. Katey, you two still have a lifetime together waitin' on you… it's just going to take a wee bit longer, that's all."

"You and Daddy didn't have to wait… go through all the things… the mess… the mix-ups that Jerry and I have to deal with. How come my life's so different?"

"Katey, your life's backwards, and it needs some tendin' to, like a garden. In my day, you fell in love, got married, and then had your babies, as it's supposed to be. That one night, that special night you and Jerry had as you've told me, changed all that forever. Your father tried to tell you… to remind you that one sin will forever haunt you 'til you and Jerry set it straight… with God, your church and with yourselves. Your father… oh your father, he has such high hopes for you… and for Jerry too."

Katey put the envelope and album back in her chest, which seemed more hopeless now than ever. "Do you think Jerry would agree to marry me as soon as he knows where he'll be stationed in the Army? If it's not overseas in Korea?"

Mary beamed again with pride at her daughter. Her good sense had returned. She hugged Katey "Why don't you ask him for yourself? He's out there patiently waiting with your father."

Mary left Katey alone in her room. Jerry rose as she approached. Mary hugged him and said, "Katey's herself again. Why don't you knock on her door, she has something she wants to ask you."

Mary and Aaron McCray watched him go to her door. He knocked. "Katey, are you all right? I'm sorry I hurt you… but it hurts me too. Can we talk?"

There was no response at first. Then through the sniffles on the other side of the door, he heard her say, "Jerry, if you don't go overseas to Korea, can we get married right away. No more waiting for even one more day?"

"Certainly Katey, if that's what you want…"

The door suddenly opened and Katey nearly catapulted into Jerry's arms. She kissed him over and over. "I'm sorry I said those, those things. I love you, Jerry Landis, I always will… remember the first day after you finish training… then we'll be married. Right?"

He felt embarrassed with Katey clinging around his neck with her non-stop show of affection in front of her parents. "Remember Katey, that's IF I don't go overseas! Deal?"

"Deal!"

Suddenly a war mostly forgotten in the American newspapers, and often relegated to their backpages, the Korean War became paramount in the lives of the McCray's and Jerry Landis. Jerry sold his used textbooks back to the student union bookstore at Sacramento State College, there'd be no need to hold onto the outdated texts by the time he returned to campus life again, if ever. Katey and her parents manned the telephones non-stop for eight hours at their house, telling disappointed friends, co-workers and relatives there'd be no candlelight wedding on Saturday night, Uncle Sam had other plans for Jerry Landis.

Monday morning arrived and two young lovers replayed their good-bye scene of over two years ago, only this time it was Jerry doing the leaving and Katey doing the staying. The irony of their situation hit each other-hard! Fate was about to demand its dues for spending one exotic, erotic night locked in each other's arms.

Then it was time to go, they threw their arms around each other and kissed and held each other so tightly, so closely that their bodies cried out for relief, for another night of ecstasy, no matter what the cost or implications. Finally, the train conductor's last call forced then to part their lips and look at each other one last time. "Katey, I'm going to sign up for a monthly allotment to you first thing when I get stationed. I'm not about to forget my responsibility toward you."

She mildly objected, "But Jerry, you told me the Army doesn't pay much… no, you'd better keep what little you get paid."

"Nonsense, Katey, I've lived on much less most of my life. This will be the first time in my life that having been poor will be an advantage. I can and have lived on next to nothing."

Katey blew him a kiss as he boarded the slowly moving train. They waved good-bye to each other and Katey called to him. "Remember Jerry, you owe me a letter within five days! No letter, and I'm calling the post commander and the Red Cross. There'll be no more letter mix-ups or messes in my life anymore. You can take that promise to the bank and cash it! I'll have it no other way!"

# CHAPTER FIFTEEN

Jerry was sent to Fort Ord, California for testing and processing. Five days later, Katey did receive his first letter telling her that he was being sent to Camp San Luis Obispo, California to complete his basic and technical training in the Army Signal Corps. She heaved a deep sigh of relief that at least he escaped being sent to infantry training with its hand-to-hand kill or-be-killed instructions, a sure ticket to the frontlines in Korea. She turned over a snapshot he'd also sent along and discovered he hadn't escaped his first G. I. haircut. Her once, golden-haired Jerry, now sported a patch of bristles, measuring an inch and a half, all over the top of his head. She showed Mary the snapshot.

"My goodness!" Mary exclaimed. "The top of his head looks like a porcupine!"

Katey could only shake her head and smile. "They're going to change him, and when he comes back to me, he'll probably never be the same, but his heart and his love will belong to me. Uncle Sam better not try to take that away from me, or he'll have another war on his hands, right here on the home front."

The U.S. Postal Service was kept busy the next four months delivering love letters, the kind that are shared with no one, the kind that bind and cement forever true love. For Katey, Jerry's letters were an affirmation of the things she'd done all her young, adult life: plan, dream, and pray for her beloved Jerry. Yet no matter what happened at work or at home, she carried a two-pronged hunger and longing for Krissy, her baby growing up in Chicago, and for Jerry, doing his boot camp and soldiering on the California coast. She prayed nightly that somehow, somewhere, her two loves, her two cares would be united, possibly when Jerry came home on his first furlough. In the meantime, she'd developed a nightly ritual of opening her clothes closet to make sure in her heart and mind that her wedding dress still hung where she'd last touched it, and Jerry's civilian clothes were where they should be, next to hers. Often Mary would find her hugging them both, down on her knees, saying a prayer. Katey would turn, and dab a bit of mist out of her eyes, and quietly say, "Mother, don't you think it's time I bought that empty chest of drawers for Krissy's and Jerry's things?"

Then Katey felt her mother's hand rest gently on her shoulder. "Patience, Lass, patience, it'll all come together in due time when God wills it. It's He who holds the calendar, not you or me, no matter how the heart longs for our loved ones."

One night Katey burst into the McCray front room, waving his latest letter. "Jerry's coming home! He's coming home! Now we can get married! He didn't say anything about going to Korea!"

Mr. McCray put down his paper, laid his pipe across the tobacco bowl, and looked across the room at his wife doing her knitting. He read her expression, so he spoke first. "Now Lass, we're about as excited at the good news as you, but by chance did Jerry say anything in your letter about setting your wedding date when he's here?"

Katey re-read her letter. The McCrays saw her long face. "No… no, he doesn't," she finally admitted, still trying to read more into the letter than was there. "But he doesn't say anything about going to Korea either…"

Mary put down her knitting. "Katey, darling, he's tryin' his best not to build your hopes up for another fall… he wants to spend all his time with you. Surely that's what you want, isn't it?"

"Yes… yes… of course that's what I want… you know that." The tears refused to stay put. She broke down sobbing her poor heart out. She went to her father. He took her in his arms, just as he'd done, all these many years. "Oh Daddy," she cried, "It hurts all the way down to my toes. Why can't my life be like most people? Why can't I have a normal life… like you and Mom have? Together each night, that's what I want. Jerry and Krissy with me in our own place."

He kissed her wet cheeks. "Patience, my KateLynn, patience."

Katey saw the irony of her predicament and laughed through the tears. "That's what Mother said the other day, and you both know darned well, that's the one thing we Irish are mighty short on is patience!"

***

Katey met Jerry at the railroad station. She flew into his arms, tears of joy unchecked, streamed freely over her make-up, but neither seemed to care or mind, so much in love, so happy to be together were those two lovebirds. Finally, after three non-stop minutes of being stuck together like glue, Katey stepped back to see what the Army had done to her Jerry. "The uniform!" she exclaimed. "You look so different… so much older! But I love you just the same!"

He gathered her back into his arms. "You'd better, Katey McCray, or else this is one big wasted trip."

He pointed to the baggage cart being wheeled by them. "There's my duffle bag, that's it Katey!"

Two jabbering magpies couldn't have said more in less time than Jerry and Katey as they stopped at one of their old high school hangouts, Wally's Drive-in, for a sandwich and coffee. Jerry got up to pay the check. He winked at Katey. "Notice anything different… besides my uniform?"

"No, Dear..." Then it hit her and she laughed out loud. "Yeah, Landis, you're not putting the bite on me to pay for it like you used to when we dated the last two years in high school. Good thing I worked at the five and dime... paid for an awful lot of shakes, fries and burgers." She feigned looking through her purse. "Let's see...must be fifty or more of those worthless I. O. U.'s you gave me still around somewhere... probably can still dig a couple up."

He looked around after they left Wally's. "Didn't the kids seem awfully young in there?"

Katey winked back and smiled. "Not any younger than we were, Dear. Guess we're getting older, that's all. We're the ones out of place, not them."

Hand-in-hand, the twosome walked away from yesterday, from flared skirts, saddle shoes, chords and Levi's, to the present, an Army uniform, spit-shined shoes, and medium-high spikes and business suits with skirts.

They reached Jerry's car. Katey started around to the passenger side. "You're doing fine, Katey, stay behind the wheel. Think I'll enjoy being taxied around. Car still looks pretty good, I see."

She got in, reached across to unlock his door. "Yes, your Chevy has really been a lifesaver, sure beats standing around next to a bus stop sign."

Katey started to turn on the ignition key, glanced over at her passenger and scooted over to him. "Oh, Lord, Jerry, how I've missed you. My days seem like nothing, then you're here, and all of a sudden, everything's all right. Man, what a hunk you've become!"

He kissed her hand, but she didn't mind in the least. "And you, Katey McCray, you're beautiful, absolutely gorgeous! Everything just right in every way about you. I'm the luckiest lug in the world to have latched onto you. You're everything I've ever admired, respected and loved"

She broke from their embrace. "Guess we'd better get on toward home. Mother'll be expecting us. Dad'll be along shortly, they'll both be tickled pink to see you."

"Sure it's okay with them to be staying at your home? I can always get a room at the Y."

"Nonsense Jerry, you're sleeping on our davenport and that's that! Both my folks want us to spend as much time together on your leave as possible."

He was glad she opened the conversation on that subject. It made his words come a bit easier. "While we're on that subject Katey… please hear me out. I don't expect an answer today, there's still seven days left, but have you given any thought, any thought at all…"

"To spending time together as man and wife?" Katey read him perfectly. "It's been on my mind a lot, especially after you wrote, telling me that you're coming home on this leave before going overseas…"

"To Korea," Jerry finished Katey's thought. "I didn't want to build your hopes up about getting married, so I never mentioned it. I figured you knew where I was headed."

"About being together that way, you know how I feel about that…" Katey never finished her thought. They rushed into each other's arms. Katey replied, "I want to Jerry, I really do, but I just don't know. I'm so afraid that I'll never see you again… something will happen to you. Then what?"

He tried to kiss her concern away. "Then we'll have shared a very precious few hours or days together, my love. You made one exception to your hard and fast rule before, Katey. I was just wondering… maybe you'd consider it again… because of the circumstances… because I'll be gone…"

"If I agreed, it would have to be a place where we truly could be alone… no motels, hotels or anything like that… I wouldn't feel right… and my folks would have to know… I won't lie to them… not anymore, Jerry…"

He turned to look out the window. "I know they'd never understand my wanting you like this, not without a wedding band. I'm sorry I brought it up, didn't mean to put any pressure on you, Katey."

She squeezed his hand. "Let me think on it, Hon. Anyway, while you're here, I'm going to get up early each morning and fix us breakfast and you can drive me to work, and have lunch with me, and then pick me up after work… no Jackson Law Office bit this week. How's that, Jerry?"

"I like it. Tell your folks I expect to do somethin' around the house while you're working. Got any garbage that needs hauling out?"

They both laughed. "Don't worry, we'll find something for you to do. First thing I imagine you'll want to do is get out of your uniform when we get home."

"Yeah, it'll be my last chance to wear civvies, and I'm going to make the most of it."

Aaron and Mary McCray went out of their way to make Jerry feel welcome. They literally turned their home over to him. That first night, Katey kissed Jerry good-night, as he was making up the davenport and then she disappeared into her bedroom. Mary followed her in. "He looks great," she commented. "Maybe Army life agrees with him."

Katey finished brushing her hair. "Not at all, Mother, he just puts up with it. All he talks about is when he gets out. The things we're going to do, and of course, going back to college to get his degree. It'll be a lot easier, moneywise. He'll have the G.I. Bill… that'll really help our budget."

Mary seemed uneasy with her next question. "Lass, this is a hard one, but I need to ask it anyway. While Jerry's here… have you two discussed bein' together as man and wife? What with him goin' overseas to the fightin' n' such?"

Katey turned around on her vanity stool. "I'm surprised at your question, but yes, that subject did come up. He knows how I feel about that. It's against everything I believe in… I'm not ready to do that. After what a mess Ricco and Molly made of their lives, I don't think it's for Jerry and me… no matter what the situation is."

Mary shrugged her shoulders. "So that's how it is, eh, Katey? Next I suppose you're going to be telling me you're against having all the happiness you can crowd into his remaining six days with you. Am I correct on that?"

Katey was perplexed. "You're really something, Mother, you know that? All my life you've been so strict with me about saving myself for my marriage vows. Now it sounds like you're trying to tell me it's okay without coming right out and saying it. How'm I doing, Mother?"

"Me thinks the question is better directed at you, Daughter! How are you doin'? Listen to me! Your whole life has been a wee bit cockeyed since that certain night with your Jerry. Have you not given more than a passin' thought that your young man is going away, maybe never to return?"

Katey burst out crying. She went to her mother. "Mother, that's all I think about when he's not looking at me or telling me how much he loves me. What am I supposed to do, let him love me because he might not come back?"

Mary stroked her daughter's hair and held her head close to her bosom. "Aye, Katey your world is no bed of roses… there's too much gray between the black and white of proper things that need doin'. Now mind ya, your father'n me could never approve such improper conduct, there'd be no blessin' of such an affair if we were to know about it…"

Katey looked up to her mother. "What would you do if you were in my shoes?"

Mary looked away for a moment. "Thank the Lord, I've been spared your situation. Yet I believe I'd take a chance knowing that I'd always have today to remember in spite of what tomorrow brings to my heart. Spendin' awhile in Father Murphy's confessional may be a small price to pay for the love and happiness I did have instead of what I might have had."

The first five days of Jerry's leave flew by. Before Katey and Jerry realized it, Friday afternoon was at hand with Jerry parked in the railroad visitor's parking space, outside the corporate headquarters building, awaiting Katey's appearance. He thought about those five days and what they'd meant to Katey and him.

What surprised him most was Aaron McCray's sudden urge to visit his cousin in San Jose, California. Given the fact that Mr. McCray had just boasted over the supper table two nights ago, he had a perfect attendance record for over eight years as foreman on his maintenance crew. Aaron's parting scene was still vivid in Jerry's mind. Mr. McCray shook his hand, hugged him mightily, he swore he heard his vertebrae pop once or twice, and then he said in his manner: "Son, you're doing us proud, our Katey couldn't have picked a better man. Come back to us. You'll have an awful nice family waitin' for you." Did he mean the McCrays or what?

Jerry was so deep in thought, mulling over those events, that Katey surprised him when she opened the door to go in. He then became aware of her sliding in next to him. They kissed passionately, again and again. "You seemed lost. Something wrong?"

He smiled at his Katey, and then answered, "No, not really… just when I think I know your family's quirks, I find out you Irish change directions."

"Like what for instance?" Katey questioned.

"Take your dad, he tells me that he's never missed work for over eight years and next thing I know your mother and I are taking him down to the railroad station yesterday afternoon."

"Oh that… that's been in the works for months. Mother's been after him to see his cousin… he's dad's only relative in this country. They should see each other more than they do. I think it's been over two years."

"Doesn't your mother usually go too?"

Katey tossed out her answer as causal as could be. "Oh yes, but with you here as our house guest and…"

He finished her thought. "Your mother wouldn't want us to be alone for a whole weekend, now would she? Didn't you tell me that in Ireland when your parents courted, they always had a chaperone?"

"Yes, dear, I did. Look, where is this conversation headed?"

He started the car. "Nowhere, I guess."

They turned down Asotin Avenue. Katey noticed the different direction.

"Darling, where are we going?"

"Down to Sam Moore's pool hall, it'll be my last chance to see Greg and Ricco… down a couple of beers… shoot some pool… bet the beer won't taste nearly as good now that I'm legal. How about pickin' me up… say, in a couple of hours? Then we'll spend the whole weekend together… do whatever you like."

Katey snuggled up next to him. "Speaking of changing directions, Landis, you're a fine one to talk about the Irish."

They stopped in front of the pool hall. They exchanged kisses again before he got out. Katey slid over under the steering wheel. "Two hours tops, dear, then I'll be back to spend our last weekend together, right?"

He tweaked her dimple. "Dang, you're some Lass, Katey. Soundin' more and more like a wife instead of my fiancée."

She gunned the engine and blew him a kiss. "Jerry, my love, I'd let you sleep down here all weekend if you wanted to…if only I were your wife."

Katey pulled into the McCray garage, got out and walked into the house. She didn't see her mother, so she called out, "Mother, where are you?"

"In here! In your bedroom!"

Katey nearly fell over. Mary had two suitcases laid out on the bed and was busy as a bee, packing them. "Glad you're here… you know Jerry's clothes a lot better than I do… can't find his pajamas."

Katey was alarmed. "Mother, what's the matter? Why the suitcases? Did you and Jerry get into it? He seemed fine when he picked me up."

Mary stopped packing. Next she opened Katey's closet door. "Here, help me with your wedding dress… mustn't get it wrinkled. Let's be real careful when we lay it in your hope chest… the cedar will protect it for years. Maybe Krissy can wear it when she grows up and gets ready for marriage."

Katey had seen enough. She stomped her high heels hard. "That's it, Mother! What's come over you? You're actin' crazy! Packing suitcases, trying to put my wedding gown away. If you don't tell me what's goin' on, I'll never speak to you!"

Mary's jaw dropped. "I'm surprised, you haven't put two and two together. This is your honeymoon, Lass, time to make the best of it."

"Honeymoon? Mother, you're nuts! There's no time now to get married! We don't have a license, and Jerry'd never go for this… not in a million years!"

Mary smiled, appreciative of Katey's thoughts. From her apron, she handed Katey an envelope. "He will once you drive up there and let him know what you have in mind for your last weekend together. There's no refund Lass, so make the most of your situation. Grab a wee bit of happiness that's come your way! Lord knows you two deserve every minute together."

Katey opened the envelope. . "It's a map and a set of keys to a cabin up in the mountains…" She looked further. "The High Sierras… close to Lake Tahoe…"

"Katey, it's got all the privacy you were crowin' about needing, just the other day." She continued with the packing. "Can't find Jerry's pajamas…"

Katey understood now. She hugged her mother and then started on Jerry's suitcase. "He doesn't wear any pajamas, never did, always wears shorts instead… now he's got those Army boxer shorts they issued him."

"Better count on cool evenings up there…need to take jackets along. I'm sending my Polaroid with you… so get out of the bedroom long enough for picture takin'. That's something he can take with him besides his honeymoon memories." Mary replied quickly.

Katey looked down at her engagement ring and wailed, "I still don't feel right about this… I know you mean well, Mother… but my wedding band's missing…"

"Take your wedding band with you, Love… and if it'll make you feel better, have Jerry slip it on the proper finger… and… and go from there."

"And of course we'll need to say our wedding vows."

Now Katey, too, was caught up in the electricity of the moment, the prospect of two lovers sharing a secluded hideaway, isolated from prying eyes, as discreet as anything she'd dare dream about or imagine. Yet there came reluctance… a sharp tug to her conscience. "Don't be surprised if I get cold feet after we get up there and you see us back in the driveway tonight…"

Mary closed Katey's suitcase. "At least you'll enjoy the drive… you can always change your mind either way when you get up there."

"Does Daddy know about this? Can't believe he'd ever approve…"

"You might say 'twas a yes and no situation in the makin'. Yes, I sent him to see his cousin so there'd be no reason for him to object to such goings on as this." Mary faced her daughter. "You must understand Lass, this weekend never happened. This must never be brought up with your father around… are we agreed?"

Katey's nod inferred as much. "When Jerry comes back from Korea, all I want is Father Murphy to marry us in a private church ceremony… with just you and daddy present… and Krissy, of course."

"You, you plan on bringing my granddaughter home soon, don'tcha Katey?"

There was an excitement in Katey's eyes that was only exceeded by the glow of love in both the McCray women's hearts. Mary knelt before her daughter and held Katey's hand close to her face. She kissed it. "Bless you, bless you, my love. I know by the looks on your brow 'tis sweet words to my ears I'll be hearin,' right Lass?"

The words came, full of determination and love, borne by a young mother in search of her place in the scheme of her own life. "Jerry leaves early Monday morning. Tuesday afternoon I'll be holdin' my Krissy in my arms forevermore. Nothing or nobody's going to ever keep us apart again, I promise you, NOTHING!!!"

A tad of a tear found a home in the misty corner of Mary's eye. "Your father, he'll welcome his granddaughter like no other since you were born, Lass. No more askin' when will he see and hold her… all he'll have to do is see for himself as Krissy sleeps peacefully in your old crib. He'll insist on spoilin' her rotten and it'll be up to us to undo his handiwork, but I don't think we'll complain too loud, eh?"

"No Mother, not after all the waiting we've all done." They finished packing. Katey put her hand to her lips. "Oh, my gosh! Oh, my gosh! My stretch marks where I carried Krissy! Jerry's bound to see them when we make love… he'll ask questions… what'll I say?"

Mary came to her rescue with a reassuring answer. "Make sure the lights are low, or better yet, turn them out before…"

"No, I want to see him and he'll expect to see me too…"

"Then keep yourself between the light and do keep it low… he'll be so caught up in the lovin' of you, there'll be no need for words or worry."

Mary walked her daughter to the garage. Katey turned to her. "Do you really think I'm doing the right thing? I'm giving up an awful lot… the way I wanted my love to go… my wedding night… no wedding dress… no wedding plans……"

"Katey," her mother answered back, "and your Jerry? He may well be giving up a lot more… like his life for instance…"

Katey reflected on her mother's words. She would be hard pressed to argue that point. "Since this will now be my honeymoon, I'm going to buy me a negligee… the thinnest, most seductive one I can find."

Mary hugged her daughter good-bye. "Now you're on the right track, Lass… though I think just the two of you being together for your last weekend would more than do the trick… yet, a wee bit more encouragement never hurts, eh, Lass?"

***

Katey picked Jerry up and to his surprise she drove straight east out of town. "Are we going somewhere special Katey?"

She smiled and said nothing for two minutes, then finally answered. "That depends on both of us Dear. Thought a drive to the Sierras would do us both a world of good. There's still plenty of daylight left and the mountains should give us a fresh prospective on a lot of things…"

He settled back on the passenger side. "Fine by me, you're the pilot. I'm just going along for the ride. A change of scenery might not be such a bad idea after all."

She puckered up her lips and blew him a kiss. "That's what I thought too!"

They left the valley and gradually climbed up into the foothills, the April weather mild and clear. An hour later they found themselves in a beautiful world of green amidst the snow-capped high peaks and deep valleys. It was breathtaking. Katey's heart raced faster than their Chevy's engine. Already, in her mind, she pictured what this very special weekend held in store for them. The beautiful background, the isolation, the perfect setting, so clear, so untouched, so unspoiled… so right for intimate moments and the sharing of love without the noise, the clutter of man-made problems and social obstacles left down on the valley floor. She drank in the awe-inspiring vistas before them. "I know you're not a believer, Jerry darling, but how in good conscience could anybody deny that God does not exist, that there isn't a natural order to things, after seeing all this?"

He moved over closer to her. "Yes," he agreed, "it would be hard to argue in the face of such overwhelming beauty. There's a real grace about things up here, Katey… Never really thought about it or what you said… before."

Twenty minutes later, Kate pulled into a turnout overlooking a deep valley wedged between craggy sentinels of stone topped with splotches of snow that managed to cling on precarious ledges and outcroppings. She rolled down the window to drink in the fresh, clean air. Far below, the cascading waters of a snow-fed stream crashing over its rock-ribbed bed echoed up and down the canyon. It was almost deafening.

"Katey, let me drive back after we've enjoyed the view. You've been doing all the driving."

She kissed him. He felt an urgency in her lips, her embrace, as though she was trying to tell him they were up here for more than just the drive or the view. "What is it, Katey? Why are we really up here in God's country as you call it?"

Katey leaned over to open the glove compartment, then thought better of it and retreated to her position behind the wheel. Jerry caught her intentions and opened the compartment. "What's so special in the jockey box, Katey?"

"Our whole life is in there Jerry. There's a map from this vista to a cabin waiting for us to be alone. I have a set of keys, and it's ours for the weekend. If you say yes, there can be no turning back for either of us, for we will be married in mind and body. I will insist on a vow to me, and before God, that our lives are committed forever as man and wife until you return to me after your tour in Korea to complete the formality of our simple ceremony by Father Murphy with my parents as our witnesses."

Jerry came alive. He realized the full implication of what Katey was proposing. "Katey, this is so unlike you… I… I just never expected you to ever surrender yourself, your wedding plans, or your dress… and your folks, what about them?"

"Mother is the one that set this up and father knows about it… sorta. He is visiting so he won't be around to object… this weekend is just between us…nothing must ever be said about it… ever, except between us… Well?"

"Katey, your religion, your own personal beliefs… what about that? Are you willing to forget them too… to be together as man and wife?"

As she looked at him, there was a radiance about her. "Because I love you so much, Jerry, you're my life, don't you see? Neither of us should deny our love any longer, and I want to share my love with you if that's what you want. Do you, Jerry?"

He got out of the car and walked over to the guardrail. He spent the next few minutes searching his conscience and his heart for the answer. They responded as one. Back to the driver's side he came. "Move over Katey, you're the co-pilot while I do the driving."

"Does that mean yes, Jerry? Are we man and wife forever?"

They sealed their fate, come what may, with a hunger, a kiss that beckoned them on. "Yes, Katey, with all my heart, mind, and soul, we will be husband and wife. We will be one with each other until death do us part. You'll have it no other way, and neither should I."

With map in hand, and Jerry behind the wheel, they soon ran out of pavement less than a mile from the main highway. "How much farther, Katey?"

"According to the map, about six miles of gravel then forest service road for another two… then our honeymoon cabin."

They climbed higher, and the gravel road became much narrower. Soon they ran into patches of snow protected from the sun by clumps of densely wooded pines and junipers. The scenery: breathtaking at each turn, each curve opened up a different vista, a better view than the one they left behind five-hundred yards before. They looked at each other, the excitement, the anticipation, the feeling of what they both knew and openly accepted, building, all the while the road became little more than an open dirt trail. Around another hairpin turn and up a steep slope and then another clump of trees that opened up into a small meadow with a brook running through the middle.

"THERE IT IS, JERRY!!" Katey pointed out, her adrenaline pumping.

# CHAPTER SIXTEEN

Sure enough, their destination, their love nest lay before them, a scant three hundred yards ahead. "Wow!" Jerry gulped. "Isn't this something? Hey, Katey, I see it even has a deck. Oh, this is better than I could ever imagine!"

She scooted over to his side. "Me too, Dearest! Our home for our very special weekend. I love you so very, very much."

They parked on the backside of the cabin. Katey, key-in-hand, lead the way while Jerry, carrying two suitcases and a train case, followed. She opened the door and gasped out loud. "A fireplace, and an electric oven! Didn't think they had electricity way up here! Where's the power line?"

"Must be buried cable."

Jerry dropped the suitcases inside the bedroom and joined Katey out on the deck. She pointed. "Look that must be Lake Tahoe way down to our right! What a spectacular view! Oh it's everything and more."

He put his arm around her and squeezed her to him. "I'd give anything to own a place like this. Do you think it'll ever happen to us, Katey?"

She put his hand through her arm and patted it. "Yes, someday, Jerry, someday it will happen to us. We both want the good life… nice things… it'll take a good amount of work, but we'll save our money and then we'll enjoy weekends with our family in our very own cabin… just like this!"

Katey went inside, while Jerry wandered around and found a small storage shed tucked away under one corner of the overhanging deck. He called out, "Katey, come here! Hurry!" She heard him call and leaned over the deck. "There's a bar-b-que, briquettes and a stack of dry firewood under here. Boy, they think of everything!"

She joined in his enthusiasm. "You oughta see the fridge, it's loaded! Even has a check-off sheet posted on the door. There's a cute little notice by it that says: 'Please check off each food item as you use it. Thanks, the management.' Oh, Jerry, this is perfect! What a wonderful place for our honeymoon!"

Hand-in-hand, they explored every foot of their cabin, oohing and aahing at its completeness, the quality of the furnishings and the forethought and effort somebody obviously had put into it.

Twenty minutes later, Katey joined Jerry again out on the deck. This time she brought out two mugs of steaming hot chocolate. They sat down at the picnic table to drink their beverage and enjoy the view. "Glad you remembered to pack my jacket… there's still a touch of winter left up here."

He raised his hand. "Feel that cool breeze? That's coming off that snow-pack just above us when we rounded that last corner."

"We'll use our fireplace, tonight Dear. You do know how, don't you, Landis?"

He tickled her in mock rough-house. "Katey, maybe I wasn't a boy scout, but I can handle the fireplace detail with the best of 'em. Nothing to it!"

"Yeah? Well, we'll see, hotshot! What do you want to eat tonight? Got steak, pork chops or ham!"

"I'd sure go for a steak, Katey. Let me bring up the barby here on deck next to the back door… think it's going to be a bit too cool outside to enjoy our dinner on the deck…"

"I'll clean some potatoes and pop them in the oven so we'll have bakers… also, there are frozen veggies, no lettuce for salad though… you have your choice of green beans, mixed veggies, or corn."

"Mixed veggies sound just fine."

"Good. After you get the barby fired up, you can make yourself useful, come set the table for me, while I thaw the mixed veggies."

"McCray, you'd make somebody a darned good platoon sergeant" he laughed. "Thought I left that all behind…"

Katey was up to his wisecrack. "All right, Landis, it's your choice, you can eat that so-called Army chow, or you do a little work around here and have dinner with me and dessert later." She winked. "Well, don't horse around, which is it?"

He picked her up and kissed her long and hard. "Dessert sounds awful good to me. I'll take both kinds… the regular and what you're offering later… that's one of a kind. I've done without that long enough, almost two and a half years since that last sample."

He knew that'd get a rise out of his Katey and it took all of two seconds not to disappoint him. "Sample? That's what it was to you, huh? Seems to me I remember us making love all the way… we gave each other everything and I do mean EVERYTHING!"

He tickled her in the ribs just as he let her feet touch the floor. "Katey, I was just kidding. Now about that chow… excuse me, dinner I believe is what you called it…" He gave her a snappy, two-finger mock salute. "Yes, sir, General McCray, Private Landis reporting for K.P. duty as ordered, SIR!"

No two people ever enjoyed each other's company, humor and good, all-round companionship more than Katey and Jerry. There was such a natural flow of communication between them that before they knew it, they'd waltzed through an entire steak dinner sitting side by side at the table, sitting across from each other would never do, they'd be too far apart!

They couldn't keep their hands off each other. Twice during the dish washing episode, Jerry lifted his Katey onto the kitchen counter and proceeded to kiss her with such fervor and move his body into hers that she was left with no doubt what he wanted next, he only waited for her signal, that it was all right to carry her to the bedroom. Katey would have none of that, not until vows would be spoken, a commitment to everlasting love and life given together, and all of that symbolized by the placing of a wedding band on the proper finger. Katey would have him no other way.

Jerry sensed his timing was off, that would come later, all in its proper due time of course, so he backed off. It was time for more conversation. "Greg said to tell you 'Hi', said he expected to see you around next summer when he starts his corporate management trainee program with the railroad. Told me he expects to make division manager within five years or so."

Katey finished wiping off the counter. "Don't suppose he has to worry about getting drafted, does he, Jerry?"

He opened up the arms of the towel rack above the sink and hung the wet towel over it. "Naw, not much chance of that Katey, he's got a deferment from the draft board. Says he's got connections all over the place… especially up in the ivory tower where you work. Wouldn't be a bit surprised to see him get that management position within five… he's got the knack for it… big time charmer and all… with a certain amount of talent to go along with it…"

Katey turned her back to him. "And what's new with our other charmer, our Amigo, Ricco Petrocelli, the skirt chaser? Don't suppose he's in any danger of getting drafted, is he, Jerry?"

He sensed the hurt, the sarcasm creeping into her conversation. Katey continued, "Oh, no, not our Ricco! Why, he's too busy exploring territory between some woman's thighs. Never mind that her lawn's been trampled worse than the '49ers' gold rush. Great prospect for a good, solid relationship between a man and a woman, isn't he Jerry?"

He grabbed her to turn her around. She began to cry. "Don't Katey, please don't do this, don't say things you don't really mean, making it all the harder between us. Ricco's changing, Katey, I know you won't believe it, but he is. He's enlisting in the Air Force, and he's starting to take some responsibility for his life. He's starting to care. The Air Force will shape him up, it's what he needs. He'll come back a changed man, he'll…"

She cut him off at the knees, hard. "He'll never change. His kind never does! He'll go right on screwing anything that looks like a woman and who lays down long enough to let him! He's proved it with Molly… look what he did to her!"

"Hold it Katey! She did that to herself, remember? Another thing, I don't much care for the way you're talking… it's not like you, 'cause I know how much you hate that word, so why use it?"

"I used it because that's what Ricco and Molly did to each other… all those times, they weren't making love… they were screwing each other! That's right, I said it! I mean it! They screwed each other right out of any real chance at happiness, out of lasting love, out of any future together, out of any permanent relationship, out of honor and respect for each other, out of everything, and she threw it all away because she loved him too much to say no and she believed all that cock and bull he was throwing at her just to get what he wanted out of her.."

Jerry'd never seen Katey so wound up, so hostile, so sarcastic, so hurt, and yes, so ready to commit. "Is this weekend going to end up like Ricco and Molly, one big mess with no way out, no clear-cut answers?"

She looked up into his face, and never batted an eyelash or flinched a facial muscle. "You tell me, Jerry Landis! I want to hear your words, judge your actions and sincerity, and then we'll see."

"Or else?"

"Or else all this is going to mean is that we played house for a weekend, and you took me to our bedroom and you did the same thing Ricco did to Molly. Then you went off to war and I'm left with nothing but some words, half-meant promises, and little hope for our future. Is that what you have in mind, Jerry?"

He brushed her aside. "Where are you going, Dear?"

"To the bedroom to pack my suitcase before you do. If you think our relationship is on the same level as Molly and Ricco's you've got another think coming. Theirs was ugly and dirty... it never had a chance. I told you so years ago when Greg and I figured out what was going on between them. You comin' to pack too?"

Katey flew into his arms again. There was the deepest smile of satisfaction on her lips he'd ever seen. "Not unless you want to, my Love. This is supposed to be our honeymoon. Now that we've cleared the air between us, how about both of us making it what it's supposed to be?"

Time and time again, Katey had tested him and each time he had more than measured up to her expectations. She now felt secure and safe having his love, for she knew their commitment was real, their relationship solid, and their future bright. If only God would hear and grant her prayer, to send him back safely to her waiting arms.

Jerry banked-up the fire and stacked more firewood near the fireplace. Katey took several cushions from the davenport and laid them on the floor immediately in front of it. Together they sat on the cushions with their backs resting comfortably against the davenport, absorbing the fire's warmth, and watching with intense fascination, the flames curl over and around the logs in the fireplace. Neither spoke, yet there was a communication of mind, body and soul that transcended the love between them. It was as beautiful and sacred as any ceremony Katey had dared imagine or dream within her church. She looked at him, the shadows of flame flickering across his face and in her eyes. She was aglow, and she was his for the taking. He waited for the ring she gave him.

As if not to break the spell, they spoke their vows in whispers, each pledging their eternal love and commitment to each other, and before God. So complete, so satisfying was Katey's' wedding scene, that their kiss somehow seemed anti-climatic, the illumination from the fireplace adding its own special effervescence to this bonding between the two. When it was over, Katey kissed her ring and snuggled against his shoulder while she curled her legs beneath her skirt and waited. He felt a reluctance to change the mood, the tranquility to their setting. They both knew and understood there was a physical side to their relationship that needed to be met, to reaffirm to one another that what happened back on a certain, special night, was about to be further enhanced. It was to be practiced as their ritual of love from this day forward for the rest of their lives.

She shared in the anticipation and excitement with her eagerness to please him, to be part of his lovemaking, to help him in every way possible, to truly be as one. Gently and ever so carefully, he slid another cushion beneath her before he laid her down. He fought hard within himself, not to rush, not to hurry, but to restrain himself, for he had very vivid memories of what happened the last time when he ended up hurting her.

She raised her legs, her skirt dropped back, exposing her thighs and her sexy black, lacey panties. She never moved or gave any indication that she felt anything but sensual satisfactions letting him fulfill his desire to make love. He raised and kissed her, his lips on fire as she arched her body slightly.

"Jerry, my darling husband, please let me freshen up a bit. I want this moment to be perfect… I want to put something else on…"

Katey slid out from under him and disappeared behind their bedroom door. The minutes passed and she returned in her sheer negligee,' the firelight doing its own seductive dance, as he feasted on every subtle curve, every hint of her petite but amply endowed figure that riveted his attention down to the very last detail.

She knelt in front of him, her perfume inviting him to touch, taste, and sample every inch of her body from head to toe. Oh, how he wanted her, yet he controlled his emotions, he must not hurry, or else it would all be over too quick. Then this sacred moment, their special time of love would vanish before it had a chance to reach full bloom.

She was surprised he made no attempt to have her, but instead he concentrated on giving her pleasure. The more he touched, kissed and caressed, the better she responded just as he had hoped until her body language left no doubt. She was ready for love. She was all over him, grabbing, and holding, pleading. "Please Jerry, now, now. I can't wait… hurry, please."

Katey kissed him hard, repeatedly, and finally she understood what he had done to her. "Oh my Darling," she murmured, "I didn't know you could do that to me… it was beautiful…like the pleasure I gave you the night you proposed to me."

He picked her up, and carried her to their bed. Slowly he untied her negligee, letting it fall freely from her shoulders, letting his eyes drink in her petite, exquisite, beauty and body. She reached back, turned the switch on the night lamp to its lowest setting before he took her to another world-one filled with yearning ecstasy.

Then it came time. She marveled at his control, his restraint, wondering how he managed to stay so collected when her eyes told her he'd been ready, more than ready when their love making first started out on the cushions in front of the fireplace.

Katey was not afraid. She swooned at that moment, when they became one, holding on with everything she had, trying to make the feeling last. She began to cry, he did not understand, fearing that somehow he'd hurt her again. "Katey, my Love, I didn't mean to hurt you… please forgive me… please…"

The tiny tears of love and joy came, she didn't mind, she let them fall freely down both cheeks. "Oh, Jerry," she whispered, "it didn't hurt… it couldn't when you made me ready for this… now I know, I understand why you got me ready on the cushions in front of the fireplace."

Again he surprised her by slowly turning their bodies together until they lay fully embraced on their sides. "Jerry, Jerry," she cried, "Oh, it's so wonderful. Please dear God, please let this moment go on forever… it's so precious, so wonderful, so blessed."

They lay together, their bodies entwined with their lips pressed together, their love enshrined forever within each other. Jerry kissed her cheek. "Don't worry, my Love, you're body will tell me when you want my love again."

She took time to whisper, "I love you. Oh, I never believed it could be this good… better than our first time… but it is…. somehow you made it happen…… how, how?"

"Because you were ready, you knew what to expect… and you let it happen."

She kissed his cheek then the tip of his nose. "We must always say how much we love each other when we make love, Dear… it has to be said… it's important to me… and I hope to you… agree?"

He returned her kiss. "Yes, yes, I agree. It must be said often… you're right, it is important… we must never forget to say it."

She stirred. "Jerry, JERRY!"

Never were two minds, two hearts or two bodies more finely tuned to each other's needs, wants or desires. His was truly a labor of love. She nipped his earlobe, begging, pleading for him to keep on. "Please… more… more … it's too precious… don't hold back… …you know what I mean…… every time… promise me"

"I promise, Katey, my darling wife… I promise." They held each other tighter than before. Their bodies and their passion spent, but their love, their beautiful bonding ritual never more complete. She cried and relaxed. "Now my Love, my Precious Love, we are one! We are one as it should be between a husband and wife… we are one as God intended our love to be… as only it can be forever between us."

They lay in each other's arms, content and satisfied beyond each other's wildest dreams, far beyond anything each dared to anticipate, much less imagine. They kissed each other goodnight, and for some strange, unexplained reason, Katey turned and nestled against his body. Instinctively she felt him drop his arm over and around her, pulling her gently back into him until every inch melted between them, as they drifted off to sleep. Katey whispered a prayer and snuggled back, even closer to her Jerry, safe in the arms of her beloved husband, safe in the care of her Savior.

She had lost track of time when she was suddenly awake, aroused by something totally unexpected. "Jerry, Jerry," she called out in the pitch dark bedroom.

He mumbled something, and then drifted back into a deep sleep.

"Jerry! Jerry!" She whispered louder, making sure he heard.

"What Katey? What's up?"

"You are, that's what."

He didn't comprehend her meaning in his sleep-dazed thoughts. Groggily she felt him stir.

"Did you hear something? Maybe I'd better get up 'n check around."

She half-giggled. "No, not that, it's you! You were fast asleep and yet you were ready…"

"Oh!" Then a full minute of silence. "Oh that! Don't worry Katey, it's perfectly normal, just a little natural reaction. Happens all the time to men…"

She turned to face him. "It does? I never knew… didn't realize… I guess…"

He kissed her tenderly and tried to downplay the whole incident. "Should'a mentioned it… forgot to… forgot that might happen… since this is our first time sleeping together."

She hated herself for asking, yet she was dying to know. "Jerry?"

"Yes."

"Did you… I mean did this happen with the others? When you slept with them?"

He didn't care for her question, but passed it off as best he could under the circumstance.

"Nope, never happened with anybody else 'cause I never slept with anybody else… all night I mean, satisfied?"

She hugged and kissed him. "Oh, I'm so glad you said that. Oh I'm so glad you told me! Just think,, another first for us! And I'm the only one! Oh, I love you so much, Jerry!"

He was far less enthusiastic about her discovery. "Let's get some sleep, Katey. Tell you what, how about you snuggling up to me again… like before?"

"But what will we do? It'll still be there and I want to snuggle up against you."

"Slide up a bit… then back against me… I'll find a place…"

She obliged and then snickered. "I'll be darned… you did find a place… a perfect place."

Katey heard him drift off to sleep. She tried to close her eyes, but nothing happened.

"Jerry?"

He awoke a bit disgruntled. "Now what Katey?"

"Shouldn't we do something about it? I mean it'd be a … well… well, a kind'a waste'n all… not to… you know what I mean…"

He laughed. Katey laughed. "Yes, Katey, I get the message."

"I mean… can you? You know what I mean, don't you? We just made love twice a few hours ago…"

He was wide awake and definitely ready. "Katey, what we have here is a marvel of design and performance. It has amazing recuperative powers most of the time… you'll be disappointed once in awhile after I get back from Korea. Are you sure you're up to any more love making?"

He looked at his wristwatch on the night stand. "It's four in the morning, Katey… we still have today and most of tomorrow… and I'm still a bit concerned…. Sure don't want to chance hurting you… not ever… not again…"

That did it! Jerry's reassuring words erased any smidgeon of doubt Katey ever had concerning her desirability as his lover and wife. Giving birth to Krissy hadn't changed a thing, not in his mind at least.

She was eager to resume where they had left off. "Katey, I'd better make sure you're okay… make sure you're really ready…"

She reached up to draw his lips to hers. "Oh Darling, I'm ready, I've been ready all night… don't know how you did it, but… I'm still that way…"

Again, Katey was his helpmate in every way. She found herself in a totally new position. "Jer-r-ree!" she exclaimed, "now what?"

He thoroughly enjoyed her self-imposed predicament. "Not a chance, Katey, my Love. You wanted this, and now I'm going to lay back and enjoy and let you do all of my work."

"Please, please," she half-pleaded. "I don't know what to do… please, Jerry!"

"Sure you do… just pretend you're me. I'll hold you… you'll be fine… … it'll come as natural as night and day… give yourself a chance, Darling."

She did and oh, what pure, pure pleasure she derived from this great new experience. "Remember Darling… all of your love… I want it all…. Oh, I love you so much, Jerry, so much!"

They fell asleep, locked in each other's arms. One, two, three, and finally four more hours passed, and they slept soundly on. There were no more dreams left in either of them. How could there be? Each love fantasy had been more than fulfilled out on their marriage bed, their coming-of-age experience as man and wife.

Outside, not twenty feet away, two deer grazed contentedly on the sparse ground cover, taking full advantage of the beautiful sunrise over their snow-capped, rugged mountain domain. Each savored the precious few dew drops Mother Nature had purposely put there on the scant foliage for their nourishment, enjoyment, and pleasure. Off in the distance above the tree line, an eagle cast a wary eye for small, moving prey, circling and circling again, looking for food to feed its young, all part of nature's scheme of things. It was a great day to be alive and in love!

# CHAPTER SEVENTEEN

It took two passes of the coffee cup with its steaming aroma filling his nostrils, before Jerry made so much as the slightest stir. Katey, looking fresh as a daisy, was up and about. She pecked him on the cheek, and held the cup close again so he could get another good whiff and feel the warmth so close to his face. "Hey, sleepyhead," she teased, "let's rise and shine! There's a great day outside, let's enjoy it and each other! What say Landis?"

He rubbed his eyes and sat up, still a bit groggy. Katey propped his pillow behind him and set the tray of breakfast on his lap. "This is our wedding breakfast, so enjoy. Couldn't find a regular breakfast tray, so I made do with this pizza pan. Don't move your legs or else you'll spill everything."

He took the coffee cup from her and mooned over it. After downing two gulps he passed it back to her and looked down at the toast, jelly, orange juice, bacon and scrambled eggs. "Where's yours? Did you eat without me?"

She smiled and picked up a crisp slice of bacon and pressed it to his lips. He opened wide and accepted the morsel. "It's share and share alike Jerry… I'll feed you and you feed me. Seems much more personal, more intimate that way for our first meal together as husband and wife. Don't you agree?"

They took turns feeding each other, and sharing the same cup of coffee. He finished the last piece of toast. "Didn't hear you make any noise, how long have you been up?"

She moved the empty pan to the corner of the night stand and gave him a great big good-morning kiss. "About an hour. Showered, and put on a fresh change of everything and then decided to go ahead with breakfast. Boy, are you ever a sound sleeper! I dropped my suitcase here in the bedroom and you never twitched… not so much as a muscle."

He surveyed his pretty bride. "Golly Katey, you look better than one of those picture postcards of Hollywood starlets that you buy in the PX." He yawned and stretched both arms out full length. "Don't know how you did it… especially after last night… with all the love makin' going on between us… and everything…"

She got up, flashed her prettiest smile of the day, and then picked up the pan. "Just goes to show that married life certainly agrees with me… now take you, Landis, you look a little the worse for wear and tear. All beat and run down, got luggage bags already growin' beneath those eyeballs. Guess it's two bowls of Wheaties from now on for you each morning!"

He made a half-hearted lunge at her, missing her by at least a yard. She jumped out of his way with the ease of a pixie, leaving him grasping air. "Man, I feel beat! Like everything's been drained right out'a me!"

She turned to glance his way, still holding the pan. "Now that's an interesting statement, if ever I heard one." She shook her head. "Tsk, tsk, tsk! Imagine letting some poor little Irish girl who didn't know what was going on half the time, do that to such a big, blonde hunk who thinks he's all man! Imagine that!"

"You come back here Katey Landis… come back'n I'll show you what manhood's all about."

Oh, how she loved to tease him. "I did… last night. Remember? Look at you now and it's only our first day as man and wife. I tell you, Landis, just don't know about you…not sure if you're up to all your new husbandly duties…"

Jerry showered, shaved and got dressed while Katey did the dishes. He too was in an exceptional mood. "Did you pack a camera by chance?"

She stacked the last dish in the cupboard. "Sure did, Love. It's in my suitcase, it's a Polaroid. That okay?"

Jerry had Katey sit on the top of the railing and turn toward the skyline, profiling her figure. "Now lean back a little more, Katey… pull your shoulders back more… WOW!"

She let out a prolonged, "Jerrr-ree!" Katey's way of telling him she really liked what he was saying about her figure but her proper upbringing demanded she say something to blunt any more remarks in the making.

"Now turn and face me, and pucker up. Pretend you've just blown me a kiss."

He finished snapping two more shots. "Okay, Katey, open up… you know, your legs, want to see those sexy black panties again…"

"Don't you dare! Jerry Landis, I'll do no such thing! They're meant for you and only you! What would your Army buddies think and say if I let you take that kind of picture! No siree, Jerry Landis! Not one picture! You hear me?!"

He put down the camera to hold it at his sides, trying to keep from rolling on the deck with laughter. "Not the camera, Katey, just show them to me! You know I've been crazy about 'em for years. C'mon, Katey, just another peek, I… I promise I'll never tell. It's just between us… you and me… Heck it all goes back, way back to the fourth grade! Remember?"

She thought about it, what he said, and decided to give in again. She let him take a good look then closed her legs quickly. "There! Are you satisfied?"

He smiled. "For now, Katey, for now!"

She got down off the railing and went to him. "Tell me, and be honest, please Hon! Is it my panties that really turn you on or is it what they're protecting?"

He embraced her, and looked down into her waiting eyes. "Up 'til last night, I was sure it was the color, the black lace, but now I'm not so sure… I… I think now it's both."

They started back across the deck, arms around each other's waist. Katey looked up and said, "I'm glad I wear them just for you… it makes me proud to do that… it's our special thing, my love… it will always be that way."

Back inside the cabin, Jerry came up with a suggestion. "Hey, Katey, let's take a drive down to Lake Tahoe… maybe stop at a casino and try our luck with those one-armed bandits. I'll treat for lunch! Shucks, we're free, white and both recently turned twenty-one, how 'bout it?"

Katey thought about it. "All right, but we'll have to stick to a limit and not go over, our budget won't stand too much abuse. About that free, white and twenty-one business… better make that married, white and twenty-one after last night. Right, Jerry?"

"Got it! Oh, I'll need a small loan to take care of lunch and a few bucks for the slot machines. Hope you brought along some extra money … I spent what I had on Ricco and Greg down at Sam Moore's on pool and beer."

Katey grinned from ear to ear, and then shook her head knowingly. She returned from the bedroom with her purse. She handed Jerry three twenties. "Those were some Amigo friends you've got Landis … you're the one going away, but I see nothing's changed… I'm still letting you put the bite on me to take us out."

They started out the door, happy as larks. Inside their car, Jerry proudly announced. "Katey, when I get back, things are going to change…no more loans, I'm going to foot the bills for both of us… well, maybe not foot the bills… 'cause you'll be working and I'll be getting my degree, but at least I should be handling our budget… after all Katey, that's what accountants are supposed to do."

She scooted over by him, a very pleased expression on her face. "Well, Landis, at last, at long last, I think we're headed in the right direction… that's progress the way I see it, how about you, Jerry? Is that the way you see it, too?"

He slipped the automatic shift lever into drive, and stepped on the gas pedal. "If you're counting the changes in both our lives… from engagement rings, to our first car, to last night, I'd say we've come a long, long way. It's going to get even better between us, darling, just wait and see"

She raised up to kiss him "Oh, Jerry, it's so good between us… and when you come home safely back to me… that's when it'll be even better… I promise."

"So do I, Katey, so do I!"

***

They arrived back at their cabin with the shank of the daylight hours about gone and dusk fast approaching. They were in a jovial mood, the afternoon had treated them far better than either had dared to expect. Katey and Jerry practically tumbled thorough the doorway still laughing and joking.

"Brrr! Hey Landis, get a move on, there's a chill in here. Better leave your jacket on 'til you get that fire going."

He immediately set about building the fire. Twenty minutes later, he had a roaring blaze. Katey had made hot tea so they sat down at the table to enjoy it while waiting for the fire's heat to penetrate the room before removing their jackets in comfort once again.

"Jerry, sure wish I had our Polaroid with us inside that casino to capture the look on old granny's face when you dropped your last three quarters." Katey scrunched up her face and did a great imitation of an old lady, cackling away. "Well, now Sonny, I told you that machine won't pay off… oughta know… been feeding that bandit for two hours… getting nothin' back but a dribble now and then… go ahead 'n try it… you'll get took just like me… that's why I moved over to this one…"

He could hardly contain his laughter at Katey's impersonation. "And, and when those triple sevens came up she dang near fell off her stool."

Katey laughed so hard her sides began to ache. "Oh Jerry, the quarters just kept coming, and coming, and coming down into the tray. Never saw so many… eight hundred of them. You grabbed one of those buckets and began scooping for dear life."

"Yeah, and finally I turned around to you and said, 'Hey Katey, don't just stand there, help me scoop 'em up!'"

Jerry's laughter was too contagious to stop. "And after I cashed them in I handed you four twenties and you promptly put 'em down on that blackjack table." He laughed on. "Talk about the luck of the Irish… Katey, I'm not much of a gambler… but you're supposed to bet progressively if you want'a stay in the game. You know, bet some, save a little when the cards go sour… not you, not my Katey… no siree! You plunk down those bills and violà! You hit twenty-one! Boy, you clammed onto that pay off and skidaddled outta there before that cocktail waitress could take your drink order."

They hugged each other and kept on laughing, Jerry nearly spilling his tea. "Do you suppose that old gal was somebody's grandmother?"

Katey roared. "Sure hope not, never saw such a miserable old sourpuss! Especially after you hit that jackpot!"

They laughed together until a couple of tears lodged in Jerry's eyes. He turned serious. "I've been meaning to say this ever since I first fell in love with you, Katey. You're the most fun, the best person I've ever had the pleasure of knowing. Yet, I know you set your limits, and there's nobody or nothing that you'll allow to alter your ways or standards… which by the way are of the highest quality. I'd be a complete fool not to have recognized that in you. You're truly one-of-a-kind, don't ever change. I'll always want you just the way you are. I love you so very, very much… and indeed, you are my one and only, you are my Katey."

Jerry's words hit her where they did the most damage. She began to cry, and then kissed him over and over. He handed her a hankie. Soon she had her sniffles under control once more. "Darling, that's exactly the way I've always felt about you… if you only knew how long I've wanted to be with you, just be around you, talk to you, and now the best part… to have you love me… as my husband. You've been my friend, then my best friend, then my Amigo, then my sweetheart and my lover, and now my husband. Every time I see you, every time we're together, every time we're close, I will always remember you are all of these to me. No woman could ask for more."

Jerry got up to bank the logs in the fireplace and close down the damper to hold the heat. Katey watched him methodically tend to the fire then stood behind him. She placed her hand on his strong shoulders before saying, "I'm not really very hungry, we had that big lunch late this afternoon. How about me grilling a couple of cheese sandwiches and heating up some chili?"

He reached up 'til their hands touched. "Fine by me, Katey, my appetite's pretty well shot too."

Then the realization of running out of time, of knowing they were spending their last evening together began to set in. It took a terrible toll on their emotions, stripping away their innermost thoughts, forcing them to come to terms with the here and now, for there may not be a tomorrow to share, tomorrow as man and wife… a tomorrow they must face but didn't want to think about.

After supper they did the dishes in silence, each carefully watching the other, each afraid to say what needed to be said, yet each seeking the proper opening to bring it up for discussion.

Jerry broke the silence. He stood by her, waiting for Katey to put the bottle of liquid soap in its holder inside the door under the sink. "Katey, let's sit by the fire… I … I … we need to talk… couple of things…"

She followed him over to the fire where, as before, he slid the cushions off the davenport onto the floor for them to sit on. She sat down beside him, knees up, skirt draped over them, clasped by her two small hands, absorbing the friendly warmth from the fireplace.

"First thing Katey, is my G.I. insurance. Just before I came home, I signed a new form naming you as my beneficiary, and since we are married I'm glad I did it. It was the right thing to do."

"Jerry, please don't talk about those things, it hurts too much. You make it sound like you're not coming back to me." She began to cry.

He comforted her as best he could. "We must talk Katey or else some things might never get said." He looked straight ahead at the flames lapping the logs. He knew she was having a hard time controlling her emotions. "Here's something else you need to know. When I received my draft notice, I was in shock, so I went to the draft board and told them we were going to be married in three more days. Would that make a difference? Could I get a deferment or something?"

She watched his face, his handsomeness never more present. "Yes, and what did they say? You never told me about this."

"You were so upset when I brought you the bad news that I never had a chance to tell you about it, and when I heard their reply, I figured the less said the better. I'd already hurt you so much, your wedding plans and everything, I couldn't face you, tell you what I'm going to tell you now, Katey."

"What did they say, Jerry?"

"They said if we were married and if you were pregnant or if we had a baby I could get a deferment as they were only taking single men and married men with no children at this time."

Katey could stand no more. She ran to the bedroom and threw herself down, sobbing away with everything she had. She suddenly knew now that keeping her secret from Jerry had cost her, dearly. Jerry watched her, her body wracked with pain, not realizing the full implication of what he had said. He knelt beside her to comfort her. She would have none of his concern, she only cried the harder.

He pleaded with her. "Katey, Katey, listen to me! It wouldn't have made any difference, don't you see? Hear me out please. I'd give anything if I hadn't hurt you. I know how much having a baby has always meant to you. We talked about it, we both wanted children, and now I fixed it so you can't. I'm sorry. We'll adopt when I get back, after I get my degree I promise. We will have children, you'll just have to wait, be patient with me a little while longer. Okay?"

She heard his words of dismay, his attempt to comfort and console her and then she, too, realized what had happened. Inadvertently, he had provided the very opening she needed to discuss bringing Krissy home. Quietly and void of any more emotion, she sat up on their bed. She came straight to the point. "Jerry, I want my baby now, not later, not after you come back, not after you finish college. NOW!!"

He heard but he didn't believe. "Katey, you're mixed up, you're not making sense. I agreed we'll adopt later, why now?"

She got up, went to the vanity to get her purse and took out her wallet. Then she sat down on the bed beside him and removed a photo. She handed it to him. "Do you trust me? Do you trust my judgment, Jerry?"

He stared at the photo of a baby girl. "Yes, Katey, absolutely. But why are you showing me this picture? Who is she?"

He saw a light in her eyes, and he sensed a warmth, a love within his Katey he'd never seen before. Almost with a reverence, she talked about the little girl in the photo. "She's everything I hold near and dear, my Love. I can't wait, please don't make me! She's the baby I took care of evenings when I went to business college. She needs a mother and I need a baby now. When you leave, I'll have no one to love and I have so much love I want to give to this baby. I need to hold her, kiss her and hug her. I need to put pretty dresses on her. I need to potty train her. I need to brush and comb her hair, put pretty bows in her long golden hair, buy new shoes for her when she outgrows her old ones. I want to put her to sleep at night, listen for her cries in the middle of the night, teach her to feed herself, be around when she starts pointing at things, be there when she starts saying mommy and daddy, help her up when she takes her first fall, kiss her hurt bumps, give her a bath, buy her a dolly to sleep with at night."

"You're pretty set on adopting her aren't' you?"

"I've never wanted anything more, except you."

He got up from the bed, left the room and stood in front of the fireplace. Katey came out to join him. They held hands in front of the fire. "If I said no, if I didn't agree, Katey, what then?"

"I'd tell you, you've made the biggest mistake of your life, Gerald Landis. Krissy is the most precious, sweetest baby girl in all the world and I'd still go back to Chicago to get her. I have to give you back to the Army Monday morning. I won't give Krissy up no matter what, Jerry! I promise, if you agree, if you go along with me on this, you'll never regret it. Don't you think there have been enough regrets between us now to last our lifetime?"

He found it awfully hard to argue against her logic, her conviction that this was the right thing to do. "Dear, tell me about her, all you know."

Katey motioned him back to the cushions. Together they looked at the photo. "She's got the deepest blue eyes I've ever seen. And her hair, Jerry, you won't believe it. It's so long, so golden, I could put it in a ponytail right now."

"What about her parents? Do you know anything about them? Are they decent? God, I hope she didn't come from lots of one-night stands. You know what I mean, anyone of a dozen or more who could be the father!"

Katey was so pleased to supply the answers to Jerry's lingering doubts. "No, my love, Krissy came from love, only love. Her mother was young. It was her first time and it just happened that way."

"What about her father? Doesn't seem like he cared a whole lot to walk out on his responsibility like that. I dunno Katey…"

"Jerry, he wanted this baby too, but both of them were so young, so unprepared to take care of her. They were teenagers, just out of high school, just getting a start in life. He had big plans for college. She was going to help him. It just didn't work out that way for them. Oh Jerry if you ever picked her up, you've never want to put her down."

He picked up the photo and looked at it carefully, very carefully. "My Lord, Katey, she looks enough like us to be our own, our very own baby. And what you said about her parents why, why, that could've been us, couldn't it, Katey? We were a lot like that back then."

A radiance came over Katey's face, an unmistakable vision of a mother's true color, her love for her baby. "Yes, Jerry, Krissy certainly could've been ours. Now do you understand why I want to be her mother? You'd certainly fit the bill on being her father in the looks department."

"So do you Katey, her face will change quite a bit, but for now, she could easily pass for yours, you have the same type, kinda round with a pixie nose."

"Jerry, I'd be the best mother I can possibly be. All I ask is your okay, your blessing on our baby, on our family."

"What about your folks? Won't they have a tizzy if you show up with our daughter and we're not legally married? You'll probably have to move out, their being so strict and proper about everything."

"No problem. They want grandchildren so they'll welcome Krissy with open arms."

Katey saw Jerry still had doubts, big doubts. He got up, went to the coffee pot on the kitchen counter, and poured a cup. Next he put on his jacket. "I dunno Katey, all this happening so fast, nothing like we'd planned all along. Maybe later, I just don't feel comfortable being a father right now. Let me go out on the deck alone, sort it out for awhile. I don't like the idea of you going over my head about this, not at all."

She watched him close the side door and disappear into the darkness, alone. She too, had second thoughts. Maybe she'd pushed him too hard, too fast. Yet in her heart and mind there was no denying what she intended on doing, she just wanted him to be a part of it now with no second guessing as to who Krissy was or how she fit into their family. Lord knows, she surmised, there'd be shock and surprise enough when she let him read the parent's names on Krissy's birth certificate the same day Father Murphy formally married them.

Ten, twenty minutes passed, and Katey had made no move to join him. She put on her jacket, picked up the coffee pot and went to look for Jerry. She stood in the open doorway and called to him. "Dear, could you use a refill?"

He surprised her, for she could not pick him out in darkness, the light from inside their cabin completely blinded her. "Sure, come out and join me if you like."

"Where are you, Jerry, I can't see you? Wouldn't it be better to talk inside where there's more light?"

He didn't answer. Next thing she knew he'd taken her by the hand and led her to the picnic table and bench just outside the side door to the kitchen. She bumped the table and gingerly felt along its edge until she found the bench to sit on. "I don't want you to see me like this. I can't come in for awhile."

Now she understood, he'd been crying and his Landis pride refused to let her see him cry. She found his hand and reeled him in to her. To her surprise, he dropped to his knees and laid his head on her lap and tried to sob out his feelings to her. She wouldn't let him, instead she hugged him saying, "Don't Jerry, don't say anything just now. Go ahead, nobody need know."

He cried quietly, still trying to hide the sounds, afraid somehow his Katey would think the lesser of him, of not quite measuring up to being a man or her husband. Finally all was still, and then he blurted it out. "I know why you have to have Krissy. It's because I'm no better than what Ricco did to Molly. I couldn't keep from wanting you and I screwed up everything that night. Oh, no, I couldn't wait 'til you could've seen a woman specialist and then gotten married so we could make love the right way. Nope! Not big stud Landis! When we did it, I was no better than Ricco. Katey, I screwed you out of ever being a mother, of having your own baby, not somebody else's. And I screwed myself out of ever getting you pregnant, of me being a father." He broke down again.

Katey raised his head gently and then slapped him crisply once, then again. There was a purpose to this, a determination in her voice as she calmly but firmly had her say. "Don't you ever use that word around me, Gerald Landis, do you hear? What we did that night was as much… no, make it more my fault than yours by far. Listen to me and listen good! I promise if you'll trust me about Krissy, when you get back from Korea and we're married legally, you'll never regret letting me get her now. Then we will truly be a family in every way."

He didn't answer, giving Katey more time to soul search. She was oh so close to telling him, he indeed, was the father, so close to spilling it out once and for all, and be done with it. Didn't he have the right to know? Especially since she realized he might never know? She agonized and agonized over her decision, a few carefully chosen words, a simple sentence, and it would be out, the big lie, the big deception.

He cut short her decision. "What's Krissy's real name?"

"Kristianne Marie."

"Did you pick it? I mean after you started babysitting her?"

"Yes. Do you like it, Jerry?"

"It's a beautiful name. You have such good taste, Katey."

"Thanks, Darling. When we're ready for a boy I want you to pick him and his name. We'll try to match our son as closely as we did on Krissy."

"That won't be 'til after I finish my degree and we get situated better. You know, me getting a good job, saving some money and maybe a down payment on our own house. That okay with you?"

"Absolutely. I'll be more than ready to welcome Krissy's little baby brother into our family and by then I think I'll have had enough of the corporate rat-race. Then I want to be a full-time mother. Okay by you?"

"It'll be about time. After all you've carried most of the load waiting for me to get ready to accept my full responsibility as husband and father. Katey, you're so wonderful. How many other women would do what you're doing? Waiting for me, working so I can finish my education, never complaining, really, and never giving up on me. You deserve much better. You could've had your pick by now of most any successful young college graduate and still you stuck it out by me, now that's dedication and commitment if I ever saw it."

"That's love, the only kind I could ever have for you. That special night when you proposed to me, you said something to me I'll never forget. I knew you were ready for marriage and commitment when you said, 'I don't have much to offer except my love, but if you'll be patient, if you'll wait for me, I won't disappoint you,' and you haven't, Jerry Landis. I picked you years ago and planned and dreamed about spending our lives together forever. And tonight, I was never more right."

He reached for her hand and together they rose from the bench. She knew he was okay now, and ready to accept Krissy into their lives. Inside, he poured her a cup of coffee. He was happy again and in good spirits. "After you get Krissy, will you write to me and tell me all about her? I don't want to miss out on any of her growing up since I'm going to be her father."

"I'll write to you every day from work during lunch break. I'll send pictures, and tell you every little detail. First thing I'll work on is getting her to look at your picture and say 'Daddy'."

"That'd be great Katey! Oh, almost forgot to tell you, I made my first stripe, I'm a private first class, didn't even have time to sew on my stripe. It'll mean a few more bucks in your allotment next month, already notified personnel before I came home on leave. Guess with a new baby'n' all, we're gonna need every spare dollar, right Katey?"

Katey was so pleased to learn of his promotion. "Jerry, you're already sending me too much. How in the world do you manage on thirty-eight dollars a month? Shouldn't I be sending you some money each month instead of the other way around?"

Jerry put his arm around her. "I get by just fine. All I need is a few bucks to buy some shaving supplies, go to a on-post movie now and then and buy a few beers down at the EM club. When I write you they even provide the postage, it's donated by some of the local businesses. Overseas, I'll even have less use for money. There'll be little to buy or spend it on. Where are we on paying your folks back?"

Katey pulled up a chair. "Let's see, this is mid-April, by the first of the year we'll be all paid up. I match your allotment each month. It's really helped out, much more than I think even you could've realized."

He opened up his billfold. "Here's my latest receipt from our savings account, the one we were gonna use as our emergency fund when we were supposed to get married. There's just over twenty-eight hundred dollars in it and here's a form for you to sign so it'll be our joint account. Use it if you need to, it's your money now. Krissy will be needing things and I don't want her to do without. Use your own judgment, don't want your folks helping out anymore, they've done enough."

Katey was flabbergasted by Jerry's generosity. "I won't touch a dime of that money, Jerry. We'll need it just as you said for emergencies when you get back in college. I'm only buying Krissy a few new dresses and shoes, she'll be wearing clean, patched-up overalls and shirts to play in. We can save plenty that way, she'll be outgrowing them so fast, it'd be a waste of good money to buy new. Daddy said he'll let us use my old baby crib. They want to buy new baby sheets and blankets, and toys, so I'll let them. She'll sleep in her crib right next to my bed at night. I want to make sure I'm right there if she needs me."

"What about babysitting, when you're working days at corporate headquarters?"

"Mother's already informed me, she's taking care of her granddaughter, not some stranger. I'll pay her, but she's already got plans for that money. It's to be used for furniture or saved for a down payment on our own home later. They're so excited about Krissy. They can hardly wait 'til I step off the plane with her in my arms."

"Just by the way you're talking about Krissy, I can tell you're more than a little excited about our new baby daughter, aren't you?"

"Does it really show, Jerry?"

He laughed. "Show? The only thing missing is a big, bright neon sign saying, Welcome Home Krissy Landis, We Love You!!!"

The two lovebirds settled down for their last evening together. Had they worn their feelings and their emotions on their sleeves, they would've witnessed the great escape, their love for each other would've found a second home in each others' heart. Jerry took down an old wire corn popper hanging on the wall next to the fireplace. "Suppose there's any popcorn around here? Seems like a good, cold night to run off a batch."

She checked through the cupboards and promptly came up with a bag of corn. Together, they took turns holding the corn over the fire, using an oven mitt to ward off the intense heat that traveled the wire handle. One by one, the kernels exploded until its crescendo of noise resembled bingo balls rotating inside their container at some Catholic church's bingo night.

Jerry salted and buttered the corn and returned with a big bowl. Katey had already removed the davenport cushions and settled in their usual spot, on the floor, awaiting his return. She scooted over as he sat down, and nestled between his legs with the big bowl resting on her lap. "We need a way of communicating, a way of saying when we want to make love, a way of telling each other when we need each other."

He reached around her, filled one hand with corn and started eating. "I think we do pretty well as it is… you always wear your black panties, so if you're ready for love you raise up a bit and let me do what comes naturally… that's pretty good communication in my book."

She pecked him on the lips. "That's your signal. How about when I want you? When I'm ready for your love, but you don't know it or you're not quite ready?"

"If it's that important to you, Katey, we'll figure something out when I get back. Maybe a certain saying, a phrase or something."

She munched on a couple of kernels, still pondering. "Wait a minute, I think I've got it, hear me out! Love tank! That's it!"

"Love tank?" He shook his head. "No, that's no good. Anyway how'd you ever come up with an expression like that?"

She toyed with one of his hands, kissed some of the butter off one finger. "It makes sense, Jerry, when you give me all your love. It feels like you're filling me almost up to the top of… of me, of my tank! My love tank! Now do you see what I'm trying to tell you? Tonight, let me say it, and you'll see how it works! Then it'll make sense! Real sense!"

"Katey, I hate to disappoint you, but I don't even have anything left in my battery. It's dead, fifty naked Marilyn Monroes couldn't get a rise out'a me. That third time, did you use some kind of muscle control on me? Did you, Katey?"

She wouldn't say yes, nor would she deny it. She bussed him a couple of times, and then partially confided in her most modest, demure manner. "And if I did Jerry Landis, it's all right, isn't it? After all, my love tank needs every spare drop it can get. It's gonna be a long dry spell come tomorrow 'til you return to me to fill it again properly."

He turned her around in his arms, almost spilling the bowl of popcorn. "Katey, Katey, what am I gonna do with you? You're old fashioned and I love you for it, and yet you're more modern, more up-to-date than any woman I've ever known. We've made love exactly four times in our lives and you're already one up on me in that department. Ricco told me once he ran into a one-night-stand that could control him that way. How in the world did you ever manage to come up with such a technique?"

Katey's casual smile came slowly, but confidently. "No problem, Landis, exercise and control is the key. Just 'cause I don't have any love-making experience doesn't mean I don't read a lot. You'd be surprised what articles can be found in our so-called, old-fashioned, conservative women's magazines now days. There's articles about everything under the sun. Most of 'em I ignore, they're not for me, but once in awhile I run across something that I figure might help our marriage, maybe make it a bit better and I'm willing to give it a go. Well, early this morning I tried and it worked, so you'd better be expecting more of the same next time. You don't mind, do you?"

"Mind? How could I? When you're done with me, I'm so used up, all I can think about is wrapping my arms around you and letting you snuggle up against me. Lord, what a sleeping pill!"

He beamed at his Katey and enjoyed her popping kernels of corn into his mouth. Then she stopped as if something or someone was calling her. She rose. "I have to be alone my Love. It's something that needs doing, something I must do if I'm to have peace and harmony within my soul."

He continued eating the popcorn, and then curiosity got the best of him. He stood outside their bedroom door, thankful it was ajar. Inside, with her back to him was his Katey, down on her knees, praying. She turned slightly, he wasn't sure if she felt his presence or not, but she continued counting her beads, the rosary he held in her hand as she prayed. Now he noticed she'd been crying, and he knew the tears and her prayers were for him, for his safe return to her and to Krissy, too.

He felt ashamed that he had eavesdropped on her in her moment of need and yet he was glad he saw and overheard, for she had honored him that way, her way with her God, her Protector. He longed to be a part of what he'd seen but he knew not how to enter, he felt much more like an intruder than a believer.

Ten minutes later she returned, her eyes were bright as ever, new make-up covering her tear-stained cheeks, cheerful and happy as before. "I'm sorry," he began, "I apologize for standing by the door. All I can say is, you honored me with your prayers and though I'm not ready to accept your God, it was beautiful in thought, and I know how sacred your God is to you. Someday, I hope I can accept and feel as you do."

Katey said nothing at first, and then decided to comment on his statement. "You will Jerry. There's so much goodness in you, God is only waiting to pick and choose his time with you. It will happen."

He went to the kitchen sink. He was restless. He kept looking out the window. The moon riveted his attention, casting its glow across the deck, the moonbeams so thick, he was tempted to go outside and bathe in them. He felt two small arms encircle his waist. "You don't want it to end," she softly whispered, "And neither do I, my Darling, but it will, it must. Our lives must go on."

He seized her to make sure she was real, afraid somehow, all that had happened between them hadn't happened, that he'd pinch himself and wake up on some Army troop ship anchored off the coast of Korea. "I'm afraid I'm not much of a soldier." He broke down sobbing.

This time she saw him cry, there was no hiding in the darkness out on the deck. She saw him cry, but she saw only the strength of his character not the weakness he imagined she felt as she let him cry and then did her best to comfort and console him. "Jerry, listen to me," she said, "Both of us are afraid, but we'll make it. Our love, our commitment will see us through. We'll be together again and our lives, our marriage will survive and grow and last forever. There is so much between us. Our love is good, there's a purity between us that will see us through. Trust me."

He wiped his eyes, and blew hard on the hankie Katey pulled from his pocket. She changed subjects. "Hey, now that your battery is all run down and no telling when I can expect a recharge, how about you and me doin' something daring? I'm ready to shower with you. Think you're man enough for this assignment, Landis?"

She saw Jerry's old cockiness flow back into his face. Man enough? His little Katey daring him? "Well, Katey, time to find out if it's all talk, all tease, or the real McCoy!"

# Chapter Eighteen

Katey started peeling off her clothes, leaving a trail a blind man could follow. Jerry tried to gather them up on the way to the shower, and then he burst out laughing. "Katey, if you don't beat anything I ever saw. I'd give a million bucks to have a Polaroid of you now. Matter of fact, I think I'll go get it."

She leaped back into his arms, partly to protect what little modesty she had left and partly to prevent him from reaching for the camera, "Don't you dare, Jerry Landis! Don't you dare! I thought you were going to join me."

Two minutes later they were crammed into the one-man shower stall, laughing, kissing, and hugging for dear life. It was so tight, their bodies so close to each other, the poor bar of soap couldn't have hit the drain if it wanted to.

Katey needled him, "Say Landis, a couple of minutes ago, you were laughing your head off. Tell me, was it because I stood in front of you with nothing except my shoes on? Come now, 'fess up!"

Between spurts of shower water he managed to answer. "The shoes, Katey, the shoes! Talking about your body, I'd sure like to check it out again."

They tried soaping down each other's backs, gave up, and let the bar rest between their bodies, part of their passionate embrace.

Katey slipped one arm down. "Say, Landis, you told me your battery's dead. Maybe you'd better check again.

Ever the ultimate teaser, Jerry downplayed Katey's new discovery. "It'll probably disappear before we even get to thinking, let alone take the time to do something about it."

"Really? It will? Just like that?"

He snapped his fingers. "Yeah, Katey, just like that."

She watched him, then his sly smile gave it away. "Darned you for trying to jerk my chain, just 'cause I don't know about such things. I'll betcha if we move back out to our bed, I'll show how I can make you into a 'Ready Teddy' in nothing flat! Well, Landis, are you game?"

They toweled each other off, still laughing and joking. Then Katey blew him a kiss. "Dear, let me get ready, I want to look extra special for you tonight, our last night as husband and wife." Then she smiled and added, "Our budget took a pretty big hit buying my negligee. Let's get our money's worth!"

He laid on their bed in his boxer shorts, hands cradled back behind his head, thoroughly content. The magic of what was about to happen, their elixir of love, foremost on his mind as he happily awaited his Irish pixie's last minute preparations.

Then she came to him, his wife, his vision of an Irish angel, still radiating an aura of innocence. Her loveliness captivated him beyond measure. He was totally at her beck and call. He was her love slave for tonight and all the numbered days of their lives.

She sat down on the edge of the bed, her perfume, her freshness, taking him to another level. He thought to himself, here is love personified, here is my Katey. She kissed him and then had him lie on his stomach. To his surprise she kissed several places on his lower back, places where she had left her fingernail marks, where in the wee hours that morning she had dug in and hung on, when he took her to another world. Then Katey rubbed body lotion on the red marks, and told him in a most delightful manner, she'd cut her fingernails way back, so there'd be no new red marks tonight.

Katey asked him to sit up and to his surprise, had him raise up while she slipped his shorts off. Tonight, she was the initiator, the innovator, tonight she was in control. She had him lay back while she went to work on him, kissing him, tantalizing, and teasing him until she had him exactly where she wanted him. He writhed in ecstasy at every kiss, every touch.

Finally he could stand no more, he had to have her.

Oh the pleasure and the joy she gave him.

He gradually relaxed in her arms, so he could give her what she wanted, controlled passion.

They vowed their undying love to each other, between passionate kisses and beautiful body rhythms.

After, they felt drowsy. A need to sleep. A time to replenish. Nestled in each other's arms, the two lovers played out the scenes from their honeymoon hideaway high in the Sierras. "Goodnight, Sweet Love," she said, "Sweet dreams."

He stroked her short hair, remembering when it was shoulder length. "Do you know, many couples go through their entire married life and never do what we just did?"

She turned to him, to read his eyes. "Yes, and do you know that what you did to me Friday night… well, many women will never know about that either."

He dead panned. "Think we got a little problem on our hands, Katey."

He got the reaction he expected. Katey raised up, alarm written all over. "What problem, Jerry? Thought everything was going just great!. What did we miss?"

"With what's happened, I'm afraid our relationship has drifted into something neither of us can do anything about. It's way too late, Katey, way too late."

She was really on edge now. "Our relationship? How could it be any better between us? Exceptin' when you come home to Krissy and me."

He played it to the hilt. "Here's the way I see it, pay attention and see if you don't agree. What started out as commitment and marriage vows has gotten way outt'a whack. What we have here is the darndest, hottest, most torrid love affair I've ever seen, and it's all wrapped around that plain gold wedding band. Katey, if you were expecting only a marriage, you certainly got that and a whole lot more when you had me slip that ring on your finger. Don'tcha see what's happened? There's no turning back for either of us. It's going to mean a whole lot of MOS, more of the same when I get back."

She tickled him, and mock-wrestled him. "Darn you, Landis, you really had me going. Well, I've got the equalizer, and I'll use it whenever you get to giving me a hard time. Remember your little Fourth-of-July accident all over my skirt?

He was still embarrassed and Katey let him stew in it. "You're never gonna let me forget about that are you?"

She kissed him with new excitement and sincerity. "Not on your life, Landis! You can take that to the bank and cash it, right along with your allotment check!"

# CHAPTER NINETEEN

Katey smelled pancakes; well at least that's what her nose told her. She sat up, rubbed her eyes and looked out their bedroom window. A bright, cheery day greeted her. She glanced over where Jerry should be. No Jerry. His pillow was next to her, a terribly poor substitute for his warm body and loving arms, her security and protection.

He stood before her, the same pizza pan loaded down with pancakes, maple syrup, butter, and one steaming coffee cup, the coffee pot, one glass of orange juice, two eggs and assorted silverware. "My turn Love," he said, "you did the honors yesterday."

They fed each other much as the morning before. After they finished, he bussed the pan to the kitchen sink and returned with a second cup of coffee. "By the way, we have a couple of loose ends to tie up, Katey. I signed over the title of the car to you and left it with Mother."

She sipped her coffee. "I like what you just said, Hon, you called her Mother."

"Why not," he shrugged, "she's always tried to treat me like a son."

"Dad thinks you're the greatest, says there's still some hope for our generation after he sees what you've done with your life.

She started for the kitchen sink, coffee cup in hand. "Any other loose ends that need tying up?"

He followed her with his cup. "Our big honeymoon trip to Chicago, you called it a nostalgic tour, see Aunt Rose, visit your business college. C'mon Katey, wasn't the real reason you talked me into that was to have me meet Krissy?"

She emptied her cup in the sink and turned on the hot water tap, letting it run before turning to answer his question. "Oh, Jerry, if only you could've met her, picked her up, kissed her, and felt her soft baby cheeks against yours, Krissy would've stolen your heart like she did mine. You'd never want to put her down again! Never!"

He got the dish rack out from under the sink, and set the drain board on the counter. "You sure answered that. One more thing?"

She squirted some liquid detergent into the running water. "Okay, shoot."

"Most of your life, you've been a planner and a dreamer with a lot of down-to-earth horse sense. You've been kinda guiding, steering me along, pointing me in the right direction. In the love and romance department, same story. Never give in but gradually a few hard-earned pleasures came my way, just enough to keep me interested, keep me wanting you so bad it about drove me nuts. It was all part of your way, wasn't it Katey?"

She'd never answer that, she didn't have to, instead she proudly kissed her wedding band and politely, but firmly announced, "If you're going to bother me with questions you already know the answer to, Gerald Landis, then it's time you put your mind on other things like… like either helping me do the dishes or showering and shaving. There's half a day owed us up here, I don't intend to waste it."

He dried the dishes without more questions or discussion. While he went to shower, Katey stripped their bed, folding and stacking the blankets, sheets, and pillowcases on the mattress. Then she took her turn in the shower while he shaved.

Afterwards, she dressed, combed and brushed her hair and then dutifully watched him finish shaving. She touched the red marks on his back. "Jerry, I hope you're not going to tell anybody how you got them. Maybe you could stay out of the shower for a few days, and then nobody'd have to know."

He put down his safety razor and laughed. "Katey, we all shower together, believe me there are mighty few secrets kept out of an Army shower room. Anybody that sees them will know. Most of the guys are smart enough not to ask questions."

She thought on his reply and accepted the fact that others would know. Thank goodness they'd all be strangers, other soldiers who'd be shipping out with him, men she'd never meet. "Dear lift me up, I want to watch you finish shaving." He helped her up on the counter then continued shaving.

"Your beard's getting darker all the time, and you being a blonde. And those are dark hairs not blonde ones, on your chest and… and you're sure not blonde down… you know where"

Jerry laughed."Yeah you're sure right about that… they're about the same color, pitch black like Poolis' beard, a sergeant I know. Katey, I wish…. you could've met Sergeant Poolis, he's quite a character. He'll be shipping out with me. He's from the hill country of eastern Kentucky, got a real nasal twang to his voice. He used to really ride my tail as my drill instructor during basic. Called me 'Private Lost Cause Landis.' Said if the Army could make a soldier out of me, there was hope for all draftees."

"How come you're still buddies after all the ribbing and riding he gave you?"

He rinsed his razor off. "You know, that's the funny part about it, Katey. After I finished basic, he was transferred as my Cadre Sergeant in tech school. We get along great now, even down a beer or two together when we shoot the bull in the EM Club. He's married, got two kids. You're not gonna believe what he told me about their wedding night!"

"I'll bite, go ahead'n tell me."

"His wife must be hill folk too. Anyway, he swears this is what happened, he's making mad, passionate love and all the while she's readin' a comic book and chewing bubble-gum. Can you believe it?"

Katey was furious. Down from the counter she jumped, her Irish hackles raised up to the nth degree. "I've never heard anything so disgusting in all my life, Jerry Landis! I've got her figured out and I've never met the lady, if you can call her that. Lay you odds she's a big, fat slob too, especially after she had those two babies."

Jerry was mystified. "Come to think of it, you're right. He's shown me pictures of her. Yep, you're right on. She's got a cute face, but the rest of her has really gone to pot."

"Did your Sergeant friend say anything about their relationship? You know what I mean!"

"Told me if it wasn't for his two boys, he'd never go home on leave. Said she wants him to make love all the time and he can't stand it, says she's too fat. Anyway, when I told him we were getting married, you know what he said?"

Hands on her hips, Katey almost dared Jerry to read her mind. "Tell me, tell me, anyway, I already know the words, the All-American fat-slob copout!"

"He says real serious-like to me, 'Lost-Cause Landis', I hope it was great before you got married 'cause after the kids come it ain't gonna be like that no more 'cause certain things do change."

That did it! Katey was mad, fighting mad. "Horse-pucky, Landis! There's no excuse, no excuse at all for being in that condition! No excuse at all!"

He turned to his wife, "Katey, get off their backs, will ya? Hey, you've never had a baby, so how do you know it isn't like that? I've heard certain things are bound to stretch and it never goes back to being like it was."

She waved her forefinger in front of his nose. "You heard wrong, Jerry, dead wrong! There are exercises you can take, it tones the abdomen, and believe it or not it helps there too! There's lots that can be done, if she'd get off her duff, leave the comic books alone, and try being an attractive, desirable woman and wife once more. Then he'd break his neck to get home to her and their family!"

He tried to shut her down, tried hard to change subjects but she wouldn't let him. He'd never seen her so wound up, so adamant about something he was convinced she knew absolutely nothing about. Finally she ran out of gas. "Katey, climb down off your soapbox! Boy, for a couple of minutes you had me going, almost had me convinced that you knew what you're talking about because you'd had a baby."

"I did!" she yelled!

Before she could catch herself, the words slipped out in the heat of the discussion. She quickly put one hand to her mouth. They looked at one another, not sure what to do or say next. Katey recovered quickly. "What I meant was I did a heckuva lot of reading on this right after we made love the first time, just in case we had a baby. Of course, Chicago changed all that. That's what I meant."

He went to her. "I'd give anything to change things Katey, to know that Krissy was really ours… that I'd gotten you pregnant that night. Hey, let's lighten up here, time to change subjects, do something crazy." He pushed the button on his shaving cream and re-applied it to his face.

"Just what do you think you're doing? You finished shaving five minutes ago."

She read his thoughts a split second too late. She made a dash to get away, but was caught at the bathroom door and hoisted up in mid-air, her legs still churning. She knew what was coming. "Jerry Landis, don't you dare kiss me all lathered up that way! Jer-ree!!"

He smothered her with shaving cream, midst her squeals, giggles, and laughter. They kissed again and again. "Hey, Katey, check yourself in the mirror. You look like Santa Claus!"

They took time out from their horseplay for Katey to get a first-hand look. "Aw for cripes sake, Jerry," she half-complained, "look what you did to me. You got it all over me, even in my hair." Then she saw that familiar gleam in his eye. "No, no don't you dare! I know what you're thinking!"

He laid her down on the counter, still squirming and wiggling and lifted both knees up together until her skirt slid back, then he went in for the prize, her panties. He kissed and wiped his face all over them. She screamed and squealed but it was too late. "Jerry Landis, you're awful! Look what you did to them! You got cream all over them!"

"Better shaving cream than something else."

She gave him a coy little smile. Her thighs and shaving cream-covered panties still very much exposed. "Oh, I don't know about that. I'll trade shaving cream for the real thing any day, anytime."

He tickled her 'til she begged him to stop. He let her up after he extracted another lather-lipped kiss from her. Katey got off the counter, her old Tomboy traits working overtime. There had to be a way to even up the score. Jerry saw an old mischievous look play hopscotch across her face. He grabbed for the towel protecting his modesty, too late!

She snatched it away a second ahead of his futile attempt and raced out into the cabin, daring him to retrieve it. "C'mon Landis, come get it if you can! I dare you! 'Course you're naked as a Jaybird! And how are you gonna cover your modesty and still chase me? Huh?"

They raced around the room, Katey enjoying his predicament to the fullest. He'd take ten steps, then crouch over and try to protect his manhood, uncoil, and run another ten steps and do it all over again. It was hilarious, at least Katey thought so. "Hey Jerry," she roared with laughter, "maybe I'd better get the Polaroid! This is worth saving!"

Suddenly he gave up the chase and retreated to their bedroom, bare buttocks, and all. A minute later, he made a grand re-entrance, his modesty well covered with a pair of boxer shorts.

"Chicken! Chicken!" she taunted him, knowing that their horseplay was over.

They cleaned up the cabin. Katey swept and dusted, while Jerry cleaned out the fireplace, making sure the ashes were dumped into a metal container located to one side of the deck, near their car.

An hour later, they celebrated their cabin cleaning duties with a fresh pot of tea, hot soup and sandwiches on plates Katey brought outside on the deck. In their jackets, they enjoyed the fabulous scenery around them, while downing Katey's delicious lunch. Jerry looked off across the high plateau to the nearest stand of timber, a quarter mile away. "How I love this place, Katey... it will always be special in our memory... our honeymoon hideaway. Think we'll ever return here?"

She came over to the railing where he was leaning. She set her cup on the railing and slipped an arm around his shoulder. "When you come back, my love, I'd like to spend a week up here again. Krissy will be old enough by then, the three of us would have a ball. Just our own little family."

He started to say something, changed his mind, clenched his fist, and then looked at his bride. "Katey… I …"

"Don't Jerry, I know what's on your mind, what you've been trying to say ever since we said our vows."

"I have to say it. It's the hardest thing I've ever had to say to you, especially after Friday night, your wedding band and then after you told me about wanting Krissy as our baby."

She flew into his arms, pleading, begging him not to say it. Finally through her tears, he had his say. "Katey if… if I don't come back…"

"Don't," she sobbed, "please don't say those words. You have to come back. You have so much to come back to… please, Jerry, tell me anything but what you're going to say. Please, please, don't…"

He tried his best to control her emotions, but she cried on, afraid to hear the most beautiful compliment man can give a woman. Finally he forced himself. "Katey, hear me out. You are love. You must have love, and you must give back love or else you will surely wither away of a broken heart and unfulfilled needs all because of love. There are so few in this world like you, and far too many like the rest of us. We don't have your capacity to give love and keep love and live love from day to day. We ignore the simple, beautiful things that you see, we are blind to the special needs you require, we push and shove, looking for love, and all the while it was there but for the askin' from you. You are the teacher of love, you are its caretaker and master. You are love. If I don't return, you must go on with your life and love again, not only for your sake, but for Krissy's as well. With you I have known love, I have tasted love, and shall keep your love locked in my heart and in my memory 'til I give up my last breath."

She wept bitterly, protesting what they both knew to be true, that she needed love. "I… I can't do what you ask. It's only you I've ever loved and will always love. All my life it's been you, only you. My whole life has been built around you. How can you ask me to love another like I've cared for and loved you? How my love? How?"

He weighed her questions and clearly responded as his heart directed. "I don't ask that you love another as you loved me, my darling Katey. I only ask that you love again. You must, it's your way, your nature, and it's the very essence, the very reason for being you."

They ended this discussion without another word on the subject. They finished lunch in silence, each not wanting to touch on it again, enough had been said. Jerry glanced at his watch. "Let me do these few dishes, Sweetheart, and you check around to see if we forget something. It's getting late. I think we'd better head back down to the valley."

He did his KP while Katey, noticeably very quiet, gave every nook and cranny her usual thorough inspection. Satisfied, she returned to the kitchen area. "About our love, what happened this weekend between us, I mean we are married, and what we have, what we did is too personal to be telling somebody else. I feel it's too intimate, too precious, and too sacred for somebody else's ears, don't you agree?"

"Absolutely Katey, our honeymoon, and how we shared our love is just between us. There'll be no conversation with anybody on that matter."

Katey felt better. "After what your sergeant buddy told you, I was beginning to wonder."

"Do you have to confess our weekend to your priest, Katey? I just don't think it's any of his business. Your confession, the whole business, still bothers me."

"Jerry, you know I must. You've always known that, at least you've accepted it, and that was part of the understanding we've had since high school graduation."

"That doesn't mean I agree. What will you tell your priest, your Father Murphy?"

"I will tell him we exchanged vows as man and wife, you slipped a wedding ring on my finger, and we lived together as man and wife for a weekend. Nothing more, none of the details. I can see you're worried about that."

He chose his reply carefully, not wanting to spark a real confrontation over religion with her. "Katey, I can understand and I do accept your need to pray and talk with your God, but what I find hard to understand… frankly, it galls the heck out of me, is the need to confess your so called sins to another mortal. Heck your priest puts his pants on just like I do. Why confess to him when I'm sure you've already confessed the same thing to your God?"

Katey's Irish was sorely tested, but she controlled her temper with remarkable poise. "I'm going to let this discussion pass, my darling, because you are a non-believer, because you don't fully know my ways, because we are committed to marriage and because I believe with all my heart and soul you will change."

Jerry got in the last parting shot. "I know nothing will stop you from another round in your church's confessional, but your priest is an unnecessary middle-man as far as I'm concerned."

Katey refused comment, opting instead to go to the bedroom to get their luggage. Jerry, obediently followed, and grabbed the two big suitcases while Katey picked up her train case. She looked wistfully at him, her eyes filled with love and longing.

"Jerry?"

"Yes, my lovely wife."

"I love you so much, so very, very much and whether I care to admit it or not, you were right. I do need love, lots of love and you're the reason, Jerry Landis. . I know I shouldn't say this, maybe it isn't even proper, but if there's anything left…anything at all…"

Three piece of luggage hit the floor simultaneously.

# CHAPTER TWENTY

Mary McCray took one look at her returning honeymooners and knew immediately that she had done the right thing. She said nothing except, "Come Katey, there's a wee bit of help I'm needin' here before supper takes shape. Jerry, why don't you take those suitcases and leave 'em in Katey's bedroom?"

Jerry was simply amazed at the two McCray women bustling about as though nothing had happened. He kept out of their way by reading the newspapers in the front parlor, sitting in Mr. McCray's chair.

Supper was eaten with nary a comment about the weekend. Instead, they talked about the wind blowing away Mrs. Feeney's washing and that the Callahans were moving since Mr. Callahan had inherited a sizable estate.

Katey and Jerry volunteered to do the dishes and clean up, so Mary let them. He scraped the plates before handing them to Katey. "Did your mother say anything or ask about the weekend?"

Katey handed the rinsed dishes back to Jerry for wiping. "No, it's not her way. After you leave there may be a few questions so that she'll be ready for father in case he decides to inquire. It's very possible there'll be no discussion whatsoever between them about us or our weekend."

Jerry finished wiping. "I don't know where these all go so I'll let you put them away."

"While I'm doing that, you can be a big help by looking for your PFC stripes."

He dug out the package of stripes from the bottom of his duffle bag. Katey sewed them on his "Ike Jacket" and his khaki shirts. "There now my Love, can't have my husband without them knowing he's a private first class…that would never do."

All too soon it came time for Jerry to make-up his bed on the davenport. With an early morning flight from Sacramento, Mary insisted that everybody should get to bed early. She said goodnight and excused herself. Katey led Jerry into her bedroom, making sure the bedroom door remained wide open. She pointed to her dresser-vanity combination. "I'm going to have daddy set up a small chest of drawers on Wednesday, next to my dresser, for Krissy's things." She pointed to the foot of her bed. "That's where daddy will set up my old baby crib for now. Mother went out yesterday to buy new crib sheets, blankets and a baby pillow, so you see, dear, I'll be pretty well set to take care of her when I step off the plane late Wednesday night. She'll be tired, maybe a bit fussy from the flight, but I'll have the rest of the week to be around her so we can get to know each other again."

"What about bottles and baby formula?"

"She's never had a baby bottle. She drinks right out of a cup since she quit nursing…from her mother, of course. Aunt Rose told me that when I started babysitting her."

He studied her face, still trying to get a read on his Katey, one that would completely satisfy. He faced her and held hands with her. "I'm glad now you insisted on bringing Krissy into our family. Between Krissy and your parents, you'll be surrounded by love and the people who mean the most to you."

She moved in so close that through their kiss and embrace, each sought out the other's body until they stuck like glue to one another. "I won't be getting much sleep, darling, not with you sleeping so close to me out there on the davenport. Oh Jerry, I miss you already, I want you in my arms in my bed…I want your love again."

He looked down into her face, read the need in her eyes, and felt the invite with her body. "Don't Katey, don't make it any harder than it is already to leave you alone tonight after what we've meant to each other, after this weekend."

They kissed goodnight, promising that the next kiss, the next embrace would have to last until morning. After the fourth kiss, they finally kept their promise.

Jerry knew she knelt beside him, the sweet scent of her perfume roused in him a longing he'd had fulfilled but a few short hours ago. Her soft, moist lips grazed his, giving him an opportunity to gather her into his body where he held her as close as his conscience allowed. For an instant she responded, then dutifully whispered, "Jerry, it's four in the morning, time to shave and get dressed. I'll make the coffee and wake mother."

Mary walked in on them, on their tender scene, then half-coughed, her way of apologizing for interrupting their privacy. "I'll see to the coffee. You warm the Danish when you're ready, Katey."

The early morning ride to the Sacramento International Airport took forty-five minutes; to the lovers it seemed more like forty-five seconds. All three were surprised at the activity going on at five forty-five inside the terminal. Jerry hurriedly checked in his duffle bag, got his seat assignment and boarding pass, and returned to the two women.

First he hugged and kissed Mary on the cheek. "Feel I should call you Mom. It's okay isn't it?"

"You'd better, my Son, after all that's the only way you're going to get by me if you've a mind to say your good-byes to Katey."

"Thanks for everything, especially the weekend."

"Haven't the faintest idea what you're carrying on about, Lad. Must've been some other Katey you're confused with. Mine was with me the whole weekend, doing her proper thing."

He smiled and knew better than to push that subject any further. He turned to his beloved, waiting wife, his Irish darling. She rushed into his arms, her eager lips full upon his before he was half ready for such a display of affection. "See," she said, "just like I promised, no tears, my eyes are dry as the Mojave Desert."

"You're doing great, Katey, just great!" He settled on her lips. "Time to say good-bye, I hear the PA system. I love you with all my heart and soul, and I'll come back. I have to! You'd never leave me alone over there if I didn't. You'd see to it somehow, some way."

She, too, tried to make light of Jerry's feeble attempt to see a bit of humor in their emotional parting. Suddenly she broke down, sobbing harder then he'd ever seen her cry. Out of desperation, he motioned for Mary to come forward to take her from him so he could board the plane.

The two McCray women watched Jerry's plane lift skyward, and then gradually disappear into a pinkish-grey bank of clouds to the east as dawn descended upon the valley. "I didn't even get to say I love him. I hope he knows and understands."

"Knows? Katey, if you'd have hung a cardboard sign around your neck with two-foot high letters you couldn't have said nor done it any better. Good thing it happened here and not in Ireland. You used far too much water to make your tears. You'd have drained the River Shannon near dry, then what a calamity the country would have to endure."

They reached the parking lot, by this time Katey had her tears pretty well under control. They sat a minute or two in the car before leaving. "I think it's a fair and proper question, Katey, now that Jerry's off to war. I noticed you wearing your wedding band when you returned at supper time last night. Did you speak your vows before God, before you become his wife?"

"Yes, that was the only way I could've, Mother."

Mary inserted the key and started the engine. "Are you happy with your life now?"

She beamed over at her mother. "I can't fully explain it, but for the first time in my life I'm at peace with myself. I know who I am, what I am and what I want out of life. It's so good between Jerry and me. It's almost too good to be true. I feel content. I know what being a wife means, and I know that love, commitment, honor, and respect all made it happen between us."

They left the parking lot, each sorting through their thoughts on what the past weekend had really meant.

Katey returned late Wednesday evening with Krissy. No home or household ever received a more widely anticipated or more welcome addition to family life than one Kristianne Marie McCray-Landis brought with her. If Katey or her parents ever harbored any serious doubts about the impact Krissy would make on their lives, that was immediately dispelled by a bundle of perpetual motion, boundless energy and a sweet disposition belonging to a golden pony tail and two deep-blue eyes.

Krissy didn't just captivate her mother and grandparents; she literally and figuratively captured their attention, their love, and most certainly their hearts. Life was never the same at the McCray home, nor was it expected to change in the near future, at least not until Jerry Landis returned to claim his Katey and his unknown daughter.

The next three months whizzed by for Katey. True, she missed Jerry terribly, but his stream of letters, which often arrived in bundles, helped fill part of the void. And Krissy saw to it that her days were filled with joy and happiness. Only at night, when Krissy was safely put to bed, snuggled under her covers, did Katey face the loneliness of another night without her man, without his love. She thanked God for Krissy's presence, for filling her days and nights with needed love and attention. After her prayers, Katey would bank an extra pillow next to her and lay awake with her thoughts. Often she hugged it, and squeezed it, hoping that somehow it would help her get through another night. At those times, her body ached for his touch, and his words of love. She wondered where he was, what he was doing, and if he, too, was thinking of her at that exact moment. Tomorrow, maybe another letter would come telling her he was on his way home to her, to a simple ceremony, and to a proper, respectable life.

# Chapter Twenty-One

Aaron McCray was a man molded by hard times and circumstances. On a certain Wednesday night, he felt a renewed sense of pride in his family and their right to a reasonable life the minute Katey stepped off the plane holding her precious baby, his beautiful granddaughter.

He couldn't help but notice the contentment and happiness the wearing of a wedding band afforded Katey. Though he never asked a single question, he knew his daughter well. She was truly a married woman in all aspects of her life now, even to the point of changing her name to Landis. True, there remained the technicality of a proper marriage ceremony and a marriage license, but he reasoned that Jerry would no doubt change that situation the first chance he got stateside. He dismissed further thoughts of Katey submitting to pleasures of the flesh by virtue of the very thing that made it all possible. Their vows, and their spoken pledge before God that Katey most assuredly got from Jerry before he dared taking her to his bed.

Now to say that when Krissy entered the McCray household, things changed, would be the understatement of the 1950s. She immediately made an impact on all those around her, especially her grandfather, Aaron McCray. Anyone who was naïve or fool enough to dispute Krissy's legitimacy would bargain for much more than he was ever prepared to take on. He'd have to deal with one-hundred seventy pounds of rib-rock steel, which carried a bit of Irish brogue.

Every other Friday, Aaron and his maintenance crew stopped by McDougal's Bar and Grill to cash their checks.. This was the custom since Aaron made crew foreman, he always bought the first round of drinks. The second round was bought by one of his crewmembers. After that, each was on his own to leave or buy more drinks. Tonight it was Mike Stradsky's turn to buy the second round. When it came his turn, he conveniently excused himself, saying he'd be back just as soon as he visited Pa Jones to relieve himself.

Aaron's crew waited and waited, but Mike did not return. One of them cracked, "I know he's ducked out on the draft, and his country's responsibilities, but this is ridiculous! How long can a guy take to pee?"

Another chimed in, "He's probably in Canada by now! Didn't want to pay up!"

That brought out as gusty a roar from the bar patrons as McDougal himself, who was bartending, had ever heard.

Another crewmember added his two-bits. "I know, let's order another round and have McDougal present him with the bill! That'll get his goat, the cheapskate!"

Sure enough, that's exactly what happened. McDougal served everybody and left one extra tap beer on the bar for Mike's return. Everybody kept an eye peeled on the door to the men's can, waiting for it to open while thoroughly enjoying the ice-cold beer at Mike's expense.

Half of the crew had downed their second round when Mike finally showed up. McDougal presented the bar tab to Stradsky.

"What's this?" He objected. "I didn't order it!"

McDougal leaned over the bar and confronted his very unpopular customer. "Yes, ya did, we took a vote on it and ya lost! Pay up or get outta my bar and don't come back! My good friend Aaron and his crew have had a gut full of your kind. I hear ya run out of the draft and everything else. I don't need your kind takin' up space at my bar."

Mike steadfastly refused to pay. "I didn't order it, and I'm not paying!"

Aaron broke the standoff, he pointed to the stack of bills and loose change McDougal had laid on the counter next to his lunchbox. "Take it out'a my money, but give his drink to anybody else who wants it. Since he didn't order it, he shouldn't have to drink it!"

That brought down the house. Old customers and other bar patrons alike joined Aaron's crew in roasting poor Mike Stradsky.

Mike moved down to the end of the bar and finally ordered a beer. He sat alone, brooding over his beer, wishing there was some way, something he could do to even the score with the crew, most especially with Aaron McCray.

Mr. McCray finished up his second beer, opened up his lunchbox, and promptly put the stack of bills and loose change in it. He was ready to leave when McDougal interrupted him. "How's that granddaughter doin'?"

Aaron rested the lunchbox back on the counter. "Oh, she's a joy to behold I tell ya! Got the sweet face of an Irish angel and she's a good sleeper at night. Katey hardly has to be up with her at all. Mary says she's so easy to please in the daytime while Katey's at work. I've been blessed, aye, that I have.

"Do you have a picture of the wee tyke? I'd like to see for myself?"

The first mention of Aaron's granddaughter brought out a measure of pride in him unmatched anywhere; there'd be no sparing of words about his Krissy. Out came his billfold and he and McDougal did their own version of Krissy's heritage. "Now ya see, she's got the long blonde hair and prettiest dark blue eyes; from her father of course! But look at her McDougal, she's the spittin' image of my daughter, KateLynn and my wife, Mary. Can ya see which she's the closer to?"

McDougal studied the picture. "Hard to say, Aaron, but you're right, she's a McCray through and through, no doubt about that."

Aaron was so pleased and so proud to be talking about his granddaughter that he wasted no time passing Krissy's picture among his crew. Their fine comments were enough to pop the buttons off his church-going vest.

Then Mike got his hands on the photo. Aaron jumped him. "I'll thank you to hand my picture back; I'll not be needin' any comments from the likes of you."

Mike gloated and refused to hand the photo back. A dirty smirk filled his face. "She's a Mick all right, and a bastard at that!"

He turned to several customers and waived Krissy's photo in their faces. "Two weeks ago he told us his daughter's fiancé was in the Army, so that means she's not married. That also means she got herself knocked up! She loose as a goose!"

Aaron hit him hard enough to knock his head off. Mike picked himself off the floor, blood tricking down one side of his mouth. "Sure, Mick, hit a guy when he's not lookin', that's about your speed!"

Aaron stood next to him, fists clenched, daring him to make a move. "Go ahead, Mike, try me out. It'll be a long afternoon, I guarantee you that!"

McDougal stepped between them. "Hey, hey, you two! Not in here! Outside's the place to settle this! No damn sense wrecking my bar!"

They emptied McDougal's establishment in a minute flat, ready to see the fight, and most certainly ready to see blood spilled.

"I still say your daughter's a knock-up job and her kid's a bastard! A Mick bastard no less!"

They circled each other, the bar crowd in a frenzy, wanting to see the fight to the finish. Still Aaron hesitated. "Mike, I'll accept your apology. We'll go into the bar, I'll buy you a beer, and come Monday when you're back on my crew, we'll forget this ever happened. What say?"

"I say you're a coward!"

Mike got in two vicious chops to Aaron's jaw, dropping him to one knee. The bar crowd went wild. Aaron rose, steadied himself, and circled his opponent, waiting for his opportunity to do some real damage. The crowd drew in tighter, forcing the two fighters ever closer to each other. Mike, adrenalin pumping, figured he had the advantage, so he came straight at Aaron, swinging wildly to the head. Aaron, quick as a cat, sidestepped the charge and landed his first blow, a solid right to the pit of Mike's stomach. It was soft. He doubled over in pain, real pain, blood gushing from his mouth.

Again, they circled one another, Aaron instinctively measuring the distance to Mike's jaw with a couple of stiff left jabs to the face. Then two more feints, then one more sharp left jab to Mike's head to reconfirm his previous measurement. He was ready.

This time Aaron moved in. Mike tried to slow him down with a hard smash to the body. That's all he remembered. Two mighty blasts to the jaw rocked him hard; the third, like a hammer finished him off in mid-air as he went down. He lay unconscious in a bloody heap at the feet of his demolisher.

Aaron stood over him. One of his crew handed Aaron his lunchbox, then slapped him on the back and sarcastically cracked, "It couldn't have happened to a nicer fella. Betcha come Monday, you'll have a brand spankin' new summer replacement. Why are you stickin' around? He's still out cold, maybe for another couple minutes or so."

"He still owes my family an apology and I'm gonna stay right here til' I get it, or else continue the knuckle drill."

***

Mary was worried. Her husband was late, way late. Even on payday nights, she knew that her husband always drove their car to and from work to avoid waiting around for his crew to finish their drinks. No, something was wrong, very wrong, or else he would've telephoned. She tried to keep her thoughts to herself and not alarm Katey who was having a hard enough time settling Krissy down. Krissy was teething and running a slight temperature.

Mary rechecked the oven and turned down the heat even more as Katey appeared out of her bedroom holding Krissy. "She's still running a little fever, glad you telephoned me so I could pick up some of those teething rings at Holme's Drug, they really help cool her gums."

Katey's mother returned to her station at the kitchen window. "I remember when you were teethin,' boy what a time! We'd just moved into a rented house in Sacramento and a neighbor lady let me keep washcloths in the freezer part of her fridge. Two weeks later, your father spent all his paycheck on a new fridge. I made ice cubes and crushed them in washcloths and let you bite down on the cloths…worked pretty good too! Didn't have such things as teething rings then." She laughed. "That fridge took new groceries right off our table for two more weeks. We got by on jelly rolled up in pancakes three times a day 'til next payday."

Katey went to the fridge to get another teething ring. Krissy began fussing again. Katey inserted a fresh, cool ring, and began rocking her and humming. Ten minutes later, Krissy's eyelids began to close. Katey quietly returned to her bedroom to lay Krissy down once more. Five minutes later, she returned, leaving her door just slightly ajar.

The two women ate their supper, each trying to reassure the other that Mr. McCray was okay and would pop in any minute. "I almost started to lay down with Krissy in my bed, and then I got to thinking that's a bad move. When Jerry comes home from Korea, naturally we'll be sleeping together, and Krissy'd really scream her lungs out if she saw a strange man sleeping with her mommy."

Mary forgot about her husband for a minute. "Yes, I see your point…'course Jerry will only be home for a short time on leave to get married. Think Krissy will know who he is?"

"I've been working with her every day. Each night after I give her a bath, I point to his picture and say, Daddy. She's a smart little scamp.. Pretty soon she'll be saying Daddy and Grandpa and Grandma and pointing to everything and asking a million questions."

They heard the car door slam in the garage. Both women rushed to the front door. What they saw was hardly what they had expected. Aaron McCray stepped inside, and then tried to turn his face so his swollen cheek and jaw would be less noticeable. Mary spoke first. "Be quiet, Katey just put Krissy down. What in the world!" She went to her husband. He handed her his lunchbox. "Aaron McCray," she continued, "There'll be no supper 'til I get to the bottom of this. You've been at it! Let me see your knuckles!"

Almost sheepishly he turned both hands over so Mary could inspect. She gasped at his red, raw, bleeding knuckles. "Katey, go ahead to the bathroom and run some cold water in the sink. That'll stop the swelling."

"You better count the money in my lunchbox, Mother. Allow for two rounds instead of one. I didn't check it after the fight."

"I'll do that later when I've settled with you, Aaron McCray. You've got some explaining to do or there'll be heck to pay with me. Grown men fightin'!"

Mary doctored his bruised, swollen jaw and then concentrated on his hands. "There's some Epsom salt under the sink, Katey, see if you can reach it. It should help cut down some of the swellin'. Well Mr. McCray, we're waitin'!"

He turned first to Katey, then to his wife. "Shoulda' seen it comin' when he welched on buying the second round…"

"Who was it, Father?"

"Aw, Katey, 'twas that new fella, that summer help we put on. He's a loser if I ever saw one."

Mary took one fist, dried it off on a hand towel, then rubbed bag balm on it and wrapped a clean rag around it. Satisfied, she began on the second fist. "Now, Father, Katey and I have heard nothing 'bout the cause. Do I have to telephone McDougal to find out what happened or are you going to tell us?"

"Mrs. McCray, there was words said…bad words, words that ladies like you should never have to let pass your tender ears."

"What was said, Aaron McCray? We'll be the judge of how bad they was."

"It started when I showed Krissy's photo to McDougal. I'd mentioned several weeks ago in passin' that Jerry was Katey's intended and that he was fighting in Korea. This Mike, he's a draft dodger if I ever saw one! He put two and two together, called our Katey a loose woman. Then I grabs him and tells him nobody calls my daughter that and I'll be needin' an apology."

"Yes, go on, Aaron!"

"He refuses, then he calls our granddaughter…a…oh, I can't say it…"

"I'll say it for you, Father." Tears welled up in Katey's eyes, but she spit out the hard, dirty words anyway. "He said I got knocked up and he called little Krissy a bastard, didn't he?"

"KATEY!" Mary was shocked at her language.

"Lass, listen to me," her father continued. "Nobody has the right to say such names about my daughter or my granddaughter. I won't allow such filthy talk in my presence. No McCray will stand for such slander on our reputation."

Katey wept bitterly. "It's never gonna go away, is it? The names behind my back, the snickers, and the dirty jokes will go on 'til I'm properly married."

Mary shook her daughter hard. "Stop it, Katey! Stop it this second! You're doing the right thing. You're raising your baby and your Jerry will come back and he'll marry you and you'll be happy and you'll have a wonderful life together. You're so close to everything you two have worked at. Just a little longer and it'll work out, you'll see."

Katey took comfort in her mother's words, and her reassurance. "Please, Daddy, don't fight anymore over my reputation or Krissy's either. We'll manage 'til Jerry gets back."

Mary finished wrapping up Aaron's second knuckle. He took Katey in his arms. "I can't promise that, Katey. What kind of a father would let such things be said? I've never met a more responsible, Christian woman than you. You and Jerry will get properly married. Let me take care of the McCray name, because it deserves the honor and respect my two women have put into it."

Aaron McCray ate his supper while Katey fed Krissy. Then a very proud grandfather rocked his pride and joy while Katey ran the bathwater for Krissy. Mary brought Krissy in and set her down in the tub. Krissy cooed and played, splashing water all over her mother. The two women toweled her off. Katey rubbed baby oil on her, powdered her cute little bottom and got her ready for bed.

Katey hugged and kissed her daughter and laid her gently down in the crib. "I just love her, especially after a bath, she smells so fresh and sweet."

Krissy bit on her teething ring and soon fell fast asleep. "She's had a long hard day," Her grandmother observed. "Even when she's fussy, she's such a joy to have around."

They left Katey's bedroom door ajar, just in case. Both women finished up the supper dishes. Katey glanced out into the parlor and saw her father in his usual chair, pipe in his mouth, trying his best to hold up the newspaper between two bandaged hands. Mary saw Katey's concern and smiled. "Don't worry about your father. He'll be all right by Monday morning. I'll cut slits in his work gloves so he can slide his sore knuckles in."

"Wonder what the other fella looks like after seeing the way he worked poor Daddy over?"

Mary dried her hands on a hand towel by the kitchen sink. "You wouldn't want to see him, Katey, not after your father finished him off. No doubt he's counting his blessings that he's still able to breathe."

"Was Daddy a good fighter? You've never mentioned it before."

Mary could only nod her head in a most positive fashion. She smiled quietly to herself with a distant faraway look in her eyes. "Good? Aye Lass, he was far better than good. None of the locals could stay in the ring with him. He was a regular will-o-the-wisp, he was. Only a very few could ever lay a boxing glove on the man. Tough, and wiry, and strong he was. When he measured 'em for his right-hand hammer, down they went, most of 'em glad for the chance not to get back up 'cause they knew his hammer would put them down again."

"Did you see any of his fights?"

"Most of them. He was boxing when he started courting me. He was a five-village boxing champion until he traveled to Dublin to take on the Irish National Boxing Champ, Paddy O'Neill."

"Did you see that fight? How'd it turn out?"

"My father took me on the bus from our village to Dublin. It was a grand, but terrible brush with the truth."

"Tell me about it, please, Mother!"

"This is old history and your father'd not like me bringing this up he's such a proud man. Your father met his match in Paddy O'Neill. Both took a terrible beating. I got up before the fight was over, I'd seen enough. I waited for my father outside the building. They called it a draw – it was the only blemish on either your father's or Paddy's record. Paddy became a professional prize fighter in America and made a lot of money. However, your father told me later that Paddy fell in with crooked dealings. Some say the fights were fixed, I don't know. What I do know is that Paddy died years later from all the beatings he took in the ring. He died without a penny in his pocket."

"How come you never told me about this?"

"Because, Lass, after your father's face healed up so I could recognize him, he came courting again and I laid the law down. It was either the prize ring or me, but not both. I wanted him as my husband, not some leftover scrap of a man in bed with me at night who might not even remember his own name the next morning."

That night Aaron McCray rested his sore, tired bones in bed, glad to at last try to catch forty winks. To his consternation, Mary was wide awake and inquisitive. "Katey was worried about you, wondered if the other guy looked beat up too."

Aaron winced a bit as he tried to use his hands to raise himself. "It was terrible Mary, the way I fought tonight. Paddy O'Neill would've turned over in his grave at such an exhibition. My timing was way off, my stance was lousy, even had to measure him not once, but twice before I put him away. Thank God, the clod had a glass jaw and went down in a heap. He even got in two good licks on me before I remembered how to measure and get to him. In the old days, he'd have never laid a glove on me."

Mary smiled and pulled the top cover back. "Me thinks your timin's still great my love. Couldn't be any better, Aaron McCray."

"All right Lass, what's on your mind? 'Tis plain there'll be no sleep in this bedroom – not before you've had your say and your way."

Then he saw a now familiar glint come prancin' into her eyes and across her warm, sweet, caring face. "No, no my sweet, not tonight. Can't you see the discomfort I'm in? My hands aren't ready to hold you … I'm in no shape tonight."

"You're in better shape than you're puttin' on. I'm goin' to be in charge of what goes on behind our closed door tonight."

"Aye, Mary, ever since you returned from Chicago you've been a changed woman."

"Now lean forward so I can slip your nightgown off." She did the same with hers. "From now on we're gonna leave the light on while we enjoy our pleasure'in. Understood, Aaron McCray?"

"Aye, my love."

# Chapter Twenty-Two

The corporate headquarters building of the California Central Railroad (CCR) was an imposing eight-story structure of concrete, steel, and glass. Located in the city of Rushton, California, some fifteen miles east of Sacramento, it had been a landmark for better than fifty years. Though not a company town, this bustling community's merchants were still dependent upon the rise and fall of the CCR fortunes. Rushton was also fast becoming a "bedroom community," judging by the steady stream of traffic headed west each workday.

Katey's recent stint subbing for all eight corporate secretaries had paid dividends. Corporate management had taken note of her professional skills and rewarded her with a substantial merit raise and a new desk location on the fourth floor. This was referred to as the mid-management level. Imagine her great surprise when she was asked to interview for the Corporate Comptroller's private secretary position. She wondered if Stephen Carlson remembered her two week's work and was duly impressed by it. Enough so that it was the reason for the job interview.

Inside the comptroller's office, she was reintroduced to Stephen Carlson, a medium built man in his mid-fifties. He had a little paunch around the stomach, and his hair was starting to thin and gray. He seemed genuinely warm and friendly and tried to put Katey at ease. "Please sit down, Mrs. Landis. Take this chair in front of me. I want to get to know you better. You're my last candidate, Mrs. Landis, perhaps you know the other two. I believe they came from the same floor as you do. Ah, let me think a moment…Mrs. Woodson and a Mrs. Reiger. Do you know them by any chance?"

"Only by sight, their work stations are at the other end of the floor from where I work." Katey replied professionally.

Mr. Carlson picked up her file and glanced through it, taking time to reread several pages. He closed the file, looked up at Katey and smiled. "Excellent, excellent work record, and in such a short time, too…just over a year and you're already on the fourth floor. Well, like I told the other two ladies, the CCR is ready to reward those who have earned the right, too! I see by your file your nickname is Katey. May I call you Katey?"

"Mrs. Landis will do for now, Sir."

"I thought we could be a little more informal…but there's certainly nothing wrong with proper formality is there Mrs. Landis? Especially at first, right?"

Katey merely nodded. Carlson got up from his chair, he seemed more nervous than Katey for some strange reason. He obviously was taken by her attractiveness, and her young age, yet he appeared to be having trouble bridging the gap on where to make his pitch. He went over to a solid oak cabinet behind his desk. He fumbled with the key to the lock then remembered it was unlocked, and opened it. "Would you care for something from my private stock? Perhaps a brandy or a bit of wine?"

"No, thank you," she politely replied. "Outside of an occasional Irish coffee to toast a special event or celebration within my family, I see no need for nor do I use alcohol in my life. Maybe I shouldn't mention this, but I believe drinking during working hours is cause for immediate dismissal at CCR."

Carlson embellished his brandy to its fullest measure, holding its glass container high, letting it swish around a bit before taking a hefty snort. "Up here, Mrs. Landis, we make the rules for the peons down below to follow and obey. Company policy is for them, not for corporate management! We have better things to do with our time."

Katey felt an immediate resentment to Carlson's remark. She stiffened, but managed to act as normal as possible. "Just exactly what would be my duties if I were selected to the position as your personal secretary, Sir?"

Carlson put his brandy glass down on his desk, and then sat on the corner closest to Katey. "There are many perks, Mrs. Landis. For starters, you'll have a brand new leased Buick for your personal use, including a mileage and travel allowance. And,I will provide a most generous clothing allowance and, of course, a key to your own personal lounge, and rest facility for freshening up. There are only eight such positions, so we're very careful about just who we select. You are in effect, our personal ambassador to the outside business world, therefore, image is everything and we demand and expect you to do your utmost to maintain that image."

Katey had the definite feeling that more, much more was expected than what Carlson had alluded to. "What about salary, Sir, and are there other duties involved?"

"You get right to it, don't you, Mrs. Landis? Good! I like that! Shows you've done your homework! Your salary will double to start with, and I can be very generous in addition to that. Above this floor, on the eighth, the CCR maintains an elegant dining facility. In short, I deal in millions of dollars every day to get the very best interest rates for the CCR to meet its business and payroll obligations at critical times. Each year, I save millions by doing this, so I do as I please. My business luncheons are the key to CCR's financial success. My secretary is responsible for running these luncheons, including the handling of all the catering.

Occasionally you would have to meet some of my out-of-town VIPs at the Sacramento airport, and handle their accommodations. At my business luncheons, it will also be your job to take shorthand notes of important conversations with the reps and, of course, follow it up with the proper correspondence from my office. How's that for a job description? Are you up to such responsibility, Mrs. Landis?"

"Yes Sir, Mr. Carlson, I can do a much better than adequate job, I'm sure, once I learn the ropes."

"Good! Now don't take this wrong, it's meant as a compliment! With your attractiveness and your obvious secretarial skills, we'd make a pretty potent team don't you think?"

Katey felt on top of the world. Jerry would bust his buttons with pride when she wrote him about her big promotion. She had the definite feeling the job was hers if she played her cards right. "Thank you for the compliment, Mr. Carlson, it's been awhile since my husband's been around to say such nice things."

Carlson was pleased, oh so pleased with the interview's progress. He swished his brandy a bit, and then chuckled to himself, before downing it. Katey, eager to show her initiative, promptly surprised Carlson by taking his empty glass. She then went to his wet bar, opened it up, rinsed and dried the glass before returning it to the glass tray. Carlson was impressed. "You do know your way around, Mrs. Landis! Yes, yes, you're the right one for this position, no doubt about it!"

One thing still bothered Katey. "Mr. Carlson, when you mentioned salary, you also said you could be very generous in addition to that. Exactly what did you mean by that, Sir?"

He colored a second, and then matter-of-factly went about what was on his mind with no reservations whatsoever. "Mrs. Landis, I had hoped that with time, after you had a chance to get settled in, after you familiarized yourself with your responsibilities… What I meant to say was, in time I'd like us to be less formal with each other. There'll be situations that come up…I'd invite you out possibly for a bit to eat…a glass of wine, some good conversation over a delicious meal…you know… companionship."

"Continue, Mr. Carslon, let's hear the rest! All of it!"

Katey listened intently, not missing a single word, especially those words that dripped with seduction. He was too practiced and too polished. He left little doubt what he was leading up to without actually saying it in so many words. He finished up with an ending that really got to her-it outraged her. "Of course, Mrs. Landis, I assure you that should any intimacy between us occur it will be treated with the utmost discretion. And when your husband returns you'll be free to continue as you see fit. I won't hesitate to be very generous concerning your paycheck as long as our relationship continues."

Katey had never felt such anger before. Then it dawned on her, she'd been violated twice, and she'd let him get away with it until the full implication had sunk in. When she first sat down at the start of the interview, he'd mentally undressed her, he obviously liked what he saw, so he proceeded to make his pitch which ended with her being propositioned, no doubt about that.

She boiled over with outrage and indignation. "How dare you imply such a thing? Mr. Carlson, do I look or act like your mistress?"

He was shocked by her accusation. "Please, Mrs. Landis, I meant no such thing. Look, we're getting off on the wrong foot. You, you misread much more than was intended. I merely meant that since your husband is overseas and, and my wife is out of town a lot as our Red Cross Regional Director,that at this time in our lives we both could use some companionship. That's all! Nothing more!"

Katey got up from her chair, eyes burning with hatred. "Nothing more, Mr. Carlson? Nothing more! What you're talking about is my marriage. That part of my life means everything to me. My marriage won't be compromised nor can it be propositioned. It's too precious, too pure and far too good for such shenanigans. I won't ever allow any tampering with it whatsoever, YOU HEAR ME? NEVER!"

Carlson tried to defuse the confrontation. He stood in front of her waving both hands. "Mrs. Landis, please! Hysterics won't get either of us anywhere! Calm down, please!"

"I've only just begun," she shouted back, raising her voice. "My husband and my little girl are my life and my commitment to them, and to my God is untouchable! How dare you try to invade our sanctity with your dirty, sordid, lonely companionship bit!

"Are you through?" He questioned arrogantly.

"Not by a long shot! Yes, I'm lonely, but only for my husband and certainly not for any phony companionship scam! I was propositioned, and I don't like it one damned bit! The interview is over! Good day!"

Katey, still boiling mad, reached for the gold-plated doorknob on the thick mahogany door. Carlson called out after her. "Then I take it the answer is no?"

She wheeled around to give him one last parting shot. "You got that right, Mr.! That's about all you got right concerning me! Why don't you try interviewing mistresses who want to be daytime secretaries, instead of the other way around? Maybe you'll have better luck!"

All the way down to the fourth floor, her nerves were still on edge, so tight that her stomach churned. She felt nauseous under the kaleidoscope of high hopes, then disillusionment, followed by disgust at what Carlson had put her through. The elevator door opened and she marched straight down the hall toward her desk, oblivious that a middle-aged lady was trying desperately to get her attention. Katey was upset at herself too, for being so gullible when Carlson first sugarcoated the interview with all its perks, then smoothly changed gears on her and actually had her listening intently about how he intended to seduce her.

"Mrs. Landis, Mrs. Landis, please wait up!"

Suddenly Katey's mind registered back to reality, someone was chasing her and trying to get her attention. Almost out of breath, the lady finally got close enough to tug at her arm.

"Mad as a wet hen, aren't you? Had the same feeling myself when Carlson tried to undress me at my interview yesterday."

Katey stopped. "I'm sorry. You're Mrs. Woodson aren't you?"

The lady was plain looking, but neatly dressed in a simple business skirt with matching blouse. Her dark hair, though carefully kept, was hopelessly out of style compared with Katey's chic, short business woman's cut. She wore no make-up whatsoever; still she was handsome in her own way with a warm, friendly face to go with a most pleasant smile. "Yes, I am and if you've a minute or two, could we talk? I know you've just interviewed with Stephen Carlson."

Katey liked her. "I haven't had my coffee break this afternoon, let's hit the cafeteria, and see if we can find a couple of empty cups that need filling."

They hit it off remarkably well together, discovering that both had much in common, Mr. Carlson. Mrs. Woodson came directly to the point. "Did Carlson give you the grand tour, the elegant dining room and kitchen up on the eighth floor?"

Katey laughed, the first time since her interview. It felt good to replace her anger and hurt. "No, we never got that far, I cut him off long before that."

Mrs. Woodson smiled appreciatively at Katey's remark. "Good girl! Well, then I take it, he didn't get the opportunity to present you with your very own key to your personal lounge and rest facility!"

Both women had a good laugh. "By the way, my name is Mora, and I believe the women down around your work station call you Katey. May I?"

"Please do. You were saying…"

"You're the youngest by far, to be interviewed up in the ivory tower, so take that as a compliment. I was here fourteen years before I used that elevator. Anyway, had you seen your private restroom you'd have noticed a very, very comfortable lounge inside the inner room, next to your private dressing table and vanity. Katey, it's first class all the way, only that's where my close friend Angella met her Waterloo…there's where it happened…"

Katey saw Mora's brown eyes narrow; she set her jaw so tight her thin lips almost disappeared. "That's where it went on day after day…" Tears appeared. They were hard, hateful tears. "That's where he ruined my best friend and made a mockery out of her marriage."

Katey's hand touched Mora's. "I'm so sorry Mora, is there anything that can be done?"

"It's too late!" Mora dried her tears on a paper napkin. "Maybe I'd better back up…tell you why there's an opening in the first place. I'm sure Carlson never so much as gave a hint in that direction did he?"

"Come to think of it, I never asked, and he sure didn't volunteer any information."

"Of course not, the slime! Have you ever heard of a group of religious people called The Society of Friends?"

Katey thought hard for a few seconds longer. "Yes, but aren't they better known as Quakers? At least, I seem to recall it that way in school."

"That's us! That's what I am and that was what I thought Angella was. We do the Lord's work. We use no make-up, nor do we wear jewelry, only a plain wedding band is allowed. We hold that our body is private and shall not be displayed or exhibited in any manner that may draw sinful attention. That's why we dress simply and wear loose clothing."

"Okay, I understand now. What happened to Angella?"

Mora shook her head in dismay. "When Angella got the big promotion, I never saw a happier or more dedicated secretary. Then little by little, things changed. Twice I caught her wearing make-up, and she kept provocative, tight-fitting clothes in her private closet. She'd change into them after she left me down here. On Wednesday nights, we'd hold prayer meetings at each other's house. She quit attending after I jumped her about the liquor I smelled on her breath."

Katey took a sip and put down her cup. "I think I can pretty well guess the rest if you don't care to go on."

Mora stiffened even more.. "No, let me go on, I need to say it, and then I'll try to put it to rest. One night just before I cleaned off my desk to go home, Angella called me. She was in a panic, very frightened. Naturally, I rushed up to the seventh floor to see if I could help her, Carlson had violated her terribly. She was a mess. He'd left her there alone with her shame, too afraid to face her husband and their son and daughter. She said she was thinking about suicide. We prayed together. I cleaned her up and we went home to face her family and beg for forgiveness. I shall never forget the look on her husband's face when she broke down and admitted she had committed adultery. The children ran to their rooms to hide from hearing anymore of the sordid details. Miracle of miracles, her husband came forward, he loved her that much. He said he could forgive her if she promised to end her affair with Carlson and look for another job. She agreed and I left their home thinking their marriage could still be saved. I was never so wrong!"

"What happened? Why didn't Angella make the necessary changes to save her marriage?"

"I found out later she told Carlson what had happened. He was angry that she had confessed but promised not to become intimate with her again. Things seemed to return to normal with Angella, except her husband kept insisting she keep her promise to change jobs. Katey, that job with all its perks and prestige was like a drug to Angella. She refused to give it up! Little by little, she fell back into the same old alcohol habit and she drank heavily this time, much worse than before. Her husband came to me, begging, pleading with me to do something, anything to get her to think straight. Nobody could reason with her!"

Katey almost felt she didn't want to hear the ending. For Mora's sake, she said, "It hurts me terribly to hear about any marriage breaking up, and I don't even know your friend."

"One night I took the elevator to the seventh floor again to check on Angella. The door to Angella's dressing room was ajar, and you can't even imagine what I saw, it was horrible. So degrading, so disgusting that I telephoned the security people in the building, saying that I thought there was a break-in up on the seventh floor and they'd better investigate."

"Did they catch Carlson in the act?"

"No, the weasel had just left. They did find Angella entertaining a banker from Montreal. I guess Carlson had no objection to sharing her after he was through."

Katey was mad, fighting mad. "I hope they catch him with his pants down! It'll happen. He'll slip up someday and I hope I'm around to make the call!"

Mora reached out to Katey. They touched hands then hugged each other. "Katey, would it be all right if we became good friends? I could sure use one about now."

"I was just thinking the same thing."

After their hug, Katey went up to the coffee urn for a refill. She returned, deep in thought while she stirred her cup. "Mrs. Reiger, do you know her?"

"Only slightly. I understand she's a strong Catholic, has two sons in high school. Her husband was called back into the service from the reserves…he's a fighter pilot. She has their pictures on the file cabinet behind her desk. Just from the little things she's said, I gather his departure really hit her hard this time. I'm sure their marriage is rock solid…a very devoted couple from the way she talks. What's your point Katey?"

"Except for you, it makes sense! Carlson undoubtedly ran the files of acceptable candidates. The one thing Mrs. Reiger and I have in common is that we're both married and we're alone because our husbands are in the war. …We're lonely, and he's banking on the fact that one of us will slip. Can't see your connection though."

"No mystery Katey, he's got three of us in the same boat. I'm vulnerable too…my husband's dying of cancer at this very minute. We haven't been together as man and wife for over fifteen months and he knows that. I am lonely, so very lonely!"

Katey embraced Mora tightly. "Don't you dare give in, Mora Woodson! I'm here for you, anytime you need a friend or a shoulder to cry on, I'll be here for you."

"Thanks Katey, it's pretty darned comforting knowing you're in my corner."

Katey blinked several times, to clear the mist from her eyes. "My husband, Jerry, always said that about me too. He says he has to succeed, 'cause I won't let him fail."

They both had a good laugh. "You must know him well."

"Yes, we've known each other practically all our lives. He came from some pretty hard circumstances…no father, an alcoholic mother who abused him, drank up every cent he turned over to her…but he's a survivor, and has he ever got a streak of independence and pride and stubbornness in him. He's such a wonderful person, and the best possible husband I could possibly want."

"Just hearing you say that about him, fills my heart with hope. I'm sure by the way you talk, Katey, God plays an important part in your life. Is your husband a devout Christian?"

"Not yet. He does believe in the Ten Commandments though and their teachings, and someday soon, God will find him. And when that happens, Jerry will serve him just as I do."

"Beautiful! What wonderful thoughts from such a lovely young Christian lady. I have a small confession to make, Katey. Care to hear it?"

Both women pushed their coffee cups aside. Katey's attentive expression was better than a verbal yes.

"I usually get to work earlier than you do. While I'm here alone, wishing with all my heart and soul, that I had my own baby to care for. While you're at home caring for your own daughter, I'm here holding that picture of her close to my heart wishing that I'd listened to my husband. Sometimes…"

Katey could see why Mora stopped talking, her lips quivered, her voice trailed off, but she continued. "Sometimes, I look at your daughter's sweet face so long that I swear she's alive, that I can touch her long golden hair, that I have just combed it, and put on a fresh, clean, cotton dress, so I can put her down to play …" She could continue no more.

Katey's heart went out to her as she touched Mora's hands. "If you wanted a child that much, why didn't you?"

"My husband said the same thing. Before they started the radium treatment that made him sterile, he begged me to consider starting a family, while there was still time for him to father one. He's so young, barely in his forties. I was convinced he'd get better and recover and then we'd start our family…" She broke down, "I didn't want to listen. He was trying to tell me he was dying, that if he could father our child, although I'd be left alone, there'd always be a part of him and a part of me that would go on living. It would be our legacy."

Mora's sad revelation of what might have been tugged at Katey's heart strings. Two women dabbed at misty, watery eyes with hankies badly overworked. Finally, Katey dried her tears enough to speak. "I'm so glad I have Krissy. Like your husband said, no matter what happens to Jerry or me, there's a part of both of us that will go on to be our own sweet legacy of love. I thank my God each night for giving Krissy to us."

"What I'm trying to say, Katey, is don't get too wrapped up with things that seem so important that you forget about your own life. My husband taught the history of religion and theology at Sacramento State College while I worked here. We thought there'd always be plenty of time to live our own lives while we did God's work. We were wrong. Don't you and your husband, make the same mistake. Find out what you want out of life and do it!"

Katey's sad face turned positive. "My mother always said I was a dreamer, a planner and best of all, a doer! I don't imagine I'll be here long enough to get another chance, for another interview up on the seventh floor. But that's all right with me because I have better things to do with my life besides getting propositioned. When my husband returns from the Army, I'm going to help him finish getting his degree and then we are going to complete our family. He's always wanted a little boy. Our own son would mean so much to both of us."

"Good for you, Katey! You know what you want and knowing you now, I'm sure nothing will stop you from completing your family."

Katey looked at her wrist watch. "Oh, guess we'd better get back to our desks. I hope Mrs. Reiger sees through his little scheme and cuts him off where it hurts the most, right at the zipper in his pants."

Both women laughed heartily at Katey's remark. They bussed their trays and said their good-byes. Mora gave Katey a great big thumbs up with both hands. "Here's to you, Katey Landis, my new-found friend. May you protect your marriage and stay with God."

She returned Mora's compliment with her own brand of kindness. "This weekend, after you've visited your husband, why not swing by my home and hold Krissy on your lap? Sure beats holding Krissy's picture!"

Mora's eyes shone brighter than the first evening star of the day. "Oh Katey, you're the best! Now that's a proposition I could never turn down! See you this weekend!"

Katey arrived home that afternoon with mixed feelings. Pure unadulterated disgust and anger concerning her interview with Stephen Carlson, and a friendly warm feeling about Mrs. Mora Woodson. Maybe it was time to move forward, meet new people and establish new ties. Somehow, her old bunch, the Amigos, weren't filling the bill anymore. With Molly gone, and Greg practically out of the picture for now with his fraternity life on campus. That left only Ricco, whom she despised for the way he treated Molly. Only Greg had remained in contact, taking her out to lunch a couple of times, trying his best to remain the great communicator. He insisted that it was still his duty to keep tabs on the other Amigos. He also insisted, though jokingly, that once he became the CCR Headquarters Division Manager, his first official capacity in his new position would be to hire her as his private secretary. Both had a good laugh over this prospect, although Katey knew he did have connections with the railroad hierarchy, through his family, so in reality it could bear fruit, if she were still around.

# CHAPTER TWENTY-THREE

The first thing Katey did, after she parked the Chevrolet, was dash to the mailbox by the gate to see if Jerry had written. Her spirits dropped to zero, the mailbox was empty. Two weeks since his last letter. Inside, she set her briefcase on the kitchen table and immediately checked on Krissy, despite her mother's intervention.

"Krissy's napping. We had a long afternoon, having lunch and doing the groceries at Bettinger's, so it's to my bedroom where I've laid out your change on my bed. How, how was your day?"

Katey was down to her bra and panties. "Always those pretty black ones with the see-through lace, eh? I know ya got a drawer full!"

"You got that right, and they're only for Jerry's eyes, and his alone. Almost called you this afternoon, now I'm glad I didn't…it was one, big fizzle. I thought I had a chance to move up to the seventh floor with a big promotion and oodles of special privileges."

A soft, all-knowing smile crossed Mary's pleasant face. "Thought you were the first one, eh? No, my Katey, you're hardly the first, and certainly not the last to get propositioned. Puts me in mind of me own first little encounter it does…though it takes me back to a place and a time I always hated."

Katey laughed. "I know Mother, those beehives you and Dad lived in with Aunt Rose in Chicago. How come you never told me about it?"

Mary's eyes softened, and then teased a bit. "Well, now KateLynn McCray Landis, I saw no need to burden you with such details and if I told two things more about me private life, what'll me and Father Murphy have to talk about at my next confession? I'd be clean as a whistle!"

They both laughed. Mary opened up, "It was my first encounter, and it nearly broke up my marriage. After you were born, your father… well the truth of the matter is he avoided me like the plague. I was barely seventeen, knew nothing 'bout this making love business that you put me onto. I'd been to the free medical clinic above Kelsey Street, where the soup kitchen lines were half a mile long on good days. They'd checked me over, said I was fine. Lord, the last thing we needed was another baby, maybe that was why you're father was afraid to come near me now that I think on it…"

"Mother, you're off track. Tell me about the proposition!"

"No, I'm not Lass, you needed most of that detail. It's important to help you see it as it t'was. Like I said, your father wasn't showing me the slightest affection, I was miserable with nobody to talk to except Aunt Rose, and she had her own problems. And if the truth be told, if we had the passage money again, I would've begged your father to send me back to our village in Ireland. I missed my family and our way of life, poor that it was. Anyway, after working 'n cleaning 'n changing bed sheets at the hotel all day, I'd clean up and put on a fresh dress to try to look extra nice for your father when he'd come home dog-tired from all those long hours. Some nights he was so tired that he'd rest his head on the table and fall asleep while I was seein' to our supper."

"The proposition, Mother," came Katey's impatient plea.

"Down the hall, 'bout two doors away, a young couple, name of Mahoney moved in straight from Dublin. We hit it off like we'd known each other all our lives. She found work soon. Seems like the women could find work when there was none for the men. So, he got to hangin' around and before long we were good friends. Days passed, then it was weeks, then a couple of months, and your father hadn't made the slightest move in my direction. I had my figure back; I felt he could at least say something about that."

"Okay, I think I understand. Tell me about Mr. Mahoney."

"Like I said, something was missing…a kind word or two; a compliment…hadn't had one of those since I got pregnant with you. A touch from your father would've set my heart on fire. Instead we turned our backs to each other when we should've been holdin' each other tight."

Katey was growing frustrated at her mother's long winded story. "Mother, MR. Mahoney."

Mary ignored Katey's frustration and continued on. "He was a good talker, I'll give him that…always puttin' the right words in their proper places. First he came on with the compliments. Said I smelled better than a soft breeze off Gallway Bay. Oh, he was a charmer that one was. Then he talked about my hair. That was my first mistake. Suddenly, you woke up and I nursed you…of course, I kept me privacy with my back to him. While I nursed you, I made sure he saw my wedding band as much as possible, thinkin' that should remind both of us we were married and that would be the end of it. It wasn't. Letting him touch my hair gave him encouragement. And to make matters worse, I mentioned how lonely I was. Not a very smart thing to do, to say the least. I put you back in your crib right beside our cot and he slid his arms around me, expectin' I'm sure, there'd be no stoppin' him. He was going to have his way with me. You woke up and started crying. Thank the Lord you did, it brought me to my senses. I laid the best part of an Irish washerwoman's pride, my backhand across his cheekbone, raised a welt it did! Then I tore into him, telling him one more move and he'd find my shoe planted in his crotch lookin' for a big payday!"

"Good for you mother! You really had me worried!"

"Had you worried? Daughter, I was worried, plenty worried! I was thinkin' there'd be no stopping' him. Your cryin' was the best thing that could've happened Lass!"

"How'd you get rid of him?"

"I told him never to visit without my husband at home and his wife with him. Well Lass, that never came to pass and I'm all the better for it!"

"How did you act when Daddy came home that night?"

"It was divine guidance it 'twas, I'll swear to it! Your father, bless his soul, paid me my first compliment that night, said my figure would turn a man's head and that he wished he had the money to buy me a present or at least a new dress. Oh, Katey, I could tell he was up to something. I couldn't hardly wait to get undressed and turn out the light. I lay beside him all a'quiver, wantin' him like never before. Finally he came to me, said he couldn't stay away any longer. We held each other tight, and when I told him that I'd been to the free clinic and knew how to keep from getting pregnant, your father couldn't hardly wait, and for the first time in my life, I actually enjoyed it."

"Did you ever consider telling Daddy about Mr. Mahoney?"

"Before your father came home late that night, I mulled it over and over in my mind. Your father hadn't a pinch of fat on him anywhere, he was rock-solid! If he'd have found out, he would've beat Mr. Mahoney to death, I'm sure of it! No, says I, it's best I leave well enough alone. I didn't fancy taking you on a bus to visit your father in prison, 'cause that's the likely place he'd have ended up!"

"Mother, what if you hadn't stopped in time, then what?"

"Oh, Katey, I could never have faced your father, having done such a thing!"

Katey rinsed her cup out at the sink and set it back on the table. "I'm so glad you told me. I know I've said this, at least one hundred times before, but you're an amazing woman."

"Up 'til then I was only a married woman with a baby. Your father never finished his business with me that night, but it didn't matter, because he fell asleep in my arms. After that night, we had a marriage and I've been thankin' God ever since for me makin' the right decision."

Katey looked out the window expecting her father to step out from his carpool ride.

Mary turned down the oven after adding a little gravy to the pot roast. Katey double checked on Krissy and then got her highchair ready to feed her. "Think I'd better wake her up. She's usually awake by the time Grandpa gets here so they can go through their tickle-bug routine before supper. That always puts her in such a good mood."

Mary watched her daughter. "You're the best mother a baby could ever have. All she needs is her father and life would be pretty good wouldn't it?"

Katey stopped at the doorway leading to her bedroom and Krissy. "Yes, and that'll happen, Mother, it must. I'm going to make sure it does, propositions or not, I'll never let them get in my way…there's only been one man in my life, and like you, that's the way it's going to be. I'll have it no other way."

"That's my Katey."

"What if you had? With Mr. Mahoney, I mean?"

"I would've packed you up and left. There'd have been a note to your father on the table when he came home. I owed him that. If it had happened, the honor and respect between us would've been gone. There'd be no divorce, I wouldn't allow such a thing, but our marriage would've been over. I would've gone back to Ireland, I could never have faced your father again nor would I have wanted to."

***

Carlson's proposition incident was a closed chapter in Katey's life, or was it? Katey and Mora Woodson became good friends, each feeding off the other's need for friendship at this particular time in their lives. Sociable lunch breaks between the two were an accepted part of their daily work routine. One thing bothered them, Mrs. Reiger, who had accepted Carlson's offer. Both women wondered just how long it would be before certain telltale signs or actions took place up on the seventh floor.

Two weeks later, during lunch break, Mrs. Reiger finally brought her pretty little bottom back down on the fourth floor. Both Mora and Katey offered to help Mrs. Reiger pack her personal things in a heavy cardboard moving carton. Mrs. Reiger, a nice looking brunette in her early forties declined the offers. "Thanks you two, I'm glad there are no hard feelings because Stephen…er, Mr. Carlson picked me instead. He said I was the best qualified."

Katey bristled at her insinuation. "Oh really now!" Then she turned to Mora. "Aren't those the very same words he used in your interview? I know he used them in mine!"

Mora nodded in agreement. The last thing Mrs. Reiger did was pack the pictures of her husband and two boys. Then she turned to stoop over to lift the heavy carton up from the floor to the top of her old desk, where it would be picked up. Instantly, Katey and Mora saw a wet, dark stain appear on Mrs. Reiger's skirt between her buttocks. They exchanged knowing glances as Mrs. Reiger noticed their stares. Her face flushed to a dark, dark red. "Oh that," she said, "I spilled some salad dressing on my chair and sat on it before I noticed the accident. Stephen told me to keep an extra change from now on in my rest facility. It saves having to deal with embarrassing explanations. That's the first thing I'm gonna do tomorrow morning."

Katey had her nailed good. "Please leave your husband's picture and those of your two sons in the shipping carton, that's where they belong. Your marriage is over, Mrs. Reiger, and you, a strong Catholic! I thought sure you'd have told Carlson where he could go the first time he tried to proposition you. Just shows how wrong I was!"

Mrs. Reiger was angry and very upset at Katey's remarks. "Who made you my judge and jury anyway? Huh?"

Katey was more then up to the task. "You did, Mrs. Reiger, when it took you over two weeks to bring you down here long enough to finally do something that should've been done on your very first day. It sure shows how important your family must be to you and where your mind's been lately."

"You don't know anything about me! What gives you the right to say anything? You're just jealous 'cause I got the job!"

"Jealous? Hardly! Disappointed in you? Very!"

Finally she offered the lamest explanation either Mora or Katey had ever heard. "I told Donald not to leave me this time with two boys to raise like he did in Germany during the last war."

Mora interrupted, "You told me your husband had no choice, they needed fighter pilots so they reactivated his reserve unit, he had to go to Korea to fly again."

"How many years were you married?"

Mrs. Reiger did not like the tone of Katey's direct question. "You're talking like it's over…"

"Isn't it?" Katey snapped.

"I'll write him, explain that I was lonely and I'll promise it'll never happen again. He'll understand, he'll take me back, he'll want to save our marriage…he'll…"

"He'll do no such thing and you know it. Tell me, be honest now… how many times?"

Mrs. Reiger finally admitted, "Three…no, it was four times. One shouldn't really count, I don't count it. He made a mess all over me and didn't really get started."

Katey shook her head in disgust. "If you were truly sorry, how come it took you another three times to decide you'd made a terrible mistake?"

Katey never got an answer, yet she waited, just in case. Mrs. Reiger sat down. She looked like paste, the life gone from her face. She wept bitterly, blaming everything and everybody but herself. Katey and Mora turned to walk away. Mrs. Reiger called out. "Your husband's over there too, isn't he? How do you know he's been faithful? Maybe he's cheating on you right at this very minute! How can you be sure?"

Mora butted in. "Aren't you going to answer her? She's trying to soothe her own conscience, don't let her get away with that!"

Katey continued down the hall 'til she was out of hearing distance from a very distraught Mrs. Reiger. Mora stayed by her side. Finally Katey answered, "I didn't answer her because she doesn't deserve an answer and I'm not about to give her a second of satisfaction when it comes to discussing any marriage, particularly mine!"

That evening Katey mentioned that Mr.Carlson was up to his old tricks again with another woman from the same floor where she worked. However, Mora Woodson said she's been around long enough to say that most of the men on the CCR management team have families and care about their reputations just like we do.

Mary was less than convinced. "Katey, I'll still be willing to bet the next check you owe me for babysitting Krissy, that not a single one of those high mucky-mucks has ever really got acquainted with real sweat and toil. The kind that comes from the satisfaction of putting in a good, hard day's work. And for sure, I'd win my money if I could inspect their hands. There'd be no dirt under any fingernails, now would there be?"

Mary McCray's lunch bucket logic had its own way of putting things in their proper perspectives.

# CHAPTER TWENTY-FOUR

The Korean War was a strange kind of war from the onset. Originally called "United Nations Police Action," this war escalated into some of the most savage, intense battles ever recorded. In 1950, General Douglas Mac Arthur was placed in charge of an American-led coalition of UN forces. He masterminded a brilliant amphibious assault behind North Korean lines to score a major victory. Mac was bent on carrying the war all the way to the Manchurian border, if necessary, to secure total victory and peace.

Many in The United Nations feared that Russia would enter the war directly if Mac was allowed to continue his master plan. Behind – the – scene bickering and undue UN political pressure was brought to bear upon Washington. The end result: Mac was relieved of command in April, 1951.

The irony of ironies was that Russia's presence was already in North Korea. Russian-built MIG fighter jets, tanks, artillery pieces, along with an army of technical support personnel were firmly in-place before MacArthur was dismissed. Add in the thousands of "Chinese volunteers," and you had the ingredients for all-out war.

American troop morale sagged badly with MacArthur's departure. Everybody knew that victory was now out of the question and that new UN rules, regulations, constraints and limitations were the only way the war would be fought. One old battle scarred Infantry sergeant likened it to stepping into the ring with Joe Louis in his prime and then being told to deliver the "knockout punch" with both arms tied behind his back And from the UN came this collective political retort, "Damn the wounded, damn the dead! We're winning the war of containment! Isn't that enough?"

Now that the UN's drastic changes were in effect, the UN ground Commanders tried a new tactic, combine air reconnaissance with closely coordinated ground support to pick and choose where to attack. This "chessboard" approach met with disaster from the start. The minute US recon jets left the wild blue yonder; the North Korean Commanders immediately moved all soldiers, tanks and heavy armored equipment to new locations, which virtually rendered all recon photos useless.

To offset this move, the UN commanders put the US Signal Corps into a very risky business, that of being the frontline's eyes and ears. Numerous communication van crews were called upon to carry out this very dangerous and critical service. Often the crews of these vans found themselves setting up in "no-man's-land" that area between the UN and North Korean lines. To make matters worse, their CARRIER and ANTRAC equipment had to have direct line-of-sight in order to operate and send out their coded signals far to the rear. North Koreas' mountainous landscape added yet another obstacle for the van crews and their "wireless wonders" to overcome.

Sergeant Poolis turned to his new Corporal –in-charge, "Landis your codeword for today is 'BLUE ANGEL'. Lately the commies have been jamming our voice channels, so don't wait around one minute longer than you have to. Use your own judgment when to pull up stakes. Have La Plante keep your van's engine running at all times while you send the coordinates. I don't need to remind you that you are down to less than two weeks before you and your crew's rotation back to the USA, so be extra careful."

Poolis left in his jeep. Ten minutes later, Jerry's crew had their equipment humming once more sending out coded grid coordinates to US heavy artillery positions far to the rear.

Everything was under control, so Jerry slipped away from his van. With a pair of very strong binoculars in hand, he wanted to see for himself just how effective his new information really was. He didn't have long to wait. Thirty seconds later the valley across from him disappeared under an ear-shattering bombardment. He raced back to his van.

Suddenly the trees and the bluff above them disappeared under round after round of heavy commie shelling. Jerry barked, "GUN IT, LA PLANTE! We're cuttin' it too darned close!"

Down the goat trail that passed for their road they went as they approached the bombed out remnants of a village. Twice within the last twenty-four hours, the village had changed hands.

KABAAM! KABOOM!

Jerry looked out the side-view mirror. His generator disappeared into thin air in a power-ball of gas-fed flames and black belching smoke.

"STOP, LAPLANTE! STOP!" he screamed.

The communication van careened crazily as LaPlante slammed the brake pedal hard with both feet. "EVERYBODY OUT! TAKE COVER BEHIND THOSE BUILDINGS!"

Seconds later, five scared-to-death soldiers watched in horror as two Russian-built MIGs finished off their van in short order. One rocket tore a gaping hole in the side of their van. The gas tank exploded, sending flames skyward licking the metal sides and interiors of the truck. The force from the blast knocked the doors off the truck cab, pitching them laterally for one-hundred fifty feet into a pile of rubble next to one of the bombed-out buildings. Then as suddenly as the MIGs appeared, they left without so much as making a strafing pass or two at Jerry and his crew huddled behind a lone standing wall.

Jerry looked up and saw the reason for the MIGs sudden departure. Two American jets were hot on their heels, chasing them away. They watched in horror and awe as they were party to a do-or-die battle for air supremacy before their very own eyes. The dogfight lasted all of five minutes at most. Then one of the MIGs plummeted down, down, trailing thick black smoke until a fireball a quarter of a mile away settled the issue for now. The other Mig turned tail and disappeared to the north, no doubt reaching the no-combat - fly -zone and a safe sanctuary across the Yalu River.

Twenty minutes later, a new storm system rolled across the skies drenching the crew until they found shelter under a partial roof still supported on two sides by a combination of rubble accumulation and support posts sticking out of the pile. "At least, the rain dowsed the fire, that's in our favor," Jerry said, trying to make something positive out of a very scary, nerve-wracking predicament.

At sundown they heard a lone sound, a low drone type of hum. Everybody listened intently. "IT'S A JEEP!" shouted LaPlante. "I'd know that sound anytime!"

Sure enough it was their shepherd, Sergeant Poolis, looking for his small flock of lost sheep, trying to round them up for some more cold, World War II surplus C-Rations and another communication assignment in the morning.

One-hundred yards below the village outskirts, the road inclined sharply up, then leveled off to form part of the high bench land where the village proper began. Jerry's crew watched Poolis jockey his jeep for the final spurt up, he shifted gears down and floored the vehicle.

SWOOSH! BAAM! Poolis looked like a bronco rider being thrown off his mount at a rodeo. The jeep took a partial hit and flipped over sideways, catapulting Poolis into mid-air precariously, trying his level best to land away from the jeep. Five stunned soldiers waited for him to land. He did.

Poolis finally hobbled up to Jerry and his crew "Where are your peashooters? Those carbines you're supposed to sleep with at all times? How in "H" do you expect to protect yourselves? There's Commies all around!"

Jerry tried to answer for his crew. "Never had a chance, Sarge, we got hit by MIG rockets." He pointed toward the van. "That burned-out heap is all that remains. Our guns were inside."

"GUNS, SOLDIER? THE ARMY DOES'NT ISSUE GUNS! THEY GAVE YOU RIFLES! Will you never learn? Well, no great loss I guess. I never did understand it! You guys had M-1's all during basic, and what do they do? They issue slingshots and BB guns soon as you get over here! Now, that's some thinkin' isn't it? Damned Signal Corps brass had their heads up their butts, as usual!"

Benevedez volunteered his thought. "Guess they didn't want us to be confused with the dirt doggies…you know, the infantry!"

Poolis roared. "Believe me, Benevedez, there's no danger of that ever happening. One look at you intellectual misfits and we should all go home and forget about fightin' this war! Oh, excuse me, I forgot, this is supposed to be United Nations Police Action!"

Poolis got up from his perch on a pile of rubble and motioned for Jerry to accompany him. He was limping badly, so they didn't go far, just out of ear range. "Got any thoughts Landis? I'm just a dog-eared Infantryman, so you guys with all the smarts better come up with something or its curtains for all of us."

"It'll be dark soon, I was going to check the van over, see if anything's still operational."

"Good idea, then we'll know if there's a chance. Damned slim one at best, I imagine."

"I told the crew during the dogfight over our heads that maybe the American pilots reported our position after the MIGs knocked us out of commission. Help could be coming don't you think?"

He shook his head regretfully. "Naw, I'm your rescue, we never received any reports."

"After they miss you not returning, Sarge, won't they send somebody out to check?"

"Too late by that time, we'd be goners! I'm surprised they haven't sent a scouting party out by now to test our strength. When they find out we got nothin' but spit to throw back at 'em. Well, I don't need to draw pictures, do I, Landis?"

Jerry already knew how desperate their situation was, Poolis only confirmed it He decided to check over what was left of his van hoping that he'd find some part of it still operational. The smell of burned and melted plastic on metal nearly gagged him, but he continued his search. He removed much of the tangled debris which used to house the carrier racks,then concentrated on the voice channel bay. Five more minutes of gingerly removing scattered pieces of debris made his heart leap. It looked intact. He reported his finding to Poolis.

LaPlante and Heron were sent to remove two batteries, one from Poolis' Jeep and the other from the van's truck cab. When wired together, they would become their power supply for only a few fading minutes, their only chance to send out a voice call for help.

Poolis, Benevedez and Jerry worked feverishly on a partially burned coil of telephone cable that Jerry scrounged from the van. This would serve as their antenna once the outer insulation was stripped away. They were careful to leave enough of the insulated cable which would have to come in contact with the van.

It was decided that Dostalek had the best resonant voice, so he would man the headset when it came time to send out their last -gasp call for help.

It was also agreed that there'd be no trial transmission to check out the voice channel to see if it was working properly or not. That would drain valuable juice from the batteries, energy they could not afford to waste if there was any hope of calling for help.

Poolis and Jerry again conferred, agreeing that the sooner they tried to send their message out, the more time it might give the Army to respond. Both were convinced that in an hour or two at the most, it would be too late for them.

Knowing how active the North Korean troops were at night was also cause for considerable alarm. Poolis offered up his own analysis of their desperate situation. "They know we're here, but with their big push probably comin' in the morning, it's just possible mind you, that we're such poor pickin's that they don't want to waste the manpower to clean us out tonight. Any second thoughts, Landis? Anything you wish you could change?

"Yes, a couple things.I spent far too much time trying to do what others wanted me to. Didn't spend nearly enough time doing the things I wanted to."

Jerry took out his billfold and removed one of Katey's pictures. He found a stub of a pencil in another pocket. "I'm writing Katey's address and phone number on the back. If you make it through and I don't, I'd consider it a personal favor if you'd look her up."

Poolis borrowed Jerry's pencil and produced a snapshot of his wife, his only one. With some effort, he managed to hen scratch her address on the backside. They exchanged photos. "Likewise, Landis, I'd be obliged if you looked up my Mardella."

They shook on it. Then Poolis gathered Jerry's crew together. "Hey, it's time to put your affairs in order, or do whatever needs doing. You got five minutes!"

Poolis, Dostalak, Heron, and Benevedez knelt to pray, each in his own way. LaPlante, convinced Jerry was a non-believer, joined him. Jerry watched the four soldiers making their peace with their God. He was humbled and inspired by what he saw.

"Ya know, Jerry, they use their religion like a crutch. It's as bad as getting hooked on drugs." He slapped Jerry's back. "Once them churches and preachers get their meat hooks into ya it's all over, you've got no life of your own. They own ya! It's a weakness, just like alcohol or drugs! Right?"

Jerry turned angrily to LaPlante. "Wrong! It's their strength! It's the natural order of things between man and nature and nature to me is God! Katey, you were right! You said he'd pick his time and place with me and he has. It's now!"

Corporal Landis brushed LaPlante aside, leaving him to his own fate. Jerry found a place outside the remains of a crumbled wall and picked his spot to have his say. "Wished I'd have paid more attention to my Katey, but this'll have to do for now. I know You don't make deals, but if somehow You could find a way I'll make You this promise. I'll serve You the rest of my days! That's all I have to say. This is Corporal Gerald Landis signing off, dear God!"

Dostalak made his way to the burned out shell, the remains of the van. He plugged in his headset, blew his breath into the headset's microphone, nothing happened. He groped around behind the pile of mangled carrier bays and came up with the second headset. Again he tested it with his breath. Thumbs up! It worked!

Quickly, Poolis had the rest of the crew uncoil the stripped telephone cable. "We need something high to run this up on for maximum transmission strength, but what?"

Jerry heard Poolis' question and looked around. Nothing close by except the crumbled shells of the village for height, except an old snag that stood guard over the desperate scene like an avenging angel. Jerry pointed to it. "That snag, it's our only chance to get any decent height to send out our signal!"

Poolis hobbled over to the base of the tree that had already withstood the brunt of the battle two days before. Stubs protruded from its gnarled lower trunk where forty-eight hours ago, limbs with branches and leaves once thrived. At its very top, what was left was only the remnants of two limbs from which the antenna wire had to be hung in order that they might have any chance for rescue. He motioned for Jerry's crew to assemble around him.

He barked his order sarcastically. "Now, don't all volunteer at once, but I need one of you to shinny up to the top and hang our antenna cable. You all had pole climbin' experience in basic. Who's it gonna be?"

Heron backed away. "Not me, pole linemen don't live long up front. That's why the Army's always replacin' them. I'll bet there're half a dozen snipers just waitin' to pick off the first sucker who makes like a tree monkey!"

Poolis was disgusted. "Okay, you jokers, if I don't get a volunteer, I'll pick one!" None of the four showed any inclination to volunteer. Then Jerry grabbed the coil out of Poolis' hand. He tied the loose end around his belt and leaped up to the first lower limb stub. Poolis fed him the wire from the coil as he climbed higher and higher. "The rest of you brave souls get back," he ordered.

Benevedez, Heron and LaPlante wasted no time leaving Poolis and Jerry to hang the antenna wire. They crouched some one-hundred feet away, under a piece of overhang, part of a roof still attached to one of the buildings. Poolis called out. "LaPlante, you tell Dostalak to start when I give you the signal once the antenna is in place."

Three long anxious minutes passed, and no sniper fire, yet. Jerry reached the top of the tree, wrapped the end of the cable around it and looked down at Poolis. "Remember, you got Katey's address."

His words hardly reached Poolis' earlobes when the sky turned from night into day above Jerry's head. One, two, three, four, five flares rose up in the night, trailing a stream of sparks, smoke, and fire from enemy positions less than one mile away.

"FREEZE, LANDIS! FREEZE! DON'T MOVE A MUSCLE!'

Poolis gradually stepped back, until he too, rejoined the others in relative safety. The flares hung an eerie light into the sky, casting fleeting shadows here and there, sending down shivers, raising the hairs on the back of five soldiers' necks. Death was close, oh so close; they could almost feel its presence as the flares streamed and hovered.

"NOW,DOSTALEK! NOW!"

"BLUE ANGEL NEEDS WINGS! BLUE ANGEL NEEDS WINGS!"

Over and over Dostalak repeated those frantic words, their call for help. LaPlante left him to rejoin the others. Benevedez gave the sign of the cross and knelt.

None of the soldiers actually saw the blinding flash or the simultaneous explosion that shook everything and everybody for one-hundred feet in all directions. They were too busy trying to hug the ground to look up. When they did, the entire snag was gone except for ten feet of trunk, near the ground, that somehow survived. Up above it, nothing! Absolutely nothing!

Poolis was the first to his feet. He blinked once, twice, straining to see if anything of the top thirty feet of the snag or Landis remained in the fading light.

He shouted at the top of his lungs. "GO LOOK FOR LANDIS! HE'S OUT THERE SOMEWHERE!" Then he added a gut- wrenching second thought. "MAYBE THERE'S SOMETHING LEFT!"

# Chapter Twenty-Five

Day after day, Katey could only stand by to watch as death exacted its toll on Mora Woodson as surely as it did on her husband.

Yet she drew from Mora's inner strength, her faith in God, and her undying love for her husband though his time was fleeting. Often Katey privately prayed to let death claim Mora's husband silently in the night. Even she was sorely tested to understand when the dignity of life has long since departed, why there should remain any vestige of the human spirit.

The thought of dying bothered Katey considerably. Mora's situation only made Katey all the more aware of the precarious thread that separated life from death; especially on the battlefields of Korea where her Jerry might be having his own encounter with death.

Payday on Friday afternoon meant another wonderful weekend to be spent being a full-time mother to Krissy, more time to be with her family, and too much time on her hands to keep from worrying about Jerry. Even Katey's car seemed, in its metallic way, to sense this day was somehow different. Especially the way its master tromped down a bit harder on the gas pedal to get to the bank and home.

Katey made a beeline for the mailbox in the front yard. This time, she was more than rewarded for her effort; a big stack of letters from Jerry. "Oh thank God, he's writing, he's okay!" she murmured.

Mary met her excited daughter at the front door. "I'll take those my sweet, there's clothes to be changed, bills to be paid and it's my payday too! Then you can sit down and enjoy your letters 'til you've worn the words right off the pages."

"Mother!"

"Ah, ah, ah! Get to my bedroom, KateLynn, that's the proper place to start."

One hurried peek at Krissy and then the quickest change of clothes Mary's bedroom had seen in days, fourteen to be exact, the last time Katey had received a letter. Katey returned to the kitchen table, checkbook in hand. Mary held out her hand. "Let me be first in line, if you don't mind, Lass."

Katey wrote out Mary's check for the month's baby-sitting. "Mother, why don't you spend some of this? Buy something for yourself, maybe a new dress or take Dad out somewhere to have a good time. I know you're socking away every dollar; I saw the savings account book you keep separate for this money. What are you and Dad going to do with it?"

"That's none of your beeswax, Katey Landis! Your father'n me got special plans for it and that'll be the last word on that subject! Now get to the other bills and then you can read me Jerry's letters, the parts that are okay for proper repeatin', that aren't too personal, as you keep tellin' me."

With the bills out of the way, Katey started opening the letters, sorting out the earliest in order right up to the last one Jerry wrote. "I've saved every letter Jerry's written since his basic days at Camp San Luis Obispo. Someday when Krissy's old enough I may let her read a few of them, it'll help her to understand how much her Mommy and Daddy loved each other then, and do now."

She continued opening and sorting then she received a surprise. Her eyes went round as buttons, she was delighted. "Here's one from Molly, I'm going to read it first!"

She scanned the letter quickly, sorting out the highlights. "Molly's still on welfare, says jobs are hard to find that pay a decent wage. She misses her old typing pool job at CCR and wishes she was back there." Katey turned to the second page. "Oh look, Mother! A picture of her little boy taped to the page!"

Mary leaned over Katey's shoulder to see for herself. "Why, that's Ricco's baby or my name's not Mary McCray! Look at the curly black hair, the dark eyes and the skin. How could the lad not own up to such a thing, Katey? How?"

"You don't know Ricco like I do. The nerve of that man to dare hint Molly was ever involved with someone else! It's his baby, no doubt about it!"

"Does she say what his name is?" Mary questioned.

"Let me read on." Katey continued with her cursory look. "Yep, here it is! She named him Ricky, but she calls him Little Ricco, and that's just what he is. Oh, she's written her phone number, and wants me to visit her as soon as possible! Think I'll call her up this weekend and tell her I'm coming down to see her next weekend. I sure do miss her, and boy, do we ever have a great deal of catchin' up to do!"

Mary popped a turkey breast into the oven while Katey continued reading Jerry's letter. "Does he say anything about the food and such over there?"

Katey scanned ahead. "No, not so far, oh, wait, here in this letter! Let's see, yep, he says tell Mom and Dad he's living the Life of Riley, three squares a day, plenty of hot water to shower in, clean fatigues to wear, and way too much sleep."

Katey put down his letter and stopped reading. Mary saw her eyes mist up. "What's the matter? Isn't that what you wanted, him bein' away from all that fightin'?"

"Jerry Landis, wait'll I get my hands on you! Living the Life of Riley, huh? When he was home on leave I tried to get him to tell me about his job in the Army. He kept putting me off, saying he'll be way back from the front lines, not to worry. Well, PFC Landis, I've got a news flash for you, I know what's goin' on! I talked to a signal corps vet who just got discharged and returned to work at the railroad. He told me Jerry's with a mobile communication unit. They're always on the run, and half the time they're out in no-man's land between the enemy lines with their cannons, planes and snipers, and our own lines to the rear. This ex-G.I. also told me, Jerry's lucky if he ever sees a hot meal or takes a shower, or has a clean pair of fatigues! That's how it is, Landis, isn't it? You bet I know!"

"Katey, Katey, calm down! Jerry's just tryin' to keep you from worryin' so much. He thinks he's doin' the right thing smoothin' over a wee bit of the hard truth."

Katey started to break down. "Oh, Mother, he's right up there, right where I don't want him to be." She tried to check her tears.

Mary tried to get Katey to see the bright side. "Lass, you're getting letters, you're hearin' from him, he's all right! As long as the letters keep comin,' he'll be comin' home to you. Read another, maybe there's better news!"

Katey went on to another letter. She got excited, and then her excitement trailed off, badly.

"Why, what is it Katey? You were happy, now you're not."

"He just got another stripe, he's a corporal now! Says he took a tech sarge's place, I know what that means, somebody in his outfit isn't coming back home. So they put Jerry in charge, says he's got a four-man crew under him now. Oh yes, he goes on to say, 'Katey, don't rush to the bank to cash in my big promotion just yet. You know the Army, my new stripe will probably get moldy before the paperwork catches up. Anyway, it'll mean a few more bucks in the Landis kitty for you and Krissy.'"

Mary went to the refrigerator to set out the bread and butter. "If Jerry got a promotion, and you said he took this other soldier's place, how come he doesn't have the same rank as that other fella?"

"You mean how come he's not a tech sergeant? It's what Jerry calls time-in-grade. Since he was drafted, he doesn't get the same chance at promotion that the regular soldiers get because he won't be in the Army long enough. So, when this tech sergeant was killed, Jerry stepped up to take his place, but doesn't get his rank or pay. He did get one more stripe along with the responsibility of the tech sarge's job."

"Your father'd never go for that, if you can do the job, you should get the pay too!"

Katey agreed. "I know, but that's the way the Army works if you're a draftee."

Both women set about getting supper underway. Katey helped peel the carrots and potatoes and checked on the turkey. She then tip-toed back to her bedroom to double-check on Krissy. Satisfied that Krissy was still asleep, it was time to read Jerry's last letter. "She's stirring a bit, seems to know Grandpa will be getting home soon. I'd better get through this one before she wakes up."

Mary poured both a cup of coffee and sat down beside Katey. "Don't let me forget tomorrow when we're shoppin' to get Krissy a baby stroller. Should have enough S&H Green Stamp books to pay for it by now. She's getting too big to pack around much longer."

"Aye, Lass, we'll put those stamps to good use. Now on with your letter! You're barely readin' a third of each, they're so full of them 'personal things' as you call it. Couldn't ya spare a few lines for my benefit? I'll not tell Jerry, I promise."

Katey opened Jerry's last letter. She turned to the second page and read aloud. "Katey, my Darling, when I get back, I plan on spending a lot of time filling your love tank, I only hope you're up to it. When Krissy's safely snuggled in bed, that's when I want you, that's when we need each other the most. And that's when I want to hold you tight. I hope you'll help me show you how much I want to give you my love, all of it, until your love tank can hold no more. Next, we'll kiss goodnight. Then you'll turn and snuggle up against me and I'll whisper sweet dreams in your ear, and you'll hear the words you day will always start and end with, I love you!"

Mary touched Katey's hand. The emotion wrought from reading Jerry's words was overwhelming. "Katey, Katey, never have I heard such words, such pure, sweet words of love. You and Jerry do have a special bond between you, such love, such feeling. Thanks for sharin' those thoughts! But tell me, what is the meanin' of this 'love tank' as he calls it?"

"Motherrr! I'm not about to tell you, it's a very personal thing between Jerry and me, and it will be the rest of lives. I'm sure if you put your mind and a little imagination to work, you'll come up with the answer."

They drank their coffee as Katey reread Jerry's last letter. Halfway down the last page, her eyes opened wide, and she let out a small, stifled squeal. She rushed to the calendar and began counting. "He's a short-timer! He's a short-timer! He's coming home soon! He's going to call me from Japan!"

Mary rushed to the calendar to join Katey. "When, Lass? When?"

"Get my letter, please, Mother, I want to make sure!"

Mary handed Katey the letter. Katey was so excited she could hardly count the days. "Let's see, from the date of his letter, he says he has only thirty days to go and that was over two weeks ago. That leaves only two more weeks! TWO MORE WEEKS! Mother, just think! He'll be safe in Japan and on the way home! Oh, I'm so excited. I can hardly wait for his call! Wonder if he's thought about the time change? Oh, I don't care if it's four o'clock in the morning, JUST SO HE CALLS ME! When he does, we'll get out Dad's Irish whisky and we'll have a real Irish cup of coffee, right?"

Mary could hardly keep from sharing Katey's excitement. They hugged and danced around the kitchen in front of the calendar next to the refrigerator. "Oh, Katey, what good news! Wait'll I tell your father tonight. He's been a bit worried about Jerry lately. Said to me, 'now don't you let on I'm worried. Katey doesn't need that, she needs all the love and help we can give her 'till he gets back safe at home'."

Near exhausted, the two women somehow found their chairs again. Katey's feelings and emotions were still a mile high. "I'm going to say one, no, make that two extra prayers each night for Jerry until he's back in my arms again."

Mary turned to look at the calendar, then back to Katey. "And to think not so long ago I saw you in your bedroom, tears streakin' down without end, tearing up your calendar into a thousand tiny bits, you said you'd never trust a calendar again. All it did was LIE! LIE! LIE! Look at you now; it's your best friend!"

Mary's observation brought Katey back to reality. "Yes, I said that and boy was I ever wrong! Now I have Krissy and I've had Jerry's love and very soon I'll have both. Oh, I feel so good, I could kiss that calendar!"

"Mommy! Mommy! Mommy!"

"You better save those kisses for your daughter, she's wide awake!"

Both women went to Katey's bedroom. There she was, standing up in her crib, waiting for Katey to pick her up. "Oh my sweet precious little one, Mommy loves you so much." Katey held her close and kissed her cheeks and hugged her tight. "She's such a warm little sleeper. Good thing Grandma only used one blanket. Krissy, listen to Mommy! Do you have to go potty? Go potty, Krissy?"

"Um huh, Mommy."

"I'll check supper," said Mary, "while you tend to Krissy's potty training."

When Krissy was through, Katey hugged her again. "Oh you did good Krissy, Mommy's so proud of you." Krissy turned around on the potty insert to point to the flush handle behind her.

"You want to flush it, right, Krissy? Here, let me wipe you, and then Mommy will help you pull the handle."

Krissy clapped her tiny hands in wild anticipation. "Pease, Mommy, pease!"

Mary rejoined them just as Krissy, with Katey's help, pulled down on the handle. Katey lifted the training insert off the toilet seat so Krissy could watch the swirling water disappear. She was totally fascinated, squealing with glee and clapping her tiny hands. "No more diapers, Mother! The training panties work great! Even with an accident or two, Krissy seems to know the difference." Katey carried her daughter back to her bedroom to finish dressing her. "Hand me the baby oil, please, Mother."

Krissy cooed and squealed while Katey rubbed the oil over all her body. "Oh you smell so fresh and sweet."

Mary hovered over the two, totally immersed with pride. Katey sat Krissy up on her lap and slipped a cotton undershirt over her head. Next she put on a clean pair of training panties. Krissy rolled her dark blue eyes from side to side, "Mommy, where's Gammpa?"

Katey started combing and brushing out her long pony tail. "Grandpa will be here soon, so let's put a pretty bow in your hair for Grandpa to see. Okay, Krissy?"

"Okay, Mommy."

Katey turned to her mother. "Did you hear that, she said 'okay' perfectly!"

"Katey darling, she'll be jabberin' a blue-streak before long and then will the questions come hot 'n heavy, eh?"

"Mother, hand me Jerry's picture, please!"

Mary took an eight by ten photo of Jerry off Katey's vanity and handed it to her daughter. Katey then let Krissy hold it. "Who's that, Krissy? Krissy, do you know who that is?"

Krissy studied the picture, and then turned to her mother. "Dah dee!"

Katey hugged her. "Oh Krissy, you do know! You're right, that's your daddy!" She turned to Mary. "I've only been working with her for two weeks now, and she remembers. She's such a smarty pants, she'll have no problem recognizing him when he steps off that plane."

Krissy's mother finished brushing and combing her ponytail.

"Oh what beautiful golden hair she has Katey." Mary happily replied.

Katey finished attaching a big, beautiful blue bow at the beginning of the ponytail. "Think I'll leave her hair this way 'til she's old enough to decide on her own. Sit still, Krissy, stop being such a wiggle-worm while Mommy slips your play clothes on."

Mary beamed again with pride. "You've a natural way with her. It's easy to see why you're such a good mother. Your father keeps saying the same thing too, Lass."

Katey was pleased by Mary's compliment. She kissed Krissy, then finished buttoning her shirt and gave her patched jeans an extra tug to make sure they were pulled up properly. "Okay snicklefritz, Mommy gets to nuzzle you two times before she puts your shoes on. Gimme an ear!"

Krissy's eyes lit up like a new set of Christmas lights. She moved her head a bit toward Katey's nose, as Katey went to work, nuzzling her hard under each ear lobe. Krissy squealed and howled in pure delight over Katey's affectionate display.

"No wonder the poor little thing's a mess of giggles and squeals the way you and Grandpa work her over. Never have I seen such shenanigans pulled off in the name of love!"

Katey rose up. "Just wait 'til Grandpa goes into his tickle-bug routine. Poor Krissy doesn't stand a chance!"

Katey finished putting on Krissy's shoes, and the threesome headed for the kitchen. Mary went to the laundry room and brought out a big cardboard box filled with old pots and pans. She took Krissy from Katey's arms and set her down smack dab in the middle of the box. "She's the easiest baby to entertain I've ever seen. We bought her a box filled with brand new toys that she never plays with, 'til Grandpa spent two dollars at St. Vincent de Paul's on this beat-up junk, and look at her take to it! Grandpa says it's the best two dollars he's ever spent!"

Katey watched Krissy at play for a minute, and then helped Mary make the gravy. "Those patched knees on that pair won't last much longer, but look at the money we've saved buying used jeans and shirts.

Next month, the Landis budget will have to spring for more patched jeans and play-shirts, she's growing like a weed!"

Mary started stirring the gravy. "Katey let your father'n me buy you more play clothes tomorrow at St. Vincent's. You father's told me time and time again, anything our Krissy needs, she's to get."

Katey hugged her mother. "Thanks, but the Landis' have to pay their own way. Jerry'd have a conniption fit if he knew how much you and Dad have done for Krissy and me already. No, we'll wait 'til he's home on leave in the next few weeks, then we'll do the shopping together. He needs to see for himself where the Landis dollars go. Come to think of it, I'll have to send him plane fare when he gets stateside again. I can hardly wait to go down to Western Union to wire him that money!"

Mary turned the burner under the gravy down to simmer. "Have you given any thought about sleepin' arrangements when Jerry's home next time? After you stop by Father Murphy's, of course!"

Katey thought for a minute. "Jerry and I will certainly need some privacy. I don't think Krissy should be in the same room with us. But she's always been sleeping next to my bed and I don't like the idea of moving her crib out of my room, even for a few days while Jerry's home on leave. If she wakes up and I'm not there, what then?"

"I'll let you think on that a spell. Meantime, can't you just see the look on his face when he really sees his own daughter for the very first time? Oh, what a glorious sight to behold! A father holdin' his very own flesh and blood! Oh, Katey, I get goose-pimples just thinkin' 'bout it!"

"That's goose-bumps Mother, not pimples! Anyway, you're right, no more deception! Thank God! I'm not cut out for this big lie stuff. Never was, never will be! All I want is for him to know the truth and then we can get on with our lives as God intended."

"You'll not be takin' Krissy and leavin' us?"

"No Mother, not 'til he's completely discharged from the Army and we live on campus at college while he finishes his degree in accounting. Anyway, I'm sure by then you'll be more than a little glad to be rid of Krissy and me, so you two can get on with your own lives."

"Get on with our lives you say! Katey, when your father steps through that front door and sets his lunch bucket down, that's when we get on with our lives! Have you not seen the pages of our kitchen calendar march back a full five years by the look on his face when he kneels down and calls out for his little Irish leprechaun to come runnin' to him? And have you not noticed his pace has quickened a step or two when he carries his grandchild to her highchair at our supper table? Oh Katey, our Krissy has brought new sunshine into our lives, and your father'll have it no other way. Of course, I haven't begun to tell you what having me own granddaughter has meant to me! When you were a wee babe, we had no money, aye, we were poorer than a field mouse looking for crumbs in a church! Now that we've saved a dollar or two, let us spoil our grandchild with the money we only wished we had when you were Krissy's age."

All three women heard the sound of a car door slamming. Krissy got so excited. Katey rushed over to lift her out of the cardboard box. Her feet were pedaling in mid-air, in perpetual motion, as she waited to see her grandpa open the front room door.

"Gammpa! Gammpa!" she screamed out, as Katey finally put her down.

Aaron McCray set his lunch bucket down. He kneeled quickly, and opened both arms up wide. "Where's my leprechaun, my blond Irish leprechaun? Where's my Krissy?"

Krissy started running toward her grandfather. "Watch her! Watch her!" shouted Mary, "She's goin' too fast! Catch her, Grandpa!"

Mr. McCray crawled on his hands and knees toward Krissy. Just in the nick of time, he scooped her up safely in his arms. "See," Katey remarked, "her shoes are too tight! First stop tomorrow is new shoes at Penney's."

"Grandpa, take that smelly old pipe out of your shirt pocket, it's the first thing she wants to play with." Mary turned away, clucking. "I tell ya Katey, when them two gets together, they're thicker than thieves, that they are! Never seen the beat of it! We do all the carin' and all the work, and she drops us like we're lower than kitchen help! There's another tomboy in the makin' in the house of McCray, that's what it is! And we're expected to stand by and let it happen?"

Katey joked, "Do we really have a choice?"

The two women busied themselves with the last-minute supper preparations while Grandpa McCray thoroughly entertained his granddaughter sitting on his lap, rocking her slowly to and fro while pretending to read the evening paper. Krissy would see a picture or advertisement drawing and point to it. "What's 'at, Gammpa?" He'd answer as best he could, then turn another page and Krissy would promptly point and ask again. They played out their game, this bonding of grandfather to granddaughter until it became their ritual, each and every evening. And God forbid anybody or anything that dared have the audacity to interrupt!

The turkey was on the table, sliced and ready to serve, Krissy's plastic food ring was filled with piping hot water to keep her cut-up food warm. Mary half-coughed to catch her husband's attention. He looked up and turned to the last page. "Well, Krissy, this is it, the last page. Maybe we should get washed up so Grandma and Mommy can feed us supper."

They rocked a few seconds longer, waiting for Krissy to ask. She did. "Peease, Gammpa, tickee-bug peease?"

Mary smiled and looked at Katey. "Why does she always say that? She knows for certain what Grandpa's going to do, yet she always says, 'please Grandpa, let the tickle-bug get me'!"

Katey could only fold her arms and wait for their final game of play to begin. Grandpa McCray picked up the paper, and pretended to look hard. "Nope, Krissy, I don't see a darned tickle-bug anywhere." He shook the paper. "None here, that's for sure! Didn't see any fall out, did you?"

Krissy shook her ponytail as if to say no, she hadn't spotted one either. Then she pointed toward the stack of newspapers on the nightstand beside them. "Gammpa! Tickee-bug, see!"

Aaron McCray squinted real hard at the stack. "By George, I believe you're right! Must've slipped in with my lunch bucket. Boy, have you got good eyes, I missed him!"

Krissy scrunched her eyes real tight, and then screamed a little, waiting for the tickle-bug to pounce on her. Nothing happened, so she kept a tiny hand over one eye while she dared to peek for the tickle-bug with the other eye. Grandpa McCray had his forefinger poised on the stack of papers, ready to leap upon his prey at an instant's notice. He waved the forefinger back and forth, like an antenna, homing in on its target, namely Krissy's ribs. "Oh, oh! Look out Krissy! I think he's spotted you. Look out!"

With one exaggerated leap, the forefinger found its target; Krissy's ribs. She screamed with wild delight as the tickle-bug showed no mercy, making sure every funny-bone in her body was thoroughly worked over. She hugged her grandpa for dear life, eyes closed as tight as possible, letting the tickle-bug work her over, while squealing and screaming at the top of her lungs.

"Mr. McCray," Mary cautioned, "you keep that up and the neighbors will have the cops knockin' at our door, wonderin' who's bein' murdered!"

"All right you two, break it up," laughed Katey, thoroughly enjoying the mock-attack, "time to wash up for supper!"

Grandpa carried his granddaughter to the highchair where he deposited her into Katey's capable hands. Katey immediately put a big plastic bib over Krissy, then clicked the tray shut and moved the highchair closer to her place. Next, she produced a washcloth to wipe Krissy's face and hands. By this time, her grandpa had returned from washing his hands. He said grace and Katey began feeding Krissy mashed potatoes with gravy. Then she cut up the carrots and meat into tiny bits. "Remind me, Mother to look for one of those baby spoons with the big round handle tomorrow at the five-and-dime. Krissy's going to start feeding herself, she's ready."

Katey finished feeding Krissy, wiped her face again and set her down in her box of pots and pans to play. She returned to the table to eat her supper

"Jerry's going to be one pleased and proud father when he sees what a fine job you've done with Krissy's raisin', Lass." Aaron proudly stated.

Katey took her father's compliment in stride. "Thanks Dad, but I'll feel a whole lot better when Jerry's here beside Krissy and me, helping to feed her too. I take pictures of her all the time, to send to Jerry and for Krissy's scrapbook, but there's nothing like being here to see for yourself."

"Aye, KateLynn, aye! No truer words were ever spoken. Is he comin' home soon, I hope?"

Katey was all smiles as she triumphantly announced to her father, "Yes, in a couple weeks. I got five letters from him today. He's going to call me from Japan to let me know the exact date so I will know what Army post he'll be stationed at to finish out his time in the States. I've checked our bank account, and there's enough money to pay for a couple leaves without too big a dent in it. He'll have quite a bit of leave time coming and we'll want to be together as much as possible."

"Katey, let us help when the time comes. You two need to spend time together, and he needs to see his daughter. Married people shouldn't be separated like you two are. You're missing out on family life. It's what marriage is all about."

"I know Dad, I know! Tell that to the U.S. Army! Back in basic, Jerry wrote that the Army told him they came first and your wife or dependents came second. I guess that's a pretty good reason why I and the Army would never get along. Anyway, thanks for offering to help, but if Jerry found out you paid for his ticket, he'd hitch-hike home instead, he's so darned proud and independent. It's Jerry's way and mine too, after he comes home."

# CHAPTER TWENTY-SIX

Mr. McCray retired to this favorite chair to enjoy his pipe and the newspaper, Krissy continued stacking and re-stacking her pots and pans. The two women worked side by side, doing the supper dishes. "We're so proud of you two, but your father and me will feel a whole lot better when you and Jerry pay a visit to see Father Murphy. That weighs on our minds, Katey. Surely, you can understand that, your vows to the Church need to be said as soon as possible, the first chance he has when he gets back!"

"Don't worry Mother. We'll take care of that the day he gets here, because we both want to be together as husband and wife again, and we know that's the proper thing to do. We've tasted love and now we know we've already missed far too many nights without being in each other's arms. Jerry's letters all say the same thing, nothing, not even the Army is going to stop us this time."

"Aye Lass, and nothin' will from this day forward." Mary happily sighed.

They were about through with the dishes when Mary stared out the kitchen window.

Katey continued putting the dishes away until she noticed her mother's gaze. "What is it Mother? Why are you staring?"

"Oh, 'tis nothing, I'm sure."

"What do you see?"

"There's a station-wagon driving around, passed our place once already, must be lost. They probably can't find the right home. Well, what do you know, they're comin' into our driveway!" She dried her hands on her apron and spoke to her husband. "Grandpa, there's a strange car in our driveway. Got a Red Cross on the door, they must be lost. You tend to 'em, while Katey and I put away the dishes."

Katey and Mary turned their attention to putting away the last few dishes while Aaron went to the front door. He conversed with the woman, and then walked back to the kitchen. Mary saw him first. He was visibly shaken. She'd never seen him so white in the face, the life drained from his cheeks. "What is it, Mr. McCray? You look like you've shook hands with a ghost! Are you all right?

Katey turned around at her mother's words. She held the last two supper plates in her hand. "Daddy, what's the matter? Are you sick?"

Twice he tried to talk, but the words wouldn't come. Finally he blurted them out. "Katey! Katey, there's bad news! BAD NEWS! IT'S JERRY!"

The two plates hit the floor, and Katey called out in anguish."NO, NO! Please dear GOD! Not my Jerry!"

Mary grabbed Katey as she slumped to the floor. Krissy saw what happened and screamed. "Grandpa, quick! Grab Krissy! She's cryin'! She's afraid! She knows something is wrong! Hurry!"

The Red Cross lady and Mary tried to revive Katey while Aaron McCray did his best to calm Krissy down. Finally, Katey responded to the damp cloth pressed to her forehead by her mother. "Katey! Katey Landis, can you hear me?"

At first there was no response, no indication of a clear mind whatsoever. Then the eyes blinked and focused, some of the color came back in her face. "Yes, I can hear you."

"Your husband's been wounded very seriously. He's still alive, but barely."

Mary shook Katey. "Listen, Katey, he's not dead yet! He's still alive!"

The two women helped Katey sag into a chair at the kitchen table. Mary turned to her husband. "Take Krissy into her bedroom, she shouldn't see her mother like this!"

Mr. McCray took Krissy to the bedroom.

The Red Cross lady held Katey's hands. "Mrs. Landis, your husband left Japan, he's on his way to a special Army hospital near Seattle, Washington. There he will get the best possible medical help the Army can give him. He's asked for you, that's why I'm here."

"Do you know what happened?"

"No, Mrs. Landis, the only thing I have is this radio-telegram asking for the Red Cross's help to notify and coordinate all travel arrangements for you."

"What do you mean?"

The lady patted Katey's hands. "Your husband's still alive, so don't give up hope, there's still a chance. There's a flight leaving Sacramento in about an hour, I have already made your reservation. You should arrive about the time your husband's military air ambulance touches down at Madagan General Hospital near Ft. Lewis, Washington. When you arrive at Seattle-Tacoma International Airport, Mrs. Graham, our Red Cross representative, will meet you there and escort you to Madagan. You have about fifteen minutes to pack, I suggest you start immediately." She looked at Mary, "Can you give her a hand with the packing? Figure on taking enough clothes for two weeks minimum!

Mrs. Landis, your being there can make a big difference; it can mean the difference between life and death!"

Mr. McCray calmed Krissy down to the point where he was able to take her back out of Katey's bedroom so the packing could get under way. Katey was still in shock, she sat on the edge of her bed while Mary started in. Finally out of desperation, Mary shook her, shook her hard. "Katey, get a hold of yourself! You're a lot stronger than you think! There'll be no shirking your duty, ya hear me? Now, tell me what outfits you're taking?"

Still numb from shock, Katey finally groped around, barely managing to make heads or tails out of Mary's packing efforts.Mary closed the suitcase. They both looked around the room to see if she'd forgotten anything major. Satisfied she hadn't, Mary thrust Katey's rosary beads into her purse, along with her checkbook. "When you get up there, you call us as soon as you know anything! Don't worry what time it is, JUST CALL! Now don't you even give one fret about Krissy, she'll be fine. You need all your thoughts up there where they'll do the most good."

Katey hugged her parents and started out the door with the Red Cross lady, not wanting to alarm Krissy any further. Outside the front door, Mary caught up to her. "You must tell Jerry about Krissy, he mustn't die without knowing. God would never forgive you, and neither will you! If he lives, that could just make the difference!"

The flight to the Seattle was a nightmare in slow motion. Somehow, some way, Katey felt detached from the trauma that nearly suffocated her; she felt like a third party, a person watching from above, having no earthly connection to the life and death drama she was nearly drowning in. Events flashed through her mind. Mindless events she hadn't thought of in years, yet they now seemed so important, though she didn't know how or why. She squeezed her rosary beads tight, until they left deep indents in her fingers, but nothing made sense, even her prayers were disjointed and jumbled. Twice during the trip, she found herself in the restroom, though she couldn't remember opening the door. She was a lady lost in time. A warp of everything that had once mattered to her, but somehow had gotten displaced. In short, she was out of sync with her own life.

Only when the wheels of the prop jet touched down on the tarmac did she regain her touch with reality and the reason she traveled to the Pacific Northwest, Jerry Landis. Barely two sentences were exchanged between Mrs. Graham, the Red Cross rep, and Katey as she found herself being whisked down the highway toward Madagan Hospital. In her mind, it was still incomprehensible that two planes, each with different missions, could somehow bring together two people who had been thousands of miles apart, under life and death circumstances. Yet that was exactly what was happening and each was powerless to do anything about it but live out the drama that had been dropped upon them.

When Katey saw the military policeman standing at the guard gate checking IDs and passes, she made the connection of why she was there and why her world came crashing down around her. Stark reality seized her, shaking emotions to their very roots. She sobbed out, "Jerry, Jerry, please don't leave me! Please, please, dear God, be merciful!"

Mrs. Graham said nothing, for there was nothing to say, Katey had said it all.

Suddenly, she was escorted down one long, antiseptic-laden hall, cloaking its reason for being, to thwart death if possible, to prolong life if medical science can be allowed to have its way for today.

Her escort, Mrs. Graham, said a hasty good-by and Katey found herself alone outside a room with simple black letters: Preparation Room B. The swinging door opened and there stood a doctor with a major's insignia on his shoulder. He appeared to be all business as he shook

Katey's hand. "Mrs. Landis, thank you for coming, I'm Major Novak, I'll be assisting Major Greenspan in surgery in a very few minutes."

"Where's my husband?"

"He's in this prep room; they're getting him ready now. Please pay very close attention to what I'm going to say. Your husband is in very serious condition. I've just gone over his medical records and the x-rays that were shipped with him from Korea and Japan. The reason he's here is that we, that is the Army, felt he had a better chance of surviving if we could get him to a specialist. It's touch and go now, since it's been almost twenty-four hours. After that, chances are almost impossible to save his type of injury."

"What happened? Why is he in such serious condition?"

"I don't have all the facts, but I can tell you he's lost an awful lot of blood. There's very serious internal bleeding and his left leg is shattered badly. We'll try to save it if we can, no promises, you understand. His back is ripped open, shell fragments are lodged deep near the spine. The x-rays don't always show the full extent of the damage and we don't have time to wait. We must operate as soon as possible if there's any hope of saving him."

"What do you want me to do, Major?"

"Above all, STAY CALM! That's a tall order, but you must do it! He's drifting in and out of consciousness and that's where you come in. You can be a big help, your being here could make the difference!"

"How?"

"Mrs. Landis, your perfume! I can smell it, it's very sensual! DROWN YOURSELF IN IT! Put it on your hands, anything that stimulates his senses. He needs to know you're here beside him, supporting him in every way. Speak to him, touch him, and tell him he's going to make it! YOU MUST BE POSITIVE, no matter what you see, smell, or hear inside that room! It's imperative you do that. Many times critically injured soldiers do respond, it can make a difference, IT CAN SAVE HIS LIFE!"

Major Novak caught the signal from one of the corpsmen, a colored man who got his attention by tapping on the small window in the swinging door.

"The prep is done on your husband, he's on a clean gurney, and we're ready to operate. When you follow me, think of only one thing, a positive meeting with your husband, stimulate him in any way that you can and don't forget the extra perfume!"

Katey opened her purse and poured her lilac-scented perfume over her fingers and hands. Major Novak waited only a few seconds. "Okay, follow me!"

He pushed on the swinging doors and Katey entered a world completely foreign to her in every aspect. There on a gurney lay Jerry, more dead than alive, with an army of people hovering around him. There were blinding lights, a maze of tubes, wires and bags on portable stands. Everybody seemed to be talking at once; it was controlled bedlam. Katey wasn't even sure they were speaking English, their words and phrases sounded so strange. "Here, here, Mrs. Landis, come over here!"

She recognized the colored corpsman who motioned her to Jerry's side. Somehow, she managed to slip between most of the tubes and wires to be at his side. She hardly recognized him. He looked so pale, so drained of life. She tried to kiss him on the cheek and discovered two week's worth of beard got in her way."JERRY DO YOU HEAR ME? IT'S KATEY! I'm by your side, and you're going to be all right. I love you!"

There was no initial response. Katey grabbed his loose hand and kissed it. "JERRY, WAKE UP! IT'S KATEY! I'm here! I'll be here! Do you hear me?"

He stirred, his eyes fluttered then opened, he tried to move his lips; she was sure he smelled the perfume. "Perfume…Katey,…that you?"

"Yes, my Love, I'm here, you're going to make it! HANG ON, JERRY!"

His eyes closed again. He tried to speak, but Katey could only see his lips part.

Major Novak stepped back into the prep room from the operating room. "We're ready! Move him!"

Katey held on to his hand as the crew wheeled him toward the operating room.

"Katey?"

He was alert and awake. "Yes, Jerry, I'm here beside you."

"What color?"

Katey smiled, oh, did she ever smile! "Your favorite, black with lots of see-through lace."

They neared the door. Katey was still alongside the gurney. One last chance. "KRISSY IS OURS, JERRY! SHE'S YOUR DAUGHTER!"

They rolled him on into the operating room. Katey had no way of knowing if he heard her last words. At long last, she felt a tremendous load had been lifted from her shoulders and off her heart. She told herself she'd done the right thing. If knowing Krissy was their baby daughter would help make the difference, then so be it! She was prepared to face the consequences of living the big deception if and when Jerry was able to confront her. She left the operating room to walk back thru the prep room on her way out to the lobby. Then she spotted the blood-stained gurney Jerry had lain on only a couple of minutes ago. She saw how thoroughly it was soaked, even a pool of blood was under one wheel and more blood was dripping down the metal tubing on one side. It was a ghastly sight! A wave of nausea swept over her, that and the Prep Room smell got to her, penetrating the thick fragrance of her own perfume.

"Quick, Mrs. Landis, over here!"

The colored corpsman helped her to the restroom. Katey barely made it, her stomach wrenched and revolted as she dropped to her knees and clung to the stool with every ounce of strength within her.

He knocked and opened the door, handing her a small paper cup. "Here, rinse your mouth out, you'll be all right."

She gratefully accepted the cup. "Thanks, I sure needed something!"

He waited outside the restroom. Five minutes later, Katey appeared, looking and feeling much better. "You were pretty green around the gills," he said, "but you hung on while you were by your husband's side. I think you did make a difference!"

His words made a big impression on Katey. "I hope so, Mr.."

"Corporal Booker T Thompson, First-Class Medical Corpsman, at your service, Mrs. Landis. People just call me Booker T!"

"Thank you, Booker T, for all your kindness, I'm pretty lost around here."

"Most of the wives are that we see here. There's a small waiting room to your right as you left the prep room.. There's coffee and blankets, and let's hope it's going to be a long night. I'll show you, if you like."

"Okay, lead the way."

Booker T escorted Katey to the waiting room. She was very anxious and concerned. "Any idea how long my husband will be in there?"

"Hard to say, he has multiple injuries, could be hours before you get any word, or it could be over very soon. That is if he doesn't make it."

"Will they tell me either way?"

"Yes, Major Novak will let you know, either way."

Katey started to settle in, and then changed her mind. "Booker T, is there a church near here?"

"I noticed you almost dropped your rosary beads out of your purse when you were hurrying to dab on the extra perfume." He pointed to his right. "There's a chapel down this hallway, then turn right, you'll see the sign, can't miss it!"

"Thanks again. I need to spend some time alone," softly Katey replied.

"With your God? Most of the wives do, seems to help them put in the long waits. It's the short waits I can never get used to, and I've been doin' this 'bout two years now."

"Where are you from?"

"Alabama, Ma'am. When I finish up my enlistment, I'm goin back home and back to college on the G.I. Bill. I was the first to graduate high school and now I'll be the first in my family to go to college. I gotta get back, just in case we get another plane, an air ambulance case from Korea."

"Do you get many here at Madagan?"

"War must be slowin' down over there, 'cause we only had two tonight, your husband and another soldier, an infantryman. You'll probably meet his wife. She's down at the chapel right now. I hope you have a long, long wait, 'cause that usually means good news."

Katey located the chapel and opened the door. Three steps inside she was engulfed by a certain quietness that helped still her emotion-racked body and soul. There came over her a calmness, a special feeling she could impart to her Maker in this, her hour of greatest need and distress. She knelt in a pew at the back of the chapel and rested her head on her forearm against the back of the next row ahead. She took out her rosary beads, but made no effort to count or pray, opting instead to close her eyes. She stayed in this tranquil repose for some time until she was aware she was not alone. A slight noise to her immediate left told her someone else had dire need of the same Master's help. She rose up slightly and let her eyes grow accustomed to the subdued lighting the chapel offered.

She heard the muffled sounds of someone crying, and then all was quite once more. Then it all came to her, the pieces of her life passed before her mind in perspective. What seemed but a short, few hours ago as unbelievable and unacceptable, now for some strange reason was totally relevant. Try as she might she had no tears to give, but she felt her body spasm as though she had already been consumed by non-stop anguish and pain 'til her tear ducts ran dry.

Katey sat back up on the bench seat beneath her and softly whispered aloud, "Please dear Lord, hear my prayer. Deliver my husband from his death bed and breathe life into his body so that we may find life again as husband and wife, so that I may not weep alone. I now understand the true nature of life and that death is an extension of that life. My husband has not tasted the full measure of our life together. And I ask that you spare him from death at this time so that we may celebrate our love as you intended it to be."

Katey looked at her beads, and then kissed them in spiritual ritual, before rising to leave. At the door she heard a warm pleasant voice call out to her. "That was a beautiful prayer. I wish I had your communication with God, but I can't seem to find the right words. I am bitter in the house of my God."

The woman rose from her bench. Even in the dim light Katey could see she was approximately her age but was a full five inches taller, and wore loose fitting clothes. She was obviously pregnant. "We could talk outside, back in the waiting room, maybe that would help both of us."

Katey's offer was snapped up in a second. "Oh, thank God, someone to talk to! Someone who knows what it's all about, this fighting and dying. Someone who's left alone to face death as I have to. My name's Paula Meyers and you are?"

They shook hands. "Katey Landis. Let's go get a cup of coffee and keep each other company. I hope we both have a long, long night ahead."

They sat in the waiting room, just down the hall from the two emergency operating rooms, two women thrown together, one bitter with the lot in life she'd drawn. The other, just as upset and unnerved, but willing to vent her fears and feelings in a more positive approach, through her abiding faith in God.

Paula spoke first. "If someone had told me twenty-four hours ago that I'd be in Washington State waiting in an Army hospital to find out if my husband will live or die, I'd have said he was nuts!"

Katey echoed her thoughts. "That goes double for me! I'd just finished feeding my baby daughter and was helping my mother do the supper dishes, and then everything changed. My world came crashing down. I'm still having a hard time accepting this, yet I know it's real, OH GOD IS IT EVER REAL! I'll never forget the look on my husband's face and all that blood! HIS BLOOD!"

"Let's change subjects! I've seen enough of my husband's torn guts and blood too, to last a lifetime! I'm from a small farm town in north eastern South Dakota, it's called Leola! If you can't speak German or Russian, you don't belong there. Especially on a Saturday night, when all the farmers and their families bring in their cream cans and use the cream-check money to buy their groceries, bib overalls and more work shoes."

Katey's smile escalated into a full-blown laugh; oh, it felt good to laugh again. "I'll bet the next thing you're gonna tell me is that nobody locks their doors."

Paula was surprised at her new friend's astuteness. "We don't! Can't remember my folks ever locking anything up! Not even sure if there are any keys around!" She put down her cup and observed Katey very carefully, trying to determine just how far she wanted their conversation to go.

Katey too, had a similar feeling. "Have you known your husband long?"

"Long? If you mean all our young years, my answer is yes. We grew up neighbors. Back in South Dakota, neighbors can mean anything from five miles to fifteen miles apart; heck, there are more people around Seattle than in our whole state put together. How about you? Where are you from and when did you first meet your husband?"

"I'm from a suburb east of Sacramento, California, guess you'd call it a commute town. The California Central Railroad has its headquarters there, that's where I work. Oh, oh, that reminds me! I'd better notify them I'm up here in Seattle on an emergency!"

"My Red Cross volunteer drove all the way up from Aberdeen to get me; when you tack on the twelve miles from town each way that's over seventy miles to the nearest airport. I'm surprised she didn't tell you they'd notify your employer. I bet they said something. You probably don't remember."

"You're probably right. I was in so much shock I don't really remember much about anything 'til we drove by that MP at the gate. That got my attention, I'll tell you! About my husband Jerry, we weren't neighbors like you and your husband, but we've known each other since the first grade. We went all the way through high school together."

Paula walked over to the coffee urn, started to refill then changed her mind. "Katey, you mentioned feeding your baby daughter, then doing dishes when the bad news arrived. I don't mean to pry, but unless your husband is a career soldier, and I'm guessing he's not. How is it that you're married, have a daughter, and yet your husband, you called him Jerry, how did he wind up drafted in the Army and then here?"

Katey didn't color at all at Paula's question or suggestion. "It's a very personal thing, and I don't think it's any of your business."

"I'm sorry, please, I didn't mean to offend."

"No, no, you had every right to wonder. It's just that it's a complicated situation. I wouldn't feel right talking about it."

"Do you happen to have a picture of your daughter, Katey?"

That overcame the small hurdle between them. Katey promptly produced her billfold and the latest photo of Krissy. "Oh, she's adorable. Look at all that blonde hair! And those deep blue eyes! What's her name?"

Katey's pride welled up. "Kristianne Marie Landis is her name, but we all call her Krissy."

Paula returned the snapshot to Katey. "What a pretty name! I can see by the way you talk about her, she's somebody pretty special in your life."

For the first time Katey showed some emotion. "She is. She's the only baby I'll ever have and I'm not even sure her daddy knows he's her father." The tears finally came. "I'm afraid I've waited too long to tell him until tonight."

That drew them together. They were strangers no more as Paula tried to console Katey.

"I kinda thought as much." Then she looked down at her stomach. "My Paul knows about our coming baby, boy does he ever! That's a long story too!"

Katey wiped her tears away and put her handkerchief back in her purse. "Well, Paula Meyers, I can't sleep, and I'm sure you feel exactly the same way, so what will we talk about to pass the time?"

"I'll go first. Maybe later, you'll feel more like telling me a little about your Jerry and your life. C'mon Katey, what's the harm? First, let me make a guess about your life and you don't have to respond if you don't feel like it. From what I saw in the chapel, you take your religion very personal and very serious and your husband has to be the only man in your life. I don't know how you got pregnant, but I'd be willing to bet anybody that he never could talk you into making love unless you wanted it that way. That's the part I don't understand! Katey, the way you carry yourself, you're a very private person. Everything about you says perfection, everything in its proper place or it's no go."

Katey was astonished by Paula's remarks. "Maybe you're in the wrong profession, Paula Mayers, have you given any serious thought to fortune telling?"

Paula laughed, she knew she'd hit Katey's nail right on the head. "Up until today, there're only two people I could predict anything about, myself and my Paul. And now I wonder if he even has any kind of future.""

Katey could see the hurt, the resentment building in Paula again. She tried to switch subjects. "Your life back in South Dakota sounds so different than anything I know about, can you tell me something about what it's like?"

Paula stood up, stretched, and then sat down next to Katey again. "What it's like, Katey? Let's see, where's a good place to start so maybe, just maybe, you can understand? Three generations ago, my grandparents and my husband's grandparents came from Germany. When they arrived in the US, they got as far west a Minneapolis. There they heard about homestead land in South Dakota. Both families settled around Leola because the land reminded them of their old country. Many immigrants changed or Americanized their last names, as did the Meyers family. My grandfather did not, my maiden name was Schumacher. How much more German can you get than that?"

"My parents came from a small village in Ireland and they have kept their customs and traditions, and of course, the Catholic faith. Even my real first name is KateLynn, which is old country, not Katey."

"Traditions? Customs? That leads me right into the mess I'm in tonight."

"I don't understand, how can those traditions of three generations ago affect what has happened here tonight with your husband?"

"Katey, when I say our German traditions brought me here tonight, believe me, they did! To this very day, my grandparents and my parents always speak German at home, and God help you if you didn't follow that custom. Now we're getting to another tradition that they insist on keeping, that of the first-born son. He's expected to continue farming on the homestead, when the parents retire, and God help him if he had other ideas. Can you see where I'm headed?"

"Yes, kind of. What happens if that doesn't work out that way?"

"Now you get to my Paul's problem. He was the youngest son, fourth in line, and he would never get that chance to farm his own land or show those other German hardheads who called themselves farmers what he could do."

Katey got up to take her turn at stretching. "I get the picture, Paula. My Jerry had a lot of proving to do as far as my folks were concerned. On our Senior Prom night, my dad took Jerry out to the garage, kicked the tires, and really read him the riot act on what it was going to take if he ever planned on marrying me. Jerry said he never wanted another session with my father again. He was a changed man from that night on!"

"How about me giving a little more background, Katey? In the early days, we harvested our grain the old-fashioned way. The grain had to be cut, bundled into shocks, and then hauled by teams of horse-drawn wagons to a stationary threshing machine. That all changed in the Forties. Huge machines called combines which were self-propelled did all the harvesting in one simple operation. They saved countless hours, days and even weeks. The one big drawback, they cost more than a single farmer could afford. They were used by crews who contracted out to grain farmers all the way from Texas to Alberta, Canada. Paul suggested that his dad, my dad, and two other neighbors do the same thing, pool their money together to buy one combine. After they finished harvesting their own fields, follow the Texas combines into North Dakota and Canada, and contract out to the farmers up there."

"What happened?"

"My dad and two other neighbors followed his suggestion, and my dad's made money ever since. Paul's dad wanted nothing to do with such a crazy idea. He scolded his own son, and told him if he ever came up with another crazy idea like that, he'd kick Paul off the farm."

"Wow, what did Paul do?"

"Paul joined the FFA in high school, but unlike the other boys and girls who raised pigs, calves, or sheep as their project, he wrote to the state agriculture college in Brookings. He gathered every bulletin, every piece of information and literature about soil conservation he could get his hands on. By his senior year, he had a library better than any farmer around. He knew how he was going to make money, lots of money when he had his own farm."

"I can already see what happened as far as his father was concerned."

"You got it, Katey! No beef to raise or sell for high school clothing money like all the other kids did, including me. Paul's father was so angry because he didn't make any money that he kicked him off the home place. Paul finished out his last two years of high school living at our place and working as our hired hand. Now comes the real problem."

"I've got a pretty strong hunch what happened next."

"Katey, your guess is partly right. When Paul was eighteen and I was sixteen, we got involved. My mother walked in on us one day while we were making love. My mother had a cow, over what happened! The legal age of consent in our state is eighteen. I was still a minor. My mother wanted to press statutory rape charges on him, have him sent to prison. Lucky for me and Paul, my father sided with us. He took Paul aside and Paul convinced him that his intentions toward me were strictly honorable. So they agreed that until I was of legal age, no dates, no nothing in exchange for not pressing charges. Dad and Paul fixed up a part of our cow barn for his living quarters until he finished high school. Then he had to leave our farm and live on his own. I was allowed only to take his meals to him, no staying and no conversations once I brought out his tray of food."

"So what did you do?"

"Well, if you're a German farmer's daughter in South Dakota, you have three choices when you're eighteen and graduate high school. You marry another German farm boy, you go to the Normal in Aberdeen to get a teaching certificate so you can teach in a country school, or you leave the state and look for work elsewhere. I went the teaching route, while I waited for Paul to get a foothold working for another farmer about fifteen miles from Aberdeen. We started corresponding while I lived in a woman's dormitory in Aberdeen, and pretty soon we started dating again."

"So, what happened?"

Paula paced back and forth, unsure of what she wanted to say. "Now comes the twist. My older brother was never a farmer, and in his way he tried to tell my folks he wanted no part of the farm. They were devastated! What, their eldest son not become a farmer? What was the world coming to? My father really got on his high horse. He called my brother everything but a German farmer, if you get my drift. Translated roughly in English, it comes out something like this, our generation is the scum of the earth, we don't know where we're going, we'd need more than a road map to get there if we did, and once we got there, we haven't the slightest idea what we'd do next."

Katey smiled, all-knowing. "Think I've heard that speech before too! Almost makes a person wonder if Ireland wasn't a lot closer to Germany than our world globe shows. I'm sorry I interrupted; please go on about the twist."

"Because we have so few people our draft quota is small. In my brother Emil's case, my dad, as a member of the draft board, volunteered him since he told my folks he didn't want to farm. My dad felt Emil would grow up in the service; they'd make a man out of him. It was the worst decision my father ever made. Emil deserted to Canada!"

Katey gasped, "Oh my gosh!"

"There are no pictures of my brother at home anymore; everything, even his clothes, is packed away and his name is never brought up. My folks have no son anymore and I have no brother. My folks were strict German Lutheran church members, now they hardly ever attend. They can't stand the shame or the humiliation my brother has heaped upon them. The night my brother fled to Canada, my father struck him and said if he ever returned to the United States, he would be the first person to turn him in to the authorities. Emil can never come home anymore!"

"Where does Paul fit in now that your brother is gone?"

"After I finished teacher's college, I boarded out for two years at several local farmers' places while I taught my students in a one-room country school. I moved back in at home to save money, money I had earmarked for Paul and me. I had a real showdown with my folks. With Emil gone, there was nobody to turn the farm over to when they retired, except Paul. I had them just where I wanted them I thought."

Katey could almost guess what happened. "You didn't win the war, only the first battle, right?"

"Correct. My mother so intimidated Paul that he never felt right about being back at our farm to start work again. I'll never forget the first Sunday dinner Paul had at our place after he moved back. My mother was so proud that everything on our table that day had been raised at home. Even the bread my mother baked came from the wheat my dad had milled locally into flour. My folks insisted that Paul sit opposite my mother instead of being seated next to me as is our custom when a young man is invited by the daughter. My mother knew what she was doing. She stared him down until he left the table and went outside. The memory of my mother walking in on us was too much. My mother would never let Paul live that down. He moved out to the barn and never ate at our table again while my folks were around."

"So how did you marry Paul?"

"To please my mother, we had to wait two more years before we married. Time, my mother insisted, Paul needed to prove himself. During this time, Paul convinced my dad to spend a little more money. Buy fertilizer and plant it with the wheat seed. Boy was he right! We had bumper crops while Paul's dad and the others barely combined enough to get their seed money back, let alone turn a profit. Then the bottom fell out of the market, wheat prices dropped, and my father was in a panic. He'd barely recover what he'd spent for seed, labor, and fuel to plant and harvest it, even though he owned his own combine."

"Don't tell me, Paul saved his bacon again."

Paula was pleased, oh, so pleased with what she had to say. "Paul wasn't even ruffled over the poor market. He calmly told my father to play the same game 'the big boys' played. They're buying millions of tons of wheat at rock bottom prices and holding it in granaries until the market rises so they can make a killing. 'What granary?' my father said, 'I can't afford to buy and store it like that!' Paul went to town and bought rolls of cheap plastic and lined our cow barn to store all our wheat, waiting for the market to rise. He had my father sell off the cows and milking equipment and live on that 'til the wheat prices rose. He also told my father to forget about milking cows anymore, there'd be plenty of money later to convert the cow barn into a permanent granary."

"Was he right?"

"Right? Oh Katey, he was better than right, my father cleaned up six months later. He made the most money he'd ever made in his life all because of Paul."

"So where's the problem? Paul certainly proved himself to everybody's satisfaction, even your mother's, didn't he?"

"Now comes the real corker! What I'm about to say I can't prove, but in my heart I know it's true. For years my folks had always talked about buying a new car and taking a vacation during the winter, maybe travel to California or possibly even down to Florida. Anyway, to make a long story short, they had the money, plenty of money, so they bought a new car and took that trip. Katey, there's not an ounce of doubt in my mind, but my mother somehow engineered it so while my father was gone, she had Paul drafted to break us up! I know it's a terrible thing to say, but I truly believe that's what happened!"

"Oh, my Lord, how could she ever do a thing like that to you?"

"After that incident with Paul, my mother and I were never close. No matter what I did, no matter how much money my folks made because of Paul's decisions, it was never enough. He would never be acceptable in her eyes. He'd done the unpardonable with me and he'd violated her trust, even though I encouraged him to love me!"

Katey was astounded by Paula's revelation. "I'm so glad my mother and I are very close. We were always that way as a family, even more so since I've had Krissy."

The two women stopped talking for awhile, each nervously glancing at their watches, counting the hours and the minutes that had elapsed since the lights were switched on in Emergency Operating Rooms A and B.

"How long has your Paul been in the operating room?"

"Better than four hours now. The doctor told me his stomach is ripped to shreds and at best he'll have part of it missing for life. Have to go on a special diet and carry one of those bags strapped to his side to hold his body waste. Some prospect for a farmer!"

"At least he's alive, the same as my Jerry is …for now." Katey asked, "Do you hope for a son?"

She looked down at her bulge. "For Paul's sake, I hope so, then at least Paul and I have done something somebody approves of. Although I'm not so sure my mother would agree or approve for that matter."

Paula returned to the couch in the room. "I was teaching school last winter while my folks enjoyed the warm sunshine in southern California. A late seasonal blizzard from Canada hit the Dakotas. We had snow drifts high as haystacks blocking the roads. Paul was home on leave and realized the danger we were all in. Because of the late season, the school board hadn't bothered to order more coal for our standing stove in the school house. I didn't dare turn the kids loose to find their way home in the blinding snowstorms. They would've frozen to death. Paul called several neighbors and they organized a farm tractor rescue operation. He told them to flatten the big tractor tires by letting the air out so they could buck the drifts. It worked, and all of us made it back home safely. I rode home in Paul's tractor and he stayed the night, and six more, to be exact. I told him I wanted his baby. We'd get married in Leola when the snowplows opened up the county roads again. Katey, it was wonderful! I never knew he was capable of such passion and caring. For once we both were doing something nobody could disapprove of at least not for six days."

"Oh, oh! I get the distinct feeling mother showed up!"

"Right on! It was late afternoon on the seventh day. Paul and I were, well, let's just say, it was at a time neither of us wanted to stop. All of a sudden there's a car honking out in front of the snowdrift blocking our garage. I swear that honking continued for a solid ten minutes. Paul knew who it was, Katey, I'm not kidding you. He absolutely froze in my arms. He got dressed, grabbed a shotgun, put on his overshoes, and faced the music, or should I say that horn, out front. You see, my mother spotted Paul's tractor and you can bet your last bushel of wheat she had the last say."

"My God, caught again!"

"The only thing that prevented a murder that day was that there were no shells in the chamber of the shotgun Paul tried to use on my mother or else all of this would be history. He'd be behind bars in the state penitentiary; there'd be no trip out here, no waiting, no nothing."

"Oh, Paula, I feel so very, very sorry for you. What can I say?"

"Nothing, my mother said it all! She called me a whore and kicked me out of the house. Paul and I got married in town and I rented a place to finish out my contract with the local school board. Paul returned to the Army and the rest you pretty well know."

"Have you had any contact with your folks since then?"

"My father came to see me without my mother finding out. He told me that when Paul got out of the Army he was going to sign over half of the farm to him as full payment for all the money he'd made because of Paul's ideas. You see, Paul never made a dime out of all those ideas he had, starting at the ripe old age of fourteen. Hard to believe, but it's true!"

"So, really, he never got to farm for himself, yet he was certainly successful! More than successful, I'd say."

"When we were alone those six days and nights, Paul really opened up to me. He had such great love! Yes, that's the word, such a great love for the land! The soil was his soul as he poured out his heart and his feelings and his love to me. He'd never been across a state line before he was drafted. I'd saved some money teaching, and I tried to talk him into taking a trip out west. See the Rockies, visit the Pacific Ocean, things like that. He said the Black Hills of South Dakota were all the mountains, forests and trees he cared to see. As for the ocean, he said to look out across the endless miles of tall, ripening wheat waving in the wind. That was his ocean, and the wind rippling the wheat was his waves, his sea of grain. That's as far as he cared to go, he so loved this land, it was his home, his only home."

Paula's words touched Katey deeply. "And to think your mother had him drafted! Incredible!

"The worst part of it was where they put him, in the infantry where you either learn to kill or get killed. He had no business in the infantry. My God, he's a wheat farmer, not a killer! His letters to me weren't regular love letters, not the kind you probably got from your husband. Paul's letters were drawings, layouts for planting windbreaks and for crop rotating, things like that. Even in Korea, he was dry-land farming in his letters to me. He never stopped farming. In his last letter, he said their machine guns ran white-hot, they killed so many North Koreans. But they ran out of ammunition, so they had to pull out. He said waves of enemy soldiers never stopped coming. It was like the wheat fields, an endless supply of wave after wave after wave. What chance would a South Dakota wheat farmer have against those odds?"

They settled down for more of the long wait, each wrapping a blanket around their bodies trying to find a minute or two of fitful rest, even though each knew there was no real chance. Tonight, sleep, that precious commodity, belonged to the dead. Come the dawn maybe it'll belong to two tired, exhausted wives in Madagan Hospital in the Evergreen State of Washington.

"Katey, you're far too private, too personal for me, but allow me this one observation, will you?"

"I won't promise I'll answer you. On some things, I can't."

"When we first talked, you said your husband was a changed man on a certain night, your prom night. Now, putting two and two together, that had to be the night when you conceived your darling baby Krissy. But something else had to happen that night or else you would never let that happen. You're too strict, too rigid. What was it?"

Katey thought a minute before answering. "Jerry committed himself and his love to me. He proposed and I accepted. How did you figure that out?"

"Don't ever play poker, Katey; your face gave you away. It was written all over it when you said he was a changed man."

Their conversation trickled down to nothing, each preparing to be alone with her thoughts. Katey checked her watch, three hours since she walked beside her Jerry trying to say the right words, trying to tell him how much she loved him, and yes, trying to tell him Krissy was theirs, really theirs.

Another half hour slipped by, then all of a sudden both women were wide awake, nostrils sensing something was about to happen. They saw the young officer, a captain, stride toward them. It must be news for Paula, because it wasn't Major Novak, Katey surmised. She was right. Paula's messenger of life or death was among them. "I'm terribly sorry, Mrs. Meyers, we did all we could to save your husband! He went into shock and never recovered!"

At first, Paula tensed and seemed to accept the news. Then she let out a horrible scream in anguish. She hammered away on the young doctor's chest, cursing and screaming and crying. She cursed everything and everybody, so complete was her bitterness, her resentment toward every living thing. Katey walked away from the scene and turned her back to them, letting Paula rant out the poison that had built up in her. Then weary of words, Paula sat alone on the couch while the doctor excused himself.

At 2:57 A.M., PFC Paul A. Meyers of Leola, South Dakota, stopped farming in his mind, in his layouts and in his letters to Paula. The official cause of death, shock caused from massive injuries and internal hemorrhaging to the vital organs of the stomach. Unofficial cause of death, insurmountable hate and hostility from an unforgiving, mistrusting, and vengeful wife of a German wheat farmer. The deceased is survived by his loving wife and their unborn child and by a first-generation Irish lady who never met him.

Then it came time to say their good-byes. These two wives thrown together in the worst of circumstances, yet they reached out and shared in their time of need. Perfect strangers, but sisters nonetheless. "When they bury my husband in our cemetery just south of town, I'm going to make sure no one ever forgets him."

Katey broke from their hug. "How will you do that?"

"On his headstone, this will be his epitaph, 'The best farmer in McPherson County,' that's all Paul Meyers ever wanted to be."

"What a beautiful tribute to a wonderful man, Paula."

"Thanks, Katey, I know what I'm going to say may hurt you, but I believe it now more than ever. There is no God. I no longer have any faith in Him or anything else for that matter. How can there be when all this is going on, and God never lifts a finger to stop it?"

"Oh, but there is! Your Paul is still farming and planting. Through God's miracle, he planted the most important crop he'll ever plant, his seed of life in your womb!"

They shook hands and Paula Meyers left Katey alone with her thoughts of Jerry. She realized it was only a matter of time before she would be visited by her messenger. She let out a silent prayer. "Please, dear Lord, please make it a messenger of life and hope."

# Chapter Twenty-Seven

Another hour moved slowly by and her thoughts dwelled on Paula for a few moments. She'd never seen a woman so bitter, so fed up with what life had dealt her. She wondered if someday Paula and her mother would reconcile or would the chasm between them always be too deep and too wide to cross? Time can heal most things she concluded, but in Paula's case, some things are better off left alone.

She huddled in one corner of the couch with a blanket wrapped around her and her back against the wall for support. She must have dozed off, because there he stood, gently shaking her. "Mrs. Landis, are you awake?"

Katey was on her feet in a second, still clutching the blanket."MY JERRY! MY JERRY! IS HE?"

The stern face softened, his cold business-like eyes melted a tad. "He's a fighter. He has the will to live. You were the difference, he knows you're here!"

The blanket hit the floor while Katey grabbed the major and hung on for dear life. "OH THANK GOD! OH THANK GOD!" She sobbed out.

The flood of tears came and Major Novak let Katey have a real good cry. Then he continued. "His vital signs are improving, the next seventy-two hours will be critical! You understand he's not out of the woods yet, but I believe he's going to make it."

"What can I do? How can I help?" Katey begged.

Major Novak looked down into the most eager, grateful pair of eyes he'd ever seen. "Ordinarily, I'd say, be patient and wait. But with you, that would never do, would it? Tell you what, I'm going to make an exception. If you promise not to get in the way, I'll let you spend an hour in the morning and an hour late in the evening in his room observing. I'll leave permission with the nurses on his charts. Now mind you, he's lost a terrific amount of blood. He's terribly weak, so he'll look awfully pale 'til we replace his blood with new plasma. He'll be sedated heavily because we want him to sleep as much as possible."

"Oh thank you, thank you, Sir, or Major, or whatever you are!"

He cracked a smile, it almost hurt, but he did smile. "Now when your husband is awake, he'll be very groggy, and we want to keep him that way. There'll be dressings to change on his back, his leg will need constant dressing and repacking. That's an awful lot of bloody dressings and the smell isn't going to be any bed of roses either. Are you sure you're up to it?"

"Just give me a chance! After what I saw in the prep room, I can take anything!"

"Okay, we'll see. Starting late tonight, we'll check you out, that'll be your first turn."

"Can I have a chair to sit by him?"

"Okay, I'll arrange for a chair to be left in his room. Remember, he's still in the critical care unit, and when he's better, we'll move him to the intensive care unit."

"How bad was it? I mean, what did you find?"

"He was very fortunate in one regard, his back and left leg took the brunt of the explosion. Had he been facing the other way, well, he wouldn't be here today. We took a dozen pieces of shrapnel out of his back, and two were very close to the spine. Anyone of those could have been fatal or left him paralyzed for life. We think we have the internal bleeding stopped, time will tell. About his leg, I made a decision, and I hope the right one for your husband."

Katey searched his face. "You did say there'll be dressings and packing to change on his leg, didn't you?"

"Yes, but maybe we should've amputated. Let me put it this way, Mrs. Landis, he has severe ligament, tissue and nerve damage in the left leg, but I voted to save it for now. That decision will put him through months of agonizing pain when they start his rehabilitation program. Some days will be three steps back and only two steps forward as far as progress goes, but I still feel I made the right decision."

"Oh thank you, thank you, Doctor! I know Jerry, he's a very proud, independent man and the loss of one leg ..."

"That's what I thought too. Anyway, this way he'll get to keep it for quite some time."

"Then what?"

"At this point, hard to say, but eventually he will probably lose it. He'll always wear a brace and special shoe and gradually over the years it will wither on him until..."

"He'll walk, won't he?"

"Oh yes, but there'll always be a foot drag, not so much of a limp as a foot drag. He'll walk with a cane."

"Okay, I can accept that."

"I think you have the full picture. You understand first we have to get him through the next seventy-two hours?"

"Absolutely, and I'm going to be there, right?"

"Are you Irish, by any chance? I seem to detect a special quality about you that suggests you have that certain bulldog tenacity, meaning no disrespect, of course."

"Yes, I am, and I'm proud of it!" she replied proudly.

"Good, 'cause you're going to need it, every ounce! You've made a hit with Booker T, he's been asking about you. I'll turn you over to his capable hands. He'll show you the ropes, get you set up in guest housing, get you a chow-line pass for our hospital cafeteria and try to make your stay as comfortable as possible."

"How long do you think I'll be here?"

"My guess, two weeks at least, then we'll see."

"I'm going to call my parents with the good news!"

Major Novak looked at his watch. "Mrs. Landis, it's nearly 4:30 in the morning!"

"Nothing's going to keep me from telephoning them right now. I wouldn't be able to sleep, or say my prayers, or give thanks to God until I keep my promise to my mother and father. I'll have it no other way."

He tried to smile again and excused himself. "Just what I expected, Mrs. Landis, good old one-hundred-proof Irish down to your pretty toenails, no doubt."

To Katey, this was the beginning of hope and life, it certainly beat Jerry's other alternative, death. For her, the twice-a-day vigil beside his bed did as much for her as it did for him. Several times, especially at night, she'd move her chair as close to his bed as possible and reach through the side rails to touch at first, and then later, hold his hand.

Often the night duty nurse would find Katey fast asleep in her chair still holding one of Jerry's hands, waiting for any response, any sign that he knew she was there. All the tubes and bags surrounding his bed didn't dampen Katey's spirits. Quite the contrary, she saw it as a good sign, things that must be done and closely monitored to preserve life and breath in her Jerry, her beloved husband.

Two days into her vigil, Katey saw and felt Jerry's first positive response. He awoke in sharp pain, but with a clear head, long enough to say he loved her and thanked her for being with him. Then he begged her to call the nurse to give him a shot. His back and his left leg were killing him.

Now, there was no stopping her as Katey quickly adapted to a military style of life at Madagan General Hospital. Something she would've thought impossible only a few short days ago. Her routine never varied. Sleep late, shower, dress, and then hit the late chow-line for the last call to breakfast. From there, her first visit to the chapel, then on to her late morning bedside vigil with Jerry. She skipped lunch, returned to her quarters, tidied them up a bit, wrote a letter to her folks, then took a walk around the post, weather permitting. Back to her quarters for a catnap, and then on to the late-dinner chow line. From there, she'd go down to the post library and read for an hour or two. Then return to the hospital for her late-night vigil with Jerry again. A second visit to the chapel and finally back to her sleeping quarters. Her own personal prayer and to bed once more. She never failed to hug and kiss the extra pillow in her room and squeeze it tight as she slept with both arms wrapped securely around it. For the most part, her dreams were pleasant ones, often taking her back to a honeymoon weekend in a special cabin high in the snow-capped Sierras. Sometimes in the middle of the night, she'd prop the extra pillow behind her, and try backing and snuggling up to it. She'd reach back and draw it up tight, a poor substitute at best for Jerry's warmth and arms. And oh how she longed to feel his arms wrapped around her, pulling her into him while they slept.

When morning came, she'd lie in bed alone with her thoughts of him, her body aching so much for his touch, with nothing to show but more of the same.

Gradually Katey saw what concerned around-the-clock medical treatment can do for a patient. Jerry's color returned and he slept more restfully, instead of chronic episodes of drug-induced, forced sleep. He was conscious for longer periods each day although he tried to stand the pain so that he'd have a few more precious minutes with Katey before he finally pushed the call button clipped to his pillow.

One bright sunny day, he awoke to find Katey asleep in her chair beside him. He pushed his call button and Nurse O'Grady came running in, thinking he was in deep pain needing another shot. To her surprise, he whispered to her and she disappeared out of his private room on the double. Two minutes later she returned with two cups of coffee. Jerry, lying flat on his back had Nurse O'Grady gradually raise him up so he could peer over the top of the side rail. Then he whispered to the nurse, "Now, pass that cup of coffee under her nose a couple of times."

The aroma of fresh-brewed coffee brought Katey out of her slumber in an instant. Jerry smiled and said, "Good morning, Mrs. Landis. Up to a cup of brew with your hubby, are ya?"

Katey laughed so hard, she nearly cried. "Landis, that's the lousiest Irish impersonation I've ever heard. Just for trying though, you get one good morning kiss, but only one. Ready to collect?"

It was almost like old times, almost. They laughed and joked and kidded each other for the next twenty minutes, by far the longest Jerry had been clear-headed without pain killers or drugs. He seemed almost upbeat.

"Hey, Katey, before I collect that kiss, I could sure do with a good shave and I need to brush my teeth. Tastes like the local stockyard stampeded through my mouth all night. I'll ring for O'Grady."

O'Grady brought in a tray of shaving supplies, lotion, along with a toothbrush and small tube of toothpaste. Next she cranked up the bed and propped another pillow behind Jerry so she could see the mirror to shave, brush his crew-cut and his teeth. Nurse O'Grady started in.

"Couldn't I do that for my husband?" asked Katey. "I need to do something."

"All right, Mrs. Landis, I'll turn this chore over to you. From now on each morning, you're stuck with this big galoot."

Katey laughed. "From now on, the name's Katey, okay?"

"And you can just keep on calling me O'Grady, haven't used my first name in years."

"What is it?"

O'Grady kidded right back. "Let's see, last Christmas, I got a card from an old boyfriend and if I remember correctly, it was addressed to Constance O'Grady. I darned near returned it to the postman, thought he had the wrong O'Grady!"

he threesome laughed. O'Grady started to leave the room after watching Katey shave Jerry, between all the tubes and bags. "You handle that pretty well for a tenderfoot. Sure you haven't been practicing up on a spare husband or two?"

Katey smiled. "No, I watched him do it on our honeymoon."

After shaving him, Katey brushed and combed Jerry's crew-cut, then held the spittoon cup under his chin while she brushed his teeth. "Next week dear, I'm gonna ask O'Grady if they can disconnect you long enough so you can do this yourself. You're comin' along just fine, darling."

Jerry turned pensive after looking at his leg still packed in a cast of dressings, heavy tape and gauze. "Not like I thought it would turn out, not like it at all."

Katey knew what he was leading up to. "Hey, none of that! Look, I'm not complaining, why should you?"

"Not complaining, Katey. Look, you're stuck with, with -"

"Go ahead Jerry, say it! It's stuck in your craw, you're choking on it, I can tell! Say it, Jerry! Say it and get it over with and then we're gonna get on with our lives."

"All right dammit, I'm a cripple! How do you think it's going to make me feel when I finally get outta here and come home to you? I didn't want it this way, Katey, I don't want people feeling sorry 'cause I'm a cripple!"

Katey finished wiping off his mouth. "Jerry Landis, you listen to me and you'd better listen real good. I never, you hear me, never, ever want to hear you say cripple again! You're only a cripple if you think that way. Where's that stubbornness and pride you always had? Sure as heck hope you didn't leave it overseas, 'cause you have so much pride and independence in you that no one, not even me, is going to worry about or even bother looking at a little foot drag. Now put a cork in your mouth and kiss me before I change my mind about what a wonderful husband I have."

They kissed long and tenderly. "Oh Jerry, Jerry my Love, I wish I could hold you like I want to. I have so much love saved up for you, I'm afraid almost to start."

He understood what she was trying to say. "Katey, sure my leg won't bother you? You know what I mean, and I'll be wearing a brace."

"Nonsense, if it does, I'll help you take it off. Now, let's have seconds on that kiss. That first one was kinda puny. It lacked a lot of oomph, if you ask me."

They settled on another hungry kiss. "This better?"

"Much better," she murmured. "This is more like it. Now we're starting to make progress on putting the pieces of our life back together." He winced slightly as she held him. "Jerry, I know your back's killing you when we kiss. Let me roll you back down."

"Not too far, Katey, I still want to see your face when I talk to you."

"Okay, but only five minutes more, then I'm ringing for O'Grady if you don't."

He lay back, but could still see her eyes and read her lips. "That first day or night or whatever it was, it's all scrambled up. I can't seem to sort some of it out."

"Such as what, Hon?"

"I remember smelling your perfume and I remember you touching me and holding my hand as they wheeled me along…I remember a few of the words you said like 'I love you' and 'I'm here.' Then it gets real mixed up. I kept having this crazy mixed-up dream over and over again and it sure doesn't make sense, but there it is and I'm stuck with it. I can't get it out of my head."

"Tell me about it."

"Well, here's how it kinda goes. You're still hanging onto me and it's like you're real worried I won't make it so you're trying to tell me something. Boy, here's the crazy part, oh, Katey, I know it's only a dream, it has to be."

"Jerry, tell me, what did you hear me say in your dream?"

"Aw Katey, it's all nonsense. It doesn't make a lick of sense. It has to be the drugs. Yeah, that's probably what happened, sure, that's it."

"Jerry, what did you hear?"

"Promise you won't laugh?"

"Promise!"

"Here goes! You said Krissy is ours—like you're her mother and I'm her real father. Does that make a lick of sense? Naw, it can't be! Can it?"

"What if that were true, Jerry, would you still go ahead with our private ceremony with Father Murphy?"

"WOULD I! Katey, if Krissy were really mine, I mean really ours, I'd get in a wheelchair if need be, to take her in my arms and tell my very own daughter how much I love her and want her. It was all a dream, wasn't it, Katey? One crazy, mixed-up dream, right?"

Katey hesitated. "Yes …it was"

"Tell me all about her, anyway, and tell me about your folks and your job. Bring me up to date on everything!"

She blew him a kiss. "Tonight, my love, tonight we'll talk again 'til you need your shots. I'm ringing for O'Grady."

She didn't really know why she answered him the way she did concerning Krissy. Perhaps she held back the truth again because he was obviously on the road to recovery and she felt a full disclosure would be much more personal and effective holding each other close with the missing snapshot pages from Krissy's album and her birth certificate close by at home. Or perhaps she still harbored second thoughts, not wanting to risk until after their private church ceremony with Father Murphy officiating. No matter, she thought, Jerry will be the happiest father and proudest husband when at last they are together as a family. Either way, Katey was never more confident of the outcome than she was now. He was committed to their lifetime relationship and learning later that Krissy was theirs only added more bliss to that relationship, one that had certainly matured, in every aspect.

# CHAPTER TWENTY-EIGHT

ay number eleven at Madagan General Hospital opened with
Katey hitting the late breakfast line at the hospital cafeteria.
A voice caught up with her. "Mrs. Landis, Mrs. Landis, wait
up!"

Katey turned to see Booker T loading up his tray with twice the
food she had. "Good Lord, Booker T, don't tell me you can put away all
that food? What do you have, a hollow leg?"

"Naw, Mrs. Landis, just an overactive tapeworm!"

They both laughed and carried their trays to an empty table and sat
down. "So, this is the big day, huh?"

Katey picked up her orange juice glass and took a sip. "Every day's
a big day for me. Jerry's doing just fine, and I'm thinking of going back
home to my daughter and my parents."

"You don't really know, do you?"

"Know what?"

"About your husband, he's a genuine, dyed-in-the-cotton, flesh and
blood war hero!"

Katey put down her piece of toast. "What are you talking about?
Jerry's never said one word about anything like that."

"Well then, let me be the first to tell you. Guess they kinda waited to see if he was going to survive to award it personally or if they'd have to award it posthumously, after his death. Anyway, this morning at ten-hundred hours, that's ten o'clock your time, Brigadier General Bransvold, the base commander himself, will present your husband with the Silver Star, a Purple Heart, and a Citation. Man oh man, will there ever be big brass all around his bed. You really didn't know, did you?"

Katey put on a slow boil. "Darn that Jerry Landis! But that's just like him, always doing it low key, never telling me anything. Heck, if you hadn't told me, I'd be over at the chapel taking my own sweet time, and I'd probably get to his room long after the ceremony! Do you know what he did?"

"Yeah, the notice and ceremony times are posted on the bulletin board at the hospital entrance. Maybe you oughta read it, don't get many Silver Stars awarded around here. Not if they're still alive to tell about it."

"Do you know, Booker T, that he's never mentioned one single word about what happened over in Korea? But that's my Jerry! Darned that husband of mine!"

"I take it then, you'll be there."

"Absolutely! Won't he be surprised when I show up an hour early this morning? He just didn't want me to know. But that's my Jerry all right! He'll never change!"

Booker T cut up his sausage. "He saved his crew, not once, but twice! How about that? First time, he ordered them out of their communication van just before the MIG jets blasted it to kingdom come! But the second time, he volunteered to climb a tree to string an antenna wire, it was their only chance to survive and it worked! That's when they blew him right outta the tree! There's lots more words on his posted Citation, but that's the meat of it. Pretty proud of him, aren't you, Mrs. Landis?"

"I'm so proud of him, I could cry, but he'll never even talk about it. That's just his way. Oh, that man can be so frustrating but I love him so!"

"Yea, kinda figured that, too!"

Promptly at ten o'clock, Katey in her best dress was privileged to attend a once-in-a-lifetime experience, an awarding of the Silver Star and Purple Heart, complete with Battlefield Citation to her husband, Corporal Gerald Landis. After the ceremony, the Post Commander shook Katey's hand.

"Mrs. Landis, your husband exemplifies all that is right with America's fighting men; none are braver, none more ready to risk their lives if the cause is just and none more ready to come home to their wives. Your husband is that kind of man, I salute both of you. You, indeed, have every right to be proud of him."

After the brass cleared out, Katey, misty eyed, embraced her husband. "Oh my darling, I'm so very, very proud of you. Wait'll I write my folks. No, tonight I'm going to call them. Mom and Dad will be so proud of you."

They talked of many things, trivial things, but important to their lives. Then Katey broached Jerry about what really happened in Korea. "I know you don't want to talk about it, and I respect those wishes, but someday I'll want to show Krissy your medals and tell her about you and how you earned them. I know you'll never do it, so I must. What should I say?"

Jerry was uncomfortable with his answer. Then his expression softened. "If you feel you should say something, say this about me. I saw something I'll never forget as long as I live. I saw four men pray to their God. Their faith? Unshakable! I saw another man, my driver, La

Plante, scoff and ridicule them as weak because he said they used their beliefs as a crutch. He was dead wrong! It was their very strength in the face of certain death! I saw an order to mankind, a natural order to things in spite of all the death and destruction around us. I now believe in God. That's what I saw and found, Katey. It will be with me always."

Katey was absolutely astonished by Jerry's moving words.

"Jerry, listen to me. I knew someday He would find you or that you would find Him. Oh, what a blessed story! What a blessed day! This is the best possible story any man could tell his daughter. I will be so pleased and so proud to tell our Krissy your story about God and how you became a believer. No battlefield citation or Silver Star could ever match this."

The next morning Katey had a surprise for Jerry, two five-by-seven enlarged photos of Krissy and herself. "Put them on my portable stand, hon, so I can see them when you're not here. How did you ever think of them?"

She planted a big kiss squarely on his mouth. "I knew you didn't have any with you, how could you after what happened? So, I took two of my billfold snapshots and had them enlarged. Jerry, I've made the rounds around this hospital. Ask me where the PX is, or commissary, or the post theater, or the library, and I can point you in the right direction. Oh, my gosh! I'm sorry, you're a long way off from finding out for yourself. I'm sorry, I wasn't thinking."

He looked at his darling Katey. "I know you're right, I am a long way off from ever visiting those facilities, but I will someday."

She kissed him again. "You have to believe that my love and you will." She switched subjects. "Say, did you know there's a great big snow-capped mountain outside? It looks like a huge dish of soft ice cream piled high with a little chocolate syrup running down it in a couple of spots."

"O'Grady told me it's called Mount Rainier. Haven't seen it yet, but I intend to when I get my legs going again. From what you describe Katey, that ice cream must be glaciers and the chocolate syrup is probably bare ridges sticking out through those glaciers. Must be some sight."

"It is! Booker T told me it's over fourteen thousand feet high. It's pretty up here when it doesn't rain, everything is so green." Katey pulled up her chair next to Jerry's bed.

Jerry seemed in good spirits, quite relaxed. He looked at the latest photo of Krissy "Gosh, Krissy's growing so much, changing her looks too, but she sure looks like she still belongs. Tell me some more about her."

"Last night, I called Mom and Dad to tell them about your big day, and they put Krissy on the phone. She's starting to put her words together, guess what she said?"

"Please come home?"

"Bingo, Jerry! Only with Krissy, it's Mommy, Mommy, Mommy, peease come home. She says 'peease' for please."

They laughed. "Dear, with me, she always says Mommy three times, and then tells me what she wants to say. Gotta tell you, I'm willing to bet we've got a tomboy on our hands. You must see the way she takes to her grandpa. That is really something!"

"Do you suppose she'll take to me? I sure hope so! Of course, at first, I know it's going to take some time before she gets used to having me around."

"I don't think so, Sweetheart, you've always liked being around kids, she'll come to you right off the bat. Kids can sense those things about adults, I'm sure."

"Does she have any favorite toys?"

Katey held Jerry's hand. "Oh, this is precious. After I brought Krissy home, Mom and Dad spent a small fortune on toys to play with. She also has a shelf on the wall above her crib lined with all kinds of dolls and stuffed animals. Does she ever want to play with any of these things? Nope! She's driving us crazy trying to figure out what she likes to play with! Then one day mother hits upon an idea, so she drags out a couple of her best pots, pans and lids and sets Krissy smack down in the middle of them. Voila! Krissy plays for hours, stacking, re-stacking and putting lids on them, just like I used to! So Grandpa heads down to St. Vincent de Paul, plunks down two bucks and walks out with a cardboard box full of the most beat-up pots, pans and lids you ever saw, and Krissy's in hog heaven every day. Dad says it's the best two dollar investment he's ever made!"

Jerry squeezed her hand. "She must be some little girl! And you must be some little mother! I'll bet there's none better.

"Thanks, love, about the mother compliment. You are also right about something else. Guess we really do know each other far better than most married couples."

He frowned. "What are you getting at, Katey?"

"Up in our honeymoon cabin, just before we locked the door to drive back, you said I needed love, lots of love, and that I should surround myself with love because I have so much love to give. But now Jerry, I'd like to add one thing to your statement, if you don't mind."

"Sure, go ahead."

"Now that you've found God, you will no longer take love, but you will give it for the rest of your life. That's one of many reasons I believe in God. For He is love."

He was moved by her words. "Jerry, I made reservations for a flight out of Sea-Tac early this evening. I called mom this morning, right after breakfast. I should be home by eight this evening."

"You're, you're not leaving after this morning are you? Say you'll come in this afternoon before you go, please, Katey, please?"

"All right, but just to say good-bye, my love. That, and nothing more! Right?"

Jerry feigned ignorance. "Don't have the slightest idea what you're getting at, Mrs. Landis."

"Oh really? Jerry, you must be feeling a lot better, 'cause I know you and I know what's on your mind. Forget it, Landis! You're in no shape to do anything about it."

"I won't deny it's been on my mind, matter of fact you've been on my mind constantly."

Late afternoon came up so abruptly, that even Katey with all her careful planning had to admit to herself she barely gave herself enough time, especially in an emotional sense to leave her husband. She called for the transportation jeep to move her and her luggage back for one last stop at Madagan General. She surprised Jerry and Nurse O'Grady by letting O'Grady order an extra supper so she could eat her last meal alone with him.

O'Grady picked up the trays and boldly announced to them. "Okay, hero, no more coddling after tonight! Tomorrow you move to the rehab ward and then it's work, work, and more work!" She changed the pitch of her voice and did a heckuva job imitating a first sergeant. "Landis, no more country club privileges. It's time to get off your butt and earn your lousy pay! You hear me? Yeah, I'll bet you do! Tomorrow all I wanta hear outta you is grunts and groans, and then in the afternoon we're gonna do it all over again. And I'd better hear more of the same, a heckuva lot more of the same! Got the picture?"

Jerry roared. "Man, what a first sergeant you'd make, O'Grady! Of course the sergeant I have in mind is a bit different equipment-wise, I mean!"

All three laughed at Jerry's remark.

O'Grady looked at Katey. "Your husband tells me you have an early flight out of Sea-Tac this evening. We'll miss you. You've been good company, Katey, and I'll do my best to get this big lug on a plane down to Sacramento as soon as possible. Of course you understand all I can do is kick him in the pants, the rest is up to him."

Katey flashed a broad smile. "You do that, O'Grady, and you'll have my undying thanks! I want him home where he belongs as soon as possible. He has a daughter waiting for him whom he's never seen."

O'Grady pointed to Krissy's picture. "Oh what a cute baby girl! Jerry's told me about you adopting her in between telling me all about you, Mrs. Landis, hope you don't mind."

"Not at all. As a matter of fact I'm flattered."

"Look, I'm in the way, so why don't I disappear for a few minutes to... leave you two alone."

Katey smiled at her, knowingly. "Thanks O'Grady, I owe you one."

O'Grady hardly closed the door before they were in each others' arms. "Darn these hook-ups," said Jerry. "I'll sure be glad to get out of them tomorrow and start my rehab. I can't even do a decent job of kissing my wife."

Katey nipped his ear, still leaning over the side rail. "Next time we kiss, it'll be at the Sacramento Airport and you'll not be tethered down like this. You'd better not be, 'cause I'm gonna expect a lot better performance out of you, got it?"

"Yes, Sergeant Landis! Anything else, Sergeant?"

They both snickered at Katey's sergeant impression, and then broke out laughing. "

" Oh, that reminds me. Take these two awards, my citation and my campaign ribbon with you. Pack them away in your hopeless chest, this hero business had gone a bit far for me. I'm no hero, Katey, never was, never will be."

"There you go again, darn you Jerry Landis! Why do you always under-cut yourself? Ever since I've known you, you've always been this way. You've proved yourself and gone way beyond anybody's expectations in everything you've ever done. Enjoy your recognition, Jerry! My Lord, how you've earned it?"

"Please Katey, just take this stuff with you! You're the one who's earned it, by putting up with and waiting for me all this time. And you're gonna be waiting some more. It isn't fair for you or Krissy for that matter. Bottom line Katey, your being by my side is what pulled me through. I was never so afraid of dying as I was that last night in Korea. All I saw, all I could think about was I wanted one more chance with you." He laughed, "Well, I got that chance, look at me now! Not exactly what I had in mind."

Before Katey answered, O'Grady came bounding back in. "Okay, okay, break it up you two!" Then she motioned with her head toward Katey. "Got a minute, Katey?"

Katey followed her back toward the rest room door, next to the entrance to Jerry's private room. "We're kind of sisters under the same shamrock, so can I speak freely for a minute or two?"

"Sure, shoot!"

"Tomorrow morning your husband is going to start a rehab program on that left leg of his. Katey, he doesn't have a clue what's in store for him. We've kept it that way. When you showed up to pull him through, Dr. Novak said leave it that way 'til you leave. He'll make it from then on."

"It's going to be pretty rough isn't it? Level with me, O'Grady!"

"The first time we wheel him into that physical therapy room he'll wish to God that Dr. Novak hadn't tried to save that left leg. Katey, the walls of that room are sound-padded for a damned good reason. We call it our 'rubber room' because his screams of pain will bounce around and around those walls before the padding absorbs them. He's going to feel such excruciating pain, that by tomorrow night after the second daily session, he'll beg us to cut it off. That's how bad it's going to get. We can't wait any longer for his shattered leg to heal, if we do, too much atrophy will set in and he'll lose it for sure. Then all we've done is prolong the amputation. Now that I know your husband, that's the last thing in the world he needs. What he needs is two legs, even if one will never be quite right."

Katey was alarmed. "I had no idea it was going to be that hard. Thank you for being so honest with me."

Katey sensed O'Grady had something else on her mind. "You told me about Jerry's rehab for another reason too, didn't you? Something personal, right?"

"I've been around you two for a couple of weeks, and what I've seen is extraordinary, such devotion, such feeling, such love between you two. Now, I've seen a lot of wives, and what I'm about to say is this! I'm reading a torrid romance novel at my apartment and it pales in comparison to the real-life romance going on every time I see you two. Your eyes, your body language, Katey, and the way he looks at you, I mean all over you, Katey, well, it's almost too good to be true. Don't know how you two did it, but somehow you two managed to turn the pages in my romance novel. I see this hunger in him. This need to have you, but knows he can't. Katey, you'll have to be the one to make it happen. Today you still have that chance."

Katey was amazed by her conversation, yet she knew O'Grady had it pegged down to the last tee. "I can't, it's too personal, too private between us, and yes, too good now to risk."

"Katey, we Irish women have one thing in common, above all else, we know how to take care of our men. You can give your Jerry a real boost to remember why he's going to sweat and scream with pain for the coming months. Get what I'm driving at?"

"Suppose you are right about us. There's no privacy, without that I'm sorry, no matter how much I think about it, it's out of the question."

"Not if I take care of that for you. Novak and his staff won't be making their rounds for another forty-five minutes and I could stand watch outside the room, just in case."

"You'd do that for us? You really would, wouldn't you?"

"Katey, I have to ask you something personal, don't take it wrong, I have my reasons. When you're intimate with your husband, can you do all of the love-making?"

Katey's cheeks burned. "I beg your pardon, O'Grady, but that's none of your darned business!"

"You're taking my question wrong. What I'm trying to say is you're going to have to make all the moves.

She thought on O'Grady's question. "If you're asking do I know how to make love with my husband with him flat on his back, the answer is yes."

"Before I leave, I'll prop an extra pillow behind his back, don't want to put any unnecessary strain on those stitches in his back. He'll get enough of that tomorrow. Good love-making, Katey! Leave him with something to remember!"

"Thanks O'Grady. I'll knock twice on the door when we're through so you won't have to wait forever out in the hall. Might look a wee bit suspicious."

"Remember, Katey, just between us shamrocks, this conversation never happened."

Katey disappeared into the restroom while O'Grady, looking professional as ever, set about unhooking Jerry and closing the blinds.

"What are you doing O'Grady?"

"It's time you were disconnected Jerry, you'll be just fine. A little prep for tomorrow's big day when I move you down into the rehab ward." She lowered the side rail all the way down.

"What's that for? Am I moving somewhere today?"

"No, your wife will be out here in a minute and she's kinda small, it'll help her really say good-bye. I'm going to raise you up to put an extra pillow behind your back so you won't have such a tough time leaning forward to kiss her goodbye. Gotta watch those stitches in your back."

Katey came out of the restroom, a glow on her pretty face, her eyes sparkling with romance in her heart and on her mind. Just the thought pushed her adrenaline to the brink. The two women exchanged glances and winked at one another as they passed in opposite directions. Katey walked on, the excitement building with every heartbeat. Suddenly, she stopped dead in her tracks, she gasped out loud as she quickly turned to call out, "O'Grady, get back here at once!"

O'Grady was mystified. "Yes, Katey?"

Katey rushed back to her. "You forgot, you forgot, O'Grady!"

O'Grady was indignant. "What do you mean, 'I forgot'?"

Katey nodded toward Jerry's bed. She whispered. "His hook-up, the most important one! I can't make love with his manhood all hooked up like that!"

O'Grady blushed 'til she turned beet-red. "Oh Lord, Katey, I'm sorry, I'll take care of it! Been nursing for twelve years, never did anything like this before."

Jerry was surprised to see O'Grady return to remove the last hook-up. She tossed it off. "Starting tonight, you're supposed to use the latrine, but make sure you call me, I'll bring the wheelchair."

O'Grady left and Katey, fully composed once more, moved her chair around to Jerry's right side of the bed, the side where O'Grady had lowered the side rail down as far as possible. Katey smiled, and with a little physical dexterity and a mountain of confidence, climbed up on the bed and sat beside him. He sized her up, God, she was pretty!

"Katey, Katey," he said, "You've got it all, the looks, the legs, and everything in between! Still think I'm the luckiest guy in the whole, wide world. And what have you got? Stuck with a cr-"

Katey's hand covered his lips. "One more time, Jerry Landis and I'm going to call for my ride to Sea-Tac."

"I'm sorry, Katey. I just kinda slipped out before I thought."

Neither spoke, they didn't have to, their eyes said it all. Suddenly, Katey moved up to him, and they threw their arms around each other and kissed! Oh how they kissed!

"Oh Katey, Katey my Love," he whispered in her ear. "Your cherry lips, they're sending signals again, they're inviting me, but I don't dare. O'Grady and Doc Novak would kill me if I tried."

Katey touched the corners of his lips like a delicate humming bird, then she found her flower, the full part of his mouth and settled down, sampling the passion he gave her.

She whispered back, "But I can. Let me love you, let me give you everything you need and want; let me make our goodbye complete. Let me love you with all my heart and soul."

He was surprised to see his Katey slip back on the floor. She removed the wide belt around her waist and then reached back behind to unzip the fastener to her skirt. Down it dropped around her ankles as she stepped out of it as though it had never graced her hips. She stopped to gather it up, and then carefully folded it at the foot of Jerry's bed. Jerry couldn't see what happened next but guessed she had just stepped out of her casual low-cut shoes as easily as she did her skirt. One quick hop up beside him and Katey began to unbutton her blouse so he could receive his first pleasure.

"Gee, what a pretty half-slip you're wearing," he commented, noting the intricate lace scallops around the bottom of her slip. "Everything about you is extra special, right down to your last stitch."

Katey smiled, oh how she loved giving him this pleasure, so intimate and so right for them.

She glanced at her wrist watch, it was time to move on, time to replenish their physical need within each other.

"Katey, we're not running out of time are we? O'Grady's standing guard outside isn't she?"

She saw the concern written all over his face. "O'Grady's outside, not to worry there's still plenty of time."

Jerry relaxed with the good news, now he could lean back and let his Katey work her magic on him. "I feel so useless, what do you want me to do?"

"Just keep my slip from getting in the way."

Ever so gradually, and with a gentleness beyond compare, Katey's fluid motion took control to bring them both to their brink of ecstasy. "Hurry, say you love me! Hurry, my Love!" she pleaded.

They embraced. Both had experienced perfection and neither wanted it to end just yet.

A minute later, Katey was back on the floor looking as though nothing in the world had ever happened between them. She glanced over. "Well, Landis, I'll say this for you, those hospital gowns sure don't do much in the way of protecting your modesty, and I now know you've got an awful lot to protect. O'Grady brought me up to speed on that."

"What've you two been doing, comparing notes?"

"Not exactly, but what I've always suspected I no longer will wonder about." Katey finished dressing. "Be back in a jiffy for one last kiss, so don't go wandering off anywhere!"

Jerry was amused. "Sure Katey, sure! I'm going to hop right outta bed and knock on the door of the John and say, hurry up, Katey, I need to use it!"

Five minutes later, Katey returned looking great as usual. Jerry could smell a fresh application of perfume and make-up.

"Got any freckles left Katey? Boy, have you ever blossomed out. What a knockout you turned out to be! And always such a proper lady too!"

Katey let him examine her face up close. "Right above my cheek bones, just under my eyes, you'll find a few. Make-up covers the rest. We've come a long, long way since that day down by the river, haven't we, Jerry?"

"Yeah, I'd say we've made a few strides in the right direction."

Katey squeezed his hand. "Got our little one to meet when you come home to Krissy and me. Then our life will be complete, the way it should be, everything in its proper place."

Jerry kissed her hand. "You like that feeling, don't you, Katey? Everything working out just the way you first dreamed it, then planned it, and finally made it happen. You like order to your life. You're so organized, so much in control."

"Yes," she admitted. "I do, and I'll do anything to keep it that way. Our life, our marriage, our daughter, my family, and our God. Who wouldn't be happy with all that?"

Katey rechecked her watch. "Jerry, it's time to go."

"Katey, Oh Lord, how I'm going to miss you!"

They kissed again, this time it was tender, and oh so sweet. Katey broke their embrace. Jerry noticed a tiny tear trickling down one cheek.

"If I don't go now, if I don't force myself out of your arms, I won't be able to leave you, that's how much I love you."

She picked up her purse and walked away, her tears were having a field day falling down both cheeks. When she reached the door, it was time for one last emotional look back.

Jerry watched her blow him one exaggerated kiss, then he called out. "It's just between us, Katey, you hear? It's far too private for confessional ears. No more trips to your priest! Got it Katey?"

She didn't reply at first, and then she felt she must. She had to answer him as her heart, her mind, and her conscience dictated. "My Love, you don't fully understand because you're not a Catholic yet. When you are, you'll see, and then you'll understand."

"Please, please, Katey! I beg you. It's nobody's business but ours! Talk to our God, pray to Him, BUT NO MORE TRIPS!"

He saw her lips move, those perfect, soft yielding lips, her cherry lips. Those same lips he'd sampled time after countless times. No one, not even Jerry Landis could mistake their meaning, what they said in perfect mime, "I love you."

# Chapter Twenty-Nine

No one was more unprepared for the trip to Washington State to see Jerry Landis at Madagan Army Hospital than Katey Landis. The reverse was equally true for Katey on her flight back to Sacramento International Airport to resume her life with her daughter Krissy and her folks. She had the warmest of feelings, an inner glow in her heart as she watched the many lights below come closer and closer, and then the slight skip when the plane's wheels touched Mother Earth again. How good it was to be alive and an integral part of the life she'd left behind only fifteen days ago. Yet the trip up to the Pacific Northwest had more than its share of compensations too. Jerry was alive and on the road to recovery, something that was very much in doubt a scant two weeks ago.

Katie felt a bit shortchanged when her welcoming committee was down to one, her father.

"Where's Krissy and Mother? Why aren't they here?"

Aaron McCray picked up her luggage. "Krissy's been a bit under the weather, Grandma says she has a touch of that flu-bug that's been goin' around, didn't want to take her out in this crowd, especially since her appetite's dropped off a wee bit."

"Did Mother take Krissy to a doctor? You're sure she's all right?"

Aaron put his arm around his daughter as they walked to the car. "She's fine, just a touch of the bug, that's all. You know your mother, if Krissy's not scampering around ninety miles an hour that gives her another excuse to mother her like a hen with chicks. I'm afraid we've spoiled our granddaughter beyond hope, not sure even you can undo the damage."

They reached the car. Katey hugged and kissed her father. "I'm sorry, Daddy, had so much on my mind lately, I nearly forgot how much I love you and missed you and Mom. Thanks for picking me up... and Dad, thanks for everything else too that you've done for Krissy and me."

He closed the trunk lid. "How is Jerry really, Katey? Your letters kept getting more hopeful and we're so proud of the medals our country has honored him with, but that only tells half the story."

Aaron opened the door and Katey got in. "He's going to be all right. He's a changed man…got the Army and the war to blame for that, seems a lot older too, somehow…didn't even want to keep his medals and campaign ribbons. He sent 'em home with me. I'm worried about his leg. He's going to go through hell in the next months on a pretty tough rehabilitation schedule in order to keep from losing it. His leg will never be quite right…"

Katey's father turned on the ignition key. The engine purred like a kitten, but he didn't move. "What about his commitment to you? To your marriage? Sometimes wars change feelings between people."

She smiled, and touched his hand. "Don't worry Daddy, that's stronger than ever between us. He told me the most incredible story. He was about to die and of all things he watched some of his crew pray, right in the face of certain death, and he became a changed man! Father, he now believes there is a God! Incredible, wouldn't you say?"

"Lass, consider what war can do to the human spirit. It can break a man, he'll be lost in mind and limb forever, or it can build a man, make him see things in a different way…in a different light. I believe that happened to Jerry and he'll be a better man for it."

"Let's get home! I want to hug Krissy and Mother!"

Mr. McCray didn't even turn out the lights in the garage before Katey was running up the steps to her home. She bounced inside and dropped to one knee. There was Krissy in her pajamas, sitting contently on her grandma's knee.

"Mommy, Mommy, Mommy," Krissy screamed as Mary McCray let her perpetual motion machine down to get revved up for a headlong dash to her mother's open arms.

"Got a kiss and a hug for me, huh, Krissy?"

Krissy squealed with delight as she made a beeline to her mother. "Oooh! That was a pretty good one, a nice big juicy kiss, Krissy! Just what the doc ordered!"

Mary came over to watch the homecoming proceedings. "Well now, 'peers the workin' class has been left out as usual. Don't I get a hug or a wee bit of a kiss, Katey?"

Katey rose up with Krissy in her arms. Together the three of them hugged and kissed each other. "Welcome home, Katey, we've all missed ya somethin' fierce, especially the wee one!"

Mr. McCray brought in the luggage to Katey's bedroom while the two women tried to get Krissy settled down in her crib. Finally they left the door ajar and retreated back to the kitchen table for coffee. Aaron found his paper, lit his pipe, and then settled down to finish reading it.

"What did you do about leaving Krissy alone in my bedroom while I was gone?

Mary looked into the parlor at her husband and back to Katey's inquisitive face. "Mr. McCray, it was your doin', so help me out! Your daughter wants to know about Krissy sleeping in her crib at night. Come clean! Spill it!"

Katey's father came in the kitchen and stood by his wife, still puffing on his pipe. "Katey, it was this way, we worried about the little tyke all alone in that big bedroom…"

"Daddy, my big bedroom?"

"Aw Aaron McCray, you started your story out wrong…"

"All right, you tell it then!"

"Since you put it that way, I will! Katey, now hear me out, it was either leave her alone in all that darkness with nobody to hear her at night…or else move the crib into our bedroom…my hearin's not what it used to be, you know, Lass…"

"Motherrr! You did it, didn't you? You had Dad move Krissy's crib into your bedroom while I was gone, didn't you?"

Aaron turned to his wife. "See, I told you not to do that!"

"Go read your paper, Aaron McCray, you're no help! All right! All right! I did and I'm not a bit sorry, either! And Father, why don't you tell your daughter who lay awake at night worryin' his poor self to death every time our granddaughter stirred or yawned. Go ahead, tell her!"

Aaron confessed. "All right, so I did! Katey'd never forgive us if she took sick or had a bad cold so I stayed awake just in case. Lord, I'm glad to see you back, maybe now I can get some sleep!"

Katey hugged them both. "If you two aren't something! But I love you both so much for takin' the time to care…and you did the right thing. Ahem…in your mind at least!"

Everybody laughed. Aaron returned to the parlor while Katey and her mother drank their coffee. Mary began. "Katey, I have some bad news. Mrs. Woodson called…and what with you up north and all your worry over Jerry not makin' it…well, when you called early that morning, I didn't want to burden you with any more. Thought it would be better to wait 'til you got back."

"When did her husband pass away?"

"The evening you left. Even Mrs. Woodson said it was a blessin' in disguise. She'd like to see you when you get back to work."

"Of course, she's one of my best friends now."

They sipped their coffee, each alone with her thoughts. "Katey? It was pretty bad up there with Jerry, wasn't it?"

Katey stirred in a spoonful of sugar. "You never took sugar before!"

"I do now, ever since that first night up there…all that waiting and waiting and waiting and not knowing. There's so much to tell, but not tonight, I'm just glad to be back. Jerry's world is so different. Military life, rules, and regulations everywhere you go. Believe it or not but I actually adjusted fairly well I think."

"Did you get to spend much time with him?

"Every day, and as he started to improve, a lot more time. Mother, I wish you could've seen him that first night. I never saw so much blood, and the smell was unreal, too! Yet he made it! The doctor told me my being there made a difference. I'm glad I was there. I never want to go through another experience like that again. Yet, in a way, I wouldn't trade it for a million dollars, the time we spent together, the award ceremony. I got to shake hands with a general, can you believe it? A real live general! He paid Jerry the highest tribute…it was something! Doubt if Jerry will ever talk about the war when he comes home. I imagine he'd just as soon forget it and leave it at that."

"His leg, Katey? And what about his back?"

"His back is going to be okay. They dug twelve pieces of shrapnel out of it, two pieces were ever so close to his spine they could've left him paralyzed for life or worse. He'll be left with a lot of big, ugly scars on his back."

"And the leg?" Mary asked hesitantly.

"That's the sixty-four-dollar question. He bled so much and there's so much damage. Dr Novak told me if Jerry had gone into shock again, that would've been it. Another lady's husband did and he didn't make it. I'll tell you about that later and it's something, her story too! Anyway his leg isn't healed, but they can't wait any longer to start therapy or he'll lose it for sure."

"Do you think they did the right thing, trying to save it?"

"Another sixty-four-dollar question. Dr Novak gambled that Jerry would rather drag it and wear a leg brace for many years instead of amputating it and fit him now for an artificial leg."

"Did he make the right choice, Katey?"

"I think so. Jerry is so darned independent and has so much pride. This way he gets to keep it for quite a while, but his nurse, O'Grady, told me that Jerry's really going to go thru an awful tough rehab program if he wants to save it."

They stopped their conversation again. Katey got up to refill their cups.

"His feelings towards you, Katey, has the war changed that too?"

"That's the one thing that hasn't changed, that, and he now believes in God. That's quite a story too, but I'll save it for tomorrow."

They sipped their coffee, each alone with their own thoughts for a moment. "Did you tell him, Katey? About Krissy?"

Katey put down her cup, Mary saw the most pleased expression work across her face. "Yes, and I've never felt better about it. There's not one pinch of doubt anymore, I feel on top of the world telling him. Our marriage is so secure, our love never stronger."

Mary put her cup down; she appeared almost as relieved as Katey. "It's good that you told him, Lass, there should never be secrets between a husband and a wife. You must be open with one another, that's the key to making it work."

Katey toyed with her spoon. "I told him, but he was under so many shots for pain and isn't certain exactly what I said. I left it that way. I tested him again and his answer was the best. He said if Krissy were really his, he'd go to her even if it had to be in a wheelchair, that's how much he wants a family."

"There's still that one thing you must do. Your Father'n me will sleep better when Father Murphy gives you and Jerry the official church blessing to your marriage. That's been put off again, but you must never let that slide. When he comes home, it must be done as quickly as possible."

"I've decided to take another day off; I'm not going back to work tomorrow. I need to spend more time with Krissy...almost feel like a stranger to her. And when she's down for her nap in the afternoon, I'll slip over to see Father Murphy for a few minutes."

"Whatever for?"

Katey fidgeted, and then got up to rinse her cup out in the kitchen sink. "It's personal ..."

"Katey! On no! You didn't! You promised me after that weekend before Jerry shipped out, you'd wait 'til the church ceremony."

Her daughter stood her ground this time. "I don't see what the fuss is all about! I'm wearing my wedding band, I've taken Jerry's name and we are married in the eyes of God when we said our vows to each other. And Mother, I want his love all the time...every chance I get when I'm around him. I can't be near him and not touch. He does things to me that I won't even try to explain. Now are you satisfied?"

"Katey, Katey, listen to yourself! I overlooked one weekend because I did understand he might not come back and he didn't want to leave you a widow, you're too young for that."

Katey snapped her fingers, and then held two barely apart for her mother to see. "See how close my fingers are? See them? That's not even in the ballpark compared to how close Jerry came to not making it. And that doesn't even begin to cover his fight for life once he got to the hospital. No, Mother, no guilt trips this time!"

"Katey, how could you?"

Katey's eyes blazed. "You mean, how could I, being such a proper Irish Catholic lady? Or how could I, with Jerry lying wounded in a hospital bed?"

"Both...I guess..."

"The first is easy to answer, 'cause Jerry sure questioned it, and I'm beginning to think he has a point, a darned good point! We're two consenting adults who have a sweet, baby daughter as a result of our love for each other, and we're responsible adults, we've paid our own way. We're Christians and we both now believe in God and we'll raise Krissy that way. Now that's a pretty good basis for any marriage, wouldn't you say? Don't answer, I know, I know, our marriage, our commitment still hasn't been recognized by the Catholic Church. But it will be the first chance we get when Jerry's discharged out of the Army and comes home to me."

"I've never doubted yours or Jerry's love for each other nor your commitment. Our church sees it only one way... you must see it that way too!"

"WE DO! NOW DROP IT!"

The two women stared at each other in silence too thick to ignore. They both recognized this was the first real rift between them, the old versus the new thinking about relationships. Suddenly they were in each other's arms, each so very, very glad to have their relationship intact, frayed a bit, but nonetheless still very strong and viable.

"Katey, Katey, your father and I, we love you, and it's only your happiness we're thinkin' 'bout. Surely you can see that, eh, Lass?"

"I do, Mother, sorry I got a little testy. That's the Brannigan Irish coming out again. About the second part, I assure you I took Jerry's condition very carefully into account…and with the help of another Irish woman, Jerry's nurse, I made it happen. That's all I'm going to say about it…it's very personal."

Mr. McCray stepped into the kitchen. "Mother, with Katey back home safe again, and that precious, sweet granddaughter of ours always in the capable hands of the two best Irish mothers I know, I think it's' high time we give our thoughts and prayers over to our son, Jerry. Katey tells us he'll be taken' on a mighty hard road to recovery so he can come home to his family. I can't think of a better way to honor him then to the sharin' of an Irish cup of coffee."

"Aye, Aaron McCray, the liftin' of our spirits will certainly be in keeping with our thoughts and prayers for him. Eh, Katey?"

# CHAPTER THIRTY

Katey never let up in keeping a daily stream of letters headed north to Jerry. Encouraging him to hang on, to see another day through, and to always remember she'd be waiting for him when his rehabilitation was over, and that her love for him was never stronger.

Even Mary saw the change in Katey, the resolve, the determination in her like nothing she'd ever seen. She remarked about it to her husband one evening while Katey was busy bathing Krissy.

"Mary McCray," he said, "what else would you expect of our daughter? She knows about life and death because she's had to see it first-hand like few others her age. Aye, she's a better person now, as fine a woman as I've ever seen, not withstandin' me own darling of course."

Mary pinched her husband on the cheek. "Thank you for such thoughts, love, I'll keep them in my heart always. Aye, we've a fine family to be proud of, each and every one. Think I'll drop Jerry a line tonight. Maybe he could stand a bit of cheering up. I'll send it along with Katey's letter in the mornin'."

Aaron was totally taken back. "Mary McCray, you take pencil to paper? Why, I can't say as I ever saw or had the pleasure of your writin,' and that's a fact."

"Tisn't so, Aaron McCray, I did write once, I wrote you on a scrap of paper a long time ago. And plainly I can see you've forgotten it already."

"When was it? And what was it about?"

"The time I slipped out to meet you without my uncle, under the stone bridge that leads up to McGaretty's Road. Surely you remember that?"

"Oh yes, your cousin passed it on to me when I was workin' in the peat bog on the other side of our village. That was a pretty nervy thing to do, Miss Mary Brannigan."

"I had to! How else was I to really get to know you? I had to be alone with you just that once. It helped to quiet a couple of doubts I'd heard about you before the proper proposal was about due."

"And were those doubts quieted? This is the first I ever heard of such things in your mind."

"Oh the old doubts I'd heard about were quieted, but new ones in my heart took their place. You were a sweet talker, Aaron McCray, and I could tell you'd had experience along those lines with other women in our village."

"So what did you decide?"

"Only that the practice you'd had before would come in very handy when you decided to turn all that sweetness in my direction."

"Well, you did say yes, with your uncle present of course."

"Aye that I did, and ever since I've been the lucky one for it."

"About your letter to Jerry, how's your spelling?"

"'Bout the same as when I wrote you over twenty-four years ago. Katey'll take care of the proper placin' for dots, and such things. It's my meanin' that I want to send along."

"Just what might that be?"

"That my son-in-law is more like a real son to the both of us and if it'd please him we'd like to think of him that way when he comes home. Then I'll close it by sayin' our door will always be open to him, and to please set down at our kitchen table when he's close by, and there'll be a meal waitin' on him shortly. I'll sign off by saying our daughter, our KateLynn, has him in her heart and in her prayers each day, because she'll have it no other way."

***

Time marches on except for those who stand and wait. For Katey, the calendar was no help at all. It treated her like a forgotten woman, oblivious to her wishes, wants, and prayers. Only when Jerry's letters began to mention a discharge date did the kitchen calendar take on any special meaning, and that at times seemed far, far into the future.

Then suddenly it's here!. What happened? Why is it here so quickly? Where did the time go? Twice Katey went to the mirror to double check her make-up and hairdo while Aaron, Mary and little Krissy waited out in the McCray car for the long-awaited drive to the Sacramento International Airport.

Eyes strained, heart pounding a mile-a-minute, emotions barely under control, Katey searched and searched the passengers getting out of the sleek, silver streak prop-jet parked on the tarmac.

"There! There he is!" She shouted, not caring if fifty other strangers heard her or not. She jumped up and down, waving frantically, "JERRY! JERRY! OVER HERE!"

As soon as he spotted her he waved back, still a good one-hundred yards from the gate. Katey turned to her parents. "Now, not a word, or one look at his cane or his leg, you got it?"

Before either Aaron or Mary could answer, Katey dashed toward the passenger exit gate. She launched herself into his arms, knocking his cane to the ground. She smothered him with kisses, crying with joy, "Oh my Darling, Darling, I thought this day would never come! Welcome home Jerry! Welcome back into our lives!"

Another passenger stooped to pick up Jerry's cane. Between more hugs and kisses, Jerry managed a muffled, "Thank you" to the friendly stranger. Then he turned his attention to his Katey. "Oh are you ever something! Man, what a knockout!"

They walked together, arms around each other's waist, the reality just beginning to hit both of them simultaneously when they passed the security guard at the exit gate. "Where's Krissy? Where's your folks?"

"Just past the sign that points to the luggage pick-up area. Jerry, I want you to meet Krissy last, this is an awfully big moment in her life too. Stay back about ten feet when we approach them, I'm hoping she'll come to you. Just follow my lead when we get there."

They stopped about ten feet from Aaron, Mary and Krissy. Jerry spoke first. "Hey, Mom, how about a great big hug?"

Mary didn't wait for a second invitation. She was almost as excited as Katey. She threw herself into his welcome arms and nearly squeezed the stuffing out of him. Jerry kissed her on the cheek. "Gosh, it's good to be back home, Mom! Think I've had about all the Army I can stand for at least the next hundred years."

Katey beamed on, standing beside Jerry and Mary still embracing. "Oh Son, it's the biggest day of our lives. Just think 'twas better'n a year ago, almost this very spot when we last said our good-byes. The wait's been somethin' I tell ya, but seein' you all splendored up in your fine uniform is something too. My eyes are a bit watery, I do hope you'll pardon my carryin' on, Lad?"

"Take your last good look, Mom, 'cause when I get to your home, Katey'd better have my civvies laid out."

"It's your home too, Son! Never forget that!"

Mary returned to her husband who handed Krissy over to her. Aaron and Jerry shook hands first then hugged each other hard. "Son, I don't have the right words, but we're all so proud of ya. Welcome back to your family!"

"Thanks Mr. McCray, it's so good to be back."

"How about calling me Dad? That Mr. McCray business doesn't belong here. From now on you're family and that's where you belong."

"Thanks for saying it. You don't know how long I've waited to hear those words from you."

They shook hands again, then Aaron stepped back. "Believe me Son, you've more than earned it!"

Then it came Krissy's turn as she hugged her grandpa's pant leg, still unsure, still a bit reluctant to be part of Jerry's welcoming committee or know just exactly where she fit in.

Jerry whispered to Katey, "Is she shy?"

Katey laughed. "Hardly, she's a tomboy! Had to fight like heck to get that new dress on her. Try dropping to one knee and hold out your arms and invite her to come to you…I'll hold your cane."

Krissy turned away and clung to her grandfather all the tighter as Jerry dropped to one knee.

"Say, those are nice black patent leather shoes you're wearing, Krissy. Who bought them for you?"

"Mommy, " Krissy replied softly.

"Did Mommy buy you that pretty blue dress with all the white dots too?"

"Uh huh."

"And who's that you're holding in your arm, Krissy?"

"Mr. Floppy!" Krissy beamed!

"Why I think that's a darned good name for your long-eared rabbit, don't you?"

"Uh huh."

"Who named him Mr. Floppy?"

"Me."

"Your mommy wrote and told me all about you. She also said you give your grandpa and grandma lots of hugs and kisses. Do you suppose I could have one of those hugs or kisses too?"

Krissy started toward Jerry then stopped about five feet away. Her deep blue eyes opened wide. "Are you my daddy?"

Jerry opened his arms wide and motioned her to him. "Yes, Krissy, I'm going to be your daddy. And daddies are supposed to get hugs and kisses too, just like grandpas and grandmas."

That broke the ice. Krissy came screaming and squealing into Jerry's arms. "Daddy, daddy, daddy, you're my daddy," she kept repeating as Jerry scooped her up into his arms.

Krissy turned on her charm, as she hugged and kissed Jerry while Katey and her parents heaved big sighs of relief.

Jerry hoisted Krissy up onto his shoulder and with Katey alongside, they started for the McCray car out in the parking lot. Aaron and Mary stayed behind to pick up Jerry's duffle bag. Mary watched them. "You know Mr. McCray, there's as fine a young couple as I'd care to see. Speak up man! What have ya to say on the matter?"

Aaron more than seconded Mary's motion. "Aye, they've more than paid their fair share of dues in this world already. Now it's time they were treated to some of the happiness the rest of us enjoy!"

They sat down at the McCray home for dinner. Krissy had changed to her patched jeans, and sat in her highchair between Jerry and Katey. They held hands and formed a circle around the table while Mr. McCray said grace. Then Mary served the Irish coffee as a toast, which was most definitely in order. Four cups clinked together and Aaron's words drifted out over as happy and joyful scene as could be found anywhere in America that evening. "God bless this family," he said, "for we are truly blessed tonight, for our family is once again together, as it should be, as God intended. No one could be happier, and no one deserves more of this than our daughter Katey, our new son Jerry, and our precious granddaughter, Krissy. Amen!'"

The first thing Jerry did after dinner was change to a sports shirt and jeans. "Oh man, this is living!" he exclaimed. "This is what it's all about! That's the last I ever want to see of my Army uniform."

The women did the dishes while the men talked in the front parlor. Krissy sat on Jerry's knee instead of doing her usual thing of playing in her cardboard box filled with pots and pans. Katey noted the change. "Look at Krissy," she said. "Boy have those two ever hit it off! She won't leave him alone for one second, not since he showed her how to spoon up the peas off her plate."

"He's going to be a very good father to her. I can see he has a way with kids, just like you do, Katey."

She smiled. "And to think I was worried about those two..."

Mary brought her hands out of the soap suds. She was so excited. "When, Katey, when are you going to tell Jerry? Tonight, maybe? Oh I would give anything to be there when you tell him…when you bring out her birth certificate!"

Katey too, was excited, but she was still in control. "I'm going to wait 'til Sunday morning, after Jerry and I have had our first night together, following our church ceremony. I'll fix breakfast at our duplex on campus and then put the manila envelope next to his breakfast plate."

"Take a picture Katey! Don't let this pass! Put it in your scrapbook!"

"Good idea Mother, I'll have the Polaroid ready."

The two finished up the dishes. "Before you two go to bed, I want to thank you and Dad for not staring at Jerry's leg brace or his cane. He felt comfortable. I could tell he was perfectly at ease. Even Krissy didn't pay much attention after her first questions. Boy were they a couple of doozies! 'Daddy, how come you have a thick leg and why do you walk so slowly?'"

"Jerry handled it well, Katey, he told Krissy, if he had a regular leg, it wouldn't be any fun catching her when they play hide 'n seek. This way, she has a better chance to get away because he's slower."

"I really think he'll adjust well when he starts classes in ten days. There's other GI's going to college, so with a somewhat older bunch of students, there shouldn't be quite as many stares or questions." She went to the parlor. "C'mon Krissy, it's bath time! Jerry, you might just as well get used to it, I'll wash her up tonight so you can see how I do it, and then you can dry her off. Some nights if I work late, you'll know how to handle it."

"Sure you want me in there? In the bathroom with her?"

"Sure, you're her father, no problem! Also you need to understand about her toilet training. I have a certain way of working with her, I'll explain while you undress her. C'mon Krissy, your daddy can carry you in!"

Katey made the transition with Krissy seem as natural as drinking a glass of milk. Jerry was impressed to say the least. Krissy thought her daddy being in there was just great, this way she got twice as much attention.

Aaron and Mary turned in about an hour later, as Friday was a work day for him. They said their goodnights, leaving Jerry and Katey alone at the kitchen table, leafing through the pages of Krissy's scrapbook. "Boy, you certainly know how to pick 'em, Katey. Krissy is such an adorable child! When you said to trust your judgment, I did and look what we wound up with! That long, blonde hair and those blue eyes! Have you ever seen anyone with eyes that dark blue?"

Katey pulled her chair around the table next to Jerry's. "Yeah, just one! You!"

"Still can't get over it, how she fits in…"

Jerry felt a tug and looked down. There in her pajamas stood Krissy with a coloring book and a box of crayons. "Daddy, can I color for you?"

"How did she get out? Didn't I just kneel with her when she said her prayers and kissed her goodnight before I lifted her into the crib?"

Katey laughed. "Get ready for more of the same when she moves to our duplex on Sunday. She stands on her pillow now and can slip over the side of the crib. Smart little stinker! Okay, Daddy will watch you color just one picture tonight, then its bedtime! Got it Krissy?"

"How long has this been going on Katey?"

"Started about three months ago. Mother and I took Krissy in her stroller into the five and dime where I used to work. My old boss gave her a coloring book and a box of crayons and she's been coloring ever since. Watch her! She does a pretty darn good job of staying inside the lines and lately, she even picks her own colors."

Jerry lifted her back onto the high chair, while Katey unsnapped her tray. "Daddy, you can slide her high chair under the table now, it fits just right since Grandpa took about two inches of the legs off. That'll be your job, Jerry, when we get over to our duplex, make sure Krissy's new high chair over there is the right height. We'll leave this one here for Grandma to use when I drop Krissy off on my way to work."

"If you aren't something, Katey Landis! Got all this figured out and more, no doubt."

"Watch her, Daddy!"

He was simply amazed at Krissy's artistic ability. "Look Katey, she's even picking the right colors to use, green for the tree top, brown for the trunk, and red, no make that orange for the oranges."

Katey's pride showed. "They were supposed to be red apples, but she decided to make them oranges tonight. Sometimes it's yellow for lemons and she draws in her own bananas and colors them"

"We've gotta encourage her to keep this up, she's got talent, no doubt about it."

"Mother and I are taking turns buying new coloring books and crayons for her. Got a stack of coloring books finished already. You'd be surprised how she's progressed since that first one, which I've saved for her scrapbook."

They stood together, arms around each other, watching Krissy finish coloring her tree. No two prouder parents could be found anywhere. Krissy finished and turned around to look at Jerry, two dimples complimented her face, her even baby teeth sparkled as she politely said, "Daddy, I'm done, time to go night, night! Kiss me and hug me, please Daddy?"

Jerry was swept off his feet, absolutely captivated by one small angelic face with the long blonde pony tail. "Okay Punkins, you've captured my heart."

"I'm not Punkins, I'm Krissy!"

He picked her up, tickled her funny bone and carried his giggling, squealing tomboy back to Mr. Floppy and her crib. A minute later he appeared out of Katey's bedroom. "I just can't get over her, Katey! What a job you've done raising her!"

"She really buttered you up tonight, Dear, I hope you realize it. Don't forget you're the new man in her life. There's another side of her you'll see soon enough. She can be stubborn, and so set in her way, especially if she wants something I won't let her have."

"Does she understand the difference between right and wrong or yes and no?"

"Better than you might think. She's at the age where she needs a father, someone who can discipline her and yet show her he loves her. The timing is perfect for you, Mr. Daddy."

They returned to the table. Katey put Krissy's scrapbook, coloring book and crayons away. "Say, Mr. Floppy looks pretty beat up. Maybe tomorrow we could buy her a new one."

Katey sat across the table, they held hands. "That would never do, not for Krissy. She takes Mr. Floppy with her everywhere she goes. She talks to him, and the other day I caught her spanking him."

"Which one of you bought her that rabbit, anyway?"

Katey smiled. "This one's hard to believe, but Krissy and I found Mr. Floppy lying all wet and soaked in the produce department of Bettinger's Supermarket about a month ago. Couldn't leave him there, oh no! So we just had to bring him home to dry him out. I sewed on those two big black buttons for eyes, and Mother made his brown pants and red checkered shirt outfit. We tried to stiffen up his long ears with starch, but that didn't work, so that's how he got his name, floppy ears. Krissy changed it to Mr. Floppy. She's got some imagination, that little scamp!"

They talked on into the night, as Katey made a fresh pot of coffee.

"How are we fixed for money?"

Katey was pleased as she produced two savings account books and handed both to Jerry. "The top one is the money you left me. It was originally our emergency fund for your college. I never touched a dime. The second is what money I've managed to save after paying the folks off, and after paying my mom to baby-sit and all the other bills."

Jerry looked at both balances. "Katey, you've almost saved another twenty-eight hundred bucks! That's great!"

Katey's eyes were aglow. "You're not disappointed that I didn't save more? I know how careful you are with money, Jerry. I tried, but I'm not the money manager you are."

He hugged her. "Nonsense, you did great, just great! Say how's our Chevy doing? On its last legs I suppose."

Katey's demure style folded. "Boy have I ever paid through the nose when it comes to driving and operating a car! That gas-guzzling, metal monster you left me with gobbles dollars up whether we eat or not! Since you've been gone, I've had a rebuilt engine put in, bought four new tires, replaced a dead battery, and had it towed twice to put in a new fuel pump and a reconditioned water pump. I think I must've been Art Kasey's best customer, it was always something. That's where the lion's share of our money went. Well, my Dear, I'm pleased to report our car is in A- number-one shape! It has to be, I've replaced everything except the transmission and the car radio! Whether it knows it or not, that car is going to run for at least another eighteen months while you're getting your degree 'cause I'm going to get back every money sucking dollar that beast has beaten me out of even if I have to push it to work! Another thing, I do know how to check the oil, the battery, the radiator and the tires, so I'm not gonna fall for anymore loose fan belt checks, or other phony garage schemes, trying to take advantage of another ignorant woman driver."

Jerry roared. "Okay, Katey, I get the picture! So now you've got everything under control for tomorrow and Saturday's ceremony, what happens first?"

Katey was in her glory. "First thing we'll get up early and surprise everybody by fixing breakfast. Then after Krissy is fed and before she takes her late morning nap, you slip into my bedroom to try on your suit to see if it still fits."

"Is that the same one I bought two years ago just before I was drafted?"

She pecked him on the cheek. "Yup, it's never been worn, had it dry-cleaned last week. So if it still fits, you're all set."

"What next?"

"We get our marriage license and then I give you the grand tour of our duplex on campus. Think you'll like how I've got everything set up. Had to make some decisions on our housing or else lose our place on the list and I wasn't about to do that."

"Knowing how much you like to plan, I'm sure you did a bang up job!"

She kissed him. "Thank you, dear, glad you appreciate the effort I put into getting our lives back on track again."

"What about the next day, Saturday, our ceremony day?"

"Got that all set up too! Our ceremony is a four sharp."

"Hope you told Father Murphy to make it short and sweet."

"I did, I told him we wanted a very simple ceremony. He promised to have us out of the church in fifteen minutes! How's that?"

"Splendid! Then what?"

"Well, my parents want to take us and Krissy out to dinner. Oh! Oh! Back up a minute! At four fifteen, right after our ceremony, Dad hired a photographer to take a couple of shots and then it's off to Templins for dinner. We have a private room reserved at 5:00 P.M. should give us plenty of time to drive to Sacramento."

"That's it, Katey?"

"You bet! Like you told me in your last two letters, make it short and sweet! Notice I never mentioned the word wedding when I told you about the plans and arrangements. As far as I'm concerned, like you, our wedding took place at a certain cabin in the High Sierras when you slipped my wedding band on my finger and we said our vows before each other and God. Saturday afternoon's ceremony makes my folks happy and it takes care of the legal requirements and officially blesses our marriage within my church."

"When do we move into our duplex officially as Mr. and Mrs. Jerry Landis?"

Katey glanced down at her wristwatch. "Well, it's officially Friday morning now, five minutes past midnight. Tomorrow night, after the folks drive Krissy back from Sacramento, you and I will officially christen our brand new queen-sized bed with all the love you'd care to give me in our duplex. We'll have all night together without a pair of padded feet in pajamas and Mr. Floppy to interrupt us. Sunday morning, we'll sleep in and have breakfast together, and then we'll show up here for an early dinner and move Krissy back with us to start life officially as the Landis family on campus. I'm taking all of next week off so we can get acquainted all over again, the three of us. How's that on our final preparations for a lifetime of togetherness and love?"

"Couldn't be better, Katey, couldn't be better! Are you gonna dress up or wear something special at our ceremony?"

"Mother and I have new dresses, and I'll be carrying a bouquet of fresh-cut flowers, that's all."

Jerry started to yawn. "It's been a long day, since leaving Sea-Tac, guess I'm ready to hit the hay. Oh that reminds me, O'Grady sends her best. Just before I left, she comes bustling in and flashes this big rock in front of me. C'mon, Katey! Take a wild guess who she's engaged to!"

"Haven't the slightest idea! Who, Jerry?"

"You nicknamed him, remember? Old Stone Lips himself, Dr. Novak!"

One tired, ex-GI and one excited lady nearly died laughing. Jerry stood up and stretched. "Level with me, Katey, let me stand up and tell me how noticeable my brace and built-up shoe really are."

"Not bad, Jerry, not bad at all! I noticed tonight around the house you didn't use your cane at all."

"Short distances are no problem, only a slight drag. It's the long walks that really get to me…then my leg fatigues and it gets pretty bad. Without the cane then, I'd be in real trouble. Oh, don't let me forget when we're downtown at city hall getting our marriage license this morning I need to stop off at Pennys or Monkey Wards for a few minutes."

"What for?"

"I'd better buy a couple sets of pajamas, tops and bottoms. Had O'Grady hold up a mirror so I could see my back…the scars are pretty bad, Katey! Don't think you'll be very enthused about wrapping your arms around that tomorrow night. The bottoms should be worn anyway, so my leg brace won't bother or dig…you know what I'm getting at."

Katey confronted Jerry by coming straight to the point. "Gerald Landis, you've never owned a pair of pajamas in your life and you're not about to start now, not if I have anything to do with it! As far as your back goes, I could care less, my arms won't mind it at all. I'm not making love to your back. As for your leg brace, let tomorrow night take care of itself. If it needs removing, or if you prefer to take it off before you sleep with me, that's up to you. I'll help you take it off, if need be. I'd better not ever, ever see anything but boxer shorts on you, got it? That's what you wore when we were married and that's what I'd better see from now on."

He mock-saluted her, "Aye, aye, Skipper! I'm just following orders Sir! Nothing personal just thought I'd better check to see where I stand."

Katey worked him over good as the two mock rough-housed on the davenport. It wound up their usual draw as they exchanged kisses and embraces. "Aye, aye, Sir!"

"Really, Landis, you are the living pits sometimes!"

"Just following orders, Sir!"

"Suppose I'll ever be able to break you from some of your one hundred or so bad habits?"

Katey had his arms pinned down. Jerry looked up in her face. "I doubt it Katey, it's all part of the package. That for better or worse bit you got stuck with when you decided to throw your good Irish sense and caution out the door and let me come into your life for good."

They kissed goodnight, four times, before Katey finally admitted that maybe it was a good time to get some sleep.

Jerry made up the davenport, pulled his clothes off and settled in for what few hours were left before Katey undoubtedly would rouse him to help get the surprise breakfast underway for her parents. He'd just turned over when he felt two moist lips firmly planted on his. "Katey! What the?"

"Shssh! She whispered, "Move over, let me lie next to you, Darling!"

"You can't do this. Your folks'd have a hemorrhage if they came out here and saw this."

"Not to worry, I'm dressed and I'll make sure there's a blanket between our bodies, I just want to be close to you…besides we're married, what's wrong with this arrangement?"

"Katey, there's still that little technicality to take care of tomorrow afternoon, remember?"

"How could I ever forget, my mother has reminded me at least a dozen times this past week."

"I'll say this about you, you're definitely not the same girl I proposed to when we were eighteen. You've changed, Katey…I think I like the change."

"You know you do, it's just that I couldn't really be the person I wanted to be until our weekend together. I told mother that too, out at the airport when you left for Korea and I wore my gold wedding band."

"Are you comfortable with who are now?"

"Never been more comfortable in my whole life, Sweetheart. I have everything I want, a husband whom I love more and more each minute and a darling, sweet baby girl whom we both adore."

"Hey, are we gonna talk some more or get some shut eye?"

They kissed good night and Katey turned over and snuggled hard against Jerry. She reached back over the light blanket, found his arm, and pulled it around her body. His strong arm, her safety net, knowing he was there again beside her was all she needed to drift off into her first peaceful sleep in many, many a night.

An hour later Katey woke him. "Honey, honey!"

"Now what?"

"You're poking me again. Even through the blanket, I know it's there."

"I'm not about to do anything about it, not here, that's for sure!"

She giggled and teased. "I know, just thought I should tell you, that's all! Now try to get some sleep, Dear."

"Thanks, Katey, you're all heart!"

Katey and Jerry had breakfast on the stove by 6 a.m. Jerry turned the flapjacks over, watched the eggs and broiled the bacon while Katey grabbed a quick shower. Aaron and Mary couldn't believe their eyes when Katey rapped on their door. "Hey you two, breakfast is ready! If you'd like to join us, get a move on!"

Aaron was long gone for work when Katey heard a familiar, "Mommy, Mommy, Mommy!"

"I'll let you go pick her up, she needs to get used to you being here too! Bring her out in her pajamas, I always feed her that way. After she goes on a potty call, I clean her up, oil her down, brush her hair and redo her pony tail. Finally it's to her dresser for training pants and undershirt, and clean play clothes and her shoes. Got it, Daddy?"

"You go through this routine every morning?"

"Every morning except when she sleeps in, then I do it, Lad," Mary added.

Jerry did pretty well with Krissy that morning with Katey's ever present help. After Jerry had set her down in her box of pots and pans with Mr. Floppy, he turned an admiring glance toward Katey. "You have my complete respect and admiration, Katey Landis. Motherhood's not for me, let me bring home the bacon!" Then he laughed, "Golly, it's going to be awhile before I can even do that! Looks like you're even stuck with bringing home the bacon!"

Mary, Katey, and Jerry laughed. Katey added, "Well, at least with your GI check and your disability payment starting soon, it'll make it that much better on our budget. Speaking of which, today Jerry Landis, I officially turn over the Landis budget to you. You're the bean counter in our family, good luck and if you need any pointers, just ask!"

They waited 'til Jerry put Krissy down for her late morning nap before leaving in their car to pay a visit to city hall for the marriage license. That out of the way, Katey drove Jerry to the married student housing section on campus at Sacramento State College. She drove past several rows of housing units, finally turned down the last row and continued to the very last unit on the street cul-de-sac. "I choose this duplex for two reasons, it's the quietest street so you can get some studying done, and it's the farthest away from the new playground the college is putting in because they have so many married GI's with families living here."

He patted her hand. "There's my Katey, planning and doing her thing. Can't thank you enough, my love."

She walked smartly up to the door, ready to insert the key, then looked back and apologized. "I'm sorry I wasn't thinking, you don't walk as fast as you used to. Give me some time, I'll get used to your pace."

While Katey waited for him to catch up, she dug into her purse and handed him a key. "Here is the extra key for you. Go ahead, open the door! It's our new home 'til you show me your sheepskin. Hope you like it!"

He turned his key and let the door swing all the way open. "Oh, Katey, this is nice, very nice! Look at all the new stuff! Boy is this ever an improvement over what I used to live in!"

She put her arm around his waist, and they stepped inside together. "Yes you've come a long way from that run-down housing development on Cicero Boulevard. I know you don't miss it one bit."

He leaned his cane up against the wall. "Nor do I miss one of the people who used to live there."

"Do you know where your mother is?"

"No, Katey, and I really don't care." He walked out into the small kitchenette area. "New toaster, new coffee pot, even new potholders."

Then he opened the top drawer under the counter. "Oh these I do recognize, Katey! They're your Betty Crocker silverware set, the ones you saved all those coupons for! They were on the top tray of your hopeless chest!"

Katey joined him. "Yes, everything on the counter is from my hopeless chest…the one Molly nicknamed because she thought it was hopeless when I told her I was going to start saving for our wedding after we started going steady. Everything here is brand new, but is almost two years old from my hope chest and the two bridal showers I had just before you were drafted. Seems more like one hundred years ago in some ways, doesn't it, Jerry?"

He didn't answer her right away. He looked down at his leg. "I know, Katey, for you, the waiting, and everything else that's happened, it must be like one hundred years. For me, it all happened eight months ago, when I climbed that old snag…my world's changed forever."

"Jerry, both our world changed forever eight months ago!" She quickly switched subjects. "Come take a look at Krissy's bedroom! It's small but I think it'll do nicely. See, all her stuffed animals are here, moved 'em over three days ago. Once in a great while, she'll ask for one of them…maybe she'll play with one for a few minutes, and then it's back to her old pal, Mr. Floppy."

Jerry followed her into Krissy's room. "New curtains, new crib, and new chest of drawers."

"I made the curtains and the folks bought the furniture." Katey went over to the crib. "See, the crib rails slide all the way down on both sides. Before long Krissy won't need the rails so it converts into a bunk bed."

"Who thought of that?"

"I did, when Mother and I picked it out."

"Good idea, you've outdone yourself. I can only say thank you, again and again."

Jerry moved back into the kitchen area. He opened the refrigerator door. "Gee! It's already stocked. I see milk, juice, fresh fruit, bread, butter, jam and bacon."

"That's for Sunday morning's breakfast. On Monday, you and I and Krissy will do our grocery shopping in a food cart. Krissy and I are old pros at it, but it'll be a whole new experience for you, Hon."

"Looks like I got a whole bunch of new experiences coming Katey. Sure hope I'm up to it."

She gave him a reassuring squeeze. "You're doing just fine, my Love, just fine. Look at how Krissy takes to you! You're her number one man!"

"Say, who did all this moving?

"You won't believe it, but my dad and Greg did most of it."

"Greg? You can't mean our old silver spoon Teddy Bear? Our old Amigo?"

"None other! He really was good help. He and I have had lunch together on and off for the past four months. He'll be finishing up his railroad management degree program in June. Says he's all ready to move up the corporate ladder on the CCR management trainee program. And with his family's connections, who knows? Asks about you all the time. I'm going to invite him over after we get settled in. Okay?"

"Fine with me. I'd like to see him again….be nice shooting the bull with old Greg."

"Good, I'll tell him when I go back to work a week from next Monday. Oh, that reminds me, your college quarter starts the same day. I've already set up your registration and counseling session next Friday at ten in the morning. They already have your grade transcripts but will need a copy of your medical discharge and disability application to process the paperwork for the government checks. Hope you brought them?"

"In my duffle bag, I'll dig them out when we move Krissy's things and the rest of our clothes over on Sunday. Speaking of Greg, don't suppose you kept tabs on Ricco, have you?"

"No, Jerry, Ricco is not one of my favorite people anymore. Greg keeps track of him. He mentioned that about a month ago."

"You're never gonna forget or forgive him, are you?"

"I doubt it, not after the way he treated Molly…let's change subjects."

"Not quite yet. Do you still write to her?"

"Yes, all the time. She's off of welfare now and is doing okay working as a secretary for an insurance agency in the LA area."

"Does she still have her baby?"

"Of course! I'm surprised you even questioned the idea that she might not."

"If you'da been in her shoes, would you have even thought about giving your baby up?"

"NEVER!"

Katey said never with such conviction it startled Jerry. "Boy, you left no doubt about where you stand on that issue! I'm glad we're not into that kind of a hassle."

She slid her arm up over his neck. "If we were, I know I could always count on you meeting your responsibility! Right? Not like someone else we know."

He put her mind and her question to bed. "Don't worry. I could never pull a Ricco on you, Katey. Thank God, we're not in the same boat, that's all I care to say on the subject."

They moved on to the one remaining room, their bedroom. "Hey, this is my favorite hang-out, Katey! This is where it all happens, tomorrow night. Hope you're gonna wear that see-through sexy negligee, the one you kept losing in our bed up at the cabin?"

She kissed him passionately. "Don't think it'll really make any difference what I wear tomorrow night, my sweet. Yes, I will wear it again…at least to start out with."

They both smiled at Katey's obvious reference.

They took a break, sitting on the foot of the bed. Jerry surveyed the room. He definitely liked what he saw. "Nice vanity and double-chest of drawers, everything new except the fridge and stove. I assume they go with the rental."

"Yes, the folks sprung for the furnishings, Dear, that was my dowry. You know, the one we never quite got around to, something always seemed to come up." She looked up at him earnestly, searching his face for continued assurance. "Please, please my Love, we're just over twenty-four hours away from the start of the best days of our lives, I don't think I could stand anymore delays or disappointments. It would hurt too much."

He took her in his arms and kissed away any lingering uneasiness. "Not to worry, Katey, nothing's going to come between us…ever, again."

She melted in his embrace. "Oh Jerry, Jerry, those are the words…that's what I want to hear. Oh I love you so much." She kissed him again and again. "I have so much…so much love for you…I can hardly wait."

# CHAPTER THIRTY-ONE

They drove back through the housing area with Katey still behind the wheel. She stopped along the curve and pointed across to an open field now under construction. "This will be the playground, and Krissy will be ready to use the swings and slide before we know it. One of us has to be with her at all times when we bring her over here to play. That's the only way I'll allow her to use the playground. If anything ever happened to her I could never live with myself…I wouldn't want to."

"Katey, you're reading my mind, loud and clear. She's so precious. I would never leave her alone, no matter what."

She pulled out from the curb. "The worst part, Krissy is so trusting and being another tomboy doesn't really help either. I haven't worked with her about not going to strangers, because I knew you'd be a stranger too, and I wanted her to overcome that with you."

"After tomorrow Katey, Krissy and I will start working on this part of her training. I think her daddy could be a real help in that situation."

"Now you're reading my mind."

They drove back to Rushton. "Hey, wanna stop at Wally's Drive-in for a Coke? My treat!"

Katey thought about Jerry's offer. "No, I'd rather go on home, there's pop in the fridge and Krissy will be waking up soon, if she hasn't already. I think it's time we left those memories at Wally's right where they belong, in our past."

"When your dad gets home from work this afternoon, I'm going to make a special point of thanking your parents for our furniture and for providing your dowry. From now on though, Katey, we pay our own way, every dollar!"

Katey nudged him with her elbow. "What took you so long, Landis? Expected that speech when you first opened the door to our duplex!"

They both cracked up. "Good Lord, Katey, guess we really do know each other pretty darned well, don't we?"

Katey gave him another nudge, a pretty good one this time. "Jerry, it's much better than pretty darned well! Mother says we're the only two people she's ever known who knew what they were doing at the age of sixteen and that includes her when she first married Dad at the same age."

They came to their more-than-familiar street, with Mrs. Feeney's grey-toned house on the corner. Katey drove into the garage. "Gonna seem strange not to be sleeping here and parking the Chevy here night after night like I've done since you were drafted."

Jerry opened the door, got out and leaned on his cane. "You said it right, Katey, time to leave our memories where they belong…in our past."

Katey came around to his side and they walked arms around each other's waist, up to the front steps. "Just got to thinking, Dear, Krissy will be in kindergarten before you get your degree in accounting."

Jerry took her thought a step further. "I think you're trying to say it's time I put a hitch in my get-a-long and get to cracking the textbooks again or else she's going to catch up."

Katey smiled, then let the laughter roll. "You said it, Landis."

"Or else what?"

"Or else you'll be stuck in college while Krissy and I go house shopping with your GI loan money. You can't come with us unless I see that diploma, that's the deal! Gonna get awful lonesome, just Krissy and me."

"You got it figured down to the last day, haven't you, Katey?"

"Yup, you can do it, eighteen months by going full-time the year around, I've already checked. That's it!"

Jerry answered Katey's challenge right back, "That's what I told Sergeant Poolis. I told him you can't fail around my Katey, she won't let you."

"How is Sergeant Poolis, Jerry? You never mentioned him in your letters when you started your rehab."

Jerry turned away and Katey saw his jaw set, then the neck chords strained. "Poolis didn't make it, Katey…I wrote to his wife after I was able to, up in Madagan General. He was out looking for my replacement crew one day, guess they strayed out in no-man's land too far. No one's ever seen or found Poolis or the crew."

"Couldn't they be prisoners, now that the truce has been signed?"

He bit his lip. He didn't really want to answer her question. "That'd be worse than dying. When the North Korean Communists put you through their torture chambers and techniques, they break you down, destroy your spirit. There's nothing left but the shell of the person you once were."

Katey could see Jerry was having a pretty hard time dealing with the subject of his Army buddy. It was time to shift to something much more palatable. She reached for the front door knob. It felt so solid, so secure in her grasp. Much like her life would be now that he was home, back in all her plans, in her future, and in her dreams as they were on the verge of being exactly where she knew they should've been all along, as family.

"Can't you just feel the excitement building in our lives, Jerry? Oh God, there were times when I truly wondered if tomorrow would ever come for us…and for Krissy too, so that we could be together again."

He sensed she needed his re-assurance now more than ever before. He waited just long enough to step inside before holding her tight. "It's because of you, Katey, what you've done, what you wanted, what needed doing. That's why I'm here with you and Krissy, that's why it's all coming together. And I thank you from the bottom of my heart for making it happen."

That night around the supper table, Jerry made a special point of thanking Aaron and Mary for their generosity. Aaron responded with a round of Irish coffee stoutly laced with more than the usual double shot of Irish whiskey. "Aye, Jerry, let the coffee speak for itself as to how much your coming back has meant to each one of us! We only wish Katey's mother and I could've done a wee bit more!"

The telephone interrupted any continuation of such tender thoughts. Katey returned from the parlor. "It was Father Murphy reminding us, Jerry…"

He set his cup down. "About what?" Then he tried to make light of it before Katey could answer. "Don't worry, Katey, I'm not about to change my mind. Nothing's going to ever change that! So what did Father Murphy want?"

"It's about stopping by before our ceremony for a little counseling." Katey replied nervously.

"You said the ceremony would be short and sweet. You didn't say anything about this…"

"And it will be, like I told you. That hasn't changed."

Jerry was still uneasy. "Why do we need counseling?"

Katey took her seat again and wiped Krissy's mouth. "It's really no big deal…since you're not Catholic yet, he wants to meet you, go over our church rules and laws, remind us that if we have any problems to come to him for guidance and counseling. That's really about it."

"Do you think we need this session, Katey?"

Aaron and Mary perked up their ears as Jerry's question nailed Katey. "Yes, Jerry, I do think we should go. Give you a chance to ask questions too! I'm sure Father Murphy can put any minor concerns you might have to rest."

Jerry wasn't satisfied. "All I want, Katey, is that fifteen-minute ceremony. That's all I've agreed to and that's all we need to do to get on with our lives together."

Katey looked at her parents, watching their reaction, and then she came down on Jerry with a firm, deliberate message. "We're less than twenty-four hours from making it all happen. Now let's get through this and everything else will fall into place. Remember the discussion at our complex?" She slowed each word to emphasize her determination. "I…told…Father   Murphy…we…will…be…there!   I…   gave… my… word… and… WE… WILL… BE… THERE! END…OF… DISCUSSION!"

Promptly at 2 p.m. on Saturday afternoon, Katey and Jerry met with Father Murphy. Twenty-five minutes later, Katey had to practically run to catch up with Jerry and his cane. He was more than a bit irritated, he was fighting mad!

Wham! He slammed their car door and waited for Katey to follow suit. She beat him to the punch. "All right, Jerry Landis, what's going on? I've never seen you act this way! You were absolutely rude to Father Murphy…no, better make that terrible! After our ceremony, I want to see you personally apologize to him. Do you hear?"

Eyes blazing, he snapped right back. "They'll be marching through snow banks in hell before I apologize to that smug, arrogant, righteous, self-centered, holier-than-thou thing that calls himself a priest! No, Katey, it'll never happen! Not in my lifetime!"

"God, you can be so exasperating! So damned stubborn! All right, tell me, what set off the large charge this time? Come on! I'm waiting and it better be a damned good explanation!"

He slid over in the seat toward her. "I'm going to try to keep our discussion from ending up into one long shouting match if I can. Are you willing to try too?"

She nodded yes.

"Good! So let me begin! I can't stomach him, Katey, I can't stomach anything about him, and I sure as heck can't stomach what he tried to shove down our throats."

"Okay, Jerry, what's bothering you? Be specific!"

"For starters, that pledge he insisted we sign for our family's contribution to the church."

"For Pete's sake, it's only a pledge! It's not a contract or a demand payment! You make it sound like we've mortgaged our lives to it."

"Haven't we? For the rest of our lives we'll be under the gun to come through to give our ten percent. No, Katey, not one dime of our money is going to that church under those conditions. WE GIVE WHAT WE CAN AFFORD, WHEN WE CAN AFFORD TO! Got it?"

"Fine! Then I'll take ten percent out of my paycheck so you won't have to! Now do you feel better?"

"You're missing my point! Not one dime of our money goes to that church under any signed pledge. We're married and your money is our money and I just told you not one dime, Katey!"

Katey let Jerry's words sink in, and then she countered. "Okay, Jerry, what is this really about?"

He moved even closer to her. "Please let me make my case, logically, one step at a time. If you'll try to keep an open mind, I think you'll not only agree with me, but that I've earned the right to at least question if not confront the issue head on."

There was only compassion and love in her response. "Yes, Jerry, nobody can or should ever deny you that, you've more than paid for that privilege and right."

"Let me back track a minute. Now think hard about this question, Katey. Back up in Washington State at Madagan General, you went to the chapel twice daily, right?'

"Yes."

"Now before I ask you why you went there, tell me what you remember most about that chapel. Were there any outstanding features that stick out in your mind?"

Katey thought hard "No, not really. Matter of fact, I remember very little about any specific features. It was so quiet and peaceful in there, I certainly do remember that. Wait a minute, I see what you're getting at! The wooden cross…it was at the front of the chapel. It commanded my attention. The minute I saw it I knew I was in a house of God."

"Exactly, it's used by every religion in the new world. Now, Katey, in your way, you've just admitted that the chapel furnishings were simple or plain, nothing outstanding, yet that cross, which is our symbol, really meant something to you. Now, dear, go one step further. What role do you think your church should play in your life?"

Katey never hesitated. "That's easy, Jerry, my church is an extension of my personal life…and when a person marries, it should be an extension of the new life created through that marriage by God. My church should be a place I can come to, it should provide me counseling and guidance to questions I have concerning my mind, my soul, and even my body."

"I couldn't agree more, Katey. Now what else besides counseling and spiritual guidance do you think should be the proper role of your church?"

Katey dwelled on Jerry's question a few seconds. "I would want our church to have an active role in helping others both outside and inside the church. By that I mean I want our church to help the needy, provide shelter for families down on their luck, and let's not forget the young people, give them things to do, give them responsibilities so that they can be shown by example, not just words, how to achieve their goals in life. That one area, Jerry, I'll admit most churches I've been around fall flat on their face...possibly with the exception of the Mormon Church."

"Textbook all the way, Katey, nobody could've said it better. Now if you had just that kind of church, wouldn't you feel that most of the money you gave would go directly to support the church on a more reasonable basis, which would leave a lot more of your contributions free to be used where they could do the most good?"

"Yes...I can't argue with that. Jerry, I smell a lesson in accounting coming on."

"Katey, when you go to your church, what's the first impression you have when you walk inside?"

"Jerry, no problem there. It's beautiful, everything is of the finest..."

"Yes, I know, I took a good look around today. Stained glass all over, beautiful statuary, rich tapestries everywhere, and the best hardwood I've ever seen, walked on, touched, or kneeled near. Now all that costs an awful lot of money to build and maintain, therefore, how much do you suppose is left to carry out the other support services that you just told me are important in your church, Katey?"

Katey didn't care for the question or its inference. "I don't like your question, Jerry, I know what you're up to. I won't answer it."

"You don't have to, because your answer just confirmed what you and I both know to be true. Speaking from an accounting standpoint, the Catholic Church is taking in dollars for salaries, maintenance, and other related expenses. Its overhead including administration must be staggering, yet it's barely putting a few measly bucks back into the church coffers to be used for the needy and other worthwhile projects that you just said should be important functions of your church."

"There's more, isn't there? This whole thing has been building inside you, hasn't it?"

"Yes Katey, I used to attend Catholic Church with you because you made sure I understood that was the only way you'd accept my love. You made it a condition of courtship, and your folks absolutely made it a condition of any continued relationship whatsoever. Your Catholic Church must change or else it's going to be in deep trouble with people like me. And another thing, I can't stand that mumbo-jumbo, that Latin your priests use on the members when they conduct their Mass. Do you really know what they're saying? C'mon, Katey, be truthful about it?"

"It's a beautiful ritual and I like it…"

"What you really mean is you've been conditioned to it for so long that you've accepted it. But do you use Latin enough to really know the language?"

"No, you've got me there…okay, so the church needs to make a few changes. Some changes?"

"Changes, Katey? The Holy Roman Catholic Church needs a complete overhaul!"

"Gee, thanks, Jerry. In less than five minutes you've completely destroyed my religion and my church!"

"But not God, Katey! We both believe in Him! Let's use some of our freedom of choice and find a church that comes a heckava lot closer to meeting the needs and goals and roles that you just told me were important to you."

Katey couldn't argue with Jerry, how could she? He had just painted her into a corner with her own words. "Jerry, please listen to me, let me explain the position you're trying to put me in. All my life I've been a devout Catholic, and yes, you're right up to a point. But you're approaching everything from a dollars and cents standpoint. My parents will not understand if I dared to make a change or leave our Catholic Church."

"Would you, Katey? Now?"

"I can't now, but I'm willing to look later, no promises that I will change, you understand."

"That's at least a start, Katey. I'll give you this, you did keep an open mind about what I've said. At least we're not shouting or screaming at one another."

"No, our life, our happiness are far too important for hysterics. Let me continue, so you can see what a predicament you've put me in. I know people, especially young people, are leaving the Catholic Church for whatever reason, probably some of the very reasons you touched on. My parents will never change and even you, Jerry, must admit that."

"I do, Katey, and let me say this about them. They are without doubt the two finest people I've ever known. They came from a country that had only one religion, so nobody, including me, would ever expect any change on their part. If there's going to be change it must come from us."

"But don't you see? That's the problem. There are no stronger Catholics than the Irish. If I leave my church I have to leave my mother and father. I can't do that, we're too close, they mean too much to me."

"Are you saying they won't have anything more to do with your? Aw, c'mon, Katey! This is America and in a couple of months it will be 1954. That kind of attitude and reasoning went out in the Dark Ages. Surely you can't be serious?"

"You'd better clean the wax out of your ears, Jerry Landis, 'cause this is how it is in my family. If I leave my church, I can never come back. My father will disown me, and I'll never be welcome in their home again." The tears came on, but Katey found a way to continue. "Krissy will never see her grandparents again! Maybe, just maybe, someday my mother will meet me away from her home, but she will never invite me to Sunday dinner again. To the day my father dies, he will never ask about me or his granddaughter. Is that the way you want me to live out my life? Is it, Jerry?"

"But they're so attached to Krissy…surely in time they'd come around. I'd be willing to invite them to our place if they won't ask you to their home."

"That won't make any difference to them, Jerry."

Katey moved over to kiss him. "Jerry, please just go through the ceremony today with me…please, please…we can work out our differences…there must be a way. I'd even be willing to go back, right now, to ask for another priest to conduct our ceremony, since Farther Murphy is the last priest in this world you'd want. I'm more than sure they'd be willing to accommodate you on that. In less than fifty minutes we can forever put the talk about and the technicalities of our marriage behind us by just going through with the ceremony. That will free both of us to work out our religious differences and with time on our side, I truly believe we can come to some compromise that both of us can live with. All I ask is you just go through the ceremony with me for now, nothing more, no church commitments."

He held her close. "If I agreed to your Catholic ceremony now, after telling you how much I despise your church, I'd be the biggest hypocrite that ever walked the face of our earth. No, Katey, I won't do that to you or myself. I can't, Katey! Don't you understand, I can't!"

The solution to their problem became crystal clear to Katey, but she couldn't accept either of the choices. "Jerry, you're forcing me to make a choice! Either way I lose! Why me?"

"I can't make your choice for you and neither should your parents. We're married, surely I would think that alone should help you make your choice in our favor."

"How much time do I have?"

"We have our marriage license, why not go to a Justice of the Peace today and get the ceremony over with? Then it would buy us time to find a way to work out our religious differences."

Jerry's solution was certainly compelling enough to cause Katey to give it some serious thought. "If we did that, as far as my folks are concerned, it would be the same as abandoning their beliefs and my church. No, I couldn't do that."

"You mean you won't do that! Katey, you have a choice, your parents and I do not have that luxury."

"Won't, can't, it's all the same! What's the difference?"

"You're the difference, you have to make the choice, there's no other way."

They were both talked out with Katey refusing to make her choice, either way. "Where do we go from here, Jerry?"

"From the way you're acting, Katey, let's give it a rest…give you time to settle it out in your mind. I can plainly see you're not ready for any decision today."

"How much time, Jerry?"

He looked out the car door window on his side. "One way or the other, Katey, we both need to get on with our lives." He turned back to her again. "Six months is reasonable…more than reasonable, I'd say."

Katey did not like putting a time limit on anything, much less their marriage prospects. "So, what do we do about today?"

"Take me to the YMCA. I'll get a room there 'til I can make arrangements at college to find some kind of student housing there next week before my classes start."

She drove him to the YMCA. As he started to get out, Katey said, "What about us, Jerry? What about our relationship? We're still married you know!"

"Think we'd better put that on hold too. Tell you what, let's continue to see each other…maybe meet somewhere after I get settled…nothing intimate…that wouldn't be right…agreed?"

"Okay." She looked at him, a lump lodged deep into her throat. "Nothing can change the way I feel about you. I'll always love you, Jerry."

"That goes for me too, Katey."

She watched him walk away, possibly out of her life for good. He stepped along, his cane and his foot-drag working in splendid coordination. Such dignity, such confidence, and so much maturity about him for all his young years, she thought to herself. This man, her Jerry, still had so much future, so much to offer to the right person… the right lucky lady who would be his wife in name and reality. Where did she fit in? She thought she had all the answers with all her dreaming and planning, until today.

She drove home slowly still trying to mull over the dilemma that had been dumped upon her. In mechanical fashion, she parked the car, and then stepped inside her home. Krissy, looking like a Christmas greeting photo in her new dress and patent leather shoes, ran to her. "Mommy, Mommy, Mommy!" she exclaimed, "hurry up!"

Katey didn't bother to pick her up, but instead she strode straight for her bedroom with her daughter close on her heels. Two minutes later, Krissy, holding Mr. Floppy in her chubby arms, came running back out, crying as though her poor little heart was about ready to break. She found her grandpa, decked out in his Sunday suit, smoking his pipe in the front parlor. "Come to grandpa, my little Irish chickadee! Come to grandpa, he'll make it right!"

Together they rocked in his chair, Krissy clutching Mr. Floppy harder than ever, trying in her baby ways to compensate for what was going on behind Katey's bedroom door. Up went a small fist to one tear-filled eye, trying her best to rub out the big tears and still keep her rabbit from tumbling off her lap onto the braided rug on the floor.

"Why are you crying, Krissy? Can you tell grandpa?"

Krissy's tiny fist went to the other deep-blue eye, trying her best to blot out its fresh pocket of tears, she only half -succeeded in checking the flow. With red eyes and glistening cheeks she gave her grandpa the bad news. "Oh Grandpa…Mommy's crying…Grandma too… Mommy says it's too grown up for me…Mommy says it hurts…it hurts something awful!" She brushed two more tears away and continued between body wrenching sobs. "But I told Mommy show me where your hurt-bump is…I'll kiss it 'n make it all better…"

The rocking continued, Aaron kissed one wet tear-stained check. "All right, Krissy, then what happened?"

"Mommy says she has too many hurt bumps for me to kiss and make them all better."

They continued to rock."Yes…yes, I suppose that's so…"

Tear stained cheeks and all, Krissy let Mr. Floppy slide from her lap, as she turned all her attention to solving the mighty big problem behind her mommy's bedroom door. "Grandpa," she whispered, "I know who can make it all better."

"You do? Who Krissy? Who?"

"My daddy can! He can do anything, 'cause he's my daddy!'

"By George, I believe you've got something there, Krissy! But he's not here! Now what will we do?"

"We have to find my daddy, but I don't know where to look… Grandpa?"

"Yes, Krissy…"

"Where's my daddy?"

# SPECIAL ACKNOWLEDGEMENTS

Battista, editor, *Press-Tribune*, Roseville, CA. Your open files and sage advice were deeply appreciated.

Karen Ellis, editor, who literally "ran" with my story and whose "editorial touch" was the perfect prescription.

Jana Rade, ABP Director of Design, who gave my cover life, real color, and intrigue.

# About the Author

Ivan Bosanko's critical research has produced his fifth novel, *The Rubber Room*, which exposed the railroad industry's "century old out-of-the-closet secret." Set in the 1950s, you're given a nostalgia tour unlike anything ever experienced. His considerable writing talent and wide range of unforgettable characters are truly showcased for your reading pleasure and enjoyment. His epic is loaded with CHANGE, COMMITMENT, and CHALLENGE.

Ivan's writing talent has been duly recognized by the national and international literary community. His online series of articles has earned him two most prestigious awards. *Who's Who* named him as their 2009 "Man of The Year." That was followed up being selected into their 2010 "Hall of Fame."

All this from a lad who first published his own newspaper at the ripe old age of twelve.